THE
WOODCUTTER

To Dave

Enjoy the Fantasy ☺

THE BALANCE SERIES
by Lorn Wolf

The Woodcutter
*The Sol'mar

*Coming Soon

THE
WOODCUTTER

LORN WOLF

A Wolfsong® Publishing Book

CANADA

Inspired by the bedtime fable my mother told me
when I was a child

For my daughter Zarria — My friend in imagination

For my Mother
Thank you for always letting my imagination run free
You're the best

For my sons, Kyle & Shade — Your music inspires me

Special thanks to Kristopher Lundine and Gordon Chapple
for their support during the creation of this fictional work

CONTENTS

CONTENTS

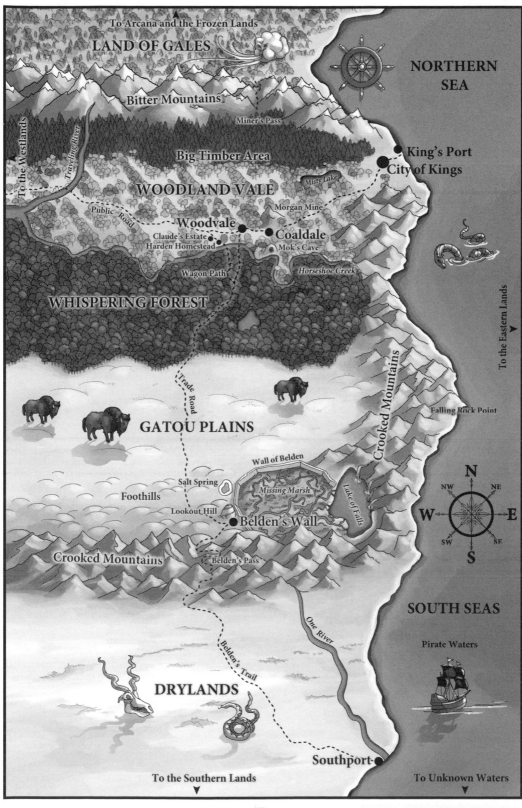

CHAPTER

1

New Hopes

T he light was barely visible through the cabin window as the woodcutter wiped his eyes and sat up in bed. He leaned over, kissed his sleeping wife on the forehead and gently got out so as not to wake her. Ivan waited as his eyes adjusted to the scant light, and after a few moments, reached for his clothes. As he donned them, even the chill of the cold leather couldn't dampen his spirits or newfound resolve on this day. He walked toward the kitchen, but stopped to look in on his children. They shared a room with a blanket hanging through the center to separate it. He could make out the two beds at opposite ends. In one was his son Cade, who was fourteen, and in the other his daughter Shyla, who was twelve years old. He could hear them breathing in the slow rhythm of slumber and it warmed him just a little.

His children, and his wife Grace, were the only reasons he had been able to hold on over the past months of hardship. If not for their support and encouragement he would have had no choice but to take that coal mining job his neighbor Claude Boyle had offered him, or that ridiculously low offer he had made on his homestead. His family understood that his true love was woodcutting or working with wood and they were

1

always there encouraging and urging him to be true to his calling, and to himself.

Now that so many people had switched from wood to coal as a source of fuel, Ivan's livelihood was slowly becoming nonexistent. He wasn't the only one to feel the pressure of change though. Most of the woodcutters in the land had either gone to work in the coal mine or taken up other occupations just to survive.

As he walked into the kitchen he recalled when he was first hailed the greatest woodcutter in the land. He remembered the respect and the good feeling of providing for his family with extra left over at the end of each month.

He lit a fire in the cookstove so the house would warm before his family awoke, then filled the kettle and set it on to boil. As he stoked the blaze, adding several larger pieces, he recalled the time when the representative from the Morgan's Coal Company had come by and asked if they would like to switch from wood to coal. The agent had explained how coal was more efficient, how it burned hotter, and how it was a cheaper source of fuel.

All of what he said had been true, and Ivan was in total agreement as he escorted the gentleman from his house and off the porch. As he warned him not to step foot on his land again, he had thought, *But coal doesn't have the friendly smell a wood fire offers, or the cozy warmth that only a wood fire can provide.*

Morgan's Coal Company, owned by Sam Morgan, had been started eight years earlier. Ivan remembered when they first broke ground because that's when Claude Boyle had moved onto the adjacent property. Claude had come to the Woodland Vale because he was joined with Morra, only child to Sam Morgan. He had been placed here as manager of the coal company by Sam as a favor to his daughter.

Morra felt that if she could get Claude out of the city, and away from the bad influences he had been associating with, he could get a fresh start. Hopefully this change and responsibility would help bring out in him the man she hoped he'd become.

She also felt that it would be good for her boy Sonny, who was ten, to grow up in the country and learn the values of clean living. That was the story that Morra had told Grace on their first brief meeting, before Claude had forbidden them to see each other.

Claude spent his time in the towns of Woodvale and Coaldale, where he drummed up new clients, made sales and oversaw the day-to-day workings of the mine. Though he was quite intelligent when it came to business dealings, most of the day he just strutted around acting important and did much the same in the evening at each town's Inn. Ivan had heard this more than once from his clients and friends and had experienced firsthand some of the shady maneuvering Claude had pulled off just to try to undermine him. This dislike, or even hatred, that he felt for Ivan was something the woodcutter had never been able to understand. He had always been respectful of Claude, but for some reason, which his wife had tried to explain to him was jealousy, he just didn't like Ivan. Of course Ivan couldn't imagine, with all that Claude had, how he could ever be jealous of a poor woodcutter.

The fire, now burning strongly, crackled its approval as the woodcutter headed for the door. He grabbed the water bucket from the counter, walked over and pulled his boots on, then stepped out onto the porch. He stood there for a moment, then looked around for his old hound-dog Rufus. *He must be off chasing something,* he thought, *or digging a hole somewhere to bury a great find.*

Rufus, a dark red mountain-hound, had been a gift from the Catcher's to Cade when he was born, but was clearly Shyla's dog and was always by her side.

Ivan took a deep breath; the air was pure and brisk. He loved mornings, the taste in the air and the way it smelled after an evening rain, and had always thought of it as a new beginning. Anything could happen today and Ivan knew that he had a big decision to make. This decision had been weighing on him for some time now and there would be no more putting it off.

This summer he would make the choice between remaining a woodcutter and becoming a coalminer. He shuddered at the prospect, but had given himself five months to find enough work to enable him to continue doing what he loved. All he needed now was a couple more woodcutting contracts like the one he would be delivering this morning, and he would have enough coins to take him well into the winter.

Ivan stepped off the porch carrying his six-foot, forty year old frame with ease. He was lean and well muscled, but not too bulky. He had dark tanned skin resulting from decades of working in the hot sun, and his chestnut hair, badly in need of a cut, framed a chiseled face as his dark eyes took in their surroundings.

The light in the morning sky had brightened as he walked along the path that led the two hundred yards south to the creek, and Ivan could hear the sounds of the woodland's early risers. To the left of the path he could see lush grass and spring flowers blooming in a collage of bright colors, and to the right he saw the five-rail fence that surrounded his neighbor's estate.

He looked back at his log house which was situated perfectly in the five acre meadow. He kept it up as much as his woodworking skills would allow, and though it was badly in need of some new windows, it was home.

As he continued along the path, Ivan studied the trees that covered the south end of his property. This land had been handed down for generations, and each one of the men in his family had known and practiced the art of woodcutting. Although his father had worked primarily as a stonemason, the land and the craft had been passed to Ivan by his grandfather. The woodcutter had learned all he could from this wise woodsman and felt honored to be a part of that heritage.

He took a closer look at the trees and could tell that some of the mature stands were hundreds of years old, providing homes and shelter to the creatures of the woods, while the newer trees and saplings fought for light and space on the forest floor.

Ivan cut and carved wood for a living, but had a deep understanding and respect for its existence. He only harvested the prime trees and left the mature and newer ones as a balance. He also lived by a code that you should *never* harvest trees or hunt near your home. As a result he only hunted and did most of his cutting to the north, in and around the Big Timber area. He had also cut to the south in the *Whispering Forest*, though not as of late. This extra traveling took more effort and organization, but it kept Ivan's little thirty-acre sanctuary untouched.

As he made his way toward the creek he marveled at his neighbor's property. From the huge manor, which could easily fit twenty of Ivan's houses inside it, to the stables and outbuildings, it was all in perfect order. He could see that the spring plowing was almost finished and ready for the new seed, with the smell of the freshly turned soil filling the air. He admired the huge trees all standing stately in rows up and down the graveled carriage path, and the blacksmith building towering in its three-story splendor. If he remembered correctly, Claude even had his own blacksmith and many hired hands to work his place, but even with all of his impressive wealth, Ivan could not respect his ways. He had seen how he treated others, including himself, and in a way he felt sorry for him. *I don't see how anyone can treat people in such a manner*, thought Ivan. *Claude must be very miserable inside to have the capacity to inflict such cruelty on others.*

He took another long gaze at his neighbor's magnificent property and wondered again how Claude could ever be jealous of him.

He resumed his walk, and within a short while was coming up on the opening that led to the north shore of the Horseshoe Creek, and beyond that, the boundary of the *Whispering Forest*.

Many believed the creek got its name because it wound through the vale so much that it looked like a line of horseshoes strung tip-to-tip. Ivan believed that if you drank the water from its cool bed it would bring you luck, but after the last few years he was starting to believe the winding theory.

As he moved closer he could see that a thin mist had blanketed the water, and on the other side, saw movement of some sort. He stopped, set down his bucket and knelt, focusing on the far shore.

He could discern three different shapes, and with a little more effort, could see the outlines of a doe deer and her two fawns. These early morning movers were visiting the creek before the start of a hot spring day.

He grabbed his bucket and crept in to get a closer look. He watched the two fawns nuzzle the liquid as the mother kept watch for any danger. The wind was blowing gently toward him so the doe couldn't detect his scent. He remained still as he watched the fawns lose interest and the cautious mother start to sip. Even as she drank she kept an eye out for danger, and was instinctively aware of her fawns' whereabouts. As she finished, Ivan reached out and picked up a small twig from off the ground. He broke it slowly between his fingers and watched the animal. Almost as soon as the twig had snapped, the doe bounded in front of her babies and chased them back into the dark forest.

The woodcutter was amazed at the keen hearing the doe possessed and the protective instincts she had for her offspring, and just for a moment it reminded him of his wife. *It's funny*, he thought, *what a common thread there is throughout all the balance.*

Ivan got up, grabbed his bucket and walked to the water's edge. The sky was brighter now and the mist had almost vanished. This allowed him a panoramic view of the *Whispering Forest*. This ancient behemoth appeared almost formidable as it loomed in seeming watch over its perimeter. It had gotten its name from the many visitors that had wandered to the east and swore they heard its windswept voices warning them away.

The wagon path leading into it on the far side, almost invisible to the untrained eye, led to the trade-road that made its way through the forest from Woodvale to the *Gatou Plains*. It was said that if you stayed to that road the forest ignored or dismissed your presence, but those who strayed from it had returned somehow changed, or *not* returned at all.

Ivan dipped his bucket into the icy water as he listened to the forest sounds. He remembered his few trips into that place, and the last one in particular which he didn't want to think about. When you entered, it always felt like you were being watched, and made the hairs on the back of your neck raise.

Ivan had gone into that forest and taken wood from it, and although he hadn't heard any voices, he always felt uneasy until he had safely reached the outer edge. After his most recent trip in he had never returned, and was now cutting all of his wood up north.

He filled his bucket and set it on the bank, then leaned down and put his lips to the water, sucking in the cool liquid. As he drank he saw a school of minnows darting around in the shallows. *Spring is such a gift,* he thought, *a gift of new beginnings and new hope.* With that in mind, the ever-present feeling of despair seemed to dissipate and his step felt lighter as he lifted his bucket and headed back up the path toward his cabin.

Ivan whistled a tune as he walked, and went over the plan he had been working on. He was saving up as much as he could for the yearly event that got him through the winter months, the Woodcutting Competition. This competition was held each summer, and the amount he would make from his delivery today, along with what he had tucked away, would cover the entry fee of five silver coins.

Ivan had won first place in this competition each season since it had been started over twenty years ago. The Baron Vero Salday, a longtime friend to the woodcutter, was a true lover of wood and its craft, and the founder and host of this event.

It was a winner-take-all contest and the prize was usually around four gold coins. Those winnings, along with his woodcutting earnings, had kept them going over the past few years. Now, because of the scarcity of jobs, even with the gold from the contest, they still had to scrimp and stretch every copper just to make it from month-to-month.

He had to smile when he thought of how that competition had become so extravagant. The baron brought in entertainers and artists, and invited anyone with merchandise or foodstuffs to set up a booth and sell their wares. It was a great festival and a chance for Ivan to feel recognized for his talents in the ways of wood, and that recognition had become all too rare these days. The funny part was that even though Ivan was feeling unappreciated, he was still a legend throughout the land and the people told stories of his woodcutting feats. This may have been one reason for Claude's dislike of him, and another may have been the fact that Claude's boy Sonny also saw Ivan as a legend.

"Yeah a legend," he chuckled to himself. "A legend that no one wants to hire."

He had almost reached his house when he heard the sound of horses' hooves. He looked across the fence and saw his neighbor, with his boy Sonny, in a brand-new double horse-drawn carriage, hurrying away from his home toward the public road. Sonny saw Ivan and lifted his arm to wave, but his father quickly grabbed it and jerked it down roughly as he whipped his horses into a frenzied pace. Ivan gave a futile wave and stepped onto his porch. *That's strange*, he thought, *Claude doesn't usually leave until well after first light. He must have some urgent business in Woodvale or at the mine.*

As he walked toward the door he could smell blueberry pancakes and knew that his love was busy in the kitchen. He could also smell the smoke from the cookstove. He loved that smell, and a momentary sadness crept over him at the thought that one day it might be completely replaced by that *stinky, sooty* coal.

He was reaching for the door as it flew open, and out ran his daughter carrying an empty basket. He steadied the water bucket in his left hand, then reached down with his right and swept his little girl up, holding her tightly.

Ivan looked down at Shyla as she squirmed to free herself. How pretty she was with her mother's bright green eyes and graceful movement. She had her grandmother's raven blue-black hair, except hers was wild and wavy, and her fine features accentuated pouting lips.

"Where are you off to in such a rush?" asked the woodcutter as he squeezed her.

"I'm going to gather eggs for breakfast Daddy!" she squealed with glee.

"I'm not Daddy!" he growled. "I'm the porch troll, and you will *not* be freed until you reveal the password!"

"You're not a troll, you're my daddy!" she chided.

The woodcutter squeezed her tighter and said, "I am the evil troll and if you don't know the password, then I must take you to my cave beneath the porch and have you for my breakfast!"

Shyla's face became very serious and she looked into her father's eyes and said, "Ah yes, I can see now that you *are* the porch troll, but I will not be joining you for breakfast this fine day. The password is Horseshoe Creek!" she bellowed in her lowest, biggest voice.

Ivan fell to his knees and released his daughter, but not before kissing her cheek. "Foiled again!" he cried, "but one day I *will* get you fair princess!"

"Not today," she giggled, and leaped off the porch, running toward the chicken pen. *That girl is wise beyond her years,* thought Ivan as he stepped inside and closed the door.

He walked to the counter and set the bucket down, then noticed that some of the water had gone missing during his dealings with the princess. He reached for the dipper that hung on a nail just above and took a drink to smooth away his troll voice.

He could see the sunlight streaming through the kitchen window, silhouetting his wife as she mixed a few more preserved blueberries into the pancake batter. She looked elegant with her auburn hair flowing down the length of her back and her petite five-foot-four physique, lithe yet muscled in perfect proportion, accented by a tiny waist. She was strikingly beautiful with her deep green eyes, rosy lips and flawless ivory skin, and it was hard to believe that at thirty-six, she looked like she was still in her twenties.

Ivan came up behind her, slid his hands around her waist and held her close. He kissed her neck and whispered, "What a vision you are, and what a fine woman."

She turned and faced him, wrapping her arms around his neck and replied, "Well if I am a fine women, it's only because you are a true man my love," and they stood there holding each other for a few magical moments. It didn't last though as the door flew open and Shyla came in with her basket of eggs.

She carried them to the counter, washed them in the basin and set them on the cupboard. "Can I flip the pancakes?" she asked.

"Sure," replied Grace, "but not until the bubbles pop."

"I *know* Mother," she answered in a frustrated voice, "you taught me that when I was seven."

Grace looked at her daughter thinking, *she is growing up so fast, I often forget she is probably a better cook than I am.*

She glanced at the ten eggs in the bowl and sighed. They used to have fifty chickens, but with the difficulties over the past years they were down to eleven. Well at least ten were still laying and the brood-hen was setting on eight more that, hopefully, would all become chicks within the next two weeks.

"How is the brood-hen and her eggs?" asked Grace.

"She is doing well," replied Shyla, as she flipped another pancake. "She is worried about her eggs and is very protective of them."

Grace looked at her daughter in wonder. "Some days I swear that child can speak with the animals," she said quietly to her husband. "Since she was old enough to talk she has been telling me that this animal wants that, and that animal feels a certain way." At first it had seemed strange, but now it was almost normal.

"Where is Cade?" asked Ivan as he moved to his favorite chair.

"He's outside loading the last of the wood for your delivery today," replied Grace. "He *is* his father's son and your approval means so much."

Ivan thought for a moment and said, "I'll take him with me today. I'd say he's old enough to learn about the business side of woodcutting. You can only learn so much from schoolbooks, and he is coming into his manhood. Why, he will be fifteen soon, can you believe it Grace?"

She just smiled and turned the last of their bacon over in the frying pan as Cade walked through the door carrying a towering armload of wood.

He was a handsome boy with blue eyes and black hair like his grandfather on his mother's side. He had grown three inches this past winter, and at five-foot-seven, he was very happy to finally be taller than his mother. He had waited for what seemed like forever to reach that goal, but his sights were set on six feet like his father. At fourteen years old his build was wiry and a bit gangly, though unusually strong for his age, and at his rate of growth, would fill out and possibly surpass his father before he was finished.

He dropped his load into the wood box and walked over to his father who had just sat down. The armload had looked effortless for him to carry, and reminded the woodcutter just how unusual his son's strength was.

Earlier that spring, Ivan and Cade had been working in the forest when the wagon lost a wheel. The woodcutter had tried to lift it and reattach the wheel, but could only move it a few inches. While he was looking for a long pole for leverage, Cade had hoisted the wagon up and held it there long enough for Ivan to slide the wheel back on. This was no ordinary strength his son possessed and made the woodcutter wonder where it had come from.

Ivan watched him and leaned back in the chair he had built with his own hands. When he thought about it, he realized he had crafted it even before he had been joined with Grace, sixteen years ago.

"I've finished loading the wagon and filled the wood box," said Cade as he stopped in front of his dad and waited.

"Well Son, you've earned your breakfast today haven't you," replied Ivan. Looking disappointed, Cade turned and walked to the washstand. "You've been working hard lately," observed Ivan, "doing the job of a man I'd say." Cade listened as he washed his hands and face, adding more hot water from the kettle. Ivan paused for just a moment and then continued. "I'd say you're ready to come on the delivery and into Woodvale with me. What do you think?"

Cade dried his hands and face and tried hard to contain his excitement. "Well," he admitted, "I have completed all the work from my lesson books, and passed the last exams. I think it would be good for me to become more familiar with some of the ways of the trade." Cade walked to the door and called back, "Just need a few more pieces of wood to fill the box, I . . . I just noticed." As soon as he was outside, the whole family could hear him jumping and yelling, "Yes, yes, yes!" which caused everyone to roar with laughter.

Ivan stood up, leaned over and grabbed the guitar that hung on the wall beside his chair. He sat back down, placed it over his knee and strummed a chord.

Grace was pouring bacon grease from the big frying pan into the smaller one, in preparation for frying eggs. Shyla was setting the table, in between spooning pancake batter onto the hot skillet and flipping it at the precise moment.

Ivan strummed another chord and looked at the old guitar. It had been traded to him by the gypsies. About two years back they had stopped on his property and asked if he could fix a couple of their unique wagons. They had asked around and he had been recommended to them by some of his neighbors.

The gypsies traveled in a caravan of about thirty-or-so wagons and wandered from town to town peddling their trinkets, telling fortunes, and selling elixirs and potions that were supposed to cure almost anything. They were great entertainers and storytellers, and the music they made wove a combination of bliss and sorrow.

Ivan had agreed to do the work, crafting two new wheels and some floorboards, but the method of payment had been an interesting negotiation. After the bargaining was finished they had settled on an old guitar, along with a few lessons—Ivan had always wanted to learn the instrument—and one silver and three coppers. Grace had also asked for some bottles full of strange colored liquids from the old gypsy woman with the blind eye. She said she needed them for her healing practice, so Ivan had agreed even though he had no idea what they contained.

Like her mother and her mother's mother, Grace was a healer. The art of healing had been passed down in her family for countless generations, and as her mother had taught her, so was she teaching Shyla. Healers used remedies and mixtures to ward off sickness, and the ones who possessed the gift also used the force that emanated from within the land to aid them. Only one out of every hundred healers was gifted in the magic of the land, and as a result, they were sought out above all others.

Grace, who was blessed with this gift, had been administering aid and fending off sickness in the surrounding areas since she had come to live with Ivan all those years ago. Before that she had lived with her mother in their mountain home in the south.

Grace's father Hawkins, who had captained a ship in the King's Navy, had mysteriously disappeared when she was ten and she and her mother had left Southport soon after to live in the mountains to the north. In fact, she had been awakened in the middle of the night by her mother and they had packed up whatever they could carry and left before the next morning.

Ivan had asked Grace what happened to her father but she wasn't sure. Her mother had never told her the details, but she had learned that it had to do with a seer, and an important foretelling that involved the family. It had all sounded strange and complicated, so Ivan had never mentioned it again.

The woodcutter kept strumming his guitar as he fell ever deeper into thought, and found himself remembering the first day he had seen Grace.

CHAPTER

2

Looking Back

I van had taken a load of building logs from the Big Timber area up north to the town of Belden's Wall in the south. What an adventure that had been. He'd driven down from the north with fifteen forty-foot logs tied down to two wagons, one on each end. They were pulled by a matched team of four workhorses that were half again the size of a normal horse. He then traveled south through the *Whispering Forest* and across the *Gatou Plains*, then southeast into the foothills for miles until he reached the town of Belden's Wall. The entire trip took seven days loaded, but it had been worth every mile. After he had delivered his load to a merchant who lived outside the town, he unhitched the horses and rode one in to pick up supplies for the journey back.

As he entered the town—Belden's Wall was smaller than the City of Kings but a lot bigger than Woodvale—he decided that he would fill his water skins first and then purchase what he needed from the marketplace. After getting directions to the town well, he approached it and was about to dismount when he saw a breathtaking creature walking toward him from the opposite side.

Ivan remembered it vividly. He was captivated by her beauty and the way she moved. With her shoulders back and her head held high, her precise yet flowing steps made her seem almost regal, even when fetching a bucket of water. Ivan's heart pounded so hard that he was sure she would hear it, and the closer she got, the less breath he was able to draw. He felt too weak to move, and it was all he could do to climb down and offer his assistance with the water. When he was near her, his skin seemed to catch fire and he had trouble speaking.

He remembered thinking to himself, *so this is what love at first sight feels like*, and he had known from that moment on, that she was the woman he wanted to spend the rest of his life with.

They talked for awhile, but then she had to get the water back to her mother who was tending a sick child. He asked if he could see her again, so she agreed to meet him at the marketplace the next day at noon's high sun.

The merchant, who was a shrewd yet kind man, offered Ivan a place to stay while he was there, which turned out to be longer than he had expected. Five days longer to be exact.

He met with the extraordinary maiden, who had introduced herself as Grace Fallow, each day in the marketplace. They talked and laughed, and she told him about her mother being a healer and how she had apprenticed in this art since she had been a little girl. Grace explained how on her twenty-first birthday—she had been born on the twenty-fifth day of the third month of summer—she would be done her apprenticeship and become an adept healer.

Each moment they shared felt natural, like they had known each other forever. She told him how her childhood had been spent living by the sea, and then later about her home in the mountains with her mother and their animals. He loved her stories, but mostly he just loved being with her.

Each day they would walk through a different part of Belden's Wall. She would point out buildings and tell Ivan who owned them and what business they ran, or what part they played in the structure of the community. When they had finally seen the entire town, she took him to the wall that it had been renamed for.

Ivan was amazed when he saw it. It was made of solid stone and was well over twelve feet high. It spanned as far in each direction as the eye could see and appeared to be very old. He asked why anyone would build such a wall, and as they headed back toward the market, she told him the history of Belden's Wall.

"The town had once been called Marshside," she explained as they walked, "because it was built next to a vast marsh. This marsh, woefully named the Missing Marsh, ran north to the *Gatou Plains* and south to the Crooked Mountains, then east, covering six hundred square miles, where it eventually drained into the Lake of Falls. The lake, which spanned for miles in each direction, was bordered by the Missing Marsh on its western shore, the *Gatou Plains* to the north, and the Crooked Mountains on its southern and eastern edges.

The lake was named for its five great waterfalls that roared out of the mountains on its eastern side and plummeted hundreds of feet into its icy depths. Being fed by the falls and the marsh, and lying in the crook of the mountains, the lake had no outlet except down the cracks and crevices of the mountain itself. For centuries it had cut its way through those chambers and eventually formed an underground river. This river ran for miles within the belly of the mountain until finally it cascaded·down the opposite side, forming the One River. The One River then wound its way south through the Drylands, as its only source of water, until it found its way to the South Seas."·

Ivan was still contemplating a river flowing under a mountain as Grace began to explain the Wall of Belden.

"Two hundred years ago," she told him, "when the people of the south came through the mountain pass—this pass was later named Belden's Pass—looking for a new place to settle and hopefully a trade route to the north, they ventured through the foothills and into the *Gatou Plains*. The plains were beautiful with tall thick grass and herds of massive black buffalo, but the wagon train was driven back by the tribes of the *Gatou*.

These warriors of the plains, led by their chief *Shadak*, were fearsome with their painted faces and wild yells. Though they were just over four feet in stature, they were *much* stronger than an average man.

The settlers tried to fight back, but when the *Gatou* attacked with their spears and great-bows, riding those wolf-like beasts, they struck terror into the hearts of the southerners.

After that first encounter, over half of the people returned to the south, and the remainder settled in the spot that is now known as Belden's Wall."

Ivan knew the plains people and had dealt with them on a few occasions, and it was hard for him to imagine them as a savage race after witnessing their gentle ways and their expertise in art and leather crafting. The garments they could fashion from a single Black Buffalo hide were incredible and highly fashionable in the City of Kings.

"With the marsh a mile from its eastern edge," she continued, "and the mountains to the south, the people were protected against attacks from either of those two directions. Once they had found this safer area, they started to build shelters and a fortification.

This is when the name Belden first appeared in the writings.

Frank Belden was a seaman from the town of Southport. He served in the Kings Army and Navy for years, fighting against invasion and the pirates of the South Seas. One day he had come home from three months of duty at sea to find that his wife had been murdered, and his ten-year-old son Marcus was being cared for by a friend. His wife had put their boy in the cellar, closed the trapdoor and placed the rug over top to conceal his whereabouts, therefore sacrificing herself for the child.

Frank had been informed that the raid was carried out by the Dryland Brigands who roamed like nomads through the south, plundering and pillaging as they went.

Feeling guilty about leaving his wife to such a fate, he packed up his son and their belongings, and headed north with a caravan to build a new life. He had made a vow on that day that he would never leave his son like that again, and he never did.

Frank was a natural leader with his brilliant strategies and easygoing manner, and was the one who organized the southerners in their first skirmish with the *Gatou*. His background in military training, both as a soldier and seaman, resulted in him taking charge and saving many lives that first day in the new land.

He was about five-foot-ten, with brown hair, hazel eyes and a lean muscular body, but people always thought he was over six feet because of his powerful demeanor.

He was the one who picked the site for the town, and the one who organized the fortifications to protect Marshside. He delegated duties to the settlers and kept everyone so busy that they hardly had a chance to think about the danger that roamed the plains to the north. He also organized the patrols and oversaw the building of the barrier that surrounded their new home.

The barrier was eight feet high and consisted of thick poles standing side-by-side, sharpened at the top and sunk into the ground four feet. This barricade was reinforced and braced on the inside, and a tower was built every three hundred feet to accommodate a lookout."

Ivan interrupted Grace as they turned onto the street that led to the marketplace, and asked how she knew the story in such detail. She explained how a woman named Maden, and later Mallah, had kept detailed writings of their journey from the south to the new land in the north, and that these documents were preserved in the archives at the library in Southport. Grace's mother had taught her to read when she was four, and when she had reached eight years old she'd read every parchment that Maden and Mallah had penned.

"Frank Belden and his son Marcus were legends in the south," she told him as they walked along. As she continued, Ivan could hear the compassion and caring in her voice when she talked about the hardships and sacrifices the people had endured.

"As spring warmed the land, they began digging a well and planting gardens with the seeds they had brought. They started building cabins for themselves and pens and outbuildings for the various animals that had survived the journey.

Frank's next task was to teach the men who had agreed to be in the hunting party, how to fight. Out of the forty-two men and boys that were big enough or fit enough to carry arms, only four were proficient with a bow or even owned one. The rest he began teaching hand-to-hand combat and melee weapons use.

Their weapons consisted mainly of axes and long knives, with a few old swords and the odd spear, but Frank managed to train them well enough to handle themselves in a frontal assault or defensive situation.

The wooden perimeter was finished as fast as possible in anticipation of an attack, but it never came. At first this puzzled Frank but he soon realized that the *Gatou* were not bloodthirsty savages, but a territorial tribe that only attacked to protect what they considered to be theirs. The problem he now faced was that the main food supply in the area was the Black Buffalo that roamed the *Gatou Plains*. With the food cache dwindling, and the first month of winter coming closer, the few deer and eating birds in the foothills were not going to be enough to feed nearly one hundred and fifty people for long.

Since the moment they had reached the north, and with all the tasks that Frank had taken on, when he was busy or overseeing a project, his son Marcus was being watched and cared for by Maden.

Maden was a heavyset woman, very stern but motherly. She was always serious about whatever task she undertook, but loved the little boy like her own and treated him with gentleness and kindness. Marcus seemed to like her also and was content to do his studies or help out with the chores while Maden, with her ink and parchment, put into words the events that occurred each day.

Frank knew that his little ragtag army didn't stand a chance against the *Gatou* warriors in an open fight. He had seen the plainsmen that first day, riding their wolves at a dead run and shooting their great-bows, hitting everything they targeted. Frank wondered how men that size could even draw the string on a great-bow, and if he hadn't seen it with his own eyes, would never have believed it.

In his life he had only known a few men that could actually pull a great-bow to full tension and shoot with any accuracy, and the *Gatou* bows looked far sturdier than any of the ones he had seen.

The problem was becoming more urgent and Frank had to find the solution. He needed the Black Buffalo to feed his people, but the plains weren't safe and that was where the herds grazed.

The men were finishing the cabins. The woman and children were out gathering berries for drying and preserving, and Frank was trying to figure a way to get into the plains unnoticed. He finally decided that they needed to skirt the edge and try to find any animals that may be close, or had wandered into the foothills. Hopefully this would work and they would get a good supply of meat without any confrontations with the *Gatou*. To be on the safe side though he had five wagons disassembled and got his craftsmen to make the armor they needed most . . . shields.

They made forty-five shields, each three feet wide and four feet long, and he made sure that every hunter had one strapped to his back and ready to use in case of an attack.

Frank kissed Marcus on the forehead and promised him he would be home by nightfall. He thanked Maden again and headed out with the others. At first light, and with his plan in place, the hunting party rode north.

They kept up a good pace and reached the southern border of the plains by midmorning. They pulled back and out of sight, moving westward and watching for any signs of the Black Buffalo. As the sun reached its highest point, a small herd was sighted grazing near a stand of trees that led into the foothills. The hunters circled and approached them from within the cover of the thicket. They crept closer, making as little noise as possible, and stayed well hidden.

Frank pointed out the two bulls to the bowmen, and the four of them took their positions and waited for his signal. When the herd had moved closer, and both bulls were broadside, he lifted his arm. The *snap!* of the bowstrings cut the silence. The first bull fell to his knees and then to his side as the arrows struck true. The other started to run toward the hunters, which seemed strange to Frank, so he scanned the horizon. Finally the majestic animal fell into the tall reddish-green grasses of the plains only ten yards from their position.

Frank's worst fears were realized as he saw unusual movement to the right of the remaining herd. Before he could warn anyone, two of the younger boys scrambled from the trees, and with their long knives drawn, ran straight to the fallen prey.

Frank yelled at the first boy and he ducked down startled as an arrow sliced the air above his head and disappeared into the ground behind him. The second arrow bit into the other boy's side and spun him around as he fell, holding the wound. The first boy jumped up and ran toward the trees. An arrow hit him hard in the back, sinking deep into the shield he was carrying. Another pierced his calf muscle as he plunged headlong into his friends, and temporary safety.

Frank ran after the injured boy, his shield at the ready and his sword drawn as he called for the longbows to cover him. They fell into position but could see no targets. The first volley of *Gatou* arrows fell as he reached the second boy, who was now silent and still. They hit his shield with such force that he was almost knocked to the ground. He grabbed the young hunter and dragged him to the trees as another volley was fended off by some of the men who had now moved in front of him with their shields placed together. They moved deeper into the brush and tended their wounded companions as best they could, but Frank knew they had to get the boys home soon.

The men were preparing for another attack, but Frank stopped them. He had a feeling the *Gatou* wouldn't be pursuing them as long as they stayed out of the plains, and with the condition of the wounded, it was a risk that he would have to take.

They got the injured boys out of danger and back to the settlement before nightfall. He reached his cabin to find Marcus busy constructing a miniature replica of their village out of small sticks and blocks of wood, and Maden buried deep in thought and parchments. He told her what had happened, then picked up his son and held him tightly. 'Just a few more years and that could have been my boy out there,' he told Maden."

Grace stopped her tale as they reached the edge of the marketplace, but Ivan wanted to know what happened next and how and why the wall was built. Grace had teased him, saying she had to be getting back, but then laughed and said that she still had some time left before her mother needed her and promised to finish the story.

They moved away from the noisy market and found a shaded place to sit down as Grace began where she had left off. The sound of her voice lilted through the air like a verbal fragrance, drawing him in like magic, and Ivan just smiled as she continued.

"The first month of autumn had touched the land and the people were very busy, both inside and outside the walls of their new haven. The hunters were combing the foothills for deer and game birds, and hopefully a stray buffalo. At only twenty-five feet down, the well had been finished and was providing more than enough fresh water to sustain them. The cabins were almost finished and they had started preparations to build a town hall. The chickens were laying again after their long refusal and the two cows were giving enough milk to satisfy the youngest children. The women had enough berries picked and readied to last into the winter and everyone was feeling much better about their situation.

Everyone that is except Frank, who had been spending his days away from the others in a little glen he had found to the south, in the shadow of the Crooked Mountains. He went there to meditate and try to find an answer to their food problem. It had to be solved soon or there was a possibility that not all the villagers would live to see the spring. The few deer and birds, and the odd bear, were enough to get by on, but they would thin out fast. The Black Buffalo were the only answer and they were abundant, but out of his reach at the moment. One of those enormous animals could feed his people for weeks, and that frustrated him completely.

As he sat cross-legged in the grass with his eyes closed, he remembered that black mass barreling toward him, eating up the plains with each stride before it fell to his bowmen. It was at least ten feet tall at the top of its horned head, and probably twelve at its massive hump and he guessed it to weigh in at nearly four thousand pounds.

Frank played the whole wasted hunting trip over in his mind and that's when the solution presented itself.

He left his thinking spot and rushed to the settlement. He stopped outside the protective wall and gave the signal. Hearing this, the guards opened the big gates and allowed him access. He hurried to his cabin and stepped inside. He walked over to his son, who was drawing on a piece of parchment, and lifted him high into the air, spinning him around. He continued this for a bit, causing Marcus to laugh out loud, then hugged him tightly before setting him down again. He then walked over, and much to Maden's surprise, kissed her cheek and gave her a big hug.

That night over dinner, which consisted of rabbit stew and greens that grew wild throughout the foothills, Frank told Marcus and Maden his plan.

He arose the next morning before daybreak and readied himself. He had no time to make breakfast so he broke off a chunk of heavy-bread that Maden had baked the day before. He was thankful he'd brought his cookstove up from Southport as he knifed some of the strawberry preserve onto the bread, eating it hurriedly. He looked in on Marcus. It wasn't cool enough to build a fire, and he knew Maden would be over long before the boy awoke, so he put on his hunting cloak and riding boots and left the cabin.

He went straight to the horse corral where he caught and saddled his mount, then saddled one of the packhorses. Without hesitation he led the horses to the supply wagons to undertake the next part of his plan.

Of the one hundred and three wagons that had left Southport, there were only sixty-seven left including the five they had made the shields from. Most of the people who had fled back to the south those first days had taken a horse and saddlebags and abandoned the bigger stuff. This left an abundance of wagons, a shortage of horses, and families who had stayed because they didn't want to take younger children or elders back over that hundred mile trail.

He approached the wagons that were located in the southeast corner of the village and went directly to the one he needed.

The wagons had been organized into six rows and Frank had overseen the inventory and distribution of supplies.

He opened the back of the wagon and looked at the twenty one-hundred pound sacks that were stored within. He lifted out the four sacks he needed and closed it back up. He then tied the sacks to the packsaddle, two on each side, and made sure they were even. The horse groaned with the added weight, so Frank told him that if his idea worked the people would be eating buffalo this winter instead of packhorse. He grabbed the lead rope, mounted his horse and rode up to the front gates. It was still dark when he reached them, so he gave the signal to announce his approach. The guards seemed confused at first, but opened up for him and he headed straight north toward the *Gatou Plains*.

Frank had only traveled a mile before the sky began to brighten. He kept the marsh on his right, and in sight, just the way he had done on that first hunting trip to the plains. He traveled a few miles more, always watching for the large circle of trees that would be his destination. He rode down a grassy slope and up a long steep incline. He ascended for awhile before reaching the crest and then stepped down to give his horses a rest. He led the two animals along the ridge of the hilltop until he found a clearing where he unloaded the packhorse. He loosened both saddles and tethered each animal with enough lead to graze.

Frank walked to the very top, which appeared to be the highest point in the foothills, and surveyed his surroundings.

To the south he could see the settlement, and from his vantage point it looked just like his son's miniature of the village. The Crooked Mountains loomed ominously in the distance and their silhouette was brilliant as the sun rose from behind and cast its life-giving light on the land. In the embrace of those mountains, where they ran east and turned north, was a lake that looked like an emerald shining in the sunlight. West of the lake, and in the shadow of those monstrous rock formations, lay the marsh. He didn't know its name, nor if it even had one, but its sheer size was staggering.

From its mazelike waterways, to its swampy bogs, guarded by those strange looking trees with their twisted limbs, it commanded an eerie presence. Half of it was covered by fog and the other half was mostly hidden by dense growth and those tall gnarled watchers.

Frank turned his attention to the north where the *Gatou Plains* stretched for miles along the border of the foothills and the marsh. To the far north he could make out a forest that ran along the plain's entire northern edge.

He could see the many herds of buffalo, and from where he stood they looked like black dots moving across a reddish-green blanket. He glanced back and forth across that grassy sea, trying to find signs of the *Gatou* tribe, but could see none. Not a building or camp could he make out. This puzzled him and he scanned so intensely that his head began to hurt. Finally he thought he could see some of the wolf-riders chasing a small herd, but he wasn't sure.

As he continued his search, he found himself admiring the hunting skill of the *Gatou* and wondered how long they had inhabited this area. He moved his focus into the foothills straight north of his position, and after a short while, found the area he was looking for. He returned to the horses, secured the sacks and tightened his cinch before starting down the hill toward what he hoped would be the salvation of his people.

After traveling a few miles across hills and valleys, with only a few rabbits and a chipmunk for company, he finally saw the thick ring of trees that towered high above the rest. He knew the reason for this abnormal growth, and that reason was exactly why he was headed there. He reached the outer trees, followed their edge until he found a well-worn trail, and started in.

As he rode through the opening, the day turned to dusk in an instant and a peaceful feeling swept over him. Even in the dim light his horse was surefooted and carried him ever closer to the center. His excitement grew when he saw the bright light only a hundred feet in the distance, and when the sky opened he had to cover his eyes for a moment to let them adjust. When he pulled his hand away he took in one of the most breathtaking sights he had ever seen.

A circular meadow, lush in grass and flora, enticed his senses. The open area was about three hundred yards across, and in the center was the spring he had ridden all this way to visit. It bubbled slowly from the ground creating a large pool and then overflowed into smaller pools around its outer edge. These outer water-traps were crisscrossed with a myriad of footprints, at least two feet below the meadow floor, that cut deep into the dirt from years of animal use.

Frank and his hunters had found this place when they traveled north to search for buffalo, and he had returned here to carry out his idea.

He rode to the edge of the watering hole and dismounted. He untied the sacks, set them on the ground and led his horses to the trees to picket them. Walking back to the spring, he surveyed it thoroughly looking for the best place to empty the contents of his sacks. Finally he decided that two of the outer pools would do nicely for what he had in mind.

He pulled one of the sacks to the edge and jumped down. He hoisted it onto his shoulder then walked over and set it down. With his knife, he cut the string and emptied one hundred pounds of salt into the clear water. He repeated this until he had emptied all four sacks into the two pools. If buffalo were anything like cattle they would be able to smell that salt for miles and would be drawn to it like a bee to a flower. If this worked, there would be a continual meat supply that would feed his people through many winters.

Frank felt warm inside as he left the spring and rode back to the settlement. The sun was moving down the western sky and a new hope was building in his heart. He would leave the trap for a few days and then return to see if any of the buffalo had entered the meadow. If his calculations were correct, about four more sacks should create the effect he wanted, and if the buffalo came they would need to build tree stands for the bowmen to await their next visit.

He was working it all out in his mind when the village walls appeared in front of him. The guards saw him and opened the gates. He entered, put his horses away and went straight to his cabin without telling anyone the reason for his trip. To reveal it now seemed premature and he wanted to wait until he was sure the buffalo were attracted and visiting the salted spring."

As she finished the sentence, Grace stopped and informed Ivan it was now called "Salt Spring".

"Marcus ran to his father, hugged him and started rambling on excitedly. Frank could make out some of what he said—there was a new design for the town hall, and drawings, and a minia-ture—but he didn't fully grasp his son's words until he showed him.

Marcus got his parchment out and presented the drawing to his father. He also showed him the replica he had created depicting the finished building. Frank was amazed at the detail of his design and promised he would propose and show the idea to the elders first thing in the morning.

He was feeling weary from the long day and sat down at the table. Maden served him some leftover rabbit stew with flatbread and it tasted extra good after his long ride. He wolfed down the food and became even more tired as he ate his fill. Thoughts of a good night's sleep filled his mind, and he was about to bed down for the night when Maden cornered him and demanded to know every detail of his trip for her writings. He was tired, but going back over the day's events seemed to solidify the reality that they just might have a chance of getting their winter's meat supply.

The blankets were inviting as he climbed into his bed, and he slept better than he had since he arrived in this harsh land. His dreams were peaceful, as though a weight had been lifted from him somehow, and he awoke the next day feeling refreshed.

He took his son's model and drawings to the morning meeting and showed them to the newly formed council. A five-sided log building that increased capacity and visibility for the types of gatherings it would be used for. Everyone agreed the design was perfect for a town hall and Frank couldn't wait to tell his son.

Marcus was thrilled; the town hall was started, and Frank waited patiently for the time when he would make his next visit to the spring.

It was a week to the day when Frank made his way back along the trail that led through the trees to the meadow. He brought four more sacks to add to the previous amount, which he thought should be enough to ensure results. Any animal within a five-mile radius should be drawn to it if this was going to work. He looked after his horses, poured the sacks into the pools and checked the area for buffalo tracks. He could see many fresh tracks and he looked them over. There were deer, bear and wolf, but no buffalo.

His hopes sank at the sight of the wolf tracks. By the size and depth of the impressions they *might* be *Gatou*, but he didn't want to jump to any conclusions. Only time would tell if the wolves that made those tracks bore riders.

Disheartened, Frank turned away. He mounted his horse and was just about to leave when he saw a single buffalo track. It appeared to be that of a buffalo cow and when he got down to check closer, it looked like there had been a calf with her. The rest of the tracks had been trampled by the other animals, so he went to the northern trail to check for more signs. As he approached the opening he could see clearly that a buffalo cow and her calf had entered the clearing only a day before. Frank tried to contain his excitement, but he knew that only one buffalo needed to visit the Salt Spring to put the next part of his plan in motion.

He hurried back to the settlement and called a town meeting. He explained to everyone what he had done and what needed to be done next. They spent the rest of the day, and the next, preparing the horses and supplies for the last part of his undertaking, and left the following morning for the spring.

When they reached the meadow, Frank started organizing things. He picked the locations for the tree stands and instructed the builders to put them twenty feet up and five feet back into the trees, with a clear view of the entire meadow. Four stands were needed, and the planks, rope and iron nails were unloaded and taken to each location. The extra packhorses were kept about half a mile south where the camp had been set up, and the bowmen awaited the completion of the stands so they could take their places and make sure the view was sufficient.

Everyone worked through the day and completed their tasks before the evening meal. It all looked good, and the bowmen were satisfied, so they loaded up the extra supplies and moved them to the south camp. They ate a quick meal, looked after the horses and turned in early. They had to be up long before daylight to prepare for what Frank hoped would be a fulfilling end to his plan.

It was well before first light when Frank and the four bowmen left for the spring. The darkness hindered their progress but it was only half a mile to the circle of trees, and then a hundred yards to the meadow. When they reached the inner circle the archers climbed the stands and strung their longbows. Frank found a good place at the edge of the trees where he could be seen by each stand's occupant. All the signals had been worked out and not an arrow would leave a bow without his say-so.

He pulled his green hunting cloak closed against the cool morning air, then sat down and leaned against a tree. It was still awhile until dawn and then who knows how long before the buffalo showed, if they showed up at all, so the hunters waited patiently.

There was no wind and the sky was just starting to brighten when the first signs of movement appeared. Two doe deer with their fawns came in from the southeastern trail and stopped just short of the spring. They lifted their heads checking the air for any unusual scent, and when they were satisfied, walked in to take a drink. They drank from the fresh pools and pawed at the salted ones, licking at the water that spilled onto the ground. The bowmen watched for a signal but Frank only wanted big game this day, so after the deer had filled their needs, they left the hunters alone in the meadow once again.

Over the next while they were visited by a black bear and her two cubs, a beautiful six point buck, and a rather curious gopher that seemed to think something was going on. Frank *was* tempted to take down the stag but didn't want to compromise the situation.

Just when it looked hopeless, their long wait was rewarded as the men saw the massive buffalo cow and her calf enter the ring. She was over ten feet tall at the hump and her calf was the size of a horse. Frank guessed their combined weight to be over thirty-five hundred pounds as he watched them amble into the watering hole. The bowmen were ready. With their arrows nocked and strings taut, they awaited the signal that would bring down the mammoth pair, but Frank never moved. He waited while they drank. He waited while they pawed at the salted pools and licked the ground. Even as they moved away from the spring and left the meadow, he waited. He could feel the gaze of the bowmen on him and knew they must be wondering why he didn't give the signal, but Frank did not want to kill a cow and calf, even though they needed the meat. Until now he had followed his plan to the letter and wasn't about to stray from it. He would wait for a bull, even if it took days.

The sun had climbed well into the eastern sky when they heard the hoof beats. He could swear the ground shook as the buffalo entered the clearing. Three young bulls were butting heads and pushing one another back and forth playfully, each nearly twelve feet high at the hump and close to four thousand pounds. Frank smiled as he ducked lower into the grass and gave the 'at ready' signal, which he knew was not needed. The bulls entered the watering area, still pushing and shoving, then drank from the spring. After drinking their fill they moved over and spent a good while just licking the ground where the saltwater had poured from the pools. When the buffalo had finished, they started squaring off again, rehearsing for the day they hoped to be the dominant male in the herd, but for them that day would never come.

Frank jumped up and shouted, stopping them in their tracks. The dark visitors looked around in bewilderment, sniffing the air, trying to locate the sound. He gave the release signal and arrows flew one-after-another until three black mountains, which appeared to grow from the meadow floor, lie still and silent.

Frank had *never* liked to kill, and as he gazed down at those once majestic animals, felt a pang of sorrow. Such a life force to be ended just like that, but their sacrifice would feed his people for a long time.

The bowmen climbed from their perches and moved to the fallen bulls. Frank had started skinning the closest animal and instructed two of them to start on the others. The two remaining men were sent back to camp to bring what they needed to pack the meat and hides.

They had nearly completed removing the thick black hides when the others returned with the pack train. It took the better part of the morning to complete the task, and when they were done, six thousand pounds of meat and six hundred pounds of hides were loaded onto the backs of twenty packhorses. They left the meadow as clean as they could and headed home with a new hope for their future.

What a sight it had been, Maden had written in her journals, Frank leading the hunting party into the village with everyone cheering and shouting his name. He had taken all forty-two horses on the expedition and returned with salvation on their backs. He was a hero to the southerners for what he had done, and would remain a hero for the achievements he made throughout the rest of his remarkable life."

Ivan remembered how he had felt when Grace stopped telling the story, saying she had to get back to help her mother. He
couldn't help but admire a man like Frank Belden, and
understood why Grace had memorized Maden's journals. Still
he wanted to know how the settlers finally made peace with the
Gatou, and why a wall was built around the marsh.

They said goodbye as Ivan held Grace and kissed her cheek.
He told her that he had one day left in Belden's Wall before he
had to go back up north for another load of logs. They agreed to
meet back at the market the next day, and Grace promised she
would finish the story then. She also told Ivan that her mother
wanted to meet the man that was taking up so much of her
daughter's time. Ivan recalled how nervous he had been at the
thought of meeting her mother, and how the butterflies had
fluttered in his stomach when he rode toward the market the next
day. He tied his horse to a hitching post and walked to their
meeting place. As he approached he saw her standing there in a
pretty yellow dress, holding a basket in one hand and a blanket in
the other. She told him she had packed a picnic lunch, so they
headed off to find a suitable spot. She finally found a grassy area
beneath a falseapple tree, so she laid the blanket down and set out
the food. They talked while they ate and when they had finished,
Ivan looked into her bright green eyes, then leaned in and kissed
her. He had wanted to do that since the first time he had seen her,
and it was even sweeter than he could have imagined. He was
afraid she might pull away but she kissed him back ever so gently,
and for a moment it felt like he was dreaming. When their lips
finally parted, Grace blushed slightly then asked him if he would
like to hear the rest of the story. In his euphoric state he could
only nod, so she continued her tale.

CHAPTER

3

Fallen Princess

The *Gatou* had monitored all of Frank's movements near the plains, from that first hunting trip to the salting of the spring, and they admired him. They called him *kau-diche*, which in their tongue meant "cunning warrior". *Shadak*, their chief, had ordered his riders not to interfere with the buffalo who made their way to the Salt Spring. He believed that it would upset the balance, and also, his respect for Frank had grown very strong. This respect though would pale in comparison to the respect they would have for his son Marcus in years to come.

Seven winters had passed since the settlers first arrived in the new land, and the people had found their place within the community. Everyone had a specific function or duty. They had built a school for the children and some new cabins for young couples who had been joined. The buffalo were using the Salt Spring regularly and everything was running smoothly in their little town.

Marcus had turned seventeen that year and was becoming a well educated, handsome young man. Between Maden's guidance and his own thirst for knowledge, at twelve years old he had completed all of his schooling and was helping the teacher instruct two days a week. His intellect was matched only by his strength and dexterity. He could wield a sword and shoot a longbow as good as anyone in the community, including his father, and his love of the land was evident. He had long black hair, dark blue eyes and looked exactly like his mother, so-much-so in fact that every time Frank looked at him it brought out an inner pain. That pain lasted only moments though when he realized that his son, whom he loved beyond words, was a part of her that *he* would have for the rest of his life.

It was the first day of the first month of summer and Marcus was up early. It was still dark, so he took his fire-rock, held it to the candle and scraped it with his long-knife until he had created enough spark to ignite the wick. He put on his clothes and searched the room for the rest of the supplies he would take. He was going on an adventure walk into the foothills today, so he grabbed his hunting cloak, walking boots and longbow.

Marcus preferred to *walk* everywhere he went, not that he had anything against horses, in fact he loved animals, but it just didn't feel right to him. He thought that the only time a horse should have to carry or pull something was when it was too much for a man to handle. For a horse to carry a man around when he had two good legs of his own, seemed ridiculous to him.

He blew out the candle, walked out of his room and into the kitchen where he saw his father at the table mulling over a parchment. He had cooked some eggs and buffalo sausage, so Marcus fixed himself a plate and sat down. Frank was busy figuring out plans to send a caravan down to Southport for some *much* needed supplies, but stopped to visit with his son. They talked briefly, and his father mentioned that both Sarah and Tisha had dropped by to visit him the day before and Marcus looked amused. He had no interest in those two, or any other girls in the settlement, but the girls sure took an interest in him.

When he helped out at the school, all the girls would sit in the front row so they could watch him. They would whisper and giggle and pass him notes. Marcus was more than just good-looking, he was *almost* beautiful. With his broad shoulders and dark tan—his skin reflected the amount of time he'd spent roaming the foothills—just one look with those piercing blue eyes would send any girl's heart fluttering.

Frank looked worried, so Marcus asked what was troubling him. Frank informed him that two more sheep and a goat had been taken, and the tracks had led into the marsh.

There had never been a threat from the marsh until this past winter. The winters since they had first come to the new land had been fairly mild, due to the large body of water that comprised most of the marsh. The last winter though brought a cold snap that lasted a month and had frozen its waterways. Frank believed that this phenomenon had unbalanced the food chain, causing the marsh-dwellers to leave their natural lair and supplement their diet with land roving animals. Marcus wasn't sure about that, but he'd sure had fun sliding across the frozen water on his birthday.

Now all the animals were being brought inside the town walls each night rather than left in their fenced areas, and many of the villagers were frightened at the thought of what might be lurking in that quagmire.

Marcus however, wasn't concerned with any of that. If he wasn't designing some new structure or practicing his sword and archery skills, you would find him either teaching at the school, which he designed, or gallivanting around the foothills. Today was no different as he said goodbye to his father, stuffed some buffalo sausages into his satchel and jogged to the front gates.

After the first year at Marshside, and no attacks coming from the *Gatou*, the guards had been removed from their posts. With this new threat from the marsh, they had been assigned there once again for continued safety. The guards knew Marcus well, in fact he was their most frequent visitor, and let him pass without hesitation.

Marcus always loved the feeling of leaving the settlement and wandering into the wilderness. He loved the sense of adventure and the fact of not knowing where his feet might take him next, but today he did know. He was going to the Salt

Spring. He went there quite often just to sit in one of the tree stands and watch the animals that came to drink or lick the salted ground. He also enjoyed visiting that magical place because Maden had told him the story of his father and the Salt Spring so many times over the years. He loved it so much that no matter how many times she told it, he always asked to hear it again.

The sun lit up a cloudless sky as he moved along the path. The day was perfect and Marcus felt great, and when he felt that way he would sing. He had a beautiful singing voice, with a deep timbre of lows and sweet resonant highs. He would never sing in public though, and had once made the mistake of singing in front of Maden, who had then tried to get him to sing in the village music group. Marcus only sang for whichever animal might be in earshot as he made his way through the rolling foothills. This morning he thought he would sing one of his favorites called, *The Foolish Maiden*, and so he began.

> *A tender young maiden lived high on a hill*
> *In her beauty well none could compare*
> *The birds sang her praises, the wind called her name*
> *And the sun paled to her golden hair*
>
> *In this land there were two mighty kingdoms*
> *And from each a young prince he did ride*
> *And rode far until, at the top of the hill*
> *Each one asked if she'd be his bride*
>
> *She told them she would not choose either*
> *And cast them aside with a wave*
> *But then she did say, Indeed that she may*
> *If one gave her all that she craved*
>
> *They searched high and low through the kingdoms*
> *And brought her all things rare and fine*

But to each she did chide, and was not satisfied
For her wants were the whimsical kind

Now for years they had vied for her favors
But a love with no answer does fade
Now she sits on the hill, awaiting them still
A lonely and bitter old maid

When he finished, he laughed out loud. He had found that song amusing since the first time he had heard it as a young boy, and it still got to him every time he sang it.

He was walking along the well-worn trail, when he saw Lookout Hill rising up in the distance. As he got closer he could see where the trail split at the bottom to either go around or climb to the top. His father had named the landmark on his first journey to the spring and Marcus would always hike up it to look around.

Climbing was easy for Marcus and he loped up the hillside, reaching the ridge where the trail flattened out and wound along its crest. He slowed his pace to a fast walk until he got to the place where his father had stood when he first gazed out over the new land. He stopped near the edge and had a look for himself. The village looked to him like it always did in his mind's-eye, and the mysterious marsh—this place had become even more mysterious since those creatures had started leaving its waterways—seemed to go on forever. Then there was the lake that Marcus wished so badly to visit, but that would mean either taking a boat through the marsh or braving the *Gatou* territory, and neither one of those choices would be a healthy one.

The *Gatou Plains* had always intrigued Marcus and he had ventured close to it many times in his travels. His main reason for this was to try to get a glimpse of those fabled wolf-riders, but unfortunately, *he* had never seen one. He studied the plains intently now, but as usual, could see no sign of them. He was beginning to wonder if they even existed, but Maden's writings were not to be refuted and neither were his dad's warnings, so he had always used caution while nearing the plains. Another landmark that caught his eye was that great forest to the north, but he knew that he would probably never get a chance to explore that either.

Marcus concluded his scanning and started off toward the Salt Spring, reaching it before the sun had barely cleared the Crooked Mountains to the east. He filled his water skin, which he had almost drained, jogged to his favorite tree stand and climbed up to await the morning visitors.

By noon he had seen some deer, a family of foxes, and a buffalo cow and calf accompanied by a dry cow. He pulled tight the string on his longbow and targeted the dry cow just to show himself that he could take her down if he decided, but then loosened it again and put it away.

He was feeling energetic, so he decided to climb the tallest tree supporting the stand. He reached the top, sat out on a limb and proceeded to eat some of the buffalo sausage he had brought. He welcomed the tasty meal and even had some entertainment as two more fox entered the meadow, taking turns chasing each other playfully.

He had finished his meal and was taking a drink from his skin, when he heard a yell. It was the voice of a girl, and he moved his focus in the direction of the sound. The cry had come from the east, so he concentrated, trying to pick out anything unusual. From his treetop perch he could see the lay of the land all the way to the marsh, which was about a mile and a half from his position. He was watching carefully, trying to discern some movement when he saw a figure moving southward along the edge of the swampy shore. About ten yards behind he could see another figure moving in the same direction and closing in. The trail they were on was about to swing west, and was the same one that entered the meadow from the southeast. It only took a moment for Marcus to commit and he climbed down quickly. He grabbed his longbow and hurried out of the stand and onto the ground. He was at full speed in moments and left the meadow on the southeast trail.

He moved through the thick trees swiftly and turned straight east toward the marsh. He heard a scream and pushed himself even harder, and within another two hundred yards, saw movement on the trail ahead. It appeared to be a young girl, but it was hard to tell for sure. Marcus stopped, readied an arrow and waited. He could see now that it *was* a girl and she was staggering badly but running as fast as possible, and not ten feet behind her was a reptilian looking creature with a fish-like head and scaly body.

He pulled his longbow taut and tried to target the fish-man, but the girl was in the way. She noticed him now and looked into his eyes as she ran at him. It took only a moment to see that hers was a look of desperation and defeat. She lunged forward, holding her side, but each time she stumbled, her pursuer would gain ground. Marcus retargeted and released the shaft. The arrow sliced through the air just above the girl's head and struck her assailant in the chest, below the right shoulder, spinning it around and onto the ground beside the trail. The girl fell at the same time and lie still.

Concern for the girl was foremost in his mind, and he barely noticed the reptile as it staggered east, back down the trail. He ran to where she had fallen, laid his longbow down and knelt beside her. She was unconscious and blood was pouring from a wound in her side. She was obviously *Gatou*, and for a moment he wondered how this situation had come to be, but now was not the time. He had to stop the bleeding and get some help soon.

Taking off his hunting cloak, he cut a strip of cloth from it. He gently lifted her shirt and assessed the wound. It was a deep bite, but didn't look like it would be fatal as long as he could stop the bleeding in time. That was assuming it wasn't infected with any venom or poison.

He washed the gash as best he could and wrapped the cloth strip around her waist to staunch the blood flow. Her breathing was labored and her face was twisted with pain, but it abated slightly and her color began to return as the bleeding lessened.

She was stable for now, but he had to get her back to his settlement if he was going to save her life. Moving her right now was
not an option, and any motion would cause the bleeding to
increase. He would wait until it was safe to carry her, or make a
litter, but either way he had to get her to safety soon.

He built a fire and filled his satchel with leaves and grass,
placing it under her head. He looked down the trail and wondered if that lizard-man had gone to get some friends to come
back and finish the job. If they did, he would be ready, and
stuck his arrows into the ground for easy access.

The fire was roaring nicely and his weapons were handy, so
he sat down and took a few deep breaths. He would always do
this when he was stressed, because it cleared his mind and
helped him focus. The girl's wound had almost quit bleeding
and there didn't look to be any infection setting in, so he looked
to her basic needs. He took his water skin, parted her lips and
poured the cool liquid into her mouth. She coughed as he did
so, but swallowed most of it. He repeated this a few more times,
then laid the skin down and really looked at her for the first
time since the incident.

She had long black hair, light green eyes and dark skin, and
to Marcus she looked absolutely stunning, even with her pained
expression. Her shirt, shoes and pants—he could not recall ever
seeing a girl wearing pants before—were all made of leather, but
not like any leather he'd ever seen. It appeared light and supple,
almost like garment material. On each of her fingers were rings
of intricate design, and around her neck was a necklace of
equally fine craftsmanship. She had a large hoop through each
ear and bracelets adorned her wrists, and each piece of her
jewelry looked like it had been crafted of solid gold.

He stroked her head and told her everything was going to
be all right, then did something he had never done before in his
life. He sang for her a song his mother had taught him as a child.
As he sang, he could see her face relax and body tremble a little
less, so he continued in hope that it would soothe her even
further.

The sun was setting as Marcus finished his song, and the fire was starting to die down, so he threw on a few more sticks. He knew they would be spending the night because of the girl's condition, but that was nothing new to Marcus. He had spent many a night out under the stars on his adventure walks, and what an adventure this had turned into.

Dusk was setting in and he was just about to cover the girl with his cloak, when he heard a noise up the trail toward the marsh. He quickly grabbed his bow and an arrow, preparing for the attack, but instantly knew his mistake and turned only in time to feel his head explode with pain . . . then darkness."

Grace stopped the story, much to Ivan's chagrin, and asked him if he would like some of the dessert she had made. He told her yes, and she handed him a big piece of cake, that she referred to as squirrel cake. He hoped it got its name from the assortment of nuts that were in it, then smiled and nodded his approval. Grace smiled back and poured them each a cup of water from the container she had brought. When they had finished their cake and washed it down, Grace continued where she had left off.

"Marcus regained consciousness, but his ears were buzzing and his head throbbed intensely. His sight was blurred as he opened his eyes, and he fought hard to focus. As he waited for his vision to return he could hear voices, but couldn't understand what they were saying. His first thoughts were of the girl. *Was she alive? Was she safe?* His head was still pounding, but his eyes had started to clear when he realized he was sitting down with his back against a pole. His hands were tied behind him and his feet had been secured as well. A moment of relief came to him when he realized that he wasn't in the marsh, but it was cut short when he saw the massive wolf watching him, only ten feet away. *Well,* he thought, *I'd rather be tied here guarded by a wolf, than to be some overgrown lizard's lunch.*

He heard voices again and turned his attention that way. He saw two young men about twenty yards away. They were both well under five feet tall, with black hair and dark skin. They were wearing that unique leather clothing, and carried spears. Now that he knew his captors were *Gatou*, he thought for *sure* the girl must be safe. That thought comforted him even more than he realized, and he sighed deeply.

He couldn't let thoughts of her distract him, and he checked his bindings. They were secure and he knew that any amount of struggling would be futile, and even if he did get loose, he had no idea what that wolf was trained to do.

He looked to the sky and realized it was well after high sun, and as far as he knew, he had been unconscious for almost a day. He thought of his father and what he would do when Marcus failed to show up at the settlement. He had stayed out overnight many times before so Frank wouldn't be worried yet, but if he wasn't back by nightfall Marcus knew a search party would be sent to look for him. The *last* outcome he wanted now was to cause trouble between his people and the *Gatou*.

The two men were still talking and it wasn't in the kingdom tongue, in fact he was fairly sure they didn't even know they were in the kingdom. They stopped talking when they realized he was conscious and ran into the thick grass, out of sight.

Marcus started to laugh when he thought of all the times he had wanted to see the *Gatou* up close. It looked like he'd got his wish even though this wasn't exactly what he'd had in mind. Just then, five *Gatou* appeared and walked up to him. He stood up and awaited them, trying not to show any fear. As they approached, the one that he assumed was the leader said something to the wolf and he moved off and laid down in the grass about fifty feet away. The *Gatou* stopped a few yards from him and were arguing about something. The older man, who had directed the wolf, was speaking in a loud tone to the younger man standing next to him. The other three, who Marcus thought must be guards, just stood there looking at the ground, pretending to hear nothing. He knew the *Gatou* were discussing him, and when the younger man seemed to convince the elder of something, he hoped it was in his favor.

As they approached, one of the guards walked up carrying a rope. He used his bone-knife to cut Marcus' hands free of the pole, then removed the bindings from his feet, leaving his hands tied behind him. The *Gatou* placed the rope around his neck and motioned for him to follow. The rope scratched his skin as the man jerked him forward. By the mood of these warriors, and the rough way he was being handled, Marcus knew the outcome of this little jaunt was not going to be pleasant. He waited for his opportunity, and the next time his captor jerked the rope, he ran at him with his full force, knocking him to the ground. He ran as fast as he could in the opposite direction, looking for escape. Not a moment later the wind was knocked from him and he was pinned to the ground on his belly, with sharp teeth at the base of his neck awaiting their master's command. It never came, or at least the lethal one didn't, and the little group continued on their way without any more foolish outbursts.

Hunger and thirst entered his mind as he walked along behind them, and he thought of the girl again. These warriors must have thought he was the one who harmed her, but surely they could see the lizard's bite mark and realize the truth of the situation. Somehow he had to make them understand before they did something that they, and especially he, would regret. He tried yelling, and received a sharp jerk on the rope, which caused a trickle of blood to flow down his neck. He could see this ending badly, and was desperately trying to think of some way to explain, when they reached their destination.

The *Gatou* camp was built in a small valley between the rolling hills. It was very simple, yet efficient. All the buildings were about six feet tall and had roofs made of living grass, explaining why they could never be seen from Lookout Hill. The outside fires, which were somehow smokeless, were all covered with the same living canopy, held up with poles and unseen from the crest of the hills. There were about forty shelters and three areas where wolves were being kept, with no need for fences. He wondered for a moment why everything was so camouflaged. Why *did* the *Gatou* want to stay hidden so? They had no enemies that he was aware of, and with their skill and hunting abilities, who did they have to fear? Maybe they were just a private race of people that wanted to stay to themselves.

As their small group reached the outer fringe of the camp, Marcus could see the *Gatou* busy at their daily tasks. The children who weren't being schooled in some ability were running and playing with the wolf pups and everyone in the camp, including the children, were wearing leather garments and gold jewelry.

Marcus saw men skinning buffalo, training wolves and practicing archery with those incredible great-bows. The women were preparing hides and meat, as well as crafting garments and jewelry. He saw rope weavers, weapon makers and builders. Everyone had a specific task. The strange part was that at each workstation there were at least three or four children learning from the adults while they worked. These people were happy and content with their existence, and Marcus could sense that they had found a deep peace and balance within their little part of the land.

The workers were stopping now and staring at him as he was being led into the center of the camp. The women started ushering children inside the grass huts, and the men moved in to get a closer look at the spectacle. They stopped, and the leader instructed them to secure Marcus to a large pole in the middle. There he stood, helplessly bound, with all these dark skinned people gathering around. Each one was at least a foot shorter than him, and he wondered what fate might befall him at their hands.

By now he had the attention of the whole tribe, but they kept their distance. Only the leader and the younger man remained close to him, and again they had words. The young man was adamant about something, but the elder held his eyes. The older man pointed at Marcus and said, '*Kau-diche-rah.*' That lessened the fury of the other man, but only a little. Finally they agreed and moved away, but then Marcus saw something that turned his blood to ice water in his veins.

He felt sick to his stomach and his knees almost gave out on him. Lined up before him, only fifty paces away, were eight bowmen with great-bows at the ready. The *Gatou* warrior who had led him to this place grabbed the rope that was still hanging from his neck and wrapped it around the pole, choking him as he pulled it tight. He tied it and moved away. The bowmen nocked their arrows at the leader's command, and awaited his signal.

Marcus couldn't believe what was happening. He thought of his father, and wished he were back home by the warm fire discussing some settlement issue, or designing a new structure, or adventure walking through some new territory. This could *not* be happening, but it was. He had to accept it and try to be brave.

The archers lifted their bows and pulled back on the strings.

He had heard about executions like this in stories, but had never witnessed any. He had sometimes wondered what he might do in this situation, but everything he had ever thought of was foolishness when it came down to actually standing here. He had only moments to live, so he closed his eyes and waited. His heart pounded like a drum and his body was shaking, but he would not beg for mercy or cry out. He would be a man and not give them the satisfaction of seeing his fear. Every breath seemed like an eternity now, and his mind was separated from his body. He could hear a scream welling in his throat and felt ashamed. *Will I wet myself also?* he thought, as the scream became louder. He was filled with self-loathing and fear, but then realized the scream was not coming from him, but from in front of him.

He opened his eyes and saw the girl. She was standing between him and the archers, holding her side and swaying in her weakened state. She was screaming something at the leader, as the younger man ran toward her.

Marcus' knees buckled, tightening the rope around his neck, and he knew darkness once more."

CHAPTER

4

Blood Brothers

G race paused her story to take a drink of water and Ivan watched her contently. She finished and asked if he was ready to meet Zarina. Ivan had never been a shy or timid person, but he remembered feeling a surge of panic at the thought of meeting her mother that day. Ivan told Grace he was looking forward to it, which was true other than the uneasy feeling in his stomach. He told her that as soon as she finished the story he was ready to meet her, and as Grace continued, he was wishing he didn't have to leave for the north the next morning.

"Marcus awakened to find himself lying in one of the grass huts, on a soft pallet covered with buffalo hide. He was being tended by a young *Gatou* maiden, and was completely free of any shackles. As soon as the girl saw him sit up, she ran out of the dwelling. He could see a water-skin and some dried meat and berries on a wooden platter, and his weapons and belongings were laid out on the table nearby. The younger man, who had argued with the leader, entered the hut and looked into his eyes. He put his fist over his heart and gave a slight bow which came across as a sign of gratitude and respect. Marcus stood and returned the gesture, and as he raised his arm, the *Gatou* grabbed his hand and held it firmly. He then took out his bone-knife and cut Marcus across the palm. He wanted to pull away, but didn't want to offend his new ally, so he gritted his teeth and waited. The warrior then cut his own in the same fashion and clasped their hands together, holding tightly. Marcus held his gaze and they stood there staring at each other until the leader entered. The young tribesman nodded, then released his grasp and left the hut.

Marcus had heard stories from Maden about the blood brother ritual, but this was the first time he had witnessed it. He was having many firsts today, and was *sure* it wasn't finished yet.

The *Gatou* elder, who Marcus thought must be the chief, gestured for him to sit, so he rested on the bed while the chief sat at the table. He motioned to the water and food, and that's when Marcus realized he was *famished* and *parched*, so he ate and drank vigorously. The old man watched quietly until he was finished, then smiled and handed him a wafer-thin piece of leather and pointed to his cut. He realized it was still bleeding, took the offer and wrapped his hand.

He had an instant respect for this man and could feel the power emanating from him. He could see a deep wisdom in the chief's eyes and sense an almost youthful presence beneath that wrinkled and timeworn face.

The old man hit his chest with his fist and said, '*Shadak*.'

He hit his chest and said, 'Marcus.'

The *Gatou* looked at him and said, '*Kau-diche-rah*.' That was the second time he had heard that and wondered what they were saying."

Grace told Ivan it meant "cunning warrior's son", and he smiled.

"Marcus asked how the girl was, but *Shadak* didn't understand, so he made a gesture for long hair and held his side as if he were hurt. The chief seemed to understand and said the word *Jadax*, then made a sleeping motion to let him know she was resting.

A boy entered and spoke to the elder, then left quickly.

So her name is Jadax, thought Marcus, and it made him smile.

The chief was looking at his belongings as Marcus moved over to him. How strange they must have seemed, his fire-rock and iron long-knife. He assumed the chief had never seen metal before, other than gold, as he'd noticed that all of their arrow-heads and knives were made of bone. *Shadak* motioned for him to follow and stepped outside. Marcus donned his belongings and followed him out of the grass hut.

The sun was bright in the western sky, and it felt great to be alive. The whole tribe was gathering around them as the chief walked him to the pole in the center of the camp. There was now a long bench there, and he sat down, as the chief had silently instructed. It felt strange to be sitting in the exact place where he was nearly killed, but it passed quickly.

The tribe started to form a line in front of him, and he sat there wondering what was next. The chief raised his arms and the people went silent. He stood, pointed at Marcus and shouted, '*Kau-diche-rah fal von Jadax!*' and the *Gatou* people began to cheer. They kept cheering wildly until the chief raised his arms again, and then one by one they approached and showed their appreciation for what he had done for *Jadax*.

Most of them knelt and bowed before him saying the word *utai*, and the warriors put their fists over their hearts and spoke the same word, which Marcus assumed meant thank you. He also received gifts. The women presented him with an outfit made of that magnificent leather. The men brought him a buffalo hide blanket, and the warriors gifted him with an intricately carved great-bow. The great-bows they used were the size of his regular longbow, but four times sturdier, and they smiled when he could only pull the string about a quarter draw.

With all the attention given him, he was starting to realize that *Jadax* wasn't just another girl in the tribe. With this kind of ceremony she *had* to be the chief's daughter, and that would, according to his estimation, make his new blood brother, the chief's son.

While he was pondering this, thanking people and trying to pull the string on his new great-bow, he realized the crowd had gone silent and formed an opening in the center. Suddenly the chief's son appeared, followed by *Shadak*, who had left without Marcus noticing. They were both dressed in formalwear. This consisted of buffalo robes with the hair still on, shaved to about an inch long and trimmed with gold rope. He was amazed and had never seen or heard of such a thing. They also wore buffalo headdresses with horns in the front, trimmed in the same rope only of a finer weave. On their feet were leather slippers, also trimmed on the tops with tiny gold rope. They looked like kings as they approached.

Shadak's son stopped in front of him, pointed at himself and said, '*Korak.*' In return Marcus gave his name. *Korak* handed him a statue made of solid gold, about eight inches high and carved in the shape of a warrior. The design was so detailed he couldn't stop staring at it. *Korak* moved away and the chief stepped up. He handed him a gold necklace made of thick rope with a wolf carving attached. Marcus removed his water skin and replaced it with the gift. The chief motioned for him to rise, and he followed him away from the crowd to one of the places where the wolves were kept. This area contained the females and younger males. The chief pointed to the circle and said, '*Vallah-von,*' which Marcus assumed was what the *Gatou* called their wolf-like companions. Next he motioned to the center and waited, so Marcus entered the ring and stood there nervously. Everything was going too well at this point to start questioning his host, and besides, he found himself gaining a deep trust for this wise man.

The wolves looked up for a moment, then continued to ignore him. He looked back at *Shadak* and shrugged. The chief just smiled and gestured for him to wait. It wasn't too long before one of the huge animals walked up. A young black wolf circled and sniffed the air around him. Marcus remembered he still had some buffalo sausage in his satchel, so he took a piece and held it out. The black hunter watched him warily and continued circling. The young wolf hadn't grown into his paws yet, but he was still almost four feet tall. He kept circling, but this time Marcus turned with him, still holding the offering. As he turned he saw the chief off in the distance, smiling. Finally the animal stopped, and he stopped with it. Then as if he had decided Marcus was no threat, he moved up and took the sausage from his fingers, swallowing it in one gulp. He then sat on his haunches and stared at Marcus with a quizzical look, tilting his head slightly.

The chief walked over and pointed at the wolf, then to Marcus. He realized that *Shadak* was giving him another gift, and wasn't about to insult him by questioning his hospitality. Not only that, but there was something about this black fellow that Marcus liked, besides the fact that it was the only black wolf he had seen so far.

He nodded at the wolf, then the chief and said, '*Utai*,' which prompted a smile and nod from *Shadak*.

They started back to the main camp and the wolf followed. Marcus wasn't sure if that was allowed, but nothing was said.

When the three reached the camp, Marcus was shown to a different dwelling. The chief motioned that they would be eating soon and left Marcus to his new quarters.

He entered the hut and sat down. The wolf stuck his head in the door, but would not enter.

He smiled at the wolf and said, 'Well boy, if we're going to travel together, you will have to have a name.' He looked at his new companion and thought, *Chance, that's what I'll call you, and there just might be a chance for peace between the Gatou and the settlers now.*

He called to the wolf but it only stepped just inside the opening, then turned three times and laid down facing the entrance. Chance looked funny with his big head and paws, but Marcus figured when he grew into them, he would be over five feet tall.

He thought of *Jadax* as he rested on the soft buffalo blanket. He felt a slight pang inside when he recalled her screams and obvious pain as she had rallied to save his life, but felt a different feeling at the thought of seeing her again. It was a feeling he had never felt before, and was unsure of its meaning. *It must be concern for her safety*, he thought, *that must be it.*

His thoughts were interrupted by a low growl and then the appearance of a young *Gatou* boy in the doorway. He looked wide-eyed at Chance, probably not used to one of the wolves acting that way toward a *Gatou*. Marcus spoke to his new protector and it calmed him, so he laid back down, seemingly oblivious to his surroundings once more. The boy, who was watching Chance warily now, made signs to tell Marcus it was time to eat, then left hastily.

Dusk was setting in and the plains looked beautiful with an orange hue dancing off the grasses. The sky was like a fire with its sunset colors, and the air was filled with the smell of wood-fires and cooking meat.

As he left the hut, he was greeted by two warriors who escorted him toward the delicious smells. Chance moved off into the grass, but kept a close watch on him with those yellow eyes.

They approached the food-laden table, which was made from half of a huge tree, and he wondered where they had gotten it from. Everyone sat around it, the only thing between them and the ground being large pillows covered in buffalo hide. As each *Gatou* acknowledged Marcus they fell silent. He noticed that *Shadak* was sitting at the head of the table with *Korak* on his right. To his left were two empty seats which he hoped were for *Jadax* and himself, but where was she? He glanced around the table but could see no sign of her. *She must still be too weak to attend*, he thought, and followed the warriors to the chief's side.

The chief and his son stood to greet him and *Shadak* spoke in a commanding tone. '*Shau-muai-din vay*,' he said, and pointed at Marcus. That was different from the other name he had been called, and wondered what it meant. '*Shau-muai-din vay. Shau-muai-din vay*,' chanted the tribe, and kept doing so until the chief raised his arms and gestured to the closest buildings.

All attention was focused to where he was pointing, and Marcus watched intently to see what new spectacle or entertainment might be taking place, when he saw a true vision.

Jadax was moving up to the table, followed by two handmaidens. She wasn't the helpless victim he had seen in their first meeting, but a magnificent princess that transcended any words of description. Her essence was power and her very presence outshone the formal attire, which, in its beauty, paled against her radiance. His mouth hung open, and he was speechless as she walked up to him. She said, '*Utai shau-mau-din vay*,' and kissed his hands. His heart raced and his ears burned crimson; he had to look away. She turned to her maidens and then back to him, holding up a buffalo robe. The robe was the same as the ones *Shadak* and *Korak* were wearing, only in his size. It was splendid, but he would have cherished *any* gift from her. He pulled on the robe and waited for everyone to be seated before he did the same.

The meal was delicious. They had prepared wild boar and buffalo in many different ways, complemented by wild potatoes and sauce covered greens, with an herb tea to wash it all down.

He watched *Jadax* closely, hoping he wasn't too obvious. He was intrigued by this girl, and when she retired for the evening he felt that sting again. It was a feeling of loss, which made no sense to him.

The rest of the evening was filled with drumming, dancing and acrobatics to rival even that of the gypsies. After a full evening, fatigue finally crept up on him, so he bid his hosts goodnight and made his way to his lodgings. Chance was by his side in an instant and they disappeared into the night.

It was a fitful and restless sleep in that little grass hut, and the *Gatou* princess filled his dreams.

He awoke the next morning with an uneasy feeling gnawing at him. Chance was lying by the opening, and Marcus could hear people milling about outside his shelter. First light hadn't even arrived and it sounded like the whole camp was busy. His uneasiness was to do with his knowing that today was the day his father would come looking for him, and he couldn't let that happen. If the *Gatou* saw a settler enter the plains he didn't think they would ask who it was before they attacked, or if that even mattered. He may have saved the princess, but he didn't know how far that deed would carry him. He *had* to meet with the chief and tell him he needed to get back to his village.

He dressed and grabbed his belongings. He wasn't sure how he would carry the gifts, but he would make do. Most importantly he had to start back before anything bad happened.

He placed all his new items by the door and stepped out into the coolness of the morning. He could make out shapes in the dim light and noticed *Korak*, not far off, kneeling over a fire pit. He had a pile of shavings cut and was working hard with his soft-bow and flame-stick to start his morning fire. Marcus walked over, grabbed one of the smaller rocks from the pit and struck his fire-rock along it, sparking the shavings into a small flame. Startled, *Korak* moved back, then looked in amazement at the black rock. Marcus held it next to his chest, then back to the young warrior to show him he meant it as a gift. *Korak* smiled and accepted it graciously. *Now he will be the talk of the camp,* thought Marcus.

He looked around and said, '*Shadak*,' which prompted *Korak* to point to a hut at the crest of the small hill. He started forward, with Chance only a pace behind, then glanced back and saw *Korak* making sparks in the darkness.

He reached the dwelling, which was a lot bigger than the others, and stopped just outside the entrance. In a moment *Shadak* was there beckoning him to enter. He took the remainder of his buffalo sausage, threw it to Chance and asked him to wait outside.

He followed the chief in and they sat opposite each other at the table. An older *Gatou* woman brought food to them and the chief motioned for Marcus to help himself.

She served some potatoes, sliced thinly and fried, and some meat cut into small chunks. Marcus said, '*Utai*,' and tried not to eat too fast, but he felt an urgency to be getting back.

They finished the meal and stepped outside. Chance wasn't far off—he could usually be seen resting in the grass—and was always watching. The chief knelt in front of his fire pit while

Marcus tried to think of a way to tell him he needed to leave very soon. *Shadak* grabbed a stick and started to cut shavings from it. Marcus grinned and presented his iron long-knife as a gift, the way he had done with *Korak* and the fire-rock. The chief accepted it and finished cutting the shavings, only much faster and easier.

He smiled and said, '*Ucho.*'

He was just getting his fire kit together when *Korak* walked up. He leaned down, struck his new fire-rock and tiny flames sprang from the newly cut wood. The chief looked on in wonderment and then spoke a few words to his son. *Korak* pointed at Marcus and said, '*Shau-muai-din vay ucho,*' and they laughed. Marcus felt desperate now and began signing to *Shadak* that he had to be leaving, and the chief nodded like he understood.

He pointed to *Korak* and then to *Shadak*. Then he pointed to himself and drew an outline of another person to indicate his father.

Shadak smiled and said, '*Kau-diche.*'

Could *kau-diche* be a name for his father? He had heard them call him, *Kau-diche-rah* when they had first captured him, so on a hunch he pointed at *Korak* and said, '*Shadak-rah,*' and the chief nodded. This was weird. Why would they have a name for his father? And why would they say it with such reverence? Well he had no time to ponder such things, and knew he needed to be getting back to the settlement.

The chief and his son followed him back to his hut and waited while he brought his belongings outside. When he had finished, he realized there was no way for him to carry all of his gear *and* the gifts from the *Gatou* by himself. Just then a young boy came up and handed him a packsaddle. He was puzzled for a moment, then realized it wasn't for a horse, but a wolf. He had a few misgivings about packing Chance, but the wolf had obviously been trained for it, so he secured the weapons and the rest of the gifts on his back.

Everything was ready now, so he thanked *Shadak* for his kindness and started moving west through the camp. As he neared the edge he found himself wishing *Jadax* was there to see him off. He stopped when he heard a loud whistle and turned to see *Shadak* behind him. Within moments a large red wolf came bounding up and stopped beside him. The whistle sounded twice more and two more wolves arrived, one gray and the other a tan color. *Korak* ran up and leaped onto the back of the gray wolf and rode off quickly. *Shadak* stroked the red wolf and motioned for Marcus to mount the tan.

He said, '*Utai*,' and shook his head no, hoping his refusal wouldn't insult the chief, and it didn't appear to.

All the times the chief or his warriors had seen Marcus, as they watched hidden in the plains, he had never been riding, so the old man just nodded and sent the wolf away. The chief sprang onto his mount and Marcus was amazed at his agility. Most men his age had trouble walking, and although Marcus knew nothing about these people, he assumed that his healthy and active lifestyle had granted him longevity.

Korak joined them now with two other wolf-riders, and the five of them started moving.

The sky was brightening as they made their way through the camp and into the western plains. The *Gatou* waved and some shouted, '*Shau-muai-din vay!*' as he passed, so he smiled and waved, still hoping to get a glimpse of *Jadax*."

Ivan stopped Grace and asked what *Shau-muai-din vay* meant and she explained that it translated to "blood brother of the plains". He told her his guess had been close and thanked her. She giggled and went on.

"When they reached the outer boundary of the camp, the riders stopped and turned their mounts to face him. He wasn't sure what was happening, until he turned and saw *Jadax* walking up. He tried to swallow but his mouth went dry. His heart picked up speed as she approached. When she finally stood before him he was glad she didn't understand kingdom tongue because anything he said right now would be nonsensical. She was so striking that all he could do was stare. She took his hand and placed a gold bracelet on his wrist.

She held it a moment and said, '*Ucho tan* Marcus,' then turned and walked away. She looked so beautiful silhouetted in the morning sun and he watched her until she disappeared into her shelter. He looked at the bracelet and saw a carving of a wolf and a girl standing on the plains, and he moved his fingers over it. He took one last look at the *Gatou* camp, then followed the riders into the tall grass.

Frank was puzzled as he stared at the ground in front of him. He had started out this morning and tracked his son to the Salt Spring. Following his tracks to the southeast trail, he saw where Marcus had ran out of the meadow to this small campsite. There were signs of a fire and a place where a child had lain. There was much blood on the ground, and on the piece of his son's cloak that he'd found. The only tracks leaving were that of wolves and one of those marsh-dwellers, and that made his stomach turn.

Frank had come alone to check on his boy and wasn't prepared for this situation. Marcus had gone out walking and stayed overnight before, so Frank thought he would catch up and surprise him with some of Maden's freshly baked heavy-cake.

This day could turn on me, he thought as he mounted his horse and followed the wolf tracks east. Concern for his son was foremost in his mind as he swung north along the trail that bordered the marsh. Just as he thought, the tracks headed straight into the *Gatou Plains*, so he stopped in the last grove of trees before the grasslands and dismounted.

The trail was over a day old, so before he went galloping into enemy territory, he scouted a route that would take him in the direction of the tracks and still keep Marcus' rescue a possibility. If Frank was captured or killed, he could do his son no good, and running headlong into the *Gatou* would ensure that.

He picked out the tallest tree and started to climb. He reached the top and positioned himself so he could see the plains clearly. He scanned the horizon and searched the grasses but could see nothing.

He picked a path that was parallel to the tracks, which to the untrained eye were invisible by now, and started down. He entered the *Gatou Plains* afoot, leading his horse. He would have tied him in the trees, but he might need the speed and who knows what animal might come along and find a nice snack tethered there.

Frank had walked about a mile along his chosen path when his horse whinnied and bolted. He let go of the reins, drew his long-knife and spun to the left where he had heard the sound.

Marcus and his unlikely companions, after traveling a half-morning, had stopped to take on food and drink. He had taken Chance's pack off, which he still felt weird about, and fed him the last of his sausage, when suddenly the wolf took off to the south at a dead run. The *Gatou* mounted and circled right and left, disappearing quickly. Marcus knew this was bad and ran in the direction his wolf had gone.

When he arrived on the scene he couldn't believe his eyes. There was his father, knife-in-hand, fending off a snarling Chance, while two wolf-riders, one on either side, had great-bows trained on him. *Korak* was behind him, great-bow locked in position, and the old chief was a few feet back watching Frank with admiration. When Frank saw his son, he let down his guard and the black wolf crouched to lunge.

'Chance!' yelled Marcus with such ferocity that he stopped and backed away. Frank looked confused as his son ran up and hugged him.

Shadak gave a command and the warriors lowered their weapons and vanished into the background. The old *Gatou* moved in closer and sat there on his wolf. Marcus introduced the two leaders and they met each other's gaze. They exchanged nods and Marcus could see a mutual respect as each man-sized up the other. The chief held up his fist, hit his chest hard and then held it out once again. Frank returned the gesture and noticed that his horse was moving toward them from the west, with a wolf-rider not far behind. Another rider bounded in from the north and dropped Chance's packsaddle on the ground in front of them. Frank turned again as the horse came running up, and when he looked back the *Gatou* were gone.

'*Utai Shadak!*' shouted Marcus into the tall, empty grass, then turned and gave his father another hug.

Frank returned the hug and told Marcus he had a lot of explaining to do. He nodded and told his father there was someone he wanted him to meet. He called Chance over and introduced him. Frank was still taking it all in as he greeted the young wolf. Marcus asked his father if he would mind walking, and proceeded to strap his possessions on the horse. He liked to see Chance running free, and it was wrong in his mind to encumber such a majestic animal. The horse was still spooked by the wolf so Marcus motioned for him to follow behind, which he seemed to understand. So with the wind in their face and a wolf at their back, they walked out of the *Gatou Plains.*

On the journey they shared some of Maden's heavy-cake and Marcus told his story, which was amazing even to Frank. He left out the part about his feelings for the princess and hoped it would pass. His detailed description of the fish-man left his father with a real problem. Frank had no idea these marsh-dwellers were that cunning, which meant they would have to keep a full watch on the shores from now on.

They reached their home just before sunset and the guard was ready to put an arrow through Chance, until he was instructed otherwise. Maden was *so* happy to see them, and had a delicious buffalo stew prepared. She didn't seem startled by the wolf and they hit it off right away. She fed him a bowl of her stew and even gave him some of her leftover heavy-cake, which he enjoyed thoroughly.

After supper she started asking Marcus questions about his adventure. She got so captivated with the details that she kept him up half the night, getting it penned while it was still fresh in his mind.

Marcus didn't arise until midmorning the next day. He ate a quick breakfast and showed Frank and Maden the gifts he had received from the *Gatou*. It was good to be home, but *again* he was feeling that tiny ache in the pit of his stomach, almost like something was missing.

While he was putting his gifts away he came up with the idea that would change the future of his people forever. It would also give him an excuse to go back to the *Gatou* camp, and hopefully see *Jadax* again. He told his father and Maden, and they thought it was brilliant.

Marcus would take items from the settlement, like fire-rocks, long-knives and whatever else the *Gatou* may want, and trade them for garments, gold and anything else they had available for offer. He would then take these items down to Southport and trade for what they needed at the settlement.

CHAPTER

5

Unlikely Alliance

M arcus took his first load into the *Gatou Plains* about a week later. He showed *Shadak* his trade goods and presented him with the idea. The chief accepted, on the condition that he deal solely with Marcus.

He and *Jadax* went for a walk during his time there and he was relieved to find out that she didn't have a mate.

He made many trips that summer trading with the *Gatou*, and managed to send two caravans to Southport. This replenished their trading stock and dried goods, as well as the livestock. They even brought back new settlers from the south that were looking to build a new life in the northern frontier.

The settlement was thriving and growing, thanks to Marcus, and so were his feelings for *Jadax*. Each time he visited the plains on business, he would spend time with her. She would teach him *Gatou* words and he would teach her the kingdom tongue. When they were able to communicate well enough, she told him she had lost her mother to the fever ten years earlier. He told her of his mother and they shared in each other's pain. With the bond of their deep mutual understanding, he felt he could accomplish anything when he was with her, and she felt safe in his arms.

Due to the new patrols, the attacks from the marsh had almost ceased, and the first month of winter was creeping up on the northland. Marshside was doing well and Marcus felt great.

He had practiced every day with his great-bow and could almost pull the string to half tension now.

His visits and trading with the chief had been going well, but he had *one* trade in mind that he wasn't sure the *Gatou* leader would agree to.

This was the big day and he wanted so badly for it to go well. He had asked *Jadax* to join with him and she had said yes, so today he would ask his father if he would accept *Jadax* as his new daughter. Then later he would ask *Shadak* if he would pledge his only daughter to Marcus. Frank didn't know *Jadax* and hadn't realized that his son had such strong feelings for the girl. He told Marcus that he would like to meet her, if *Shadak* agreed to the pledge, and that he was sure he would love her if Marcus did.

He arrived at the *Gatou* encampment by midday, and finished his trading business just before the evening meal. Marcus decided to wait until after they had finished eating to ask *Shadak* for his consent. His voice trembled as he stumbled over the words and *Shadak* listened carefully to his proposal. When he was finished the old chief began to grin and then became serious again as he considered his request. He told Marcus that *Jadax* was only sixteen summers, and that when she was nineteen summers, if they were still fond of each other, he would give his blessing. He hated to wait, but respected the wise old chief and ran out to tell *Jadax*. She was a little disappointed, though not surprised by her father's decision.

It didn't matter whether they took the pledge now or three summers from now, they still saw each other frequently and it didn't change how they felt. Marcus was just excited that *Shadak* had said yes, and before he and Chance left, he stopped in and asked the chief if it would be all right if his father came to meet *Jadax* on his next trip.

The chief agreed readily saying, '*Kau-diche.*'

With his wagon loaded, he returned to Marshside to tell Frank and Maden the good news. His father commended *Shadak* on his decision, and told Marcus he couldn't wait to meet the girl his son was so smitten by.

Frank and *Shadak* became friends instantly and formed a strong relationship over the next three years. *Jadax* and Marcus fell deeper and deeper in love, and the anticipation grew as the summer drew near. Marcus had since brought Maden along on a few trips and she and *Jadax* had become extremely close. Maden was like a mother to Marcus, and it meant a lot to him that they like each other.

They took the pledge and were joined that summer in the *Gatou* village, with Frank and Maden on his side to witness the joining. *Shadak* and *Korak* walked *Jadax* across the fertility line and left her under the protection of Marcus. Chance, who was over five feet at the shoulders now, and the biggest wolf in the *Gatou* pack, looked on with indifference, but could sense his master's happiness and had always liked the smell of the princess.

They spent the rest of the summer at the *Gatou* camp and then the winter in Marshside. Marcus could speak fluent *Gatou* now and *Jadax* had caught on to the settlement speech quickly.

The next summer *Jadax* gave birth to a baby boy and they named him Frank *Shadak* Belden. He took after Marcus in size and looks, but it was apparent right away that he possessed the *Gatou* strength. The two leaders loved their new grandson and were both honored to have him named after them.

Over the next six years the little family was blessed with both health and happiness, not to mention wealth. Frank Junior had started attending school that year, and when he arrived at the doors of his father's building he could already read and write, thanks to the extensive tutelage from Maden.

Chance had been very protective of him since birth and the two had become inseparable. When he was finished school each day, Chance would be there waiting. He would bend down so Frank Junior could get on his back, and they would race home where Maden would have some wonderful treat prepared for both of them. He would run to his mother, who would be preparing dinner or crafting some wonderful *Gatou* item, and give her a big hug. He would then climb onto Chance's back and dash off to find his father, who would be out-and-about doing settlement business. When they found him, Marcus would gather his son in his arms and swing him around, then hold him close. He would carry him for awhile, then set him back on the gentle giant and they would walk home together.

The next spring they were blessed again, but this time it was twin boys, both taking after the *Gatou* side. They named them *Adan* and *Sada*, which in *Gatou* meant "moon and sun", and they were their mother's light.

For the next ten years the community thrived and Marcus and his family remained happy and prosperous in every way. He and Frank Junior spent a lot of time together, and he was growing into his father's son. The twins preferred the *Gatou* village and never felt quite at home in Marshside, even though they were loved dearly by everyone. *Shadak* and *Korak* spoiled them terribly, but also taught them the ways of the *Gatou*, and they had been chosen by their own wolves already.

Life for Marcus and *Jadax* couldn't have been better, until the year of the black winter. This was a strange year to say the least, and by the last month of autumn the temperature had dropped well below normal and stayed that way until the first month of spring. This was the coldest winter Marshside had seen since they arrived in the north, but worst of all there was no snow. Hardly a flake fell that year and the ground had frozen deep. Everyone survived the unusual drop in temperature and everything seemed normal, until someone found a half dead marsh-dweller lying on the shore. He was obviously starving to death and died shortly after he was found.

That's when the attacks started again, only this time more frequent and intense. The livestock, now too numerous to keep inside the walls, were watched night and day, but even with the steady guard, the strays and stragglers went missing. A few cattle, sheep and goats weren't a high price to pay, but when one of the guards was attacked and almost killed, Frank and Marcus called a town meeting.

The council decided that with the threat to their food supply, and the impending danger to the people, the watch needed to be doubled and concentrated on the shores of the marsh to stop the attackers before they could advance. No guard was to be alone at any time, and there should be at least two men at each post, rotating three shifts per day.

After the meeting, Frank and Marcus informed Maden, *Jadax* and Frank Junior, who was now coming into his manhood, of the new plan that was about to be implemented.

Korak arrived with the twins, who had been visiting the *Gatou*, just before evening meal. He explained that the trouble was not isolated to Marshside, and that many buffalo had been killed up and down the northern shore of the marsh. He knew the attacks would soon move inland and was readying his warriors for that day. He described the spear-like weapons they used and how they had been hunting in packs.

Marcus felt a chill when he heard those words. *Korak's* story corresponded with the wounds on the guard, which brought his worst fear to light. It meant that they were dealing with an organized group and not just animals acting on a survival instinct. Now instead of guarding their livestock from predators, they were in a war against an intelligent, calculating race of lizard-men who would stop at nothing to ensure their survival.

Maden set the table and everyone ate mechanically as each of them started to realize what this new information had revealed, everyone that is except the twins. They were always hungry and had little concern for adult matters. They had been big eaters since birth and actually ate more than their older brother, who also had a hearty appetite. They looked up to their brother like a hero and loved it when they were allowed to go with him on a hunt. Marcus had never liked this idea, but it was the way of the *Gatou*, and he never questioned it.

From the age of nine, every male child was taken on the hunt to participate as much as possible and learn the ways of a warrior. Frank Junior, who the *Gatou* called *Zalak diche*, which meant "strong warrior", had been on the hunt from the age of six, and could handle a great-bow since he was thirteen. He now had a custom-made bow crafted from the heaviest wood that was half again the size of a regular one.

This bow, which a normal man could barely draw a few inches, he handled with ease. Marcus, who had never fully mastered his great-bow, could only draw his son's quarter way, and marveled at the strength his boy possessed. *Zalak*, as everyone now called him, could hit a target as far as the eye could see, and had easily surpassed both his father and grandfather as a bowman. At only sixteen, he was most likely the greatest archer in the known kingdom.

The twins ate their fill and then ran outside to play with their wolves. Marcus just sat there going over the things in his mind that bothered him about this new information. He had no idea what this enemy was capable of, nor did he know its intent or strength. There was no way he knew of to communicate with them or any reasonable means of attack, other than when they showed aggression. To enter that swamp would be suicide, and right now Marcus' main concern was for the safety and continued well-being of his people.

He barely slept that night as he made mental preparations for the days to come. *Korak* left before daybreak, after going over strategies with Frank and Marcus. *Korak* would gather the *Gatou* warriors and patrol the north shore, as-well-as send reinforcements to Marshside where most of the attacks were taking place.

Marcus called another town meeting and informed the people of the new danger, and asked that every male able to wield a weapon report for duty that afternoon. His existing fighters were to be assigned to groups of fifteen, with a captain appointed to each, while an elite group of thirty men, captained by *Zalak*, would be created to guard the shores nearest Marshside itself. Frank remained with the men, forming the different war parties and delegating duties, while Marcus and *Zalak* returned to their home to prepare.

As *Zalak* got ready to lead his small army, the twins burst into his room and quizzed him on his actions. They could always sense when a hunt was about to take place, and they *loved* the hunt. *Zalak* was so preoccupied with his duties that he ignored his little brothers. When they received no answer to their query, they pounced, and he allowed them to wrestle him to the ground. They held him down, as *Zalak* pretended to be overpowered, and demanded to know. He relented and revealed his mission, which prompted them to jump up and dash out of his bedroom. They ran through the small hallway and into the kitchen, where they cornered their father. They asked if they could go on the hunt with *Zalak* and received a firm, 'No.' Then they pleaded with him, which caused him to sit down and place them one on each knee. He explained that this wasn't an ordinary hunt and there was a war coming. He also explained the difference between confronting an enemy and hunting an animal, and tried to make them see the danger. He chose his words carefully so they would see his meaning and understand that they were just *too* young to join the fighting men. They argued, but gave in when they realized that their father meant what he said.

Everyone hustled and bustled around the twins for the next few days, and they were quite put out because they were the only ones without a job to do. School had been postponed and everyone was too busy to acknowledge them. Marcus would return each night with news from the scouts that the attacks were increasing, and the need for more fighters was imperative. What the twins got from this information was that their brother was short of men and needed their help. They were bright beyond their years and immediately devised a plan to help *Zalak*.

The next morning, after everyone had gone about their daily regimen, the twins snuck out and mounted their wolves.

They skirted the central areas of the town and made their way to the armory. They informed the guard that their father had instructed them to fetch him more bundles of arrows. The guard would never question Marcus' orders and produced the arrows without question. *Adan* and *Sada* rode in the direction of the front gates, still skirting the main roads, and reached them without any confrontations. This guard was more skeptical than the last, but opened the gates when they told him they needed to replenish the arrows at the weapon shack, about a half mile out toward the marsh."

Grace looked into Ivan's eyes before she continued, and he could see a deep sadness.

"The next pieces of Maden's writings were sketchy," she began, "and were pieced together from two different accounts.

Marcus and *Zalak* searched frantically for the twins once they realized they were missing. With Chance in the lead, they tracked the wolves to a sandy place near the marsh's edge. *Sada's* wolf, *Kast*, lie cold and still on the ground, his fur matted with blood from countless spear wounds, but his life had cost the enemy dearly. There were lizard men lying all around his lifeless body, and he still had one of those foul creatures locked in his once powerful jaws. *Adan's* wolf, *Fanta*, was closer to the water's edge, and she too was matted with blood and lie still. Standing over her, spear in his clawed hand, was one of those creatures. Before he could thrust his weapon, Chance was there and left him lying quietly with the rest of his kind.

Fanta was still alive, though barely, and Chance stood over her, watching for any other movement in the area. Marcus felt panic forming deep inside and was sick to his stomach when he could see no trace of his sons. He searched the shore in desperation for any sign of them, but all he could find were lizard tracks leading into the murky water. He searched harder, and still nothing.

Zalak was truly afraid for the first time in his life and felt helpless, as he too searched in vain for some sign or track that would suggest anything but the obvious. He told his father he was sorry for telling the boys his plans, but Marcus assured him he was not to blame. Still the guilt welled in him, but he pushed it away to keep a clear head.

Marcus was looking around frantically now. Panic stricken, he ran straight into the icy shallows. *Zalak* was quick to move and pulled him up onto the bank. Marcus fought him, but his son was too strong. Tears fell from *Zalak's* eyes as he held his father, who was screaming his sons' names in anguish. Marcus finally went limp and stared into the marsh, sobbing quietly. *Zalak* kept holding him, but did so as much to ease his own pain, as his father's.

Suddenly Marcus ceased his grieving and stood up. *Zalak* waited beside him to see what he would do next. Marcus just stood there for awhile with a look in his eyes that his eldest son had never seen before. He remained still until, without a word, he turned and ran toward the settlement.

Jadax began wailing when Marcus told her what he had found, then went silent and sat on the bed rocking back and forth as if something inside her was broken. Maden tried to comfort her but she was too grief-stricken herself to do any good. Frank remained calm, holding his emotions inside as he tried to help his family cope with the situation. *Zalak* had carried *Fanta* back and was tending her wounds, even though it seemed futile. She was so badly hurt, she probably wouldn't last the night.

Word spread quickly through Marshside that Marcus was forming a search party, and a scout was sent to inform *Shadak* and *Korak* of the tragedy. One of the longboats that had been brought up from the south was being rigged and fitted for an expedition into the marsh. Marcus was going into that maze of waterways and was going to find his sons, if there was any possibility of doing so. No one could talk him out of it, no matter how hard they tried. Even when the elders told him it was suicide, he just kept preparing. Chance could feel the emotions from the man he had protected for so long, but stayed by *Fanta's* side, softly licking her wounds and watching over her.

Early the next morning Marcus was busy packing his horse with the supplies he needed for the journey when *Korak* arrived with two of his warriors. They were worn from traveling, but Marcus stopped them briefly to explain his plans and share a few moments with his blood brother. There was no time for sadness and action was needed.

Maden served up a quick breakfast as Marcus finished his task. *Korak* informed him that he and his warriors would be joining the rescue, and it made Marcus feel better to know *Korak* would be at his side. When all was ready, Marcus, and what seemed like half the town, left the settlement and headed for the marsh. Chance, who could sense that *Fanta* was getting stronger, arose and loped to the front of the group, leading his master to an uncertain fate.

The *Gatou* warriors, and the two captains Marcus had chosen to accompany him, finished loading the supplies, then boarded the vessel and waited. Marcus said goodbye to his father, who hugged him and stood there ever so stoic, even though he knew he may never see his son again. *Zalak*, who thought *he* should be going, had agreed to stay behind and safeguard the settlement at his father's request. Marcus clasped his son's hand, held him and kissed his forehead. He then said farewell to Maden and the rest of the townspeople.

Jadax was standing alone by the shore. She stared into the mist that had gathered over the glassy surface. Marcus felt a chill as he approached her and was hesitant to interrupt her trance-like thoughts. He could see the pain that twisted her insides as she turned and looked him in the eyes. The only words she said to him were, 'Bring back my moon and sun,' then turned and walked away. As he watched her go, she appeared to have aged ten years in the last day. That sight caused a flame in his guts to burn and he felt a growing hatred that would fuel the drive he needed to find his boys. As he watched his love disappear into the crowd, he made a silent vow that those lizards would pay for tearing out his heart.

He turned toward the longboat and there was Chance looking at him, almost eye-to-eye. He sometimes forgot how big his companion truly was, and gently stroked his head. He asked him to watch out for *Zalak* when he was gone, and then walked over to *Korak*, who was just entering the boat. Chance tried to follow but Marcus stopped him, pointed at *Zalak* and said, 'Stay boy!' The old wolf sat on his haunches and tilted his head, just like he had done all those years ago, and Marcus knew he didn't understand.

Everyone was in the boat now, so Marcus joined them and prepared to shove off. They used the oars to push away from the shore, then sat down, placed them in the oarlocks and took their positions.

Marcus felt a pang of sorrow when he saw Chance's expression. He must have thought his master was abandoning him. The wolf hesitated only a moment, then bounded to the shore and sprang through the air, landing squarely in the center of the floating contraption, almost capsizing it. When the commotion had settled down and the boat had stopped rocking, Marcus looked at Chance and smiled. *Well I guess it won't hurt to have a wolf along,* he thought, as they disappeared into the mist.

Jadax sat by the shore as she had done every day since her husband had left. At first *Zalak* tried to stop her but realized there was no use, so he reorganized the troops and stayed with her while she awaited Marcus' return. It had been almost a month since his departure, but she waited patiently every day for him to bring her children back to her.

Always ready and on full alert, *Zalak* watched the shore for any signs of danger. *Fanta*, who had become well enough to join the daily routine, patrolled the area instinctively. There had been a few incidents over the last while but *Zalak's* great-bow had made short work of the reptiles and discouraged any further attacks along that part of the marsh's edge. He admired his mother's strength and determination, but could also feel her pain. She felt distanced now, almost unapproachable in her sorrow.

He was taking another survey of the tree-line on the far side when he noticed ripples coming from the misty waterway. The ripples were growing larger, so he moved up to the bank and readied his great-bow. He could make out movement in the water now and pulled back on the string, waiting to get a clear shot. He was about to release his arrow when he recognized the swimmer. Chance was making his way to shore, rope clenched in his teeth, towing a listing boat behind him.

Jadax didn't move as Chance reached the edge. She just stood there staring at the boat, waiting for her prayers to be answered. *Zalak* pulled two forms from the waterlogged craft and laid them on the grass. Holding her breath, *Jadax* watched him return to the wooden vessel, but her heart sank when all he brought out were some weapons and supplies. She jumped up and ran over to the figures. As she got closer, she saw it was her husband and *Korak*, and a small glimmer of hope returned to her. She knelt beside Marcus. He had a ghostly pallor and was badly bruised and cut, but his chest rose and fell ever so slightly. Her brother was in bad condition also, but conscious. He had a makeshift splint on his leg and she could see he was in a great deal of pain. She looked at *Korak* and he returned her gaze. He could see the question in her eyes and shook his head sadly.

Fanta returned from her patrol and trotted up to Chance who was lying off a short distance from the others. He was still breathing heavily from all the swimming but arose to greet her. When they had finished reacquainting, *Fanta* trotted over to the others and waited for Chance who, though limping badly, moved along behind her. *Zalak* tied the weapons and what was left of the supplies onto *Fanta*, then taking his father in his arms, carried him from the shore. *Korak* could stand and walk with the help of his sister, and Chance, even with his wounds, was strong enough to follow. So the ragtag group made the trek back to the settlement and the warmth of their home that was once again, almost whole.

The next day *Shadak* arrived with a healer and six warriors. This was strange because no one had sent word yet. It was the first time he had been to Marshside, and it was a shock to everyone. He sent his warriors out with the patrols and put his healer to work on the wounded.

Over the next few weeks, with the help of Maden and *Chintau*–the *Gatou* healer–the physical and emotional injuries of the family began to mend. Marcus was back on his feet, though still too weak to continue his normal duties, *Korak's* leg was healing nicely and Chance was as good as new, spending most of his time with *Fanta*. It was obvious he had taken her as his and the wolves of the plains only ever took one mate for life. The old chief returned home with his healer, but left the warriors to help take up the slack so *Zalak* and Marcus could be with their family. *Korak* also decided to stay on awhile longer because he was worried about his sister and wanted to be there for her.

The attacks continued, and *Zalak* took over the charge of the little army to ease the pressure on his father, who seemed otherwise preoccupied most of the time."

Ivan remembered stopping Grace right then and playfully demanding to know what had happened on Marcus' journey through the marsh. Grace informed him that, though she was sure Marcus had told Maden all that had happened, there had never been a document of the telling on public display. She admitted that she had spent more time trying to find that information than she liked to admit, but had always come up empty-handed. She had asked around and snooped, but couldn't find a trace of that part of the story. Ivan had felt disappointed when he heard that, but sat back and listened as she went on.

"Marcus became distant and very private over the next while, and *Jadax* went through her daily routine methodically. It wasn't until Marcus insisted that she join him for a picnic at his father's old thinking spot that there was any change. They spent the entire day there and when they got back she looked as though a weight had been lifted from her, returning the light to her eyes. No one knew what Marcus had said to her, or what had taken place, and no one questioned it. They were just relieved to have her back.

That night the entire family sat down to a heartily prepared meal, and for the first time in what seemed like forever, they laughed together. Now instead of mourning the loss of the twins, they celebrated their lives and the brief time they had been blessed to share it with them. Marcus however, still had a distant look in his eyes. He lifted his glass in a toast to his boys, then arose, and for the first time in his life, he sang for his family.

As the resonant beauty of his voice cascaded through the room, each listener became transfixed. Cold shivers ran through the small gathering and tears streamed down every face. Not only did his voice and the song touch them, but somehow they each knew that this was the last song he would ever sing. Maden felt a sense of motherly pride as she listened to Marcus deliver his sorrowfully haunting song.

> Lead me down to the hanging tree
> And end this fateful misery
> Toss my soul where the four winds blow
> And cast my body to the sea
> Despair has won and life is done
> For it's been torn from me
> Oh it's been torn from me
>
> When lights fade it's time to leave
> And take our lost and broken dreams
> But still I cry to a darkened sky
> Although I know it's an empty plea
> Despair has won and life is done
> For it's been torn from me
> Oh it's been torn from me
>
> Ne'er again will I kiss their cheeks
> Or gently lay them down to sleep

Instead I pray for a peaceful day
Oh bless the hardened heart that weeps
Despair has won and life is done
For it's been torn from me
Oh it's been torn from me

When Marcus finished, the only sounds were sniffles and the clearing of throats. Maden smiled at him through her tears and *Jadax* walked up and held him tightly. Marcus returned her hug, then addressed his family. He told them that he was calling a town meeting the next day and had made an important decision that would affect everyone. He then said goodnight and retired to his bedroom. *Jadax* thanked everyone for their kindness and support, then saw them out and joined her husband.

The town of Marshside was busy the next morning with the news of an important meeting, and the town hall was buzzing as Marcus and his family entered the overcrowded building. When they approached the platform there was whispering and the air was filled with a heightened sense of excitement. This was when Marcus announced the building of the wall.

He would design a wall fourteen feet high and eight feet across. It would stretch from the Crooked Mountains in the south, along the western shore of the marsh, then turn and follow the northern shore to where the Crooked Mountains cradled the Lake of Falls in the east.

This announcement caused an uproar. People wanted to know everything all-at-once, and were all yelling questions simultaneously. Frank stood, and the crowd fell silent. He took each question in turn and Marcus answered, explaining how the task would be accomplished and why he thought it was imperative to do so. He told them the marsh-dwellers had caused enough pain and suffering in all of their lives, and it was time to end it. He called for volunteers with masonry experience and asked them to report to his father and *Zalak*. They would be starting the wall from its southern point using stones from the Crooked Mountains. He then informed the townspeople that he and *Jadax* would be moving to the *Gatou* village to live, and be spearheading the start of construction from the eastern edge of the mountains. He felt that it would go faster if they began at each end and worked toward the middle. *Shadak* agreed instantly to the proposal and proceeded to allocate the main force of his warriors to the project. Within a week preparations were made and construction was started.

The wall took over thirty years to complete and cost many lives. Frank lived to see the final stone placed atop the stately structure, and see the town's name changed from Marshside to Belden's Wall. He died of natural causes a year later, and in his honor the people erected a life-size statue in front of the town hall. Maden only lived a short time after that and had stayed with *Zalak* for over twenty-five years helping look after her great-grandsons and great-granddaughter. *Zalak* had met a girl from Southport on the fifth year of building the wall, and they had been joined the following summer. Chance lost *Fanta* a few years before the wall was completed. There was some white showing in his coat, but he'd had a good life, and now there were a *few* black wolves roaming the *Gatou Plains*.

Marcus and *Jadax* lived in the *Gatou* village and looked after *Shadak*. He was getting on in years even for a plainsman, whose life span was much greater than that of kingdom folk, and appreciated the company.

Zalak and his wife Mina had brought the grandchildren to the *Gatou* village each week since they were small. Now that they were getting older they tried to visit regularly, except the girl Mallah who had moved to Southport to care for her sick grandmother.

Korak, who was now chief of his own village nearby, was a regular guest at their fire. He had taken a mate, who had borne him twin sons six years earlier, and a daughter who was now two. *Jadax* spoiled her niece and nephews and sometimes called the twins *Adan* and *Sada* by mistake. She would then correct herself and say that her mind wasn't what it used to be.

In Southport, Mallah, who had taken up writing under the influence and training of Maden, was the sole founder and curator of the library and museum. She had dedicated her life and large inheritance from her grandmother to the creation and preservation of written works and antiques. She would also ride north from time to time, to keep up the writing on the Belden history.

CHAPTER
6

The Joining

A nd that's the story of Belden's Wall," Grace had told Ivan, and smiled as she gathered the picnic stuff. As she finished, she reminded him it was time to meet her mother. Ivan remembered those words like it was yesterday, and could still feel that twisting in his stomach at the thought of it.

They held hands as they walked to the place where she and her mother were staying. It must have looked sweet; him leading his horse and her with the picnic basket and blanket in her hand.

She stopped outside a small house, so Ivan tied his horse and followed her to the front door. They entered and Ivan remembered thinking it looked a lot bigger on the inside. Grace asked him to sit, and disappeared into the next room. After a few long moments she returned, followed by an older woman. Grace turned to him and introduced her mother as Zarina Fallow, then told her mother his name as they stood face-to-face.

She was taller than her daughter, with black hair, but those same green eyes. Hers were colder though, almost as if they had seen too much pain. Zarina looked at him, and he would never forget that moment. It felt as if she was staring into his soul, and the power she exuded was staggering. He remembered feeling smaller somehow, and at that moment all the air seemed to leave the room, but he held her gaze and didn't falter.

After what seemed like an eternity she spoke, and when she did it sounded almost hypnotic. She didn't say much, but Ivan remembered her words. *You are not one of us, but your heart is strong and true, and I welcome you.* That was all she had told him and then continued her duties. He looked at Grace. She was smiling, so he decided that the meeting must have gone well. They talked some more, but he knew he had to go and get supplies for his early morning trip up north. She walked him to the door, and it was hard to leave her. He told her he would be back in two months with another load and would like to see her again. She said she would talk to her mother and try to arrange to be back in Belden's Wall upon his return. They shared a kiss and he left, but his trip back seemed a lot longer than it had coming down.

Ivan realized he was still strumming his guitar when he heard Grace ask Shyla to go and get Cade for breakfast. He was only focused for an instant and then his mind wandered back to his next trip to The Wall.

He had reached the town two months to the day from his previous visit, and hurried through his dealings with the merchant. They had already agreed on the price so it was just a matter of unloading, counting and settling up. Ivan's mind wasn't on business this time as the merchant handed him a pouch full of coins. Ivan took it and shook his head when the merchant asked him if he was going to count it. The merchant laughed and told him he must have a girl on his mind. It was getting late, so Ivan took his usual room, turned in and dreamed of his fair maiden.

He was up before daybreak, had a quick breakfast, readied his horse and started into town before first light. The air here was a lot warmer than it was back home and he was enjoying his ride, but as he neared the town his stomach fluttered with the anticipation of seeing Grace again. He went to the place in the market where they had agreed to meet, and waited. He had arrived early because, if she *was* in the city, he didn't want to take the chance of missing her. He watched the traders and peddlers slowly fill the square with their wares and produce, but he was only interested in one sight.

He was listening to an old woman haggling with a shopkeeper when he saw her walking toward him, and once again it felt like the first time. When he held her in his arms he felt whole again, almost like he had been missing something his entire life. They spent the next five days together, and on their final day, Ivan asked her to take the pledge with him. He remembered the look on her face when he asked her, and without hesitation, she said yes. They set a date to be joined in Belden's Wall on the twenty-fifth day of the third month of summer, which was her twenty-first birthday as well as the day she would become an adept healer. This was a lot to happen on the same day, but she was so happy that it felt like it was meant to be.

The next month dragged on for Ivan as he prepared the logs for the merchant in the south. All he could think about was his true love as he searched the forest for the best building logs. They needed to be straight and not tapered too much along their forty foot length. He had the load ready far in advance of his intended departure date, so he decided to leave for The Wall ahead of schedule. He had nothing to wear on the special day and wanted to get there early so he could be as prepared as possible for the joining. He set out for Belden's Wall the next morning and arrived there on the twentieth.

When he rode into the town, the people he passed stopped and stared. Everyone seemed to recognize him or know who he was as they tipped their hats and waved. He rode along until he saw his destination, and on a big sign above the door it read, "Booker's Fine Garments". He dismounted and entered the shop. He was sized, fitted and quoted a two-day wait on his suit of clothes, which was fine because he still had four days until the joining.

As he rode to the market to pick up some supplies, he saw the reason for all the attention he had been getting. At the entrance, tied between two falseapple trees, was a banner with his and Grace's likeness and details of their special day written on it. This made Ivan wonder just how many people Grace knew in Belden's Wall, and had a funny feeling it might be a lot.

The next morning he unloaded the shipment and received his pay. The merchant added some extra coins as a gift of joining, which Ivan accepted, though he hadn't told him his intentions yet. By this time Ivan guessed that everyone in Belden's Wall must know.

He traveled into town the following morning to purchase a ring for Grace. He wasn't sure what kind he wanted for her, but he would know it when he saw it. He was in a rush because he was meeting Grace the next day and wanted to surprise her. *I will find her a beautiful one*, he thought, as he entered a shop called, "The Jewel House". The owner ignored him as he looked into the cases filled with rings and jewelry of every description. He recognized the *Gatou* works right away because they were so finely crafted, but he was there for a ring. Ivan knew why the clerk was ignoring him, and smiled when he thought of how he must appear in his woodsman's garb.

Ivan knew he must look like a simple woodcutter to the shopkeeper, but he had spent many boyhood years living at the palace in the City of Kings.

He plopped his sack of coins on the counter and that got the Clerk's attention. In fact he was now falling all over himself trying to accommodate Ivan. He showed him every ring he had in the store and some from the back room, but Ivan didn't find what he was looking for. The clerk brought out a case bound in leather and opened it for him. There were all types of fine rings displayed in it, but still nothing that caught his eye. The clerk seemed worried when he brought out a wooden box, which was his last container of rings, and Ivan guessed that his fear had to do with the possibility of not receiving any coins from the pouch.

As soon as the owner opened the box Ivan saw it, a perfect pearl in a solitaire setting with a silver band. It reminded him of Grace somehow, with the purity and warmth of the stone and the wholesome feeling it emanated. The clerk took the coins greedily and handed him the ring. Ivan placed it in his pocket and then walked along the street until he found a flower peddler. He ordered a large bouquet and told the man he would be picking it up the next day. He paid for the flowers then rode back to the merchants to prepare his words of joining. As he got ready for the following day when he would see his future wife, the woodcutter realized he would never have to leave her again.

When he saw her in the market he felt nervous, almost like a schoolboy. Her essence overwhelmed him and he knew he must have a silly grin on his face. She looked so beautiful and free, like a wild flower, and his bouquet paled when he handed it to her. She accepted it gratefully and took pleasure in the sweet aroma.

Even though Ivan didn't know anyone, they were mobbed by people who congratulated them and informed them their coins would be no good at the market for the rest of the week.

On the twenty-fourth they had the joining rehearsal at the town hall. This was the same location as the original hall, but had been restored and expanded to accommodate the growing population. Ivan had asked the merchant, Shamus, to be his witness in the joining, and the old man had accepted with honor. As he went through the rituals of the blessed event, Ivan felt as though he had two more witnesses as he gazed at the statues of Frank and Marcus Belden, who stood there on either side silently guarding the courtyard.

After the rehearsal they went to the house where Grace and Zarina were staying and that's when Ivan presented her with the ring. When she saw it, tears came to her eyes and she ran from the room crying. Ivan wasn't sure if he'd done something wrong, so he just sat there confused. He had felt bad and was about to take the ring back to the jeweler, when Grace came back carrying a wooden jewelry case. It was carved with detailed designs of a ship and mermaids resting on the rocks. She opened it and then explained why the ring had affected her that way. From it she removed a beautiful necklace made of pearls. She told him how the case and necklace had been a present for her tenth birthday, and the last gift her father had ever given her. He had placed her on his knee and told her it was a lucky jewelry case and she should keep it with her always. Grace told Ivan how much she loved the ring and how much it meant coming from him.

The next day the courtyard was full of townspeople as the couple was joined and it seemed his new wife *did* know everyone in Belden's Wall. The ceremony was short but the day was everlasting. Zarina walked Grace across the fertility line and under the protection of Ivan, and Shamus, along with Frank and Marcus, witnessed the event on his behalf.

At the end of the joining, Ivan looked into Grace's eyes and gave the vow he had prepared for her. He started with, "My heart and soul I pledge to thee," and ended with, "My love, my life, my wife," and then it was complete. They were pledged to each other and their journey together had begun.

On their way to the joining cottage that the town had prepared for them, Ivan wished Grace a happy birthday and congratulated her on becoming an adept healer. She just smiled and told him he was the only thing she cared about, and started kissing him. Ivan had cherished those words all the years they had been together.

They stayed in Belden's Wall for two more days and then it was time to take his new bride home. Grace said goodbye to her mother, while Zarina looked at Ivan and told him to take care. The way she said it had so many different meanings, but he got the message and told her he would. Ivan was glad that he had brought two wagons with him. With Grace's belongings, and all of the gifts they had received, there wasn't much space left.

They started out early for the long journey north and were crossing the *Gatou Plains* by midmorning. They were talking and laughing when one of the horses started to get jumpy. Not long after, a wolf-rider appeared from out of the grass. Ivan greeted the *Gatou*, but the warrior's attention was on Grace. Ivan wasn't sure what was going to happen, especially when he heard his new wife speaking to them in *Gatou*, which in itself was a surprise.

He remembered thinking how much about each other they didn't know, but was happy they had a lifetime to explore it.

When they finished speaking, Grace told Ivan the *Gatou* knew of their joining and had invited them to a celebration in their honor. Ivan scratched his head. *Why does this not surprise me?* he thought, as he agreed to the offer. There was more to this girl than met the eye, and what met the eye was extraordinary.

He asked about the horses and wagons and Grace assured him they would be all right, but somehow he'd known the answer already.

She said something to the wolf-rider and he gave a loud whistle. Two more warriors arrived with three riderless wolves. Ivan had never ridden a wolf before and approached with caution. Grace however, walked right up to the largest one and greeted her as though they knew each other, then turned and acknowledged the other two. Again Ivan wasn't surprised, nor was he surprised that her wolf was black. Grace mounted the wolf with ease and Ivan knew this wasn't her first ride. He was a bit unnerved as he climbed onto his wolf's back, but was amazed how smooth it was once they were traveling. The other wolf, although it had no rider, ran beside Grace and kept pace with her mount.

When they arrived at the *Gatou* village they were taken straight to the chief's lodge. He introduced himself as *Korak* and Ivan looked at Grace. She explained that he was a descendant to the one in her story.

The evening was incredible. They were each given new out-fits made of that amazing leather fabric, which they wore in honor of their hosts. They were then treated to a fabulous meal and entertainment. Then they were each given a gift from the chief. Grace received a statue of a princess, and Ivan was given an antique bracelet, and he could just make out the engraving of a wolf and a girl standing on the plains.

Could this be . . . no, he thought, and said, "*Utai,*" which brought laughter from Grace and the rest of the *Gatou.* Ivan was curious as to why the *Gatou* were going to such extravagant lengths to celebrate their joining, so he asked Grace. She told him that her and her mother had made many trips to the villages when they were in need of healers. Ivan felt there was more to it, but didn't question her any further.

After the festivities had finished, he and Grace were taken to a joining hut for the night. Ivan smiled. *I could get used to this treatment*, he thought as he closed the flap.

When they awoke, breakfast was waiting for them. They dressed and ate, then stepped into the morning air. All the *Gatou* were there to greet them, the older women giggling and the men all smiles. Grace talked with the chief while the wolves were being brought over, then they mounted and were off to where they had left the wagons.

As they reached the area where their possessions were being guarded, Ivan dismounted and started hooking up the team. Grace took awhile saying goodbye to her wolf, who she called Faline, then turned to the older gray wolf that had been following riderless, and referred to her as Jinda. She explained to Ivan that the big gray wolf was her mother's and that they were both chosen by their wolves when they had first come as healers to the *Gatou* camps when she was a little girl.

When all was ready, and the *Gatou* had disappeared into the tall grass, Ivan and Grace climbed aboard the wagon and continued north to their new home.

"Ivan . . . Ivan." He was pulled from his daydream and found himself staring into Grace's eyes. Sixteen years later and she was still as lovely as she'd been on that first day.

"Breakfast is ready dear," she said, and walked back to the table. Ivan stood up, hung his guitar back on the wall and moved to the basin to wash up. By the time he had finished, Shyla and Cade were back inside and they all sat down to breakfast.

He loved mealtime because it was one part of the day when the entire family was together.

"The wagon is loaded and ready," remarked Cade, as he fixed a plate. "I fed Old Bill and walked him . . . but he's still favoring his right front leg," he added, between bites of pancake.

Bill, the woodcutter's blue-roan workhorse, was getting on in years and was the only one left out of the original team he had taken down to Belden's Wall on that first trip. He'd had to sell his other horses to pay his costs, but he and Old Bill had been working side-by-side for twenty years now, and he was like one of the family. That old horse had more heart than most people he'd met and Ivan knew, if you asked it of him, he would give you his last breath in faithful service. Ivan couldn't wait for the day when he could put him out to pasture though and not have to work him anymore.

"How badly off is the Starling boy?" asked Ivan, knowing how worried Grace was.

"Well, he's getting worse and they're not sure why," she replied in a concerned tone. "We'll know more when we see him today, but I'm sure it's just something they've overlooked."

Little Ben Starling had been sick for over a month now and the soother from Woodvale couldn't diagnose the problem. Every time he would start to recover, it would hit him again and he had been getting worse with each relapse. They had finally contacted Grace and asked her to have a look at him, and that was where the two healers were off to this morning.

Healers versus soothers. Wood versus coal. Everything was moving fast and Ivan knew he was on the wrong side of change.

"Do you have all the remedies and supplies we need for our visit today Shyla?" Grace asked her daughter.

"Yes Mother, the healing bag is complete," she said with pride. Shyla was such a perfectionist, and took her duties so seriously that sometimes it was hard to believe she was only twelve years old. "I hope we can cure the little boy," she offered sadly.

"We will do our best," replied Grace, "and that is all anyone can ask of us."

Cade finished his breakfast quickly and asked if he could be excused.

Ivan replied, "Yes you may, as soon as we're done our break-fast tradition." Ivan stood up and held out his hands. The others stood and they all joined hands in a circle around the table. Everyone bowed their heads, closed their eyes and stood there in silence, just enjoying the closeness. This was something they had done in Ivan's family as long as he could remember, and he wasn't sure how far back it went.

"All right boy," Ivan said, breaking the silence. "You go ahead and hitch up Old Bill and I'll be out shortly." Cade was excited to be going with his father and rushed out the door to make sure everything was ready. Shyla finished what was on her plate and took hers and Cade's dishes to the cupboard.

"You're excused," teased her mother.

"Oh Mom," she said in an exasperated tone. "You know that once the first person leaves the table the chain is broken."

Grace smiled and asked Shyla to take the healing bag and wait for her at the wagon, to which her daughter replied, "I will Mom, but don't be too long, that sick boy is waiting for us."

Grace looked at Ivan. "Don't look at me," he laughed. "She takes after you."

When the children had gone, Ivan turned to Grace and rubbed her arm. "I'm sorry things have come to this," he said. "I wish I could provide more."

She placed her hands on his cheeks and looked deep into his eyes. "You give me more than I could ever dream of," she told him. "We have enough to eat and material possessions are not important to me. Your love and kindness are more than I could wish for."

Ivan looked at his wife with affection as she continued.

"Claude's wife, Morra, has every material possession a woman could wish for, and is she happy? No," she answered herself. "You're going to collect the payment for your shipment today, then you're going to enter the Woodcutting Competition and win it, and we will be just fine." She looked so serious, how could he argue.

"What if I don't win this year?" he asked her. "I'm getting old you know, and I'm not the woodsman I once was."

"Nonsense!" she scolded. "You are the greatest woodcutter that ever lived, and will be for many years to come." He sat there looking at her. She had enough confidence in him for both of them.

"What did I ever do to deserve you?" he asked softly and kissed her.

Grace and Ivan did a quick cleanup, then grabbed their coats and boots and held hands as they walked from the cabin.

"Mom, Cade pulled my hair!" yelled Shyla as she ran behind her father.

"I just gave it a tug," he defended sheepishly.

"Why are you tormenting your sister?" demanded Grace, as she walked over and looked up at her son.

"She laughed at me when I missed the bull's-eye with my axe," he explained.

Grace huffed, "You're both acting—."

"Your age," finished Ivan and winked at his wife as he picked his daughter up and set her in the wagon.

"Dad could you show me again how to hold and throw the axe, *please*?" Cade pleaded.

"Sure, Son," agreed Ivan. "Pass me my hatchet." The boy handed it to him and he removed it from the scabbard. The hatchet felt like an old friend with its smooth handle and perfect balance. Instantly he pivoted and let it fly. *Thunk!* it hit the target right in the center of the bull's-eye.

Cade watched in amazement. "Do you ever miss, Dad?" he asked.

"Why would I do that?" Ivan replied with a smile. Cade retrieved the hatchet, and this time his father showed him exactly how to hold it, how to stand and how to throw. Cade took aim and made his attempt, but it hit the target low and to the left. He looked at Shyla, who sat there with a straight face.

"Don't worry," Ivan reassured him, "you're doing great for your age. All you need is more practice." Cade nodded and ran to grab the hatchet but Ivan could see the disappointment in his face, so he walked over to the wagon and got his longbow. When his son returned, he handed it to him and said, "Try this."

Cade nocked an arrow and pulled back on the string. Everything fell into slow motion, like it always did as he targeted, and he let go of the shaft. *Twang!* the bowstring snapped and the arrow buried itself deep in the center. He looked at Shyla again, and this time she smiled.

As a small child Cade had always had an unusual gift for the bow, and his father had always tried to encourage this natural ability.

"Nice shot Son," Ivan said with pride, as he placed the hatchet back in its scabbard.

Cade retrieved the arrow and returned to the wagon. "Thanks Dad," he replied, but still felt disappointed. He wanted so much to be like his father, and that meant being good with the axe.

They placed the weapons in the wagon, climbed aboard and got Old Bill moving up the dirt path toward the public road.

"Where's Rufus?" asked Ivan, as they reached the edge of their property.

"He caught wind of something this morning and I haven't seen him since," answered Shyla.

They swung right and headed east along the hard-packed road that led into the town of Woodvale.

The family was silent and lost in thought as the wagon creaked its way along. Shyla's only thoughts were for the Starling boy and how she could make him well again.

Cade was thinking about hitting the center of the target with the axe. He was concerned for the Starling boy as well, but his thoughts wandered more to the Starling girl. Wanda Starling was close to his age and very pretty in his eyes. He hadn't seen her for some time, but today he was going to get his chance when they dropped the girls off.

Grace felt concern for the boy, as she did with all her healings. She was also thinking about what she was going to fix for the evening meal. It was always a challenge when you had limited supplies to work with, but she would make do as always.

She smiled as she thought of her daughter. Shyla was born with the gift strong in her, much stronger than Grace, and was learning so fast. At the rate she was grasping the ways of healing, she would be an adept by her fourteenth birthday. That would make her the youngest adept healer in the history of their family. Her thoughts then turned to her mother, and she wondered how she was doing in her mountain home. She never worried about Zarina, she just missed her.

Ivan held the reins in his hands but wasn't concentrating on driving. He was thinking about providing for his family, and the Woodcutting Competition was the key. He'd heard rumors that there would be some new blood this year, and that meant a bigger prize pool, but it also meant more entrants and more men to beat. It was always fun to watch the young woodsmen come in and try to make a name for themselves. The ironic predicament he found himself in was that sitting at their home in his wife's jewelry case was a pearl necklace, an antique bracelet and a solid gold statue, which if sold, would support their family for years. They had discussed that possibility only once and had both agreed that they would rather beg for coppers in the streets of Woodvale than to even entertain the thought of parting with one of those gifts.

He was pulled from his thoughts by the sound of Cade's voice. "There's the turnoff Dad," he said, pointing to the opening. He turned Old Bill and faced the big wooden gate with the sign above that read, "Starling Horse Ranch".

Ben and Maggie Starling had been breeding and raising horses in the vale for many years. They only worked with purebreds, and then only with the Kings Breed. These were snow-white, gaited horses used for riding or pulling carriages.

Cade jumped out, opened the gate and waited for his dad to drive through. He tied it shut again, climbed back onto the wooden seat and they continued up the road that led to the Starling ranch house.

They had only traveled two hundred yards when Cade said, "Look Dad." Ivan turned in the direction he was pointing and saw two little grizzly cubs on the right side of the roadway, near the tree-line. Ivan looked around quickly and saw what his instincts had warned him of. On the left was a mother grizzly just coming out of the trees. Old Bill stopped and reared. Ivan kept him steadied and didn't make any sudden movements as he watched the bear's actions. With his family between her and her cubs, he wasn't sure what would happen, so he reached down and readied his longbow. His hatchet would only make the bear mad and a longbow would only be effective if the shot was accurate, but the last thing he wanted to do was take that shot.

The bear was on her hind legs now and stood over seven feet tall. She chopped her jaws together as a warning and moved her head from side-to-side, trying to see her babies.

Cade took the reins and was working hard to maintain control of the horse. Ivan had an arrow ready, while Grace held her daughter and looked on warily from the backseat. The mother grizzly was becoming more aggressive now because she couldn't see if her cubs were all right, so she got down on all fours and started ripping chunks of dirt from the ground, and shaking her head back and forth.

Ivan had been a woodsman for a long time now and knew that she was getting ready to charge. He lifted his bow and pulled back the string. *What a shame*, he thought as he targeted the left eye. *She's just trying to protect her family the same as I am.*

He had to make sure of his aim, so he steadied himself again. Suddenly he heard singing, but the words made no sense to him. He was ready to take the shot but the bear had stopped moving and seemed distracted. He waited as the singing continued. Now the bear was sitting down and seemed almost docile. Ivan lowered his bow and looked back. Shyla was standing on the wagon seat, her arms out, chanting in a language he didn't recognize. He turned around again and the bear was lying down in the grass. He could hear the chanting rise to a new intensity, which caused the big old bear to roll over and put her paws in the air like Rufus would do when he wanted his belly scratched.

Ivan grabbed the reins and started Bill moving, which didn't take much coaxing. Grace held Shyla, and Cade sat there looking puzzled. Once his family was out of danger, Ivan looked around and saw the two cubs walking over to their mother, probably wondering what interesting item she'd found in the grass.

"Shyla, what was that you just did back there?" Ivan asked his daughter. In all his days the woodcutter had never seen anything quite like it.

"That was a calming chant for animals." She replied, still feeling weak from the ordeal. "I learned it from the old gypsy woman with the blind eye. She said I had much strength in the gift."

At that moment Ivan realized there was so much depth and mystery surrounding the two women in his life that he would probably only ever understand a small portion of it. He didn't care though, he loved them both dearly and that's all that mattered to him.

As they moved farther along, the trees began to thin, then turn into fields filled with beautiful white horses. There was a six-rail wooden fence on each side, and the ranch house was just ahead. Grace grabbed the healing bag that was resting on the load of wood behind her, and Shyla went through it again just to make sure they had everything they needed.

Cade was feeling anxious at the thought of seeing Wanda, and combed his hair with his fingers. Their visits were so infrequent that he wondered what she looked like now and wanted her to see how tall he was.

They pulled up to the house and everyone climbed down. Maggie was there to greet them and Grace and Shyla went straight in to tend to the boy. Ben Senior came out, walked up to Ivan and Cade and shook their hands.

"Would you like to come in for awhile?" he asked. "I've just made a fresh pot of tea."

"We'd love to," said the woodcutter, "but we've got a delivery to make, and we're already running behind."

Ben Starling had always been a big, easygoing man, constantly making jokes and teasing people, but when he looked at Ivan his face seemed strained and tired.

"Thanks so much for bringing Grace," he said in a serious tone. "We've been sick with worry and no one can tell us what's wrong with our son."

Ivan looked at him reassuringly and said, "Grace will do everything she can to help Little Ben."

Putting on his happy face once more, Big Ben walked over to the wagon. "Old Bill is looking good," he said, smiling. "I always forget how big he is until I see him again. He makes my horses look like ponies." They all chuckled and the old workhorse perked up, almost like he understood.

Cade turned his head to see Wanda Starling come through the front door, and she was no longer a little girl. He felt his mouth go dry and tried to swallow. "H-hi Wanda," he croaked.

"Hi yourself Cade Harden," she replied, offering him a cup of water. "A little something to cut the traveling dust," she said quaintly, then offered one to Ivan.

The woodcutter took it, emptied its contents and handed it back to her. "Thank you Wanda, and aren't you growing into a beautiful young lady," he complimented, and then continued his conversation with Ben.

She watched Cade as he finished the last of his water, then with the sweetest smile, took the cup and disappeared back inside. Cade stood there with his mouth open and Ivan had to almost lift him onto the wagon.

As they headed back the way they'd come, Ben called out, "Thanks again, and don't worry about Grace and Shyla, I'll see they get home safely."

CHAPTER

7

Into Woodvale

They reached the public road with no more incidents and proceeded to their next stop. Cade sat there for awhile and then turned to Ivan. "Dad, how do you know if a girl likes you or not?" he questioned.

"Well, just ask her I guess," Ivan offered. Cade looked at him and shook his head. *Can life really be as simple as father makes out*, he wondered, *or is that just his way of looking at it?*

As they rolled along, Ivan thought of his parents, William and Marrine Harden. His father, Will, as everyone called him, had been one of the best woodcutters and stonemasons in the land, and Ivan's mother had worked right alongside him. Everyone considered this to be unusual, but Ivan had grown up with it so it seemed normal to him. His father would help with the cooking and cleaning, and then together they would go to whatever job they were working on at the time.

Ivan remembered a time when this burly man from the north said something negative about his mother working with the men. After Will, who had a short temper, physically showed him the error in his judgment, there had been no more opinions voiced. Ivan had to smile when he thought of his father. Well over six feet tall and layered with corded muscle, he was intimidating to say the least. Despite his stature and powerful presence though, he was a gentle and caring man. The only people that ever experienced his dark side were the ones who pushed him too far, and even then he handled it quickly and efficiently, gaining the respect of those around him. Only by Marrine could he be pushed to any limit. Not only did he love her with every ounce of his being, he respected her more than any other. The woodcutter thought back and could not recall his father ever laying a hand on him either. Ivan had seen the lines though and had always had enough fear and common sense not to cross them.

He loved his parents and missed them dearly. For eight years they had worked as head masons on the palace in the City of Kings, and oversaw the completion of that magnificent structure. They then boarded a ship and set out to see the eastern lands. They'd been gone twenty-three years now, and he had only the few letters they had sent to let him know where and how they were. Their last correspondence had described a land of dark skinned people who used song to communicate. *What a time they must be having,* he thought, *and what a childhood he'd had with his unusual family.*

His parents had worked a lot and taken him with them on any job that lasted over two weeks, but when the jobs were shorter he had been left at the homestead with his grandfather, Barrem Harden. He'd called him Papa Bar and had learned many of the woodcutting skills from him. Barrem was a kind and patient man who hardly ever lost his composure and everyone said that Ivan took after him with his leaner muscle and laid-back temperament. He even had the same twinkle in his eye and dry sense of humor as Papa Bar. Ivan had loved staying with his grandpa when his parents worked, but he had also loved to go with them on the job.

His favorite time had been the eight years at the palace, partly because Papa Bar had come with them, and because he was treated like royalty there. The king had no son yet, so he had taken Ivan under his wing and taught him many things about life and the ways of the court. His most memorable adventures took place when the baron's son, Vero, would visit. They would run through the castle slaying monsters and rescuing at least three damsels each day.

He had stayed at the palace from age nine to seventeen and then decided to go back to the homestead with his grandfather rather than sail the seas with his parents. He and his grandfather worked the Big Timber area for the next three years until Papa Bar passed to the balance. After that he worked and stayed alone until he was joined with Grace. He smiled when he looked back on his life. How interesting and unusual it had been so far, with never a dull moment, and not one regret. That last thought brought him back from his daydream, and for some reason, Claude Boyle crossed his mind for just an instant.

They reached the turn that led into Brundle's Brickyard, and took the well-worn path that wound its way to where he was to deliver his load of wood. This payment would, with what he had saved, more than make up the entry fee for the Woodcutting Competition.

The hot sun warmed his face as he drove Old Bill behind the ovens to the place where he had unloaded his cargo for years. Suddenly the sun's warmth diminished compared with the heat he felt inside at the sight of the huge pile of coal sitting in his spot. He pulled Bill to a stop and sat there staring at the coal that, to him, was more vile and dangerous than any grizzly.

His attention was diverted from the black mound by a figure approaching the wagon.

Tad Brundle, owner of the brickyard, stopped beside him and said, "Good morning Ivan, I'm glad I caught you before you unloaded. We need to talk about the wood shipment." The patterns started forming in Ivan's mind, the way they always did when something didn't feel right. Claude's unusually early ride this morning had now cleared itself up.

Before Tad could say another word, Ivan interjected. "I see you've procured the services of one, Claude Boyle."

"Now just wait Ivan," Tad said defensively. "I can explain."

"There's no need to," Ivan assured him, holding back his anger. "You can deal with whomever you choose. I just wished you would have let me know."

"I would have," offered Tad, "but it happened this morning, and the offer was so good, I couldn't pass it up. He told me I had to take it then, or there would *be* no deal. Funny thing was," he added, "the wagon arrived only a short while after Mr. Boyle left the yard."

Ivan had to hand it to Claude. He really knew how to hit a man where it hurt. To think he had his driver waiting on the public road while he made his deal, and then had him deliver the goods before Ivan could arrive and spoil his plans. *What a devious mind he has,* thought Ivan, but how had he known about the delivery and where it would be delivered.

"What's done is done," he relented, as he turned his rig around.

"I'm real sorry," Tad apologized, "but I've got my wife Camille and my five children to support, and a man has to look after his family."

"I know the feeling," Ivan agreed, and started the wagon back down the path.

When the reality of the situation struck him, Ivan felt sick. This had been his chance to get the entry fee, and now it was gone. He might be able to peddle the load of wood, but for only a quarter of its value. Tad was the only customer in the area who needed this much burning wood year-round.

He was trying to think of which places might purchase some of the load when Tad yelled "Wait!" Ivan stopped the wagon and looked back. "I ordered that shipment darn it and I'm going to take it no matter what Claude Boyle or anyone else says or does. Just unload it beside the coal," he instructed, "and I'll be back out shortly to settle up."

Ivan looked at Cade as he turned the wagon around. "You see Son, there is also good in the land."

They had the wagon almost unloaded when Tad returned, along with his wife. Camille walked up and handed Ivan a cloth wrapped with twine. "Some cookies for the road," she offered, "and this must be your son." Ivan made the introductions, then Camille whispered something to Tad and walked back to the house.

"Thanks for doing this," said Ivan, "but are you sure you can afford two shipments today?"

"Don't worry," he replied, "I got the load of coal for free."

They all laughed and Ivan said, "Well at least this morning Claude got paid what he was worth." They laughed again but Ivan felt bad. "I shouldn't say things like that, but his under-handed dealings are *very* wearing on my patience."

Tad paid for the wood and Ivan and Cade made their way to the public road.

Now he had enough for his entry fee and some supplies. This day was shaping up, but one thing still bothered him. How had Claude known about his delivery? He was sure Tad hadn't told him.

"So what do you think of commerce so far?" he asked his son.

"Well it sure can change in a hurry, depending on the situa-tion," he answered as he watched a hawk flying overhead.

"I'm still wondering how Claude knew my business inten-tions enough to be able to counter them," puzzled Ivan.

Cade looked away and then back to his father. "Well," he muttered, "I might have mentioned something to Sonny the other day."

Ivan looked at Cade and said, "You know Son, if you tell people your business, soon you won't have any."

"I guess," Cade responded, "but Sonny is always bragging about his stuff, and he got this new horse and . . . I just wanted to have something important too."

"I understand," replied the woodcutter, "but a man cannot be measured by the possessions he can accumulate in life. He is measured by his word and his honesty, and most importantly, the way he treats himself and others."

Cade thought it through and answered, "I know you're right, but it irks me when he shows off with all his fancy things."

"I know Son," his father said softly, "but remember that he never earned any of them, and those things are truly unimportant. They are fulfilling for a short time, but true happiness comes from within."

Cade smiled, "Okay Dad, I'll try to remember that the next time he calls me poor."

Ivan felt bad for his son. He knew how hard it was for a boy his age to understand about the things that really meant something in life, and that made him wonder how Grace was doing.

They came to a fork in the road and Cade looked at the sign. On the left side, with arrows pointing accordingly, it read, "Coaldale—fifteen miles" and under that it read, "City of Kings and King's Port—sixty-five miles". On the right side it read, "Woodvale—one mile ". Ivan swung the wagon to the right and hurried Bill along.

As they entered the town it seemed busier than usual. They stopped at the common-trough and watered Bill, then made their way to the general store.

Brown's General would have most of the supplies they needed, and a table was set up outside for those who wanted to post their entry for the Woodcutting Competition. It was about two weeks away now, and if the rumors were true, it should be the biggest one yet. They stopped in front of the hitching post outside the store and Cade secured the reins. He left his father and ran inside to get what they needed and have a look around. He loved to glance over all the different items for sale, but mainly he liked to look at the assortment of candies displayed on the front counter.

Ivan walked over to the table and placed five silver pieces in front of the event coordinator. As he waited for the official to write down his name, he browsed over the many hatchets and axes that lie there for sale. He lifted each one and tested it, but none even came close to the weight and balance of his. He had just thanked the man, when he heard someone behind him.

"Ladies and gentlemen," bellowed a deep voice, "Ivan Harden, the greatest woodcutter in the land, has just entered my humble contest." Ivan turned and saw his childhood friend, the Baron Vero Salday, who was escorting the Duchess Cavillade. Everyone cheered his words and the baron applauded.

Vero looked great as he approached, with his short golden-blonde hair, neatly trimmed beard and smile that almost sparkled. The duchess appeared so regal as she carried her tall, slim body with deliberate poise. Her hair was blonde as well, but long and thick, and her eyes were big and brown, with a wisdom that almost contradicted her generous beauty.

"Sir Ivan," said the baron, earnestly. "How have you been?"

Ivan smiled. "I don't believe I warrant a title . . . but fine considering the present plight of the woodcutter. And you baron?" he asked, bowing slightly to the duchess, who looked regal with her long gown and parasol.

"I'm fine," he replied. "A title has never done anything for me except cause headaches . . . and call me Vero."

Ivan nodded and asked, "What brings you to Woodvale . . . Vero?"

"I've taken a room at the Inn until my pavilion on the competition grounds is ready," he answered. "And what a competition it's going to be!"

Ivan nodded again. "Yes," he agreed. "If the rumors are true, there should be a few young woodsmen from the north testing their axes this year."

Vero looked at him in amazement. "Don't tell me you haven't heard the news!" he exclaimed.

A small warning sounded in Ivan's head. "I only just arrived," he said slowly, "and you're the first I've talked to."

"Well," said Vero eagerly. "It appears your good friend Claude Boyle has imported a giant from the north to make the competition that much more interesting," and he gestured to a poster fastened to one of the timbers along the walkway. Ivan's ears burned as he walked over and looked at it.

In the center was the likeness of a thick, muscular man standing as tall as the tree beside him, holding a double-bitted axe that was proportionate to his massive size. On top it read, "Come see

Tamarack Jack the Giant with the Axe at this year's Woodcutting Competition". On the bottom it read, "Sponsored by Morgan's Coal Company, and brought to you by Claude Boyle, manager extraordinaire". Under that was a flattering likeness of Claude.

Ivan walked back over to the baron and the duchess. *This day just keeps getting better,* he thought.

"I wouldn't worry too much about that brute," said Vero confidently. "No one can match your woodcutting skills, no matter how big." Ivan didn't respond. He just stood there trying to calm himself.

"Speak of the storm and it shall appear," said the duchess, as she glanced up the walkway. Ivan didn't want to look but turned and faced the oncoming.

About fifty yards away, and walking toward him, was Claude and Sonny Boyle, along with another associate he didn't recognize. Behind them lumbered the biggest man Ivan had ever seen. He hadn't even heard of anything that size except maybe the Black Buffalo of the plains, or in *The Tale of the Twelve Foot Gnome.* Before now Ivan's father had been the largest man he'd ever seen, but this Tamarack Jack made Will look like a child. He had to be over ten feet tall, with his head almost touching the bottom of the balcony covering.

The three people in front were walking side-by-side comfortably down the walkway, and the giant took up that width easily as he followed slowly behind, resting that huge axe on his shoulder. Claude greeted the baron and the Duchess Cavillade, then faced Ivan.

"Having a good day?" he sneered, obviously feeling good about his early morning ride.

"I've had better," responded Ivan coldly, wishing he could thank him personally.

"There's someone I'd like you to meet," boasted Claude, ignoring the man beside him.

Claude was shorter than Ivan, but very stocky. He had dark hair and prominent features that seemed to enhance his arrogant need to be the center of attention and always get the last word in.

"This is Tamarack Jack from Arcana," he said with a smirk.

Up close the giant looked even more extraordinary, with his massive frame and skin that looked more like granite. Ivan held out his hand and said, "Nice to meet you Jack."

The giant reached out, engulfing Ivan's hand, and the woodcutter knew that with a little more effort he could have crushed it. "I long admire you," he said slowly and his voice sounded like thunder mixed with gravel.

"Yes, well enough admiration," Claude said darkly. "We have things to do. . . . Oh, and by the way Ivan, how did your delivery go this morning?" Claude laughed in his face before continuing to lead the group along the walkway. Ivan was burning all over now and was starting to shake.

"Ivan . . . ." said Vero in a concerned tone.

The woodcutter moved like the wind. He grabbed a hatchet from the table and threw with all his might. End over end it whirred through the air and then sank deep into Claude's picture on the poster, just as the man was passing it. He jumped sideways, startled, then hurried past the building and around the corner. The giant looked at the hatchet buried deep in the timber, square in the middle of Claude's likeness, and his lips curled into a huge grin. He waved back at Ivan, then followed his employer. Sonny, following the giant's example, also smiled and waved before running to catch up with his father.

When he had finally calmed down, Ivan felt embarrassed. "I'm sorry," he said to the baron and duchess, but they didn't respond. They just stood there watching him. He looked around and people were staring in disbelief. No one had ever seen him lose his temper before and they seemed shocked, and even scared. He saw Cade standing in the doorway of the store, wide-eyed, with a stunned look on his face.

"Well that hatchet should sell for a good price now," said the baron, trying to lighten the mood. Ivan forced a smile, then went and removed the axe from the timber. *I must have really thrown it,* he thought as he struggled to pull it from the wood. He brought it back, set it on the table and apologized again.

Cade rushed up and blurted, "That was incredible Dad. I've never seen anyone move that fast, and with perfect accuracy."

The woodcutter shook his head. "I shouldn't have done that Son, and there's nothing incredible about it," he muttered, still angry with himself.

"Well, look on the bright side," said Vero. "When you beat his giant in the competition it will be a sweet victory, knowing he intentionally brought him in to defeat you. It will be like beating Claude himself," he finished with a hand gesture. Ivan had to smile. The baron had such flare and enthusiasm, and more charisma than any *two* men.

"Did you find the supplies we need?" he asked his son.

"Yeah, they're loaded on the wagon and Mr. Brown is just awaiting payment," he answered back.

"All right, you go and tell him I'll be in directly, and don't forget to grab a stick of that candy for you and Shyla."

The baron motioned to the table and said, "What did I tell you Ivan. There are three people arguing over who will buy that hatchet, and imagine how the story will magnify with each telling."

Ivan looked at his wagon. "Speaking of buying," he said, "I had better go and pay for my goods. It was good to see you both again, and I hope I didn't cause you any discomfort Duchess."

"Nonsense!" she reprimanded. "I enjoy your company. There's never a dull moment when you two are together."

They shook hands again and Vero said, "I'll see you at the competition. Oh and Ivan, don't worry about paying for your supplies. I think you've had enough stress for one day." Ivan knew better than to argue, so he thanked him and walked over to the wagon where Cade was already waiting with a piece of candy stuck in his mouth. Ivan climbed aboard, sat down and grabbed the reins.

"Did you get everything on the list?" he quizzed.

"Yes, they had everything that was written down," he answered, still sucking on the candy, "but I wish there would have been enough left over to buy those dresses for Mom and Shyla."

Ivan looked over at him. "Well, as luck would have it, we do," he chuckled. Cade was excited because it had been so long since his mother had bought anything for herself, and he knew the very one she had picked out in the dress shop. Shyla had also been looking at one for over a year now and he knew how bad she wanted it.

Considering how everything had gone back and forth so many times today, Ivan wasn't sure if they would make it to the dress shop or not before something else unusual happened. At least he didn't have to worry about picking out the right dresses; Cade was in charge of that. Ivan thought about what Grace would say when he gave it to her. *Ivan,* she would start, *you know we can't afford frivolous things like this when we're having enough trouble putting food on the table.* He could just hear her, but it didn't matter. He was buying her and Shyla dresses, and that was that . . . besides, he could always tell her it was Cade's idea.

They had passed the livery stable and the goldsmiths now, and were almost to the dress shop when Ivan saw the building where Sam Morgan, the owner of the Morgan's Coal Company, kept his Woodvale office. Despite Claude and his dealings carried out in Sam's name, Ivan liked Mr. Morgan. He was always courteous, and had donated generously to the community to improve the school building and build a larger town hall. Ivan had always got a good feeling around him, but knew better than to try to do business with him. Sam was a shrewd fellow and always came out on top in his dealings. He had started in coal eight years ago, taking a little watering stop northeast of Woodvale and single-handedly building the town of Coaldale up around it. Sam loved his daughter Moira deeply and basically put up with Claude because they were joined. Sam was getting on in years and hoped that one day Sonny, his grandson, would show an interest in the family business and eventually take over for his grandpa.

I wonder if Sam knows that Claude is giving coal away? he wondered, as they pulled up to the dress shop.

He handed Cade the coins and watched as he hurried into the store. Ivan stayed in the wagon and his mind drifted to the giant. How good was he? Was he just a big guy with an axe, or a true woodcutter? The latter thought worried Ivan. A man with that much raw power, skilled in the woodcutting arts, would be both daunting and nearly impossible to compete against. Ivan's speed would be a huge advantage, but would it be enough? *Well there's no use fretting over it,* he thought, as he noticed the passersby pointing and whispering. It reminded him of the time in Belden's Wall when the whole town knew of his joining with Grace, but this was different and he guessed the reason. Word had traveled through the town about the incident that had just occurred over at the general store, and he was sure the telling had been exaggerated already. *It's funny,* he thought, *usually the ones who know the true events of a story don't talk about it . . . or want to.*

Cade walked out of the building with two packages and a big smile. He set them on the rear seat and hopped into the front. "Mom and Shyla will be so surprised," he chuckled, "and there were even three coppers left over." He handed Ivan the coins and they made their way to the edge of town.

"That was quite a throw you made back there," said Cade with pride.

Ivan frowned. "It was a foolish thing to do Son," he admonished himself, "and I am ashamed that I sank to Claude's level."

"Yeah, but it was still the best throw I've ever seen," Cade stated adamantly.

"Well, I have to admit, it was a pretty decent toss," he agreed, and winked at his son.

Ivan wondered how Grace was doing with the sick child as they started Old Bill down the well-traveled road that would take them home.

CHAPTER

8

Sol'mar

Grace looked down at the little boy. He was fevered and trembling in his unconscious state. "How long has he been like this?" she asked in a concerned tone.

"About three days," replied Maggie, as she replaced the wet cloth on his forehead with a cooler one, "but it gets better and then worse again just when we think he's cured. The soother can't figure out what he has, and we're at our wits end!" she sobbed.

"Be strong Maggie," Grace calmed her. "Your son needs *you* and the rest of us to have clear minds." She turned to her daughter. Shyla was sitting on a chair beside the bed holding a washbasin full of cool water and looking on with a worried expression. She had watched her mother examine the boy thoroughly and find nothing, but something didn't feel right. She couldn't place it, but it was there nonetheless and it needled her senses like a memory that you can't quite discern. She'd never felt anything like it before, and the closer she came to focusing on it, the darker it appeared.

Grace smiled at her and asked, "Are you all right honey?"

Shyla looked confused. "I'm fine," she answered dryly, "but there's a wrong in this boy."

"Yes," whispered Grace, "and I have to take my findings out to the table to try to figure out what isn't wrong with him, so we can start to understand what is."

Maggie moved toward the door. "Ben has made some fresh tea if you would like a cup while you work," she offered, forcing a smile.

"That would be nice," replied Grace, gathering what she needed.

Shyla remained seated. "I'll stay with the boy," she said matter-of-factly, then walked up and sat on the edge of the bed. Grace nodded and left the room with Maggie.

Shyla gazed down at Little Ben and the sense of wrong grew stronger. She knew her mother would be upset if she tried anything without her approval and supervision, but she didn't see how a routine exploration could hurt. Slowly she reached in with her mind and began to try to find the sensation she had felt earlier. When she touched its edge it made her skin crawl. She pulled back involuntarily and felt a shudder go through her body.

Her mother would be so angry if she attempted any kind of healing alone, but now that she was aware of it, and knew her mother hadn't found anything, it seemed only right to try to help this boy. She started to probe for the wrong again and could tell instantly that she would have to do this alone. She knew instinctively how much concentration it would take to proceed, and that meant no noise, no distractions, or interruptions. Her mother was a brilliant healer, but Shyla was aware of a presence that had somehow eluded Grace, and she had to do what she could for Little Ben.

She placed her fingers on the top of his head, and the sensation almost made her vomit. The wrong seemed to be located in the center of his body, but she had to be sure. She moved her hands down and placed one on each temple. She could feel the vibrations emanating from his mind and gave in to them. He was dreaming, and it was violent. It wasn't like she could see the dream. It was more like flashes of images, like when she communicated with animals, and they vanished as fast as they came. His body and spirit were fighting as hard as they could, but this black malignance was too powerful. Sweat poured down her face now but she didn't notice. Moving her hands to his chest, she never broke contact with him. The wrong, which now felt like a tainted piece of darkness, was becoming easier to visualize and harder to stomach at the same time. The disgust she felt made it difficult not to jump up and run out of the room, but with only a slight waver, she moved her right hand and placed it over his heart. She shifted her left hand to his abdomen and pushed down gently to strengthen her connection. Small convulsions tried to overtake her as she pinpointed the sickness within, but she fought them off and focused the center of her being on the ill force. She became one with the child now and lost all sense of self. It was as if her whole essence had become pure energy in the form of a white light, and she surrounded the darkness. The foul, putrid taint filled her with loathing, but she held on.

She was oblivious to everything now except the wrong, and put all of herself into purging it. The energy's intensity was overwhelming, almost out of control as she brought it to a climax.

The darkness fled the boy and came at Shyla. She quickly pulled her thoughts from the child and gathered the searing light within, expanding it until she was physically awakened. Aware of her body once more, she could feel the foulness dancing along her skin like worms trying to burrow their way inside. She arched her back and brought the blinding radiance to a frenzy. Then with all of her might, she gathered it and forced it outward in one final assault. It ripped through her like a raging storm and incinerated the wormy darkness in an instant. Shyla screamed and then fell to the floor in a motionless heap.

Grace rushed in and ran to her daughter. "Shyla!" she cried out. "What have you done my girl?"

Maggie came in and hurried to the bed. "What's wrong with Shyla?" she asked, as she looked down at her son.

Little Ben opened his eyes and said, "Mommy I'm thirsty," and Maggie burst into tears, hugging her little boy as she wept.

Grace didn't answer. She just sat on the floor holding her daughter. She examined her quickly to make sure she was breathing properly, and checked her pulse and color. Grace knew she had performed a healing, but none of this added up. She lifted Shyla and placed her on the bed beside the boy, who was now eagerly drinking the water his mother had brought.

Physically she seemed fine, but why was she unconscious? She didn't appear to have hit her head, and she had no broken bones, so Grace took a deep breath to clear her thoughts. *Come on Grace think,* she told herself. She knew the answer was right in front of her but she just couldn't see it, so she went over the facts in her mind.

The little boy had been healed, she could feel that. There had seen a blinding flash of light at the same moment Shyla had screamed and her clothes were soaked with sweat. Grace racked her brain as she placed a damp cloth on Shyla's forehead.

She closed her eyes and tried to let all the information fall into place. Then, just as quick as that it came to her, but the answer was almost impossible to believe. *Could it be?* she thought. *Could my little girl be a Sol'mar?*

There hadn't been one for centuries, but it was the only explanation for what had taken place. Suddenly she was scared for her daughter and held her close.

Zarina had told her and Shyla about the *Sol'mar* and how they performed their healings. They used energy in the form of light and concentrated it inside the sick person to extract the illness. It was very dangerous, but effective, and no *Sol'mar* in history had ever perfected the art. Each one had burned themselves out before their twenty-second year and spent the rest of their useless lives in the care of another healer . . . if they lived. *Oh Shyla,* she thought, *please be all right.*

Now that she had *hopefully* figured out what had taken place, she had to help her daughter somehow. "Maggie," she urged. "Please ask Big Ben to hitch up the team. I have to get Shyla home where I can care for her properly." Maggie ran out of the room, and Grace wrapped Shyla in a blanket. She dabbed her head with the cool cloth and waited for Maggie's return. Little Ben had fallen asleep and his expression was peaceful. "Well, you cured that little boy Shyla, but at what cost to yourself?" she said quietly.

Maggie came back in and told Grace the carriage would be ready right away. "What happened to Shyla?" she asked again.

"She must have hit her head when she fell," Grace answered in an evasive manner. "Don't worry. She'll be all right."

Maggie looked down at Shyla. "I wanted to thank her for curing my boy, but I guess it will have to wait until another time," she said, her voice mixed with disappointment and sympathy.

"That's fine," Grace assured her as she picked up Shyla and walked from the room with Maggie following behind.

"I want to pay you for the healing before you leave," Maggie told her.

"We don't take payment for our healings," Grace reminded her. "We do it to help others."

Maggie smiled. "That is your custom, but I won't feel right unless you at least take some of the venison that my husband has in the cold cellar."

"I will accept that," she agreed, and carried her daughter outside and over to the carriage. She handed Shyla to Ben, then stepped up and took her back once she was seated. Maggie returned with a cut of venison wrapped in cloth and set it on the seat beside her husband. "Thank you both so much for all that you've done for my son," she said. "It's been so hard this past month."

Grace smiled at her and said, "Make sure you let us know if there is any change in his condition."

"I will," she agreed, "and I hope Shyla isn't hurt too badly." Grace held her daughter tightly as the carriage began moving up the drive.

It was a lot smoother ride than the old wagon, and a lot faster with those white horses trotting in perfect unison. They reached the public road quickly and would be home soon. They had almost reached the turnoff when Shyla's eyes fluttered and then opened. She looked up and asked "Did I hurt the boy, Mother?"

"Oh Shyla," Grace said with tears in her eyes. "The boy is healed and doing well, but you need to rest, so just lie still."

When they reached the cabin, Shyla insisted on walking, so Grace thanked Ben and followed her in. She set the meat on the counter and checked her daughter over once again. She seemed fine, but Grace didn't want to take any chances, so she asked her to rest until the evening meal was prepared.

She wasn't sure if Shyla remembered the tales of the *Sol'mar*, but she could sense that her daughter was aware of the danger. Grace needed to let her mother know and ask her guidance in the matter, and there were so many other uncertainties that needed to be addressed. *It will all wait until tomorrow*, she told herself, and started preparing the venison for cooking.

Ivan, Cade and Rufus arrived back just before sunset. Cade unhitched Old Bill and helped his dad unload the supplies. They set everything on the porch, then Cade put the wagon away and Ivan went inside to see if Grace and Shyla had returned.

Ivan walked up and gave Grace a hug and they both started talking at the same time.

"Go ahead," said Ivan. "You first."

Grace curtsied, "Why thank you my good man," she said playfully, but her face still had a look of worry underneath. "I've got good news and bad," she explained, trying to think of the right way to tell him, "The good news is that the Starling boy is healed and we have venison for our evening meal. The bad news is that Shyla performed the healing when I wasn't there to supervise, and ended up unconscious for most of the trip back."

"Is she all right?" he asked. "Where is she?"

"She's fine," Grace assured him. "She's just resting until mealtime."

"Well it sounds like you've had a rough day," he said with concern. "So here's my good and bad news just to cheer you up. First my customer didn't want my shipment because

Claude gave him free coal. Then he took it anyway and paid me. I entered the Woodcutting Competition, where I saw the baron and Duchess Cavillade. They informed me that Claude had hired a giant woodsman to beat me. Then Claude came over with the giant and rubbed everything in my face, so I got angry and threw an axe at him . . . well, beside him. Then the baron paid for our supplies, so we used some of the extra coins to buy you and Shyla each a gift. That's the *good* and *bad* of my day all mixed together." When he was finished, he took a deep breath. "Oh and I almost forgot," he added. "We saw Rufus carrying a rabbit down the road, so we gave him a ride back."

"Wow!" said Grace, and laughed, "that was certainly a nice introduction for Cade's first business trip. I hope he was prepared for what the day held."

"He took it better than I did," Ivan grimaced. "I can't believe I let that blowhard get to me like that."

"You shouldn't let a man like Claude Boyle get under your skin," she teased, "you could get an infection."

They were both laughing as Shyla came in from her room. "What's funny Mom?" she asked.

"Oh your father had some excitement in town," she explained, "and I *thought* I heard something about gifts." Cade walked through the door carrying a rabbit that he had skinned and dressed, and placed it in a bowl of cold water.

"Did I hear someone say gifts?" he asked innocently. "I do believe I know something about that," and left again. He returned with two packages and handed them to the girls.

Grace opened hers and lifted the dress from its wrapping, holding it up. It was the pretty green summer-dress she had been admiring for some time now. Shyla already had hers open and was holding it up to herself. It was the pink one she had picked out and she ran to her room to put it on. "Are you sure we can afford this?" Grace asked in a worried voice.

"Well, I'm not sure," the woodcutter admitted, "but it feels great."

"Thank you *so* much," she fawned. "Now I have something to wear to the Woodcutting Competition." Shyla came running back with her dress on and did a pirouette, and then another. Cade and Ivan applauded, and she curtsied in acknowledgment of her admirers.

"Aren't you going to try yours on, Grace?" the woodcutter asked with a glint in his eye.

"You'll have to wait until competition day," she teased. "I'll wear it to bring you luck." Grace put her dress back in its wrapping and asked Shyla to go get changed and set the table.

"Can I wear my new dress to dinner?" she pleaded.

Grace looked at her beautiful daughter. "Yes of course you can, but hurry with the table, the meal's almost ready."

Ivan and Cade brought in the supplies, Grace and Shyla got the evening meal on the table, and they all sat down to eat.

The venison was good and there wasn't much distraction, except for Shyla acting like a princess in her new dress which brought a smile to everyone's face. Grace was glad to see she had recovered so quickly from her healing, and was also glad to see her acting like a little girl for a change, instead of a grown up.

When they had finished, Ivan said, "It's been an eventful and exhausting day and I think we should all turn in early. You kids get washed up and ready for bed."

"All right Daddy," said Shyla, "but could you tell me a bedtime story?"

"Sure I will sweetheart," he answered. "What about you Cade? Do you want a story?"

"I promised Rufus we would go hunting in the morning, so I should get some sleep. Besides, I'm kind of old for that sort of thing," he replied with a yawn, and left for his half of the bedroom.

Ivan had been planning to add another room for some time now, but it hadn't worked out yet.

Shyla walked to the bedroom, then turned and said, "Don't forget Daddy."

"I'll be right in," he told her, as she disappeared through the doorway.

When the children were gone, Grace turned to Ivan. "I need to tell you about the healing today," she began. "It was no ordinary healing that she performed." Ivan got a chill and his face showed concern as she continued. "The type of healing she undertook is one that only a *Sol'mar* could perform, and it hasn't been done in centuries.

"Why do I get a bad feeling when you say that?" Ivan asked in a grave tone. "Has it not been performed in that long because it's dangerous, or does this go deeper?"

Grace explained as calmly as she could about healing with the light and the eventual fate of every *Sol'mar*. Now they had to decide what to do to prevent the same fate from happening to their daughter.

"Well she just won't heal anymore," Ivan said dryly.

"I love you husband, but you don't understand what we are dealing with," she told him gently. "To ask a healer not to heal is like asking the sun not to shine, or the wind not to blow."

"Well, I don't truly understand," he admitted, but can't she refrain from that type of healing and do what you do?"

"It doesn't work that way," she sighed. "If only it were that easy. Let's take your woodcutting for example," she explained. "Is that not your calling?"

"Well yes, but if it was hurting me, or was potentially dangerous I wouldn't. . . ." He stopped and looked at Grace. "I get the point. You have to be true to who and what you are no matter how much suffering or hardship comes along with it."

He felt like a little boy sometimes when he talked to her. Her wisdom and knowledge about people and their inner workings was insightful.

"I have to send word to my mother," she said. "She needs to know of this, if she doesn't already."

"How could she. . . ." Again Ivan stopped and thought, *why do I even open my mouth?*

"Zarina has many gifts and qualities," she explained. "One of them is a precognitive sense of events, especially if they are in line with the forces that are in close proximity to her inner-mind."

Ivan shook his head. "Did you just say that your mother can sense when something happens to someone close to her?"

"Yes of course, and I apologize," she reprimanded herself. "I get carried away sometimes when I'm worried."

Many times throughout his life Ivan had been glad of his eight years spent at the palace, and this was definitely one. If not for the teachings there, he would be even more confused than he already was with many of the statements she made. It was there that he had learned the importance of education and how it expands your ability to comprehend.

Grace interrupted his thoughts. "Shyla and the part of her that has surfaced is our main concern and I can only help her to a point. Zarina is as versed in the *Sol'mar* as anyone, and has studied it as extensively as you can without actually being with one. I think we should ask for her guidance in this matter as soon as possible," she concluded.

"You know best in the ways of healing and I trust your judgment," Ivan agreed, "and if your mother can help teach Shyla what she needs to know to keep from hurting herself, then we should seek her counsel immediately." So with a mutual optimism, they agreed to send word to Zarina in the hope of ensuring the future safety of their child.

"Daddy!" Shyla called from the bedroom, "I'm washed and under the covers, waiting to be tucked in and told a story."

"Stop yelling!" shouted Cade. "I was just about asleep."

"Oh be quiet!" she retorted, "you're grumpier than that old mother grizzly we saw today."

Ivan and Grace went to the bedroom and into Shyla's half where she was sitting up and motioning to them. She asked her mother to lie on one side of her and her father to lay on the other while he told the story. They got on the bed and each turned on their side, snuggling close to her. Ivan's heart almost burst with the love he felt for his sweet child and it almost made him weep to think of anything bad happening to her.

"So what story do you want to hear?" he asked. "Do you want the one about the Angry Troll, or the one about the Twelve Foot Gnome?"

"No Daddy, can you tell me a new one tonight?" she pleaded.

"I know," he laughed, "how about The Woodcutter story."

"Daddy!" she giggled, "there's no story about a woodcutter, you're just teasing me."

"You're right," he relented, "but there ought to be." Ivan kissed Shyla on the forehead and said, "How would you like to hear a story that was told to me when I was a child living at the palace?"

Shyla's eyes got wide. "Is it a good story Daddy?" she asked.

"It better be," he replied. "It was told to me by the wisest man in the kingdom, and he swore it to be the truth."

She frowned at him and said, "You told me the Twelve Foot Gnome was real when I was little."

Ivan laughed. "You got me there," he responded, and growled like a troll.

Grace looked at her daughter and asked her if she was feeling any better, and she replied, "Yes, except I can sense the energy that I used on the boy, and it's burning deep in my center. It's always there, and it calls to me, just waiting for us to become one again."

Grace felt that scary feeling creep back in. "Please don't use it again until we know more about it . . . is that all right Shyla?" she asked, trying not to sound too demanding.

"Sure Mom, I was just trying to tell you how it feels," she explained.

"I know sweetie, but it scared me when I saw you lying on the floor unconscious, and I'm still a bit shaken," she admitted.

Shyla looked at her mother and said, "Don't worry, I'm fine, but maybe Daddy's new story will make us both feel better," she offered, looking at him with a big grin.

"Okay, okay," he said, pretending to be exasperated. "I'll tell it, but I've got to keep it quiet because we don't want to wake up Cade.

This story takes place a very, very long time ago," he began in a voice just above a whisper, "back before any people lived in the lands."

Shyla interrupted him. "Was there really a time like that Daddy?" she asked in a tone of wonderment.

"Well according to the wisest man in the kingdom there certainly was, and who can argue with him?"

"What's the story called?" she asked before he could continue.

"This story is called, *The Children of Balance*," he told her, "and it starts a long way from our little vale, out among the stars. You see, far, far away, in a place that is hard to imagine, there was a mother and her four children. She had two daughters and two sons, but they had no place to live. The mother had been searching for a place they could call home since her children had come into existence, but she wasn't an ordinary mother, and they weren't ordinary children. She was the mother of balance, and was the kind of being that kept the stars from falling out of the sky and the sun shining brightly. She was a being that held things together and formed the laws that keep the balance, and her children were just as unique.

Her youngest girl was water and her oldest was air. Her youngest boy was fire and the eldest was land. Not like the water you and I drink or the air we breathe, but a pure concentrated type that was magical. The brothers' essences were just as wonderful with their fire and land, the hottest and richest imaginable. They were so powerful in fact that they could take on different forms of their element and travel where they would at incredible speeds, but still they were homeless.

The mother and her children roamed the stars for thousands of years trying to find a place they could call their own.

Finally their long search ended when they found our lands, but it wasn't like the lands we know today. There weren't any people yet, and no animals or plant life. It was a harsh and violent place, with massive lightning storms and flooding. It was constantly being ripped apart by ground-shakes and scarred by fiery hot liquid that spewed from its depths, forming molten rivers that scorched the land.

When the mother of balance saw the devastation, she knew she was needed, and had finally found a true home for her children. She left her starry search and brought them down to rest upon the ground. Once she felt the core of our land, she could sense where the main turmoil was located and started her search for order. She and her children flew all over, at speeds you can't imagine, until she found places for them all. She created a paradise for each, that suited their specific talents and needs, and when she had them all situated in exactly the right areas, she burrowed deep underground into the very center of the chaos. She continued until she was at the perfect point in which to attach to her children and start the balance.

She reached out from her underground lair and connected with them. They in turn secured the Lines of Balance to their sanctuaries and the foundation for order was created. Once this had been accomplished, everything fell into place. The storms abated and the flooding ceased. The ground settled and the rivers of fire seeped back into the cracks from whence they had come. The land started to heal and soon plant life began to appear, along with small animals. After a while, people came into existence and started to work the land.

It was said that in the early days of man and woman, the mother of balance used to communicate with them from the heart of the land, but after centuries had gone by, she stopped. Then after enough time had passed it became legend and the people referred to the mother of balance as the heart of the land, and her children were forgotten. There are some though who still remember the tales. They understand that the only reason the sun rises and sets without fail, is because the mother, who rests deep in the heart of the land with her lines stretched tightly to each of her children, keeps everything in balance to this very day."

After he was done, Shyla asked intently, "Is that *really* true Daddy?"

"Well it must be," he replied. "It was *sworn* to be by the wisest man in the kingdom."

"Yeah well, maybe he's *also* the one that said he was the wisest man in the kingdom," she answered back with a smile.

Ivan chuckled and said, "Well it's not really a bedtime type story, but did you like it?"

She thought for a moment and then answered, "It's a very interesting story, but if it's true, then it's kind of scary. It's nice that they came down and made a home for themselves, and all of us, but what if they decide to move?"

"That's a good point," Ivan told her, "but I'm sure it's just an old wives-tale." He paused for a moment then looked at Grace. "And you know how those old wives like to tell tales," he said, and winked at her.

"Why, Ivan William Harden, are you calling me old?" she asked, as she jumped over Shyla and started to tickle him. Ivan burst into uncontrollable laughter and it got even worse when Shyla joined in.

One of Ivan's weaknesses was being ticklish and it almost paralyzed him if someone even threatened to do it. The girls continued despite his pleading. "Stop!" he cried, in between gales of laughter. "Please stop it!"

"Yes, please stop it!" called a voice from the other side of the partition. "Some of us have to work in the morning you know!"

"Oh really," said Grace, and gestured to Shyla and Ivan. They all jumped off the bed, lifted the blanket that separated the room and pounced on Cade, tickling him mercilessly into submission.

They all laughed and talked for awhile and then Cade, who admitted to having listened to the story, said to his father, "I thought it was good, but how could that man have thought it to be true? What I mean to say," he continued, "is that if the children were so powerful and magical, then why didn't they just create a home for themselves and their mother, instead of searching the stars for thousands of years?"

"Well," said Ivan, "I don't presume to know of such things, but I believe you're thinking of magic in the wrong way. It's not like the kind of magic in those tales of fairies. There *is* true magic in the land, but it is bound by laws just like anything else.

Take for example the sister and the brother in the story. One is water and the other is fire. Now say they wanted to harm you. By the laws that bind them the sister could not burn you but could freeze or drown you, and the brother could only burn you or suffocate you with smoke. This would be magical, but still bound by a set of laws and rules. People consider your mother's magical abilities to be quite normal, but only because they are used to it."

Then he thought of Shyla and what had happened earlier that day and was sure that was *way* up on the scale.

"Do you understand what I mean Cade?" he asked, as he stood up and grabbed the candle from Shyla's side of the room.

"Yeah, I think so, but I like the idea of three magical wishes and having anything you ask for granted instantly," he admitted. "I guess there's magic all around though, if you just look for it."

Ivan and Grace tucked Shyla back in and kissed her goodnight. Then they said goodnight to Cade and retired to their bedroom. As soon as they were under the blankets Ivan said, "I'm worried about Shyla. With all this talk of magic and healing with light and energy I feel scared and helpless when it comes down to it. I mean if that isn't the most powerful kind of magic, then what is?" he asked, hoping for another explanation.

"Well, whatever you call it, it's a part of her and nothing we *do* or *say* can change it. Just remember you're not alone in your feelings. I'm frightened to death over this whole ordeal," she admitted, and Ivan could hear it in her voice.

"I guess it's just how the situation is and we will have to accept it," Ivan agreed, and turned to face her. "Have I told you yet today how beautiful you are?" he asked her and placed his hand on the small of her back, pulling her closer.

"You may have," she answered, "but I never get tired of hearing it."

"That's good," he said with a smile, "but I think that's enough talking about it," and reached up and snuffed out the candle with his fingers.

CHAPTER
9

Practice Makes Perfect

Ivan was first up the next morning and had a fire built before anyone else came into the kitchen. Cade was next to rise and proceeded to top up the wood box, then grabbed the water bucket and went down to the creek to fill it. There were enough venison steaks left over for breakfast, so Ivan started heating them. When they were sizzling, he greased another pan with a bacon rind and started frying eggs. Once the steaks were hot he moved the pan to the edge of the cookstove to keep them warm. He sliced the left over potatoes and dumped them into the pan, then added some onions for flavor. *It's nice to have a few supplies again,* he thought as he watched Grace enter the room and take back her kitchen.

"I'll finish cooking breakfast, if you'll go feed the chickens and gather the eggs," she said. "I want to let Shyla sleep as long as possible." Ivan nodded and grabbed the egg basket. He went out and looked after the chickens, returning with the eggs at the same time Cade arrived with the water.

"Big mist on the creek this morning," Cade mentioned, as they stepped inside.

"It's cooler than normal," Ivan offered as an explanation. He closed the door, but not before seeing Rufus waiting in anticipation of the hunt Cade had promised him. It made him wonder how many more years of hunting the old boy had in him.

Ivan set the eggs on the counter, followed Cade to the washbasin and then sat down with his wife and son to a hearty breakfast. He was glad Shyla was getting well rested and hoped she would be able to sleep in today. Ivan was so used to getting up before first light that, when he did have a day off, he would still awake at the same time and not be able to get back to sleep.

After they had finished breakfast, and their ritual, Cade grabbed his hunting gear, and with Rufus at his side, headed north. Grace made a plate for Shyla and set it on the warming side of the stove. Then she cleaned off the table, did up the dishes and started preparing the rabbit for stewing. Ivan got his axe and hatchet and brought them over to his chair. He then grabbed the sharpening stone and a bowl of water, and started honing the axe blade to a fine edge.

He always kept it sharp because it meant more efficient work and fewer accidents. A dull axe had caused more men to be hurt than he cared to remember. The blade would simply glance off the wood, where it should have bitten in, and strike the man's leg or foot. Not a pretty sight, but most of the time preventable by a sharpened axe. Ivan used to have three different axes, but now he only had the one. He had been forced to sell the others about three years back when times had really started getting bad. This one was good though, and cut true if you handled it properly.

As he worked his axe against the stone, he thought of the giant again. He *had* to beat him, so in his mind he went over the five events that made up the Woodcutting Competition.

First was the wood splitting. The woodcutters went head-to-head splitting twenty-five blocks of wood and stacking them, and the first one finished was the winner. The four men who won the first trials went into the semi-finals and then the fastest two from there would go against each other for the championship. No one was faster than Ivan in this part of the competition, no matter how big or strong.

The second round was the tree falling round. With the size of the giants axe and the power he possessed, if he had any accuracy, Ivan would be hard-pressed to take that one.

The third round was the log chopping. Each man would stand on a ten foot log and simply chop it in two. Ivan was also worried about this one because of the strength factor involved in completing it quickly.

The fourth part of the competition was the tree climbing. Four men at a time would each climb a hundred foot log with a bell positioned at the top. The first one to ring it would move on to the next round. Ivan felt good about this one, due to his speed and agility with the tree spurs, and he couldn't imagine a man the size of Tamarack Jack moving up the tree too swiftly.

The fifth and final challenge was the axe throw. This was Ivan's best event and he had never been beaten. Most woods-men used an axe in this part of the competition, but Ivan preferred his hatchet. It carried a disadvantage at distance, but he liked its perfect weight and balance, besides, it meant a lot to him.

Going back over the five rounds of competition in his mind, and even if the giant was a true woodcutter, he felt confident he could beat the big man. That thought made him smile as he finished his axe and started in on the hatchet.

Today he would go into the woods and practice for the competition. He had a place north of their home that was set up for practicing the different events he would be doing on the actual day. In the early years of the competition he was so busy doing real woodcutting that he had never had to practice. In the last while though he felt as if he needed to fine tune his skills because of the lack of work, and therefore practice, he had been experiencing.

He was just finishing the hatchet when he heard a voice outside calling Grace. He didn't recognize the sound, so he met his wife at the kitchen window and they looked out. On the other side of the fence, straight across from their cabin, stood

Morra Boyle, and she looked frantic. "Oh my," said Grace, "I'd better go and see what's wrong."

Ivan set down his little axe. "I'll go with you," he offered, "just in case." So they left the cabin and walked over to see what was wrong.

"What is it?" asked Grace, and could see the woman was hysterical. "Just calm down and tell me."

"It's Sonny!" she yelled. "There's something wrong!" Grace asked Ivan to go get her healing bag while she talked with Morra, so he ran to the house while she tried to get more information.

Grace had only talked to Morra once before, when she had first moved in next door, and had forgotten how pretty she was with her long blonde hair, blue eyes and shapely figure. As she listened to her go on about Sonny, she couldn't help but wonder how a woman with such beauty, charm and wealth, could have ended up with a man like Claude Boyle.

"Please Morra, slow down and tell me exactly what happened," she instructed in a soothing tone. "Just breathe deeply and try to concentrate," she added, trying to get her to relax.

"It started this morning," she began, "before breakfast. Sonny started retching violently and shivering. Now he's delirious and has a fever."

Ivan came back with the bag, helped Grace over the fence, and the two women made their way to Morra's house.

"What did Sonny have for his evening meal?" Grace asked Morra as they entered the front door of her home.

"The only dish he had that differed from our meal was some preserved meat I made for him instead of the liver I had prepared."

Grace seemed concerned by her answer. "Do you have the jar handy?" she asked. "I'd like to have a look at it if I could." Morra told Grace that Sonny's room was on the right at the top of the stairs, then went to find the jar.

Grace glanced to either side, admiring the Boyle's mansion as she climbed the spiral staircase. It was the biggest, and most extravagant in the valley, other than the baron's west of the City of Kings. She thought of Sam Morgan for an instant, and how ironic it was that he had a smaller place than Claude, but Sam had always been about making the deal rather than flaunting his wealth.

Sonny lie curled up on his huge bed in a room that was half the size of Grace's cabin. She went over and checked on him. He was holding his stomach and his breathing was labored. He had a pail beside him that had obviously been used frequently, and he used it again while she was checking him for fever. His forehead was warmer than usual and he was definitely dehydrated. Grace administered one of her remedies for stomach sickness to help slow down the vomiting, and made him drink a glass of water. As she treated him, she noticed how much he resembled his mother, with his blue eyes and white-blonde hair, and thought how he must be her pride and joy.

Morra came in with the jar of meat and handed it to her. Grace smelled it and asked her if it was sealed properly when she opened it.

"I'm not sure," Morra told her. "Claude opened it when I was setting the table."

Grace checked the jar again. "This must not have been properly sealed when it was preserved, because the meat has turned," she explained. "Your son has a mild case of food poisoning, so I've given him a remedy that will settle his stomach. See that he gets plenty of rest and liquids, and he should be fine in a couple of days." Morra thanked her and asked if she'd like a cup of tea before she left. "Sure," answered Grace, and followed her down the stairs to the sitting room.

Grace was taking in the furnishings, sculptures and paintings when Morra returned with the tea. "What a beautiful home you have," she complimented her.

"Thank you," replied Morra. "I'm just sorry that it took Sonny being sick for us to finally visit, but Claude forbids it."

"Yes it is a shame," agreed Grace, "and I have never fully understood the feud that exists between our husbands. Maybe it's the difference in occupations," she added.

"Well I'm not sure either," Morra confessed. "Claude never discusses business with me. He even forbade me from calling you over to look at Sonny."

"Well," said Grace, "who could ever really understand the ways of men and their pride, but we love them in spite of it." They both laughed and took a sip of tea.

As she watched Morra drink, ever so daintily, she noticed the diamond ring on her right hand and commented on it. This prompted Morra to smile and tell her the story of the ring and its matching pieces, but first she ran and got the set and placed it on the tea-table.

It looked stunning, laid out in its magnificence. There was a diamond encrusted tiara, a diamond necklace and earrings, a bracelet and brooch, both set with diamonds, and of course the ring she wore on her finger.

"This set," she began, "was given to my late mother by my father on the day they were pledged to be joined. My father worshipped her, but would never ask to be joined until he was able to provide her with all the fine comforts he thought she deserved. He courted her for years, but only asked to join once he had made his fortune. She agreed instantly, and that's when he presented her with the diamond set as a token of his undying love. Mother wore them on her joining day and father said she looked like a queen as she stepped over the fertility line and under his protection."

Morra stopped for a moment and took another drink of her tea. "She died a year later because of complications at childbirth," Morra recalled, her eyes filling with tears. "My father explained to me that it wasn't my fault, and told me that my mother wanted me to know how much she loved me. She also told him that she wanted me to have the diamond set, and hopefully one day, wear it at my joining. This set means more to me than any possession and I cherish it beyond words."

There was silence as they drank their tea, then Grace spoke. "I can understand how that gift from your mother can mean so much," she told her. "My father gave me an intricately carved jewelry case and a pearl necklace for my tenth birthday, and that was the last time I saw him. So I know what it means to treasure something someone gives you."

Morra nodded. "I guess we have a lot more in common than my husband would like to believe," she said, and finished her tea.

"I had better be getting back," Grace told her as she set her cup down. "I'm glad it wasn't anything serious with your boy." Morra thanked her again as she showed her to the door. She slipped a silver coin into her hand and smiled.

"I can't accept this," Grace said, and handed it back to Morra. "We don't take payment for our healing, and this was barely that."

"Nonsense," replied Morra. "Just think of it as a gesture of goodwill to help balance the ongoing rivalry that has cost you so much more."

Grace smiled. "In that case I accept," she said, and placed the coin in her bag. "It was good to finally have a chance to get to know you better, and I hope it doesn't end here."

Morra winked at her and said, "We will just have to continue our new friendship in between Claude's trips to town." With that, Grace turned and made her way back to her cabin.

Morra went back inside, walked into the sitting room and started gathering her jewelry. She held it in her hands, staring at it. With a heavy heart she sat down, clutched it to her breast and began to cry.

Ivan had all the equipment he needed for his practicing. He had his axe and his hatchet, his tree spurs and climbing rope, and his water skin. He was ready to go, but wanted to check in on Shyla first. He looked in her room and she was still sleeping, which was unusual for her. *That healing must have taken more out of her than she let on*, he thought, and walked back into the kitchen. Ivan took Shyla's breakfast dish off the cookstove, set it on the table and covered it with a cloth, then grabbed his woodcutting tools and stepped outside.

He wasn't sure how long Grace would be, but they had never worried about leaving Shyla alone. At least not until the *Sol'mar* incident had occurred, but she had promised not to experiment with her newfound power until she received some guidance. Personally Ivan wished it had never surfaced, but that was a wasted thought.

He pulled his rope through the tree spurs and hung them over his shoulder. He grabbed his axe, hatchet and water skin and started the long walk north to where his practice area could be found.

As soon as he entered the stand of timber, Ivan's senses came alive. He could smell the spring sap that ran under the bark of each tree and feel the vigorous life that thrived within. Ivan never felt more vigorous than when he was in the woods. Somehow it was like an old friend.

He reached his destination and checked to make sure everything was in order. He had the blocks of wood sitting there ready for splitting. They had all been sawn into two-foot lengths so they could be split standing on their end.

Many woodcutters used saws in all of their work, but Ivan preferred to use one only when necessary.

He had a log secured vertically for falling practice, because he didn't want to cut down any trees if he didn't have to, and had another lying on the ground that he used for practicing the log chopping event. All the logs and blocks in the competition were sized according to the dimensions of your axe, except the tree used for climbing, which was thirty inches through. For practicing his climbing he had a tree limbed to a hundred feet, like the one they had in the competition, but left the bark on so as not to kill it. Lastly he had targets set up to practice his axe throwing. This last event Ivan never worried about too much. He had always had a natural feel for throwing, and knew just where it was going to strike, but he still liked to practice, if just to reaffirm himself.

He started with the wood splitting. In the competition you had to split twenty-five blocks in sections of four and stack them, but he would practice with only ten. He began with the first piece on the chopping block and then split and stacked them all as fast as he could. He moved like lightning in his task and proved to himself that he was as ready as he'd ever been. When he was through he realized that he had, over all the years at his practice area, cut and stacked many wagon loads of wood. He chuckled, then made a mental note to pick up this stack for the competition.

He took his water skin, drank some of the cool liquid and moved to the log he had set up for the tree falling. He stood alongside it and readied himself. He imagined he heard the turnkeeper and started into the wood. He chopped once . . . then again on an upward angle. Then downward, as big chips flew from the log. He spun and attacked the other side in the same manner until he was almost through, then spun back for the final blow. The top fell right where he wanted and he stood there pleased, though somewhat out of breath.

He was glad this wasn't an endurance competition because he knew he didn't have the wind he'd had in his youth, and each year the contestants were getting younger and stronger.

The log chopping was much the same as the tree falling as far as technique went, except that you stood on the log to chop through instead of standing beside it. He cut his way through the practice log in good time and was pleased with his performance in the three events thus far.

Next was the tree climbing and was for sure the most physically demanding, but he had been doing it since he was old enough to strap on a pair of spurs, and his leg muscles were conditioned for it. He approached the limbed tree and gazed to the top. A hundred feet seemed much further looking straight up, but that was the distance he would have to climb in the competition, so he put on his tree spurs and grabbed his rope.

Tree spurs were made of iron and attached to your boots with straps. Like their name, they had sharp spurs on the inside edges used for digging into the wood and propelling yourself upward as fast as possible. The rope was used for balance and grip, and placed around the back of the tree, with the ends held in each hand. This act looked like a dance with the tree if it was performed properly, but Ivan hadn't seen many woodsmen who had mastered it.

He held one end of his rope, then swung the other end around the back of the tree and grabbed it with his other hand. He dug in his spurs and started to climb. Rope up, hold. Lift legs, dig spurs in and thrust. It all came back in an instant. He did this continuously, making his way up the hundred foot span. His legs started burning at about fifty feet, but his muscles remembered this routine and he spurred his way through it. He reached a hundred feet and pretended to ring the bell that would be there on the day, then stopped to rest.

He couldn't see much from his position because the timber in this area was well over a hundred feet tall, but he still enjoyed the sensation of being up so high, and had made great time on his ascent. He stayed up there swaying with the forest for awhile, feeling good about everything he had tried so far, and felt even better because the axe throw was next.

Coming down was much faster and easier, but Ivan had seen many men lose control and hurt themselves trying to do it too fast, so he took his time. At the bottom he removed his spurs and made his way over to the area where he had the targets set up.

He had them placed at twenty-five, fifty, seventy-five and one hundred feet, but paced them off again just to be sure. He removed the hatchet from its scabbard and held it in his hand. It felt just right and he let it fly. *Thud!* it hit the twenty-five foot target dead center. As he went over to retrieve the axe, he noticed he had an audience, and bowed to the two squirrels that sat high on a branch curiously watching the show. "Come one, come all, and see Ivan, the greatest woodcutter in the land!" he shouted to his new onlookers, and then laughed.

Ivan took aim at the fifty foot target and placed the hatchet square in the center of the bull's-eye. The seventy-five foot target fell to his expertise as well, although, with the lighter axe, the distance was more difficult to judge.

Ivan faced the hundred foot target and stared it down. He checked the wind and asked his audience for silence. The squirrels, in seeming recognition, remained quiet as they sat there watching. This was the competition target range for the final day, and Ivan concentrated the way he always did before a long throw. All he had to do was see the spot he wanted to hit, then hone in on it and release, but keeping your eye on the target was the key to a successful throw.

His gaze narrowed and he flung the hatchet. He had to toss it hard at this distance, but once again he hit the target in the middle at the perfect height. He waited but received no response from the elevated gathering, which had recently grown by one. The three squirrels watched him intently as he walked over and pulled the blade from the wooden surface. Ivan turned to face his silent critics, who sat high on a branch about two hundred feet away. He looked at the squirrels, then at the tree they were perched in, and noticed a small black discoloring about six feet up the trunk. With a single movement, almost faster than the eye could see, he threw the hatchet. It sliced through the air, spinning over and over until it found its home right on the black mark, dividing it perfectly. When it hit the tree, the squirrels started chattering in chorus and moving about. "Thank you, thank you," boasted Ivan, bowing and waving as he strutted over to remove the hatchet. "Let's see Tamarack Jack do that," he said under his breath, and trotted back to his belongings.

The squirrels were still chattering his praises as he started for home, and he smiled up at them as he passed. He was feeling more confident now than when he'd started, and was looking forward to the competition.

Cade reached the north end of his property and crossed the public road with Rufus in the lead. He never hunted on his own land, partly because his father forbid it, but mainly because he felt as strongly as Ivan did about preserving their property. The terrain began to incline and the foliage became a lot denser as they moved closer to the Big Timber area. Rufus, nose to the ground, darted this way and that, taking on an almost youthful appearance. That old hound seemed to grow young again each time they went hunting and his aches and pains appeared to vanish for that brief time.

He had scared up a few animals on the trip so far, but didn't seem concerned when Cade passed them up. He loved the hunt and the excitement of what he might find in the next thicket or patch of tall grass.

Cade called Rufus back as they approached a small stream. He returned, tail wagging, and found himself a nice grassy area. He laid down and began licking his paws, in between scenting the air.

The sound of the water trickling over the rocks was mesmerizing and soothing to Cade so he stood there for awhile enjoying the music of the forest. He felt calm as he knelt down. He cupped his hands and drew the liquid to his lips. It was ice cold and tasted great, so he drank his fill. When he was finished he stood and looked at his companion. "Well boy!" he called out, "are you ready to get serious now?"

He could see the excitement in the old dog's eyes as he readied his bow. Rufus exuded a renewed mantle of vigor as he moved up the slope and into the underbrush. Cade followed, but had to increase his stride to keep up, smiling all the while at the stamina his old friend still possessed.

The sun had moved up the sky now and burned away the morning mist, leaving a crisp, clear view, perfect for the hunt. The terrain continued its incline as the two pushed forward in the direction of the Big Timber area, and again Cade was hard-pressed to match the pace set by Rufus.

They maintained their speed and course for another couple of miles until the land leveled out once more and they came to the edge of a large flat. Cade was out of breath and Rufus was panting heavily and moving his nose back and forth the way he always did when prey was near. Cade stopped and called to him. He returned reluctantly to his side, but didn't lie down this time. He stood there, whining softly, waiting for his master's command.

Cade took a deep breath and his heart rate slowed. He needed to prepare himself for what was coming. A steady hand, focused thoughts and clear vision were a must to execute his part of the hunt. He could sense the increasing excitement in his furry friend, but needed to regain his composure before sending him in. Rufus' whine turned into a low howl now and he knew that holding him back would be almost impossible. He knew his target would be game birds, but wasn't sure in which area of the opening Rufus would flush them out, so he positioned himself on a small rise to create the best possible vantage point.

The grass was lush and deep and the late spring flowers were blooming brilliantly, creating a mixture of exhilarating smells that filled the air with their sweet and pungent blend. He focused and readied himself.

The bow felt like an old friend as he grasped its smooth grip with his left hand. So many days he had spent practicing with it after his mediocre skills with the axe had frustrated him. The axe had always felt awkward, but the bow somehow felt natural, almost like they were connected when he held it. He wanted so much to be like his father and make him proud, but the ways of woodcutting eluded him and held no passion for him whatsoever.

He pulled on the bowstring and it gave way to his touch. He quickly drew it to full tension and then let it return slowly. His longbow was full-size and made from a denser wood than normal. Most grown men could barely pull the string all the way, but for Cade it was easy. The combination of his unusual strength and natural ability made for a perfect match, and after all the failed attempts at trying to be a woodcutter he was finally starting to embrace his true talent.

He moved his hand along the bow until it was perfectly balanced. He pulled the string and let it *twang*. It felt good. He reached back and fingered his arrows. They were right there waiting for him and were his favorites for hunting. Some of them had been with him a long time, having retrieved them from many past kills.

He was ready, and Rufus was more than ready, so he gave the command. The old dog raced into the thick green grass and disappeared. The only way that Cade could follow his movement was the continuous howl he made when the hunt was heated, so he nocked an arrow and waited for the climax he knew was only moments away. He grinned as four large game birds fled cover and winged their way skyward.

Everything began to move in slow motion now the way it always did when Cade shot his bow. He could almost count the feathers on each wing as he let the first shaft go. Then in a fluid movement, the second, third and fourth arrow left the bow in what looked like an almost simultaneous motion.

If anyone would have witnessed what had just taken place they would not have believed it. The fourth bird was falling from the sky before the first one hit the ground.

Rufus' howl was in full force now as he circled the fallen prey, waiting for his master to arrive. Cade's vision had returned to normal now and he stood there looking at his bow. He pulled it close and kissed the polished wood, then headed over to his old buddy, and their evening meal. Cade had never understood what happened to him when he used his bow, but never really thought about it. The unusual events that occurred during the act had always come natural to him.

CHAPTER
10

Darkness Comes

S hyla awoke to find herself lying on a hard surface. It was rough and cold to the touch and felt like some type of stone. She could hear the steady dripping of water nearby, but could see nothing in the pitch-black. She started to panic, wondering where she was and how she had ended up here. She sat up, then moved slowly to her feet, reaching above her head to make sure there was room to stand. She waved both hands in front of her face, but could see no movement. Apprehension threatened to overtake her, so she pushed it down, calling on her remaining senses to assist her. She stood there quietly and concentrated, taking in what she could of her new surroundings.

The air was dank and still and carried a stale, pungent odor, so she breathed in reluctantly as her vision attempted to adjust to the ever-present darkness. Suddenly a feeling of nausea hit her and she almost fell as she stumbled into a nearby wall. She could feel the dark filth enter her, only this time it was magnified and concentrated, making her stomach lurch and her knees buckle. She leaned against the wall to steady herself. Her breathing was strained now as she fought to keep the burrowing parasite from going deeper, but still it settled in, surrounding her heart like a hungry demon. She shuddered as the wrong secured itself, and she knew instinctively that she didn't have the skill to vanquish or drive it from her. Panic welled as she realized that its vileness and potency were tenfold compared with the darkness she had encountered in the sick boy. Then only a moment after it had captured her center, the cancerous symbiont started moving upward. Fear mounted in her, and she knew if that foulness reached her mind she would be lost.

She had made a promise to her mother, but now she had no choice. She called to the awaiting light and it answered her instantly. It expanded within her and raced through her veins like wildfire. The feeling was euphoric and she bathed in its brilliance.

She moved the light ever closer to the shadow that crept toward her thoughts, driving it back and surrounding it, holding it there with all her will. The darkness recoiled, then lashed out trying to penetrate the light's hold, but Shyla tightened her grasp and kept it contained.

With the searing light coursing through her, and the evil trapped deep within, Shyla could relax a little for the first time since she had awakened in this strange place. The nausea was still intense but had abated somewhat, allowing her to move again, yet where would she go?

First she examined the wall she was leaning against. It was stone like the floor and she couldn't find any seams. It was like it had been carved from one big rock. She moved toward the dripping sound, feeling her way along the rough surface. Finding its source, she traced the small trickle up the wall as far as she could reach, which made her wonder how high, or even if there was a ceiling. It was ridiculous trying to assess the situation without being able to see, so she leaned back against the wall and cleared her mind.

She could feel the disgusting visitor moving within her, testing every inch of its enclosure, trying to find an outlet or weak spot. She checked her illuminated net with a thought, finding it secure, but tightened it again just to make sure. It was at that moment that she got an idea. She relaxed as much as possible and focused her attention on the light inside. As she immersed herself in it, it cascaded over her in a scintillating shower that warmed and comforted her. She gave in to it without losing control, then began to channel a small portion outward. Keeping the wrong imprisoned, and channeling the light was harder than she had expected, but she steadied herself and continued. She had to try her idea even if there was only a small chance of success.

Shyla moved the light's energy down her extended arm and into her hand where its shimmering essence danced in anticipation just below the skin. She steadied herself once more and released it into the air. Nothing happened. She stood there disappointed for a moment, then thought it through.

The energy itself was not the light. The light was created from the energy through her manipulation, or was there any actual physical light involved, or was that concept merely a way for her mind to comprehend the way she used the energy? Her brain started to hurt. *Way to go*, she thought, *overanalyzing everything as usual.*

She turned her attention back to the energy, and this time she formed the light first and then released it. It flickered above the palm of her hand and then went out. Excitement overtook her for just an instant and she wavered, then caught herself and quickly regained her composure. The being within was moving faster now, sensing her moment of weakness, but she bore down and locked in her rigid control once more. She tried again, and this time she created a ball of light, reinforced it with a shell of energy and released it. The ball floated in the air above her palm. Its brightness caused her to close her eyes, and the effort it took to maintain the light outside her body began draining her rapidly. She knew she didn't have much time, so she forced her eyes open and looked around.

She stood in a tunnel about eight feet wide and eight feet high, that looked to be hewn out of solid stone. It sloped down to her right and up to her left, and there was a small puddle of water that ran down the hallway and out of sight. Shyla could no longer hold the light *and* the wrong, so she pulled the ball back into her and the night closed in once more.

She took a deep breath and realized she was covered in sweat and her heart was racing from the exertion she had just undergone. This maneuver had cost her but at least she had a greater knowledge of her predicament and more insight into the wild energy that ran through her.

Her choices had been made simple by her experiment. She could move up the tunnel or down. Up seemed like a logical choice and quite possibly a way out of this place, so she started following the wall in that direction. She traced the wall up the incline, but as she walked it felt like she was moving away from something, so she stopped.

Shyla had always been one to follow her feelings, and down was the way her gut was telling her. She just hoped it *was* her own instinct and not the putrid taint that was leading her.

Down she went, not knowing where she was or where she was going, and all the while her strength was being drained by her unwanted companion.

As she continued her descent, she lost all track of time and had no way to gauge her distance, except by counting her steps. She did this not so much to measure her progress as to keep her mind from imagining where each step might be taking her. She started to feel a faint sense of urgency, and increased her speed almost without realizing it. Moving as fast as she could along the tunnel, Shyla plunged deeper and deeper into the unknown, but the blackness had not lessened from within or without, and all she could do was hold on and keep going.

Suddenly she came to an abrupt halt, bumping her head as the wall she was following veered sharply to the left. Pausing only briefly to clear her thoughts, she started moving again, but now the floor beneath her fell at a much steeper angle, and she had to slow her progress to compensate.

My family will be worried sick when they realize I'm gone, she thought. *And how have I been transported to this foreboding place?*

When it felt her mind wander, the presence within her tried to break free, but she quickly regained her grasp. She realized now that her full attention must be directed toward its containment and the task before her, which was reaching her unknown destination. She gave a hollow laugh as she thought about her situation. She had no clue where she was headed, but was blindly charging into the abyss on a whim and an inkling, which she wasn't even sure was her own.

Again she felt her prisoner trying to take advantage of her relapse. She caught it quickly and strengthened her resolve, placing one foot in front of the other intently, her hand on the wall as her only link to any form of reality.

Shyla kept walking, venturing further and further down the tunnel. The air around her became warmer now and more humid with each step, and the feeling that drove her had become more of a beckoning, urging her onward. Her sightless trek continued until she rounded a gradual bend in the tunnel and saw a dim glow in the darkness below. She stopped and stared, blinking her eyes repeatedly, trying to make out any movement or shape, but the flickering was barely visible.

Excitement and fear filled her simultaneously and she leaned against the wall to steady herself. She closed her eyes tightly and took a deep breath. *What could that light be?* she wondered. *Is it even real or just my imagination playing tricks because I want it so bad?* She opened her eyes slowly expecting it to be gone, but there it was deep in the distance, a twinkling ember of hope. Excitement rose in her again but her logical side kept it from overwhelming her. She knew that this tiny beacon didn't necessarily mean good or friendly, but anything was better than this unending blindness that falsely afflicted her.

She strengthened the integrity of the radiant sphere within and moved toward her visual destination as fast as her external conditions would allow.

After traveling for what seemed to be at least half a day, the only indication that she had gone any distance at all was the light below, which was now steady and brighter. She stopped and studied it again, but still there was no sign of movement. She wondered for a moment what the source of the light might be, but only time would tell, so she readied herself to continue.

Before she could move, a tingling sensation covered her body, almost like it had been draped over her, and was gone again just as fast. She felt a chill and trembled slightly as she tried to understand what had just taken place. Suddenly her thoughts were interrupted by a violent movement inside. The malignant sludge that had violated her earlier, was now pounding against the walls she had placed around it. Shyla reached to the depths of her being to keep it at bay, and went rigid with the strain. The energy inside burned with frenzy now, and the attacks continued with an even greater urgency and determination. Her nightgown was drenched in sweat and her breast heaved as she did everything she could to keep her assailant from overtaking her. Tears streamed down her face, and she wasn't sure how long she could hold on if the assault continued at this magnitude.

It was at the time that most people would have given in to despair that Shyla reached a sudden clarity. At that moment she realized the pattern of her foes exertion was focused outward and not upward. It no longer wanted to possess her, but wanted only to escape.

She moved quickly, tightening her hold with the last of her strength, causing a flailing inside that almost seemed like panic. She held it as long as she could, then created a small opening in the front. This was taken advantage of immediately as the vile occupant left her and disappeared beyond her range of acuity.

The energy ran wildly through her now and she tried desperately to control it. It was almost impossible in her exhausted state, but she managed to harness it once again. She remembered the boy and how purging his sickness had left her unconscious. She wasn't about to let that happen again so she decided to experiment a little, in case the foulness returned.

She knew it wasn't the purging, but the speed at which she had expelled the energy that had harmed her previously, so this time she started slowly, gathering it all and moving it to her center. Once it was there she began distributing it evenly down her outstretched arms. Now the energy was concentrated in her hands and she literally had all that power at her fingertips. She smiled and relished the thought of releasing it.

Even in her fatigued condition it made her feel so fulfilled and alive, but she knew that as soon as she let it go, she would be alone and helpless once more. This frightened her.

As she prepared to send the energy from her, she knew that it was more than that. She loved the feeling of it; the way it filled her with purpose. It was like an old friend, yet foreign at the same time, and it caressed her as it slowly made its way back up her arms. She snapped out of her trance and pushed it back into her hands. She shook her head as her mother's warning returned, then clenched her teeth and continued.

Before she started the expulsion, she decided to create the globe again and have another look around. She began slowly, but this time instead of wrapping the light in a ball, she wove a circle of energy above each of her hands. She released the light in a steady stream until there were radiant spheres above each palm, that grew larger with each push.

She squinted at the brightness, but blinked her way through it and found that nothing much had changed since her last viewing. She was still in a tunnel leading down to who knows what, and still didn't know where she was.

The wild energy was much easier to manipulate now that the black filth was gone, but the burden was still enormous, and she fought to control the output. When she was finished, she stood there marveling at the sparkling globes before her. They were dazzling with swirling vibrant hues, and reached almost to the ceiling. She was completely spent now, and knew she would have to let go. She held on for a few more moments . . . then released.

Her sight was veiled instantly, and all she could see were two white spots in the night that faded quickly. She felt weak and empty and sagged against the wall, trying to cope with the loss. Her grieving was interrupted with the cold realization that her luminary display had been a grave mistake. Terror immo-bilized her as she sensed something terrible coming toward her from the depths. Something so rancid and malicious that it made the wrong she had dealt with earlier seem irrelevant. She tried to run, but fear gripped her heart and she was powerless in its clutch. The foul being moved closer at a staggering rate and this time despair overwhelmed her. Her arms hung limp at her sides and she stood there shaking, committed to whatever fate awaited her.

The first wave hit her, knocking her to her knees. She wretched violently, tasting the bile in her mouth as it spewed onto the stone. Scorching worms covered her and her body twisted in pain. They went to work quickly, trying to burn their way inside. She writhed in agony and tried to scream, but her voice would not respond. Her mind tried to escape the torment, but a second wave hit, knocking her to her back and into reality once more. Snakes slithered over her body now, causing her to squirm and roll. She sat up and tried to slap them away, but they were too fast. The snakes wrapped themselves around her wrists and ankles, jerking her to the floor. Her hands were pulled over her head, and her ankles were tightly secured. She sobbed as she laid there stretched out on that hard surface like a maiden ready for sacrifice.

The worms were starting to penetrate her skin and she could do nothing. Her living shackles were like iron and kept continuous pressure, pulling her body taut. Suddenly the excruciating pain abated, and she blinked her tears away. Her eyes widened as she saw a large, shadowlike cloud move up and hover over her. She wasn't sure how something could be darker than black, but there it was, and it was a lot darker. The cloud seemed dense, almost solid as it moved within itself, roiling and billowing ever inward. In her agony, Shyla thought, *if ever there was such a thing as pure evil, then this is it.*

A smell worse than rotten eggs filled her nostrils causing her body to convulse involuntarily. She wretched again, but there was nothing left in her stomach, so she coughed and swallowed the acid in her throat. Low rumbling laughter filled the corridor and she could see tiny bolts of red lightning within the cloud. It was on top of her now, only inches from her skin. She tried to break free but the snakes' hold on her was like a vice, and each of the fiery worms felt like a hot poker pressing into her.

Her mind couldn't take much more and she knew for certain that if that vile creature entered her, she would cease to exist. The cloud was upon her now and she could feel its filth wash over her, and it was sickening. Her fear and loathing turned to anger and she yelled, "Who do you think you are!" This caused the cloud to draw back for just a moment and she used that brief interval to call on the light. She had been afraid to bring it forth because she didn't think she had enough strength left to control it, but she decided that she would rather have the light overtake her than the foul entity she now faced.

The energy came to her in a single thought and she cleansed herself, turning worms and snakes into nothing but ash and wisps of smoke. It was too much for her though, too wild and unpredictable and far too powerful to wield in her diminished state, but it was her only means of protection against this deadly adversary. The cloud moved swiftly now sensing the change, but she was quicker, channeling the light and readying herself for its embrace. Just before she opened herself to it, she remembered the ball she had created before and how she had made that happen. Then, with all of her will she encased herself in a shell of pure energy.

The cloud came down on her and sparks flew in all directions as darkness met the light, and she was safe beneath her shield. She knew she couldn't last long and already her will was being siphoned. The thought of what would happen when it collapsed almost made her lose heart, but she was alive and sane for now, and that at least gave her a small glimmer of hope.

The cloud above grew now and its surface looked like a raging storm on a black sea with bolts of bloodred lightning feeding its anger. It came down hard this time and another shower of sparks shot violently outward, hitting the tunnel walls with unnatural force. Shyla's eyes filled with tears. One more strike like that and she would no longer be able to hold the energy. As the being sensed her weakened condition, the laughter started again, only louder this time like thunder echoing down the halls.

Shyla lay on the cold floor waiting for the final assault on her failing cocoon, when she heard a whisper. It was a loud whisper and the voice was beautiful but strained. *Shyla, come to me, I need your help.* Then it repeated. *Shyla, come to me, I need your help.* Before she could wonder what the voice was, or where it had come from, the cloud was upon her again. This time it came down slow, merging with her outer protection. The place where it touched began to glow like the metal in a blacksmith's forge; first red, then orange, until finally it was white-hot. Shyla could feel her shield unraveling, and in a few moments she would have to let go of the light and let the evil take her completely. She closed her eyes and held on with all her might. She started to shake with the effort and then her strength failed. The darkness bore down and started to enter her . . . and then another voice.

"Shyla! Shyla!" She opened her eyes and saw her mother leaning down, shaking her. "Shyla wake up!" she urged. "You're having a nightmare." She threw her arms around her mother's neck and clung to her, sobbing. "It's all right my girl," Grace consoled her. "You were having a bad dream is all."

Mother and Daughter held each other for awhile, then Shyla realized she was on the floor and not in the bed where she had started out in what seemed like so very long ago. Her mother helped her up and told her to rest while she fetched a basin of warm water. She could see that her daughter's hair was damp and matted and her nightgown was drenched with sweat, so on her way out she opened the curtain that hung across the window.

The midmorning sun shone brightly through the panes of window-glass. It hurt Shyla's eyes, but she welcomed the warm rays like a long lost friend. She had not realized how much that warmth and brightness meant to her until now. Spending all that time in complete darkness made her cherish the sunshine that beamed in from outside, and she told herself, *that was just a dream.*

Everything that had happened to her *couldn't* be real, but it had seemed as real as anything she felt now. The foul smell of that black cloud still lingered in her nostrils and she could still feel a faint residue of the darkness that had violated her so savagely, but it *had* to be her imagination. She knew it was impossible to be whisked away like that, but the wicked laughter was still ringing in her ears and that beautiful, sorrow-filled voice that had called to her was a sound she would never forget.

She removed her wet nightgown and sat up on the bed as her mother returned with the basin. She wrung out the wash-cloth and proceeded to wipe the sticky sweat from Shyla's body. Grace hadn't bathed her like this since she was a little girl and Shyla welcomed the warmth and closeness. Her mother's touch was so gentle and caring that she began to relax. The cloth moved over her face now and she closed her eyes. Her mother pushed back her hair to wash her forehead, which caused Shyla to flinch. "You've got a nasty bump there," commented Grace. "You must have hit your head when you fell out of bed."

Shyla felt cold again and fear started to form in the pit of her stomach. She kept it quelled though and thought her way through the coincidence. *I must have dreamed it at the same time I fell,* she reasoned silently, and felt slightly better. Her mother finished cleaning her forehead, being careful of the bruise, then asked her to lean over the basin so she could wash her hair.

When they were finished Grace wrapped the wet strands in a cloth and helped her into a fresh nightgown, then asked if she wanted to talk about her nightmare. Shyla told her certain details about the wrong that had invaded her body, but was reluctant to say more for some reason. Her mother listened carefully to her story and then replied, "It was probably a mental reaction to your newfound gift that caused the wild dream."

Shyla nodded and smiled. "That's better," said Grace, tracing her daughters smile with her fingers. "Everything is fine now." She kissed her daughter's cheek and stood up. "I want you to rest until you feel well enough to get up." She instructed. "Then we will make some healing salve to replenish our supply." Shyla nodded again and looked at her mother with pride. She was such a kind and thoughtful person, and Shyla loved her so much.

As Grace picked up the basin, they heard a knock at the door. "Now you lie still and I'll go see who it is." she instructed, and left the room.

Shyla tried to rest but her mind was busy with all that had taken place in the past day, and even if she could have, she sure didn't want to sleep anymore. She could hear her mother talking to someone outside, but couldn't make out what they were saying, so she settled down again and tried to slow her heart rate. She started thinking about her dream and began wondering if all the actions she had performed with the light could actually be done in reality. *Had she learned how to control the light a little more, or had it all been a fantasy concocted by events and a great imagination?* Well, she wasn't about to try to find out, and was relieved that she hadn't truly broken the promise she had made to her mother.

After trying for awhile, the resting idea just wasn't working, so she got dressed and joined Grace in the kitchen.

They spent most of the afternoon making healing remedies. They didn't talk at all except when Shyla asked, "Who was at the door earlier?" to which her mother replied, "Brant the dog-man. He wants me to look in on his wife tomorrow. She has some-thing that she can't shake, and he is getting concerned."

"Can I come with you Mom . . . please?" she implored.

Grace looked at Shyla and replied, "I don't see why not, as long as you're feeling up to it."

The Catcher Dog Ranch was famous throughout the king-dom and Shyla loved going there. Brant and Leslie Catcher owned it and had lived there for over forty years breeding every type of dog imaginable. Between her excitement over all the new puppies she would be playing with the next day, and helping her mother, Shyla all but forgot about her disturbing experience.

Working side-by-side the girls lost all track of time, until Ivan walked through the door. When Grace saw him standing there so majestic in his woodcutting garb, her heart started to flutter. He was such a rugged man with his broad shoulders and muscular build that there was no way to keep from blushing. The butterflies arose in her and she wondered, *after all these years, how can he still make me feel this way?* With her face still flushed, she regained her composure enough to ask him how his practicing went. He told her it had gone well, while putting away his woodcutting equipment. Cade arrived awhile later, dressed out the birds and handed them over to Grace who began preparing dinner. She was glad to have more fresh meat to cook, and this meal was going to be much better than the salt pork stew she had been planning to make.

Shyla put all the remedies into the healing bag and the table set. Cade finished his chores and was helping his father repair the pull-harness, and everyone was famished and happy to hear Grace ring the mealtime bell. This bell had been hanging on that porch since before she was joined with Ivan, but it seemed no one ever tired of hearing that sound.

They washed up quickly and sat down to the meal they had all been looking forward to.

The food looked and smelled wonderful. Not only was Grace a fantastic cook, but she had a way of presenting it, with her little garnishes and decorations, that made you feel as though you were dining at the royal court. It was no surprise to anyone though, because they all knew what pride she took in everything she did, and it always tasted as good as it looked.

Their concerns melted away as they joked and teased and enjoyed one another as a family. Their fears and worries didn't exist for this brief time and they laughed without reservation, recalling events that had taken place and funny stories they remembered.

"I'm going to see the new puppies tomorrow," Shyla told her father. "Brant's wife is under the weather, so I am going to help Mother find out what's wrong."

Ivan looked at Grace, but she gave him that knowing look, so he smiled at his daughter and said, "That sounds like fun, but you had better leave early. I think I heard the porch troll when I came in," and he raised his eyebrows.

"Oh Daddy!" she huffed and scrunched up her nose. Ivan was glad she was going to the Catcher's place and hoped the dogs would be a positive distraction to what she'd had to deal with lately. Not only that, but the Catchers were good people.

Ivan had known Brant all his life and the Catcher family had been breeding dogs as far back as anyone could remember. They had supplied everyone from royalty to common folk with every dog from house pet to elite hunter. The king himself had purchased a matched pair of Royal Hunters for an undisclosed amount of gold that was said to be enough to refurnish their entire home. Ivan had been glad when he heard that story because it always seemed like they pampered those dogs more than they did themselves. The Hardens and the Catchers had always had a mutual admiration and respect for one another, and Ivan was pleased that Grace and Shyla were going over to help them.

"You should take Rufus with you and see if some of his brothers and sisters are still around," offered Ivan. "If not, I'm sure he would like to see some of his own kind anyway."

"That's a great idea," replied Grace.

"Yeah," interjected Shyla, "maybe seeing old Rufus again will cheer up Mrs. Catcher," and that excited her even more.

Ivan raised his cup of water in the air. "Thank you Cade for bringing this food to our home, and thank you my sweetheart for preparing it with such love," and they all clinked their cups together.

"And I'd like to thank me for setting the table so beautifully," giggled Shyla uncontrollably, and the whole family joined in.

When Grace had caught her breath she said, "I'm sorry but I don't have anything for dessert tonight."

"Really?" asked Ivan, and winked at her.

She blushed and replied, "No, but berry season is coming soon, so we will be able to replenish our preserves and have fresh desserts more often."

That reminded Grace that most of the preserves in the cold cellar were running low and needed to be restocked. After the Woodcutting Competition she would buy all the supplies needed for preserving, and the items she needed to plant this year's garden. It was never too early to start stocking up for winter.

They all sat around the table talking and laughing until well after they were done eating, then as a family they all pitched in and helped clean up. When they had finished, Cade took the leftovers out to Rufus who enjoyed a well-deserved feast while the others washed up and got ready to turn in for the night.

It had been an exhausting day for all, but especially Shyla, who could barely keep her eyes open. She was asleep as soon as her head hit the pillow and she began to dream. This time she dreamed of meadows filled with flowers and cute fluffy puppies. Her grandmother Zarina was there also, soothing her thoughts with words of kindness and encouragement. When her mother went in to check on her, her breathing was slow and even and she had a calm and peaceful look on her face.

Grace was relieved as she climbed into bed. She moved to her man, melting into his strong embrace. She loved that feeling and wanted it to last forever. She was safe in his arms and it made her believe everything would be all right. They cuddled for awhile and enjoyed the intimacy that could only come from the deep, unconditional love that they felt for each other. The sensation was so overwhelming that Grace began to weep.

"What's wrong?" Ivan asked gently.

"Oh there's nothing wrong," replied Grace. "It's just that I love you so much it almost hurts."

With that, he held her even closer and kissed her softly. "You are everything to me," he told her. "I love you more than life itself." She returned his kiss and rested her head on his powerful chest.

The long sweet silence was broken by Ivan. "I saw a bruise on Shyla's forehead but didn't want to mention it."

"She had a nightmare last night and fell out of her bed," Grace explained quietly. "She seems to be recuperating from her ordeal, but I really need to get word to my mother so we can best figure out what is happening. Brant insisted on picking us up in the morning, but when I'm finished I will find out who is traveling down to Belden's Wall and ask them to deliver a message for me."

"That sounds good," replied Ivan. "And if no one is traveling that way I will borrow one of Ben's fastest horses and take it down myself. That will still give me plenty of time to return for the Woodcutting Competition," he assured her, stroking her hair. It was settled then. The next day, one way or another, they would get a message sent to Zarina.

"Goodnight my man," whispered Grace, snuggling closer.

"Goodnight my love," returned Ivan, and the crickets sang them to sleep.

CHAPTER

11

Puppy Dog Tales

The next day Ivan was up before daybreak like he was most mornings, and made his way toward the creek, bucket in hand. Rufus was off somewhere again, which made the woodcutter feel good. He knew that as long as the old dog kept active he would live a longer life, and he was sure some rabbit or squirrel was getting their exercise this morning as well.

It was earlier than usual, even for Ivan, and the moon brightened the surrounding area as it waited for dawn's first light. The air was cool and he could see his breath against the moonlight. The mornings would be warmer soon as the first month of summer approached, but for now it was still very brisk this early in the day.

Suddenly the path opened up, and in the pale light he could see the outline of the *Whispering Forest*. He stopped and took in the view. The birds weren't singing yet, but he could hear an owl in the distance and a mixture of other sounds coming from that mysterious labyrinth. The creek was covered from shore to shore by a thick mist and he could hear the constant rush of water as it pushed its way westward. The woodcutter could only see about twenty feet ahead, but he knew that the back-eddy where they drew the water was about a hundred feet straight south of his position, so he continued in that direction. He chuckled at his need to always know the distance of everything and calculated in the darkness. It was a hundred feet to the creek, fifty feet across the water at its widest point, and another hundred and fifty feet to the edge of that dark silhouette. All-in-all it was only a hundred yards from the Harden Forest to the *Whispering Forest*, but the difference was vast. He didn't even want to think of why that forest was the way it was. Just knowing *what* it was and respecting it was all he needed.

As he approached the water's edge, he tried to make out the position of the invisible trail that granted access to those forbidden woods, but it was too dark and foggy to see. He knew the approximate place where it should be, but couldn't see it. If he was going to be taking the letter to Zarina today he would use the old wagon path. If they found someone who was going down to The Wall, they would take the main trade-road, which was about nine miles southeast of where he stood. The trade-road had been cut later, and went straight into the town of Woodvale. The wagon path eventually joined up with it, but for Ivan, cutting any distance off that trip was a good idea.

It was thirty miles through that forest, and considering how the trail turned this way and that, suggested that the men who first made it had tried to follow the lay of the land. He assumed it was to avoid as much contact with the trees as possible. *A wise choice*, thought Ivan.

The next leg of the journey was a fifty mile ride through the *Gatou Plains*, which nowadays was fairly safe at least, and then another twenty or so miles through the foothills to the town of Belden's Wall. Grace had told him her mother would be in Belden's Wall for the next two weeks, so if he had to go, he would meet with her there. The Woodcutting Competition was less than two weeks away, but with only himself on a single horse he could make it there and back in little more than a week, giving him enough time for the journey.

The woodcutter stood on the bank watching the current swirl into the deep pool where they had dipped their water from for so many years. The mist was thicker this close to the creek and he could only see about ten feet in front of him. It was only five feet above the surface though, making it look like a fluffy white blanket draped over the entire creek bed. Ivan knelt down and filled the bucket. He then set it aside, got down on his stomach, pursed his lips and took a cool draught. He could feel it going all the way down and it was refreshing. As he stood and grabbed the bucket he could smell the wood smoke from the fire he had built in the cookstove, and he knew he would never tire of that scent.

The moon came out from behind the small cloud that had been masking it and shone its silvery light on the vale. With his new vision, Ivan could make out the virtually seamless entrance to the wagon path, and he smiled. He could see it above the mist at the tree's edge, and it was satisfying to know that his eyes were still as keen as ever.

He was about to turn and start back when he saw a large shadow exit the old path and move onto the far bank. His smile faded and he strained to identify the on-comer, but it had been swallowed by the mist. His hawk-like eyes picked out movement again and he concentrated on its location. By the time he had focused on it he could hear water splashing from the far side.

Whatever it was, it moved quickly and straight at him. He could make out its head now above the white covering and it was massive. *It must be a grizzly,* he thought, and a chill ran through him. He dropped the bucket and instinctively reached for his hatchet, but it wasn't there. It was hanging inside his front door alongside his hunting knife and bow.

For a moment he thought of making a run for it but knew that with the speed at which the animal was traveling, he wouldn't make it far before it was upon him. There was also the fact that he, like his father, wasn't much for running from anything, so he reached down, picked up the bucket and stood there grimly awaiting the charge.

Above the mist, moonlight glinted off two rows of long white fangs that were bared in a deadly grin. Ivan tightened his grip on the handle of his awkward weapon and widened his stance. The attack was only a few heartbeats away now, but all Ivan could think about was his family and how much he loved them. *Well,* he thought, *this bear is gonna have one huge headache while he's trying to enjoy his breakfast this morning.*

He could hear course breathing as the beast began to emerge from the fog in front of him. He drew back the bucket and poised himself for his one strike. His heart raced in anticipation of the encounter and sweat beaded on his brow. His only hope was to daze the predator and throw it of balance. He was counting on his aggressiveness to either confuse it enough to make it retreat, or buy him enough time to escape. Ivan knew his chances were slim, but it was all he had.

The moon went behind a cloud and he cursed its timing, but could still see those teeth approaching, so he targeted just above them and braced himself for impact. He knew he would only get one hit and it had to be precise. Suddenly, without any apparent reason, the animal stopped a few feet in front of him and stood there. Ivan faced it, heart pounding and sweat trickling down his forehead. His muscles were cramping from the strain, but he remained prepared for the onslaught. The woodcutter cursed the darkness again, but as long as he could see those jagged razors, he would be ready. The scene remained unchanged in a deadlock of uncertainty as man and beast blindly stared each other down. Finally the moon interjected as it climbed out from behind its sanctum, and shed some light on the situation.

Ivan found himself staring into the eyes of a giant wolf, and relief swept through him as he recognized the huge, dark-gray animal. It was Jinda, Zarina's mount, and she looked exhausted. Ivan relaxed and his muscles started to cramp, but he ignored the pain and spoke. "Hi Jinda, how are you girl?" he said in a soothing tone, but the wolf just stood there breathing heavily and watching him.

The wolves of the *Gatou* were a mystery to Ivan and he had only ever ridden one once when he and Grace had been joined, but he knew that this one meant him no harm. Letting out a sigh, he walked to the creek, refilled his bucket and headed back to his warm home. The wolf didn't move except for its eyes, which followed everything he did. From the side, Ivan could see that the wolf was carrying a pack, and it appeared to be full. He passed his new guest, who followed a few paces behind, and made his way up the trail to the cabin.

What a coincidence, he thought for a fleeting moment, but quickly remembered that nothing Zarina did could be thought of that way. *How could she have known that her daughter needed to speak with her?* Such things were beyond his comprehension and he had grown to accept that fact, even if he didn't like it.

Most of the men that he knew didn't understand their women at all, but it was nothing compared to Ivan. He dearly loved the girls in his life, but many of their ways were a mystery to him. A mystery he was glad he had the time to try to solve. *Good luck,* he thought, as he approached the house.

When he reached the porch, Jinda stayed back and waited by the trees. Rufus had returned from his morning excursion and didn't pay any mind to the wolf. He had already gotten to know Jinda on Zarina's previous visits and preferred to keep a goodly distance from his overgrown cousin.

Ivan went inside and set the bucket on the counter. Grace entered the kitchen and said, "You were up earlier than usual."

"True," replied Ivan. "I didn't sleep that well. You know I always get anxious when the competition is close. Oh and there's someone here to see you," he added with a smile.

"Did you ask them in?" she queried.

"I don't think she wants to come in," he replied, chuckling.

"She?" asked Grace with a puzzled look, and walked to the door. Ivan followed her out, glancing at his hatchet on the way by.

"Jinda!" yelled Grace, and moved over to the wolf.

Even though she had grown up with the old girl, she knew that without Zarina here to allow it, the animal would be reluctant to be touched, so she gently placed an arm around her thick neck.

"Look at you," she said, concerned. "You are worn out." She checked her over from top to bottom to make sure she was all right. After discerning that it was only fatigue that ailed her, she hugged her friend again and said, "Let's get this pack off you." With that, Ivan stepped in and undid the harness and set the saddle and its attachments on the porch.

"By the look of it you must have traveled nonstop from the south," Grace said in a worried tone. "You are a true and loyal friend. Now get some rest and I'll find you something to eat." Without hesitation, Jinda moved into the trees to lie down.

"I'll get her something," offered Ivan. "You had better check and see what's so important that she almost killed herself to bring it to you."

Grace gave her man a nod of appreciation and hurried to the porch. She sat down and opened the large baskets. Inside she found preserved goods and medicines, along with dried and fresh meat. There were breads, pastries and candies for the children. Her mother had sent a real care package, but she had in her hand the one item from the loving hamper that she wanted . . . a letter from Zarina. It was scribed on fine parchment, with bloodred ribbons at each end, and bore the Healer's Seal.

Grace remembered when she was given her seal. When each apprentice became an adept they received a ring engraved with the emblem of the healers; the design being a circle divided in two with a rising sun on top and a crescent moon with three stars surrounding it in the lower half. The band was carved with circling horn-vines, one of the most powerful healing plants. This signified the balance and the healers' dedication to preserving it. When a scroll or letter was sealed this way it was only to be opened by another adept.

Grace broke the seal and opened the parchment. Her mother's handwriting was beautiful, flowing exquisitely across the paper. *My dear Daughter*, it began. *I am concerned about Shyla*. Grace smiled. That was her mother, always straight to the point. She read on.

I know she is in no immediate peril or I would have come in person, but I feel she could still be in danger if this situation is not dealt with properly. I have sensed the awakening of the Sol'mar and have felt a darkness attached. Please send word of her condition and your insight into my feeling. Also, please give Jinda a day's rest before you pack her and send her back. If you don't make her stay, she will run herself to death trying to accomplish what I have set her to do. Say hello to your husband and the children. Bring Shyla on your trip to see me this summer. Don't let her use this new power until we can study it. I love you dearly my child.

Zarina

Grace's eyes filled with tears and they fell onto the note. She missed her mother so much and looked forward to their visits each year. She sat there for a moment, staring at the words and wondered what her mother meant by darkness.

Her thoughts were interrupted by Shyla who came out of the cabin carrying her egg basket, followed by Ivan who had a slab of bacon in his hand. She looked at her daughter. "You're up early," she said, handing her the raw piece of meat from the pack. "Look who came to visit."

Shyla took the item and stood there puzzled until she saw the big gray wolf resting in the trees, then ran to her, calling her by name. She gave her a big hug, stroked her head, then offered her the food she had been given. Jinda licked Shyla's face, accepted the offer of sustenance, and began eating ravenously.

Ivan stood on the porch, the bacon in his hand, watching his daughter run up to the huge animal without the slightest hint of fear. "Zarina sent a meal for Jinda so I'll use the bacon for *our* breakfast," offered Grace, "just as soon as I get these supplies put away."

Ivan handed her the meat and picked up the pack. "Zarina knows about Shyla then?" he asked.

"Well she doesn't know the details exactly, but she can sense something is going on with her."

The woodcutter shook his head. "She is an amazing woman," he said as they entered the house, "and so is her daughter," and he kissed her cheek.

Cade was up now and had the fire in the cookstove roaring nicely. The kettle was steaming and the little cabin was warm and cozy as Grace began to prepare breakfast for her family. After the meal, she busied herself with arranging all the new remedies and filling her healing bag with the ones she needed for today's trip. Brant would be over to pick them up soon and she wanted to be ready when he arrived.

Shyla was outside playing with Jinda, much to the dismay of Rufus, and Ivan and Cade were rigging old Bill with a pull-harness for the summer-sleigh. This morning they would make a trip to Ivan's practice area to pick up the load of wood that had accumulated since last year's competition.

Each year he would gather the wood he had stacked up from all of his practicing and donate it to his many friends and business associates. It was his way of supporting the event, and saying hello to everyone who showed up faithfully every summer to cheer him on.

Shyla was right in the middle of teaching Jinda to shake-a-paw, when the big wolf ran off and disappeared into the trees. She was confused for a moment until she saw Brant pull into the yard.

The wolves of the *Gatou* were only seen when they wanted to be, and this was *not* one of those times.

Grace helped Shyla into the carriage and motioned for Jinda to stay put. She wanted to give the old girl plenty of rest before her return to Belden's Wall, and knew the animal's fatigue was far deeper than she let on. She waved back at Ivan and Cade as the three headed out for the Catcher place followed by Rufus, who hung back, matching their pace. The boys waved back and then finished the last of the preparations for their own little journey.

The trip was uneventful and seemed to pass quickly as Brant dropped the girls off at the Catcher house and continued to the stables. Grace walked along the path, through the small gate and up the steps to the front door. Shyla, who was usually the first one in getting the healing supplies ready, stopped and said, "Mother, is it all right if I just go and look at the puppies? I *really* don't feel like healing today."

Normally her mother would have told her that a healer must do her duty no matter how she feels, but considering the circumstances, she told her it was fine. In fact Grace was glad to see her daughter acting once more like a child rather than the responsible, wiser-than-her-years girl she was used to seeing. She watched as Shyla skipped over to the dog kennels, followed by a panting Rufus, then went inside to tend the sick woman.

Shyla loved the puppies and made sure she played with each one of them. She thought about her mother and wanted to help her, but the thought of healing again scared her. Not wanting to think about it, she snuggled another puppy, while Rufus, who had plopped himself down a few feet away, looked on with a slightly jealous eye. It was all so calming, and for awhile at least there was just her and the animals comforted by the warmth of a calm spring day.

The summer-sleigh moved easily over the uneven ground as Ivan and Cade made their way along the trail that led to the practice area. The sun shone down in patches as it peeked its way through the openings in the leaves and branches of the tall trees. The huge evergreens were even more resistant in letting through any of the life-giving light as they swayed ever so slightly in the gentle breeze that moved through the forest. Father and Son walked at a steady pace followed by Old Bill who, despite his advancing years, was more than a match for the object he had in tow. It was peaceful and the three strode along quietly, accompanied only by the multiple choruses of nature that made up the sounds of spring.

Ivan's senses came alive when he entered the woods. Every little noise, smell and vision were like a part of him, imprinted from so many years of woodcutting. He felt invigorated and wondered if Cade felt the same.

Ever since his son could walk and talk he had pleaded with his father to try his axe and tell him stories about his adventures and competitions. Then when he was old enough, which was quite young because of his incredible strength, he had joined him when he harvested timber or practiced for the next yearly event. Cade idolized Ivan and would mimic his every move. While he was growing up he had told everyone that one day he was going to be a woodcutter just like his father.

It was every man's ambition for his son to take after him, and he encouraged and guided Cade as much as possible, even though he had known for some time that the boy's heart wasn't in it. He had almost mentioned that observation a few times, but who was he to extinguish someone's dream. It was something that Cade would have to figure out on his own and anything he said would just end up hurting him. Keeping that silence wasn't a problem for Ivan and he carried it gladly, but he could see the disappointment and frustration in his son's eyes whenever he would attempt any of the woodcutting arts. He wasn't bad at it, but he didn't have the natural ability or, more importantly, the love for it that would allow him to excel. It was all taking its natural course, but sadly Ivan had noticed a resentment forming which had now become a wedge, causing him and his son to drift apart. That was the pain he bore with his silence. Grace had reassured him that it was just a part of Cade's growing into manhood and finding his own way, but Ivan could feel that his son thought of himself as a failure in his eyes. There was no way to assure him that he wasn't without breaking the silence, and his son's heart. *You cast a huge shadow Ivan Harden,* his wife had told him, *and any two men couldn't fill the boots you walk in. So imagine how a young boy feels.* The woodcutter understood what she was saying, but understanding didn't help the situation. Through the years he had encountered many men who were intimidated and resentful of him, but this was entirely different. This was his son, and he wished he knew some way to fix it.

He looked over at Cade and smiled. "It's a good day for it, hey Son?" Cade smiled back and nodded. His smile was genuine and Ivan could feel the love, but there was an invisible wall between them that caused his smile to fade.

The practice area was close now, about a mile by Ivan's calculation, so he increased his pace slightly in anticipation. The mere thought of woodcutting thrilled him and even though he knew that he was only here to pick up a load of wood, his heart rate increased as he drew nearer.

Suddenly, off to the right, they heard a stick break and the rustle of leaves as something ran through the forest. Almost instantly they each grabbed their bows, waiting for the next sound. It never came, as whatever it was moved away silently, dashing their hopes of fresh game.

Ivan hadn't been out on a real hunt yet this year, but with the preserves almost depleted and the scarcity of small game, he was going to have to plan a serious outing before the Woodcutting Competition. The boys shouldered their bows and replaced the arrows as the trail opened up, revealing the practice spot.

The potency of the meadow permeated Ivan's senses as the smell of years of accumulated wood chips filled the air. Adding to the woody fragrance were stacks of logs, some old and dried, and some freshly cut. Ivan breathed in deeply through his nostrils and an involuntary grin appeared on his face.

Cade led Bill next to the stacks of wood and got ready to load the summer-sleigh. He proceeded to unhook the old horse so he could graze while they did their job. Bill never wandered off too far and always came when called, so they never worried about him leaving for home earlier than he should.

By the position of the sun the woodcutter could see that it was just past noon. "We better get this loaded and head back right away if we hope to be home before dusk," he observed, and started stacking the first layer onto the sleigh. "We'll put the dry stuff on the bottom and the greener logs on top," he told Cade, as they continued their efforts.

The task was going well, and they were almost halfway done when Ivan saw a large buck deer bound into the opening from the southern edge of the glade. It was moving swiftly, almost like it had been scared by something, which didn't give Ivan much time. He ran to his bow, picked it up and grabbed an arrow. By this time Cade had noticed his movements and stopped working. The deer had only a few jumps left before he would be back in the thick trees, so Ivan took his shot. His arrow flew straight and swift but was low by a few inches and he knew he didn't have time for a second attempt.

Cade moved without thinking, as though it were engrained in his very soul. In a blink he had his bow ready and had released two arrows almost simultaneously. Only after the act did he realize he had broken the vow he had made to himself to never allow anyone to observe his extraordinary ability with the bow.

Ivan watched as his son moved with unnatural speed. He was almost a blur as he let one, then another arrow go, faster than any bowman could get one shot off. What made it even more unbelievable was the fact that the first arrow struck the stag just below the ear, killing it instantly, and only a moment after, the other one struck the neck. Immediately the majestic animal fell to the ground and lie still.

Ivan stood there stupefied by what he had just witnessed. Never in his life had he ever seen anyone move like that except the *Gatou*, and he doubted if they could have matched it. Ivan stared at his son, his brow furled. Cade met his gaze and the two locked eyes. He could see the bewilderment and concern on his father's face, and felt embarrassed at his slip up. No matter though. He knew he couldn't hide it forever and felt relieved to have it out in the open. His father was speechless and felt astonished by what had just occurred. For someone who had seen *many* things in his time, he was left astounded by his son's actions and stood there in awe as his favorite audience chattered loudly from the treetops.

The air grew thick with tension as the two stood facing each other, so the woodcutter interrupted the onlookers and spoke to his son. "Never in all my days have I seen anything like that," he began. "Where did you learn how to shoot that way?"

Cade looked away and then to the ground. He felt a mix of emotions but looked up and answered, "It's been like this since I was old enough to draw a bowstring."

Ivan shook his head and sighed. "First Shyla with her mysterious magic, and now you with yours," he chuckled. "One is never bored in this family"

"It's not magic," he protested. "It's more like a natural ability."

"That ability is anything but natural," replied Ivan with a smile.

"You know what I mean Dad," Cade retorted in a frustrated tone. "It's like a calm comes over me when I grasp the bow. Then my clarity increases and my vision seems to magnify. After that everything around me slows and I am one with the weapon and the arrow becomes an extension of myself."

Ivan could sense excitement, frustration and relief all mixed together, so he chose his next words carefully. "All right Son, I see what you mean," he said softly. "What you're describing does sound more like a talent than magic." Ivan wasn't convinced even when he heard his own words, but it did have a calming effect on his son. "I think we should keep this between you and me for now," requested Ivan. "No need to concern the girls with it." Then thought, *Well at least until we figure out what's going on with Shyla. Besides, Cade's ability doesn't appear dangerous, except to an animal he might be hunting,* and smiled again.

"Well," said Cade, "I've kept it to myself for too long and don't feel like hiding my talent any longer."

Ivan listened to his son's words, and understood why he didn't want to keep it a secret any longer, then held out his hand. Cade looked at him for a moment and clasped it. Ivan shook his son's hand and said, "Nice shooting boy . . . I mean young man."

Cade beamed with pride and grinned from ear to ear. "Thanks Dad and you made a good shot too," he said, winking. Ivan burst out laughing and Cade joined in, along with every squirrel within earshot.

The two grabbed their hunting knives and headed toward the fallen animal. They would bleed it and dress it out skin on because of the time factor, and then finish the rest back home.

They were only halfway to the deer when Cade stopped and said, "Dad, there's something I need to tell you." Ivan tried not to worry as he turned to face his son. Tears welled in Cade's eyes and his lips were quivering. Ivan felt for him as he watched his son struggle to speak. *By the Mother of Balance, what can it be?* he thought, and waited for his son's words. Tears were streaming down Cade's face when he finally spoke. "Dad," he started again. "You know I respect you and your craft, and I want you to know you are my hero." Ivan stood and waited, respecting his son's turmoil. "Well the thing is. . . ." He paused as the tears surfaced again. He wiped them away and continued. "No matter how hard I try, or how much I want to, I just can't be a woodcutter like you."

Ivan grabbed his son and held him tightly. He hugged his father, sobbing. "It's going to be fine Son," he said soothingly. "I will be proud of you no matter what you decide to do, and we both know woodcutting isn't exactly a going concern," and he squeezed him tighter.

For the first time in a long time his son was hugging him for real. No barriers, no invisible walls, just a true loving hug, and he began to tear up. When Cade regained his composure, he released his father and said in a relieved tone, "I thought you would be disappointed."

"I could never be disappointed in a son like you." he reassured him, and gave him another hug.

After they readied the deer, Cade asked, "Do you think we could keep what just happened between us, a secret though?"

"Hmm," teased Ivan, then smiled and said, "Of course, Son."

"Well," replied Cade, "if Shyla found out I was crying like a baby, she would tease me unmercifully."

"That is very true," responded Ivan, and began dressing out the animal.

They finished the deer quickly, carried it over to the sleigh and continued loading the wood. They talked about the weather and hunting, but mostly about the upcoming contest. "I'm going to enter the Archery Tournament this year," Cade told Ivan, as he stacked the last of the wood onto the sleigh.

"Well you stand a good chance of winning," his father replied, wiping the sweat from his brow. "The only trouble you may have is, of course, the *Gatou* who will be returning to defend their ongoing domination in the event. No one has ever beaten them since the beginning, over . . . well, let me see now, I guess it's been over fifteen years since the baron brought in the first bowmen. Well anyway, this will be the first year the *Gatou* get a challenge at their own game, and personally I can't wait to see their faces when you shoot against them."

Cade became serious. "I will do my best to win. Not only will it feel good to compete against the greatest bowmen in the land, but the first place finisher gets a fat purse of silver coins, and we could sure use that right now."

The woodcutter looked at his son. "Those would be your coins to spend as you see fit."

"True," replied Cade, "and helping our family fits me just fine." Ivan nodded and thought, *He really is becoming a man,* and felt a sadness wash over him at the reality of what that meant. It was also a great thing though, especially if *he* won the woodcutting event and Cade won the archery. What a celebration that would be.

Like the *Gatou* with their archery, Ivan had won the Woodcutting Competition each year since its inception, so his former thoughts were not far-fetched. Of course there always has to be a downside to every happy moment and his mind drifted to Claude and Tamarack Jack the Giant with the Axe. He had been sure he was done worrying about that, but obviously he was still bothered by what had taken place in Woodvale, and again he began to doubt his abilities. *Oh well,* he thought. *May the bigger man . . . I mean better man win,* he corrected himself, then strode off to find Old Bill who was belly deep in a patch of grass.

He returned with the horse and secured the harness once again. Cade tied the deer over the back end of the load and they were ready to go. Ivan gave Bill the word and he began to pull. He groaned at the initial weight, but once the summer-sleigh started moving, its wide smooth runners glided easily over the terrain.

The majority of the way from the practice area to the public road was downhill so the three made good time as they raced the sun home. The tension that had silenced Father and Son on the way there was no longer an issue, and they talked and joked with an ease that neither had enjoyed in years. They had finally found a common ground with each other. Cade could feel that an enormous weight had been lifted, allowing him the freedom to express himself without reserve. Ivan could no longer feel that ever-present resentment, and had gained a new respect for the young man who walked beside him.

The woodcutter glanced at the deer that lay stretched over the back of the sleigh. *I'll have to get the smokehouse fired up,* he thought. It was a decent sized animal and would provide some good eating in the next few days, and a lot of cured meat in the weeks ahead. He hadn't used the smoker for awhile and looked forward to the distraction it would bring. He needed any diversion he could get to keep the anxiety to a minimum before the baron's big festival. *This is a great day,* he thought, and as they made their way homeward, started explaining the art of smoking meat to his son.

Grace looked down at Leslie Catcher. She wasn't much older than Grace, but had a few more wrinkles from long days spent out in the sun with her dogs. She and her husband had always worked together raising and training the animals, and it showed. She had a dark complexion, with dark hair and eyes. Those features, along with her slender figure, could have made her appear mean if not for her laughing eyes. They had a twinkle that made everyone she met like her instantly. That luster was dulled today though, replaced by the sadness that comes with too many bedridden days.

"How do you feel now?" asked Grace, after administering one of her remedies. She had looked over her symptoms and narrowed it down to two different possibilities and then made an educated judgment as to which to treat her for.

"I feel surprisingly better already," she said in an astonished tone. "The chills have subsided and the pressure in my head has all but vanished. You are amazing!" she exclaimed with a smile, and the spark in her eyes was brightening quickly.

"Actually your body had almost beaten the bug. It just needed a little help. Your excellent physical condition and constitution deserve most of the credit. I just gave it a nudge," she gestured, smiling back. "It shouldn't be more than a day or so now and your strength should return."

Leslie pulled the covers down a little. "Well that is good news," she replied. "I was afraid I was going to miss the festival in Woodvale, and that just wouldn't do."

Grace began putting her medicines away. "Well, unless something unforeseen happens, you should be as right as rain well before then." With that news, Leslie smiled again.

"Did you hear about all the new and wonderful attractions that are supposed to be at the festival this year?" asked Leslie, changing the subject.

"No," answered Grace, "but I did hear it's supposed to be the biggest one so far."

Leslie sat up. "I heard from Maggie Starling, who heard it from the Lady Cavillade herself, that the circus is coming to the entertainment quarter for the festivities. There will be exotic animals, jugglers, fire-eaters and of course my favorite, the Freaks of Balance. They say there's a man there completely covered in hair that they call the Wolfman, and they have a woman who is half girl and half fish that they call a Mer-maiden." She coughed in her excitement and Grace reacted quickly, placing her head back on the pillow.

"You need to rest or you won't be going anywhere," Grace said in a half jesting tone.

"I know, I know," Leslie agreed. "I just love all the excitement and unusual sights."

"As do I," admitted Grace, "but mainly I go to support my husband and cheer him on in the woodcutting events."

She held out a glass. Leslie accepted the drink of water and thanked her friend. She handed it back and said, "You're man doesn't need much cheering, he wins it every year. Everyone knows he's the best."

Grace nodded, "Yes he is, but this year Morgan's Coal Company has sponsored a giant from the north, and everyone is saying he can't be beaten."

Leslie's eyes widened, "Yes I heard!" she blurted, her eyes lighting up even more. "Is he really as big as they say?"

Grace thought for a moment. "Well, I haven't seen him, but Ivan tells me he is at least ten feet tall."

Leslie closed her eyes, "I'm sure it will all work out," she said with a yawn.

Grace put the rest of her supplies in the bag and picked it up. "You need sleep now so your body can recover," she said quietly. The other woman just nodded and remained still.

Brant met Grace in the doorway. She put a finger to her lips, and gestured for him to follow. She explained the situation to him and instructed him in his wife's future care, giving him a small packet of the remedy to dole out as needed.

"I can't thank you enough," he told her, "and I know you won't accept any payment, but there must be something I can do for you." Grace looked at the grateful man. She had seen that expression on so many faces throughout her years of healing, but it never got old. That look and her admiration for her mother were the reasons she had wanted to be a healer. To help others and be recognized for her talent was payment enough.

"Please," he said, pleading with her, "You must take something." He scratched his head. "I know. I will let Shyla pick any puppy she wants from the kennels."

After his offer she thought for a moment then replied, "I'll tell you what. I'll take you up on that offer, but not right away. Shyla is at a sensitive time in her life and can't handle looking after anyone but herself right now, but when the time is right I'll tell her, and thank you very much for your generous gift."

Brant looked pleased. "Sounds like a deal," he replied, and escorted her outside.

More time had passed than she'd realized and the sun was well down the western sky. Shyla didn't notice though. When her mother found her she was playing with a black puppy that had snow-white ears. Shyla looked up, "I named him Loner," she told her mom, "because he doesn't look like any other dog in the kennel."

Grace looked at Brant, then winked and nodded. "Are you ready to go my girl?" she asked.

"If we have to," Shyla replied disappointedly. "Just let me say goodbye to Loner. He's going to miss me."

Rufus, who was farther up the hill, looked ready to go and didn't seem too happy to be sharing his master's affections with any other four-legged friends. Shyla said her goodbyes and they walked to the stables where Brant proceeded to get the horse and carriage ready for their departure.

They were on the road shortly and moving at a brisk pace. The warm breeze felt good, and of course Grace always had that calm feeling of satisfaction after helping someone.

She couldn't help but notice how beautiful the carriage was, and mentioned it to Brant. "It *is* rather nice," he admitted. "I thought we would ride in style on the way back, and you can thank your neighbor Claude Boyle for his generous contribution."

Grace looked at Brant with a puzzled expression. He laughed and began to explain.

"About two months back I believe . . . yes, it was the first month of spring, Claude came over and asked to look at my hunting dogs. Well you don't have to ask me twice, so I took him to the upper kennels and he picked out my last Royal Hunter and paid me in gold right there on the spot. I had heard rumors about his unkind ways with animals but gave him the benefit of the doubt. Before he left though, I warned him not to mistreat the dog in any way or I would be over to retrieve the retriever." Brant chuckled at his own play on words and Grace joined in. Shyla, who was in the back, was thinking about Loner and wasn't paying much attention to the adults, who continued their conversation.

"Well I don't much care for Claude's way with animals or people," Grace said in a cold tone, "but the carriage is very beautiful and I'm glad some good comes from his dealings."

The dog-man leaned back in the seat. "I hear you," he said more seriously. "I've watched Claude since he moved into the area and I've not been impressed, but he is a good businessman."

"Yes," said Grace sarcastically, "He's all business and not much of a man." With that, the group continued on their way to the Harden homestead with very little conversation.

"Here we are," announced Brant, as they drove into the yard and up to the cabin. "Thanks again for helping my wife. It means a lot to me."

Grace smiled as he helped her down. "No need to thank me, I enjoy helping those who require my services, especially when they are good people like you and Leslie."

He met her gaze. "Well don't forget our agreement," he said, and glanced at Shyla, who had already jumped down and was over by the trees looking around. "I'll be glad to honor it whenever you are ready."

She nodded as she watched him climb onto the seat and rein his horse back toward the public road.

"I'll see you at the Woodvale festival!" he called back.

Grace waved at the dog-man and replied, "That sounds good, and take care of that girl of yours, I kind of like her."

"Me too," he conceded, and continued up the path. She folded her arms and watched until he was out of sight, then turned and scanned the trees for Shyla. She saw her little girl just inside, playing with Jinda. She had the old wolf on her back and was scratching her stomach.

The wolves of the *Gatwu*, as a rule, never let anyone except their chosen rider touch them. They might allow a pat on the head from someone close, or allow themselves to be packed, but in general they never allowed the hand of another upon them. Due to Shyla's unusual connection with animals though, Grace wasn't surprised to see her sliding over the wolf's stomach or wrapping her arms around its neck, and was so glad to see her distracted from the recent events. She left her to her fun and went inside to put the healing supplies away, and see about the evening meal.

The air in the cabin smelled stale, so she opened some windows. She tidied up a bit and decided they would have leftovers for supper. She wasn't sure when the boys would return, and it was too warm to start a fire right away, so she readied the ingredients and waited.

When she had finished with everything, she cleared her mind and decided to write her mother a reply to send back with Jinda. She grabbed her parchment and quill, along with the ink, and set it all on the table in front of her. Grace pulled the stopper from the bottle, but as she thought back to all the events she wanted to write about, she began to weep. Suddenly the reality of what was happening came crashing down on her, and her gentle weeping turned into all out crying. Her baby girl *was* a *Sol'mar*. She would never lead a normal life and how could she ever have a home and family. When the Council of Healers heard of this they would insist on studying her and do their manipulating in the name of research. She couldn't allow that to happen. She had to protect her child from what they would do in her so called 'best interest', and still try to find a way to help her through it. If anyone could make that happen it was Zarina. She was the wisest and most powerful healer in the land, and together they would find an answer to Shyla's unfortunate evolution.

Grace believed there were reasons for all things that occurred, but what could be the reason for one little girl to be given that much power? It was beyond her for now, but Grace had a way of figuring problems out, and with her mother's help she would find a way to teach Shyla to control her talents before it was too late.

She wiped her eyes and waited for the tears on the parchment to dry, then took her quill, dipped it in the ink and started to write. She was going to draft a one-piece summary of the situation, but as she began the words flooded onto the surface uncontrollably. It was like a release of frustration and emotion that she had been holding back since it started, and it felt good to let go. She told her mother everything. She didn't leave out one detail of her daughter's crisis, and when she was done a relief washed over her, and she sat there starring at six full pages of parchment.

As she waited for the ink to dry she added to the last one.

> *Zarina, do not let the Council of Healers know about*
> *this unless we have to. You know what they will do.*
> *Grace*

She wrote it in bold lettering, but knew that her mother understood full well what was done with the last *Sol'mar* that surfaced. Not that the Council had bad intentions, but their fear of the unknown and their hunger for knowledge, blinded them to the fact that they were dealing with a person and not just a subject. The Council had of course changed since the last *Sol'mar*, but she knew what would happen nonetheless.

She lit a candle in preparation for sealing her document and waited for the last words to dry. As she rolled up the parchment and tied it at either end with her mother's ribbon, she marveled at how fine and white it was compared to the kind she had written on as a child. The older scrolls were no more than glorified tree bark, but they had done the job. It was unbelievable, though, how much everything was progressing.

She held the candle to the stick of wax and it dripped bloodred onto the document. She picked it up and pushed her ring firmly into the wax, revealing the Healer's Seal.

Shyla came in, poured herself a drink and asked, "What are you doing Mom?"

Her mother turned and replied, "Just getting a letter ready to send to Zarina." The children had always referred to their grandmother as Zarina, at her request.

"Oh!" said Shyla excitedly, "can I send her one too?"

She took her daughter in her arms and held her tightly, never wanting to let go. "Of course you can," she said, releasing her. Shyla ran to the table and began writing a note to her grandmother.

The room smelled fresh now and the air was beginning to chill as the sun sank low in the sky, so Grace closed the windows and started a small fire in the cookstove. She was helping Shyla with her letter when she heard hoof beats and the creaking of the loaded down summer-sleigh. "It looks like the boys have returned," she said. "I'll get the food started."

She had just stoked the fire and began filling the frying pan when Ivan stuck his head in the doorway and shouted, "We have fresh deer meat for supper. I'll bring it in after we unhitch!" Before she could answer he was out the door, so she set the frying pan aside and went back to helping Shyla.

The woodcutter and his son took the sleigh into the back and found the easiest place to make the transfer into the wagon. They finished skinning the deer and hung it in the smokehouse. Ivan cut the back-straps from the animal and headed to the house. "Might as well eat some of the best now," he told Cade. "The rest is going to be smoked and cured anyway, and it won't make much difference after that."

The meat he carried in would feed them for a few meals. By that time he would have the rest of it well on the way to being smoked, which meant they would be able to eat it at anytime they wished.

Some people smoked meat for flavor as they cooked it, but to actually cure it in a smokehouse took about six to eight days. This gave him just enough time before the competition, plus it would keep his mind occupied until then.

He handed the meat to Grace, kissing her cheek as he passed, filled the washbasin and began cleaning up for supper. "I'm writing a letter to Zarina," Shyla told Cade as he came in from outside.

"Can I write one too?" he asked.

"Certainly," Grace replied, "but don't take too long. Supper will be ready right away."

The letters were finished and the family enjoyed a wonderful meal together, then turned in for the night, the Woodcutting Competition first and foremost in their minds.

First light found the Harden family busy packing Jinda for her return to Belden's Wall. She was well rested now and Grace asked Shyla to convey the lack of urgency to the old girl so she would pace herself on the trip back. She wasn't quite sure how Shyla did it, but she knew that she could make her understand. They made sure she was well-fed for her journey, then placed the letters inside the pouches along with a few gifts for Zarina, and sent Jinda on her way. They waved and called out as they watched her padding down the trail toward the creek. She didn't turn around, but her ears perked up in acknowledgment.

The only one who wasn't sad to see her go was Rufus. Not that he disliked the wolf, but she had taken up far too much of Shyla's time.

CHAPTER

12

Festival Preparations

The next week went by faster than expected because everyone managed to keep themselves busy. Ivan had all the deer meat in the smokehouse finished in good time, and had even taught Cade the fundamentals of the craft. The smoked venison was great and had the strong taste of the chickory willow saturating the meat with its rich, dark spicy flavoring. When they were done, they had just about enough cured to last a month.

The girls were busy making preparations for the wagon ride, and the weeklong stay in the baron's guest quarters outside Woodvale. The actual competition spanned over five days, but the family always left a couple of days early just to settle in, say hello to everyone and deliver the wood. Grace packed a big bag of healing remedies, as it seemed she spent almost as much time healing, as she did taking in the events and festivities each year. It was as if people saved up their ailments, or made them up, just to get checked out for their yearly visit. Grace didn't mind though, and it was always good to see her near and distant neighbors, even if it was only in a professional sense.

The day before they were leaving for the competition each member of the Harden family was making their own individual, final preparations for the trip. Grace was double-checking her remedies, making sure she had enough. She brought extra in anticipation of the expected turnout due to the unusual circumstances of this year's competition. People were saying the attendance should almost double with the advertisement of *Ivan vs. Tamarack Jack the Giant with the Axe*. Inside she wondered if the crowds were coming to see if her husband would finally be defeated. Well it didn't matter. Her man was the greatest no matter the outcome. She suddenly felt ashamed for doubting her husband for even a moment, and cast the idea from her thoughts.

There was no room for negativity on this day. It was a day of new hope as they were about to embark on a journey that could set their family up for awhile. The winds that blow were saying that not only the crowds were doubling, but the entrants to the woodcutting events as well. Last report had the tally at well over fifty entry fees paid. It seemed that even the woodsmen who didn't have a chance of winning were signing up, just to be able to tell their stories of how they were part of the competition where the legend met the giant. Grace sighed, that would be almost twelve gold to the winner. That kind of payday would last them for at least two years. Excitement rose in her just thinking about it. Not for hers, but for her husband's sake. It would take the pressure off him, and relieve the worry he had of not being a good provider.

Over the past few years, she could see his doubt creeping in and she knew how heartbreaking it was for him. *Well,* she thought, *in about eight days all that will be but a faded memory.*

She held up her new dress and looked at herself in the mirror. She had never owned a full-length mirror before and this one had been a gift from the baron the year previous. His words were still as clear in her mind as the day he offered them. *Such beauty should not go unseen, especially by the one who wields it.* She flushed slightly at the memory, but felt a feeling of reassurance just knowing there was another true gentleman in the land besides her husband. She took one last look around and decided she was done packing. She left the trunk open for Shyla, who was sharing it with her for the trip, then went out to the kitchen to start fixing breakfast.

She saw Ivan sitting in the living area as she walked to the stove to throw a couple more sticks in the firebox. He was sharpening his axe methodically and had that look on his face. The look he always got before a competition. It was like a trigger that he had where he could shut out everything around him, along with his distracting emotions. It was his way of meditating, and the honing of the axe helped him reach that place. Grace knew better than to interrupt him when he was in that state. Not because she feared any reprimand, but out of respect for him and his ways. Besides, he would be back to normal before long. He just needed to revisit that part of himself so he would be ready to go there at a moment's notice in the days ahead. She left him to his thoughts and started preparing the pancake batter.

Shyla bowed low and in good courtly fashion, her new dress almost touching the floor, then turned to face the other direction and bowed again. "Thank you so much for coming," she crooned in a high-pitched voice, "and thank you so much for the lovely gifts." She held out her basket of eggs for all to see, but the chickens were paying more attention to the feed she had just given them than her regal gestures, and the rooster was ignoring her completely. She waved her finger in the air. "You are all insolent peasants and I shall have each one of you punished severely for your impertinence." She looked around and hoped she had gotten that word right.

Now all the chickens were staring at her as though they understood what she had just said, but the waving of the hand only meant more food to them. Shyla didn't care and exclaimed, "That's more like it! I expected better manners at the royal court, and you can be assured that the baron himself will hear of this!"

And with that, she spun around, causing her dress to flip up and down, and stormed out of the chicken coop.

She skipped toward the house, giggling as she went, but got distracted by a *thudding* noise. She looked where the sound was coming from and saw her brother shooting his bow at a target he had set up by the woodpile. She skipped over and engaged him in conversation.

"Oh kind knight, would you help a damsel in distress? I have been disgraced before the entire kingdom and my honor is at stake. You must take your trusty bow and put an arrow into each wicked heart that has spurned me."

Cade looked at his sister and shook his head. "I don't have time to play games Shyla," he admonished her, "and what are you doing wearing your brand-new dress to fetch the eggs?"

Shyla looked disgusted. "I'm a lady, and we ladies must practice our ways if we are to marry a gentleman," she said in a sweet tone, throwing a little curtsy in at the end.

"*You*, a lady?" he laughed out loud. "I've never seen a lady with chicken manure on her worn out shoes." Shyla's face turned red and she grabbed an egg from the basket and cocked her arm. "Don't you dare!" yelled Cade, not sure what she would do next.

"I'll have you know that I'll be getting new shoes of the highest fashion as my gift this year from the baron himself, and a new hat from father." That thought calmed her and she placed the egg back in the basket.

"That's nice," he scoffed, "but I need to practice, and I think I hear Mom calling you."

Shyla scrunched up her nose, "Yeah right. And what do you need to practice for anyway. It's not like the forest animals are going to care."

Cade smiled. "The one I set my sights on might." He walked over to the target and retrieved his arrows. "The fact is that I am entering the Archery Tournament at this year's festival."

It was Shyla's turn to laugh out loud and she didn't hold back. "You are going to shoot against the legendary *Gatou* warriors?" She could barely contain herself, almost dropping the egg basket with her contortions.

"What's so dang funny?" You know I'm good with a bow."

"Yes Brother," she said, getting her laughter under control, "but they are great. They are born with a bow in their hands and are taught to hunt as soon as they can walk. They are ridiculously strong as well, not to mention the fact that, since anyone can remember, their ancestors have been the greatest bowmen in the land. Did I leave anything out?" she teased, raising an eyebrow and making a funny face.

"Just leave me alone!" he said in a raised voice, while sticking the arrows in the dirt beside him for easy access.

Shyla turned on her heels and skipped up to the cabin singing, "Cade can't beat the *Gatou*. Cade can't beat the *Gatou*." Her voice faded as she disappeared around the corner of the building.

Cade took his frustration out on the target. "I'll show you!" he scowled, grabbing an arrow from the dirt. With lightning speed he let the arrow fly, hitting the center of the circle. He then grabbed another even faster and let it go with such accuracy that it split the shaft of the first arrow. The rage welled inside as he grabbed another and then another, splitting each shaft in turn, until there were none left.

After his anger subsided, Cade stood there with a silly look on his face. He felt like a fool and looked around to see if anyone had witnessed his idiocy. He skulked over to the target and dug the arrowheads out of the wood. He salvaged as many of the feathers as he could from the splintered shafts and took the whole mess to the work-shed, where he would need to craft new ones before the next morning. As he began the long tedious chore, he thought, *I can't believe how easily my little sister can get to me*, and had to smile just thinking back on the whole ordeal.

Shyla skipped around to the front of the cabin and up onto the porch. *No porch troll today I guess*, she observed, but never really expected there to be. Her father was preoccupied with more important things right now. There was just no one to play with around this stuffy place. Not even the chickens. "*Humph,*" she grumbled, which caused Rufus to lift his head and look at her. "Well," she said aloud, "maybe one," and with a giggle she took the eggs inside.

"So that's where your new dress went," Grace said to her daughter in a stern tone.

"I know Mother, but I wanted to practice for the Woodcutter's Ball," she replied, her mouth turning down into a small pout.

"Well no matter," said Grace, looking down at her little girl. "Just go and change, then set the table please. Breakfast will be ready soon." She took the eggs and watched Shyla pirouette into her room. *Even at twelve summers the girl's beauty is remarkable,* she thought, then continued fixing the morning meal.

Cade was relieved when he heard the mealtime bell. He hadn't even replaced one of his arrows yet, but was glad of the diversion. It was such meticulous work, and he just wasn't in the mood right now. He grabbed an armload of wood on his way in, placed it in the wood box and sat down at the table.

"Aren't you forgetting something?" his mother asked, pointing at the washstand.

"I'm sorry," he said, standing up. "My mind is not quite here today."

"Speaking of which," Grace said, gesturing toward Ivan who was working on his hatchet now. "We all seem quite preoccupied today."

Cade finished washing up and sat down to breakfast. Grace took her spot and waited. After a short time she announced, "Last chance for breakfast. If I don't see two bodies in these chairs soon I will feed yours to Rufus."

Ivan snapped out of his trance and looked over at his wife. "You sure know how to get a man's attention." he said, then smiled and winked at her. She blushed slightly and looked down. Shyla came running out of her room and jumped into her father's arms. He caught her and spun her around.

"I didn't see the porch troll today," she said in a disappointed voice.

Ivan kissed her forehead. "He knows how smart you are getting, so he is probably under there scheming up new ways to capture you." With that, he growled and grabbed her, squeezing her tightly. He spun her around one more time and then gently sat her in her chair. Cade glared at her when she asked him to pass the hotcakes, so in retaliation she stuck her tongue out at him.

"What is it with you two?" Grace demanded. "I heard you yelling at each other earlier, and now you are barely being civil." She looked at one then the other. "You are acting like small children."

"He started it," Shyla interjected. "He was trying to tell me what I can wear, and made fun of my shoes." She looked at her mother and continued in an exasperated expulsion. "And he won't ever play with me anymore!" She then directed her attention to Cade. "I bet if little Miss Wanda Starling came strolling through the yard in *her* new dress, you wouldn't notice any chicken manure on *her* shoes!"

Cades ears turned crimson and his mouth dropped open, but no words came out. Grace's eyes widened and Ivan fought hard to keep a straight face. Finally Cade found his voice. "W-well," he stammered, "she interrupted my practice, and she's always talking weird and trying to get me to play silly make-believe games."

Grace shot glances at each of the children and then spoke in a soft voice. "This just won't do," she started. "We need to have balance in this family, now more than ever. We can't fight among ourselves and expect to face the obstacles that threaten our way of life. We need to pull together as a family and keep our bond strong and positive." She turned to Shyla. "You my girl are so smart and beautiful and wise beyond your years, with an imagination as big as the Crooked Mountains, not to mention your other gifts." She turned to Cade and continued. "And you son are strong, handsome and bright, and are just realizing your talent and potential." She stood up. "I want you two to apologize to each other before we continue with our meal."

Shyla was first to respond. "I am *so* sorry kind sir if my harsh words have caused you any discomfort." Then she stood and held up her hand, in true ladylike fashion.

Cade shook his head and said, "I'm sorry I made fun of your shoes, but I'm *not* kissing your hand." Shyla pretended to be distraught, which brought a smile from Ivan and Grace. The woodcutter stood, followed by Cade, and the family held hands and gave thanks for all they had been blessed with. As they looked across the table at one another, they felt strong and united enough to face any challenges that might lie ahead.

Cade spent the rest of the day replacing his arrows and helping his father with the wagon. They loaded the last of the wood from the summer-sleigh, and checked the harness, replacing one of the straps that had broken. They hung the smoked venison in the cold cellar, and made sure the chickens had plenty of food. Grace helped Shyla finish packing, then double-checked her healing bags to make sure she hadn't forgotten anything. As the day wound down, she cooked up the last of the fresh deer meat and made sure that everyone had what they needed for the morning trip. They went to bed early that night, but no one could get to sleep. When they did, their dreams were filled with all the marvels the festival might hold.

They were up early the next day and the excitement was apparent, especially with Cade and Shyla. They were talking nonstop, and couldn't wait to get their belongings loaded on the wagon. Ivan was returning from the creek with the water for breakfast, when he noticed a man on horseback galloping up Claude's roadway. When the man reached the house he jumped off the horse, ran onto the veranda and banged on the door. Not a moment later, Claude appeared from inside and started talking with the man. The talking soon turned to yelling, which eventually sent the fellow back to his horse and down the road at a dead gallop. Ivan was curious, but shrugged it off. Claude's dealings weren't his concern . . . at least not usually. He still harbored resentment toward the man. No matter how hard he tried to follow his wife's advice he couldn't help but feel a touch of anger when he saw Claude or even thought about him, but he couldn't afford to let himself be distracted, especially right now.

They had a quick breakfast and the children were eager to help clean up. Grace had to smile watching them scurry about. Ivan stacked his woodcutting gear by the door and pulled the wagon around so he could load it. "You know what I miss?" he asked out of the blue. "Fresh milk and butter," he answered himself before anyone could speak. "The first thing I'm going to do with my winnings is buy us a milk cow. Then I'm going to get the supplies to fix up our place. In fact," he looked at Shyla, "winning the competition this year will give me the gold, and time I need to build you your very own bedroom."

Shyla ran over and gave her dad a big hug. "Thank you so much," she said, and hugged him again. "I'm so excited for the festival this year."

Ivan's face became serious and he looked concerned. "I know you are," he began, "but there may be a problem with that."

Shyla looked worried, "What do you mean?" she asked, her voice wavering slightly.

Ivan held his daughter's arms and looked her in the eyes. "I saw the porch troll on the way in and he said there is no way that he is allowing you to go anywhere today."

Shyla's mouth opened and she pushed her way past her father. "I'd just like to see him try to stop me!" she exclaimed, and climbed onto the wagon.

Ivan chuckled as he secured his woodcutting gear in the back and stepped into the driver's seat. "Let's go Bill!" he shouted, and the wagon started moving toward Woodvale.

CHAPTER
13

To the Pavilion

The air was already starting to warm as the family made their way along the public road. With the first month of summer underway, all the Mother's wonders were in full bloom. The roadway on either side was lush with grass and filled with wild flowers. Ivan took in the beauty and felt at peace for the first time in a long time. He loved being with his family and knowing that each clippity-clop from Old Bill's hooves brought him one step closer to giving them a better life. Not that they had ever complained, or that gold was everything, but it would be nice for a change not to have to scrimp and save all the time. He didn't mind going without for his love of woodcutting, but his family shouldn't have to suffer for it. Just knowing that in the next few days he had a chance to make it right again, gave him new purpose.

He looked back at his children and then over at Grace, who had her eyes closed and her head tilted back. She was taking in the hot sunshine, and he put his arm around her, causing her to snuggle in close to him. *What a perfect day,* he thought. *If there's such a thing as paradise, this is very close.*

His thoughts were interrupted by a loud obnoxious voice. "Hiya! Hiya!" and there was no doubt whose voice it was. Ivan turned around to see Claude Boyle coming up fast behind them.

His horses were already lathered and he wasn't sparing the whip. As he closed in on them he yelled, "Out of my way!" so Ivan drove to the side and let him pass. A cloud of dust followed him, but died quickly as the frantic man turned the next corner and disappeared from sight.

"What a rude person," Grace said in disgust.

Ivan pulled her closer. "We're not going to worry about Claude Boyle this week," he said, and urged Bill forward again.

As they came closer to Woodvale, they began to see signs of the festivities. About five miles out it started with bright purple banners on each side of the road. They were attached to tall poles and adorned the baron's crest, framed on the top and bottom by crossed axes. These banners could be seen every quarter mile along the public road with their purple and white coloring. There were many camps appearing along the ditches now, which could only mean one thing; the festival grounds were full already and the rumors had been correct. Judging from the number of people they passed, Ivan thought the early predictions might have underestimated the actual turn out.

The wagon creaked and groaned to the steady pull of the old horse. As they passed, Ivan could hear the sounds and smell the various aromas that accompanied each cooking fire from the surrounding camps. His stomach rumbled as the mouthwatering flavor of broiled meat hit his nostrils, which made him think that it must be getting close to mealtime. Apprehension had stifled his appetite this morning, but it was returning swiftly with each new scent, and he was looking forward to lunch at the baron's pavilion.

They moved steadily along, but the closer they got to the town the more crowded the roadsides became, and Ivan suddenly realized that he didn't recognize anyone. In all the years that the competition had been going on he had gotten to know almost everyone who attended, or at least knew their faces, but he had never seen any of these people before. His stomach tightened when he realized it must be the giant's presence that had attracted these crowds, or at least the challenge between him and the oversized woodsman. *Have they come to see me beaten,* he wondered, *or see me topple the giant? Either way I guess they came for a show,* he thought, and started to feel like the whole thing was getting a little big for him. He swallowed hard and reminded himself that he was the reigning champion. *If it's a show they want, then a show they will get.*

He repeated those words over in his head a few times, but there was always that nagging doubt at the edges. He had never felt this feeling before, at least when it came to woodcutting, but this year it was crouching there waiting and it had him second-guessing his abilities. The more he thought about it, the gloomier the day seemed around him, until he was jarred from his doldrums by a child's voice.

"It's him!" screeched a young boy, pointing at the wagon. "It's The Woodcutter!" Ivan looked down and saw a scrawny little fellow that looked to be about his daughter's age, moving closer to them. "Wait mister!" called the boy, so Ivan pulled back on the reins.

Shyla and Cade stood up to get a look, and Grace opened her eyes to see what the commotion was. The boy ran onto the road, then stopped and stared at the woodcutter in awe. "How are you today young man?" asked Ivan, nodding at the child.

The boy grinned from ear to ear and stuttered, "G-g-good sir," and then giggled uncontrollably. When he finally regained his composure, he said, "My name is Simon, and you got to tell my friends that no giant can beat the legendary woodcutter. My dad says it, and *so do I.*"

"Well Simon," replied Ivan, with a short pause. "Let's go say hello to your friends."

The boy's eyes widened. "R-really sir. . . . I mean yes sir. . . . I mean all right," he stumbled through his words in disbelief.

"Lead the way," prompted the woodcutter, waiting for the boy to move, but he just stood there staring for a moment, then turned and hurried to the first opening at the road's edge.

Ivan followed and found himself in a small camp surrounded by a group of boys who stared up at him like he was the king himself. "I told you it was him," said Simon, in a defiant tone.

The oldest boy spoke up. "Do you really know Simon and his dad?" he sneered, looking at the smaller boy.

Ivan saw the worried look on Simon's face and replied, "Well let me see. I have met many people over the years. What does your dad do?"

Simon looked sheepish. "He's the town blacksmith sir," he replied, and kicked a clump of dirt that wasn't quite in his way.

"Is his name Albert?" Ivan asked.

The young boy grinned again. "Yes," he answered, looking at the older boy.

"I do know Albert *and* his son," he told all the boys, who looked at one another and then back at Simon.

"That doesn't even matter," the oldest boy chimed in. "My dad says the giant is going to beat you this year, and *I* think so too."

Ivan looked down at the boy and smiled. "Well Son, your father is entitled to his opinion, as well as you. That's one of the great advantages of living in this kingdom. We are all allowed to believe in what we choose."

There was silence for awhile and then one of the boys said, "I think you are the best."

Then another boy said, "My dad says you are a legend and can't be beaten, no matter the size of the man." Then one after another each of the rest of them made a similar comment.

Ivan nodded in gratitude. "Thank you for the confidence boys. I feel like I could take on ten giants now." The woodcutter bent down on one knee and grasped Simon's hand. "It was so good to see you again," he said, then shook his hand and winked. "I will see you at the competition. . . . Oh, and say hi to your father for me, and tell him I will be bringing Bill in for some new shoes very soon."

"Thank you mister," replied the boy, then stepped away and ran off.

Ivan nodded to the others and turned to go, but noticed that Simon had gone over to a small wooden target and was pulling an old hatchet from it. He ran back with the axe and handed it to Ivan.

"Would you carve a W in the handle for me please? I've been practicing for a couple of years now, and when I grow up I want to be just like you." Ivan felt pride welling inside and thought, *it's so funny that one moment you can be down and feeling sorry for yourself and in the next instant a young boy can give you your confidence back, just like that.*

He took the axe and told the boy he would be honored to do it. He walked over to the wagon and took his hunting knife from its sheath. He carved the initial into the hilt and turned around to take it back, but noticed that all the boys had followed him. All except the older one who was standing by the fire talking to a man he presumed was his father. He handed the hatchet back to the boy, who ran his fingers over the new carving. All the boys gathered around Simon and *oohed* and *aahed* at the sight of his new treasure.

"Thanks again mister woodcutter. I'm gonna practice so hard with this, and one day I will be just like you!"

Ivan glanced at Cade, who was smiling at him, then turned to Simon. "Can I see your hatchet for a moment?" he asked the boy.

"Of course," he replied handing it over.

Ivan took the axe in his hand and felt the balance. It was surprisingly good for a regular hatchet. He pulled it back and released, sending it end over end through the air until it bit into the center of the target that Simon had originally pulled it from.

"Did you see that!" yelled Simon, and all the boys started whooping and hollering as they ran over to the target.

The older boy and his father just stood there frowning, and Cade said, "Show off," then smiled.

Ivan put his knife away and climbed back onto the wagon. All of his family was looking at him with comical expressions on their faces. "What?" he asked in a slightly confused tone, which caused all of them to burst into laughter. "Giddy up!" he called to Bill, then joined his family in their mirth.

The camps grew increasingly more frequent as they reached the crossroads. The signs were there pointing to Woodvale, Coaldale and the City of Kings, so Ivan pulled Old Bill to the left because the turnoff to the festival grounds was about two miles further along the public road.

The banners were spaced only fifty feet apart now and seemed to be encouraging travelers to enjoy the festive spirit. They weren't really necessary though because every new camp they passed was either playing music, dancing, or involved in some other form of entertainment.

Ivan started to recognize a lot more of the faces now as they drew closer to the turn, and they all waved and wished him good luck in the tournament.

In the past they had always wished him luck, but this year there was a worry in their voices that gave him a slight chill, and he knew exactly why.

They had reached the turnoff and just started in, when Ivan yelled, "Whoa Bill!" and pulled back on the reins. The wagon came to an abrupt halt and he just sat there staring forward. Grace glanced at him with a puzzled expression until she realized what he was looking at.

The festival grounds were beautiful. There, outstretched before them, was a hundred acre meadow that was divided in the center by a steep incline that separated the huge field into an upper and lower shelf. The entire outer edge was lined with the purple banners, and the interior was decorated according to the theme of woodcutting. It looked like each of the camps in the lower northern quarter had been given a color and event, and had tried to outdo their neighbor in decorating according to their assignment. There were red-and-blues mixed with yellows-and-greens that turned the lower camps into a collage of vivid designs that were awe inspiring.

Ivan drank in his surroundings. Everything was so spectacular he could hardly believe it, but with all the beauty, his eyes couldn't help but rest on one thing. There in the center of the lower camps was a wooden statue which appeared to be carved from a single tree. The detail was amazing, even from a distance, and the likeness it bore him was incredible. There he stood holding his axe and looking out over the festival grounds.

Ivan knew instantly the baron was behind it, which made the fact that his likeness, standing about a head taller than the giant, was both a statement and a humorous gesture on his behalf. Ivan didn't know a man with more class and wit than the Baron Vero Salday, and he understood all too well what that statue signified.

The woodcutter gazed upon the spectacular view for a few moments more and then took the reins again, moving Bill onward through the camps.

Ivan could see the baron's pavilion and outer tents on the upper half of the field and looked forward to seeing his old friend again. He had known Vero since they were boys at the castle. Vero was a couple of years younger than him, so he had always looked up to Ivan. They had liked each other from the first time the young boy had visited from his country estate and had become instant friends. He thought that Vero was the son of the queen's brother or maybe the king's sister. He couldn't remember his royal bloodline, but he had never acted as though he thought himself any better than a mason's son, and for that Ivan had always held him in high regard.

As they entered the open area, they got their first look at the entire field. It was sectioned into quarters. The lower half had been set up with camps to the north, and markets and entertainment to the south. The upper shelf was occupied by the baron and his guests on the northern side and to the south were the grounds where the Woodcutting Competition took place, along with the archery and lesser activities.

Ivan remembered the competition area very well. For over twenty years he had bested every challenger that had tried to take his title. His heart raced when he thought of it, and he could feel himself starting into the woodcutting mind-set.

They came to the edge of the field and moved along the grassy trail that wove its way between the temporary dwellings.

As the people recognized him, they started to cheer and clap and voice their appreciation and reverence for the woodcutter. This public adoration, though sincere, embarrassed him somewhat but he smiled as he waved and took it all in. He was uncomfortable at how powerful it made him feel, but needed all the power he could get in the days ahead. It didn't matter if it took a young boy and a crowd of people to give him strength, as long as the outcome was positive. Without *them* he might as well be back at his practice area entertaining the squirrels.

The greetings and outbursts continued as they wound their way toward the upper grounds and the woodcutter took it all in stride. He knew most of these folks, and it calmed his earlier trepidations. Old Bill gave a nicker that broke into a whinny as they got close to the statue. Ivan wondered if he was saying hello, or had smelled another horse. He could hear his children in the back now making a fuss about something, so he turned to see what it was.

"Look Father," remarked Shyla, pointing to the south. "They're setting up the circus." There was excitement in her voice and he knew why. She loved the strange and exotic animals as well as the unusual people that came with the show.

He could kind of understand, with his limited knowledge on the subject, why she was so interested in them. When someone is different, they are attracted to others who don't quite fit in. Maybe it is because they have a mutual understanding of rejection, or are just trying to find their own kind.

This type of thinking always made his head hurt, so he dismissed it and corrected Bill, who was wandering unchecked toward a barrel of oats in a nearby camp.

The aromas from the cooking fires were really getting to him now so he hastened the old horse forward, being careful of the comings and goings of the people. When they reached the statue, Ivan stopped the wagon to get a better look. Grace observed it with admiration, and the children acknowledged it quickly, before turning their attentions back to the entertainment area. Ivan couldn't believe the detail of the work. He'd had many people paint and draw his likeness over the years, so the sculptor had obviously captured his image from a good source, but this carving was truly amazing.

The Harden family sat lost in thought, each anticipating a different activity and exciting possibility that may occur at this year's festival, when they heard the sound of hoof beats coming up fast behind them.

"Make way. Baron's business. Make way!" shouted a messenger on horseback. He raced passed them, almost knocking a man over as he made haste to the upper shelf.

"What is it with these rude people today?" Grace complained in an exasperated tone. "What can be so urgent that you endanger others just to convey it?" Ivan nodded in agreement and wondered if she could appear any more beautiful than she did when she was concerned for others.

After the dust had settled they continued along the path, accepting acknowledgments and greeting people until they reached the steep incline that would take them to the upper section of the field. As they started up, Old Bill let out a groan and dug in against the weight of the loaded wagon and its cargo.

Ivan stopped him instantly and backed him onto the flat again. "I think we can walk the rest of the way," he said in a cheerful voice. "Bill has done his share today I believe." The family climbed down from the wagon and proceeded up the hill on foot with Old Bill taking up the rear, looking less strained with the lighter load.

When they reached the top it was quite a spectacle. The baron's pavilion was circular and situated directly in the center of the area. It was huge, rising twenty feet up and a hundred feet across, and was surrounded by a series of guest tents supplied for his family, closest friends and honored visitors. The outer ring of tents was also provided by the baron for his workers, and the people who had done business with the royal family over the years. Much to their delight, the first camp they came to on the way to the center, was that of Brant and Leslie Catcher. Leslie saw the family and waved them over.

"How are you feeling today?" asked Grace, as they entered the camp.

"Never better," replied Leslie. "Whatever you gave me, or did to me, fixed me up right. In fact I feel more energetic than I have in years."

Brant was out of the tent now and shaking hands with Ivan and Cade, but Shyla was scanning the many cages and pens that housed the dogs that Brant and his wife would be showing at their market quarter booth. Finally her search ended and she let out a yell. "Loner!" she cried, and ran over to a small pen that was right next to the tent.

Grace shook Brant's hand and commented, "I see you brought the puppy."

Brant nodded. "It would appear so," he said, and his smile widened. Then his face became serious. "I can't thank you enough for what you did for my wife," he said in a grateful tone. "She's been improving daily since your visit." Grace nodded her acceptance of his appreciation, then glanced over at Shyla, then back at Brant and raised an eyebrow. "I had to bring him," he said with affirmation. "He really misses Shyla." Grace shook her head and began talking with Leslie about women's matters.

Meanwhile, Cade was doing some scanning of his own, but it wasn't for a puppy. He knew that Wanda Starling would be, camped somewhere on the upper section, and he was trying to search out exactly where that might be without looking *too* obvious. He had no doubt the Starlings would be in this area because they had supplied the royal family with the finest horses for decades. He kept looking around until it was time to go, but saw no sign of her or her family. *Oh well,* he thought, *I've got eight days here and I'm sure we will run into each other.*

Grace walked over to Shyla, who was busy scratching Loner's fluffy white ears and talking to him as if he could understand. "It's time to go dear," she said softly.

"Look Mother, it's Loner!" her voice full of excitement. "He missed me," Shyla affirmed, as the little dog licked her face.

"That's so sweet Shyla, but we do have to be going. I want to get settled in, and then we can do our visiting."

"All right," she said disappointedly, "but let me say good-bye." Grace nodded and walked back to the others. Shyla ruffled the little dog's fur and stroked his head. "I've got to go now Loner," she said quietly, "but I'll be back to play with you very soon." She ran her hand over his head one more time, then skipped over to the wagon to wait for her family.

Grace turned to Ivan. "We had better go and say hello to our host. He *is* expecting us today."

Leslie hugged her and said, "Thanks for stopping by, and hopefully we will continue to see each other over the next few days."

"That's a guarantee," replied Grace, "and especially if Shyla has any say in the matter." They all laughed and then finished with their goodbyes.

On the way back to the wagon, Ivan turned and said, "Brant, after we get situated and have something to eat, I'll bring a load of firewood over for your camp."

Brant waved and answered, "Much appreciated."

When they got to the wagon, Grace said, "What a nice couple they are, so polite and good-hearted."

"Yes," agreed Ivan. "They are some of the best people in the land."

With a familiar movement he reached down, picked up the reins, and guided Bill through the outer ring to the baron's pavilion.

When they reached the entrance they were greeted by four servants who escorted them directly to their rooms. Ivan and Grace shared a spacious, richly decorated chamber, while Cade and Shyla enjoyed adjoining rooms which boasted equal splendor. Their possessions arrived only moments after they did, and the servants instructed them in directions, facility locations and mealtimes. Grace had never felt comfortable being waited on, but this once a year pampering, she would enjoy to the fullest.

Ivan had spent many years of his childhood around this type of surrounding, but Grace had grown up in the mountains and looked *forward* to this part of the Woodcutting Competition.

"This is perfect," she commented, looking around the room.

Ivan put his arms around her waist and pulled her close. "It wasn't always like this," he told her, as he kissed her gently. "Back before we met, there were just a few of us woodsmen who got together each year to test our skill against one another. Now it has become the social event of the year." He leaned in again to kiss her, but was interrupted by Cade and Shyla, who came racing through the curtains.

"Children!" scolded Grace. "You are supposed to ring the bell before you enter."

Shyla looked ready to burst. "Oh Mother," she began, "My room is so beautiful. It has pink velvet curtains with lace trim. It has satin pillows and a feather bed . . . and it's all mine. I feel as though I belong here," she finished, batting her eyelashes ever so slightly.

Cade cleared his throat. "You say you belong here?" he smirked. "Well I don't see any chickens." Shyla's face turned red and she started chasing her brother around the room.

"That's enough!" cried Grace, stopping the children in their tracks. "We are guests in this place, so please be on your best behavior. We don't want people thinking you were raised in a barn."

Shyla frowned. "Sorry Mother," she said, and curtsied. Cade just stood there trying to look innocent.

A moment later the entrance bell rang. "I wonder who that could be?" asked Grace, as she walked over to the curtain that covered the entryway. She pulled it aside, revealing a tall boy dressed in formal attire.

"Sorry to interrupt," he began, "but the noon meal is prepared, and will be served in the main hall momentarily." He bowed and scurried back up the hallway.

No cooking or cleaning for a whole week, thought Grace, *how wonderful*. "Well kids, you heard the man. Go wash off the road dust, change into something fitting and meet us back here." She handed Shyla her clothes from the trunk and picked out a dress for herself. Cade and Shyla went to their rooms, leaving Ivan and Grace alone once again. Of course the mood had passed, so they washed up and started dressing for the afternoon meal.

The children returned all too quickly with excited and anxious looks on their faces. Grace gave them a stern look, but thought better than to question them on the thoroughness of their washing. This week was to be enjoyed and she didn't want to start it off by nagging, so she changed her expression and led her family into the hallway.

They made their way down until they came to a wider corridor. They were greeted by an escort who motioned for them to follow, then proceeded to lead them to the eating area. When they entered, they were amazed again by the effort and detail that had been put forth in keeping with the woodcutting theme.

The long table in the center was crafted from half of a large tree and the seats were constructed the same way, with smaller logs made into benches and covered with cushions for comfort. Axes, hatchets and longbows adorned the walls, and the tapestries that hung along the edges depicted scenes from each of the five woodcutting events. Cade was glad to see at least one longbow mixed in with all the different kinds of axes, and was pointing it out to Shyla when he heard a loud, musical voice.

"And how is my favorite woodcutter?" asked Vero, as he walked into the room from a side entrance. Ivan looked over and saw his childhood pal. He was dressed exquisitely and appeared even more dashing than usual.

"Doing great," answered Ivan. "And how's my favorite baron?"

Vero smiled. "Very well and glad to be your favorite," he said.

"As am I," returned Ivan.

Vero walked up and faced Ivan. "It's good to see you again old friend," he said, and the two men embraced. The embrace lasted only moments, then the baron turned and said, "My dear

Grace, you are a vision to behold. How is it that you become exceedingly more beautiful with each passing year?" And with that, he bowed deeply and kissed her hand.

Grace blushed and replied, "You are most kind sir."

He straightened and said, "It is you who are most kind lovely lady, for you honor me with your presence at my humble home-away-from-home." Grace blushed again and couldn't help but smile. "And Master Cade," he said, addressing the young man, "you look like you've grown since I saw you in Woodvale. Will you be entering the woodcutting this year? You definitely look man enough, and have the best teacher."

"Actually," interjected Ivan, "Cade will be entering the Archery Tournament. It seems he has quite a knack with the bow."

The baron looked pleasantly surprised. "Well," he said. "It will be good to have another competitor that will, hopefully, give the *Gatou* a run for the silver this year."

Cade nodded and said, "Thank you sir," shaking the baron's extended hand.

"And Miss Shyla," he said, bowing even deeper and kissing her hand, which brought forth a titter, "you are a rare beauty and so wise for your years. You are the jewel of your family and shine ever so brightly. There's a light inside you that, if we put out the candles, would illuminate the entire room."

If he only knew, she thought, and smiled, performing what she thought was her best curtsy yet.

"Forgive me," the baron said in an embarrassed voice. "You must be famished after your trip. Let us sit down to this wonderful meal. We can talk while we eat, and believe me," he said looking at Ivan, "there is much to discuss." Ivan knew that look and was sure that something serious had happened, or was about to.

Cade was the first to sit down and couldn't believe the amount of food that was on the table. There were at least five different types of meats and cheeses, along with breads and salads and some vegetables he'd never seen before. He couldn't imagine why all of this was prepared just for them, but his father *was* the champion and a legend, so it made sense in that way.

Once everyone was served and enjoying the meal, the baron looked at Ivan and said, "The giant is withdrawing from the competition."

Ivan dropped his knife and stared at Vero. "Are you positive?" he asked slowly, his mind racing.

"I just got word from a very trusted source not long before you arrived," replied the baron, backing it up with a nod. Ivan's emotions were spinning as Vero continued. "It happened early this morning according to my man, but he wasn't sure of the reason."

The baron didn't know what reaction his news would invoke, but was surprised when everyone at the table was silent and sat staring at a bewildered Ivan. A part of him was relieved that the giant was dropping out, but another part of him, a part he hadn't known about, was disappointed in losing the chance to have some real competition this year. This surprised him, but at the same time made him feel good about himself. He had been feeling a bit like a coward, what with his anxiety and trepidation toward facing that huge obstacle, but now that it was gone he knew he had been truly looking forward to the challenge.

All eyes were on him as he picked up his knife and said, "Well I hope it's nothing too serious," and continued eating. The tension left the room and the conversation continued again.

Grace spoke first. "I feel bad for Jack if there's something wrong with him, but I don't feel bad for Claude," she said with disdain. "I'm glad his little plan has failed. He only did this to try to force my husband to work for him, and I can't stand that man." Everyone looked a little surprised, then returned to the meal.

The baron was next to speak. "Well Cade," he said, his attention on the boy. "I've got good news and bad news for you." Cade swallowed the food he was chewing and waited. "The bad news is that the archery signups were closed as of yesterday." He paused to let the statement sink in. "The good news is that miraculously your name is now on the list and your entry fee has been paid." Cade's eyes widened and the baron winked at him. "For you ladies," he continued, "I'm sorry but. . . ." he paused again and his face saddened. Grace met his gaze with an interested expression, but Shyla's stomach dropped and she looked like she might be sick. Vero continued his pause for a few more moments and then continued. "I'm afraid that I only have good news for you." Grace smiled, and Shyla felt so relieved she thought she was going to pass out. "The lady Cavillade is arriving tomorrow, and the first thing she plans to do is take you girls shopping for the traditional, annual gift of your choice. This year it's even better though, for I will also be bestowing upon each of you a gift of my choice." Shyla was so excited she got the hiccups, and Grace thanked the baron for his generosity. *Two gifts*, thought Shyla, in between hiccups, *this just keeps getting better.*

Out of nowhere Shyla said, "I'm worried about Rufus. We haven't seen him all day."

The baron turned his attention to her and spoke softly. "Don't worry about that wise old dog. Last year he didn't show until the third day of the competition, if you recall."

"True," replied Shyla, "I'm sure he's fine. I just worry about him, that's all."

"That's understandable," said Vero. "I'll have the guards keep an eye out for the old boy, if that will make you feel better."

"Yes, thank you," she replied gratefully.

The baron picked up the bell that sat beside his plate, and rang it. Servants appeared and took away the dirty plates, replacing them with clean ones. Then another group of servants entered carrying at least ten different types of desserts and placed them in front of the family. *Oh my,* thought Shyla, *this must be a dream,* and proceeded to try a sample of each different kind.

When the meal was over everyone had eaten way too much, but it was a time of celebration and the food was so good that no one complained. Shyla's stomach hurt, but she still managed to fit one more pastry in her mouth. It was unladylike she knew, but it tasted so wonderful that she allowed herself to overlook the implication.

"You seem preoccupied today," said Ivan to Vero, as he wiped his mouth with his napkin.

"Well normally I wouldn't be," he replied, "but with the giant dropping out, there is going to be an outrage and many fires to put out. There are a lot of people who purchased tickets to see you and Jack square off and they will want an explanation, and some retribution once the word spreads."

They hadn't sold tickets for the competition until the last few years, with the proceeds going to the orphanage in Kingstown—that's what everyone called the City of Kings now—and Ivan felt good each time someone purchased a ticket to see him perform his craft.

The baron slid his chair back and stood up. "Ladies," he bowed slightly to Grace and Shyla. "Gentlemen," he bowed again. "I hate to leave you, but duty calls. This whole giant business is going to erupt at any time now and I've got to prepare for it." He rang the bell again and more servants appeared. He instructed them to see to the needs of his guests in his absence and turned to go.

Ivan spoke up just before he left the room. "I brought you half a load of firewood. Where would you like it dropped off?" The baron nodded his appreciation and asked him to talk to his gateman. Ivan returned the nod, and the baron exited the hall.

"What a kind and generous man," commented Grace after the baron had gone.

"Yes," agreed Ivan wholeheartedly. "He was always that way, even as a child. He is really worried about the reaction to the rumor though. I've never seen him leave the table like that before."

"I imagine there will be quite a few unhappy people," said Shyla, as she dabbed her mouth daintily with her napkin and placed it on her plate. "Most of them traveled a long way to see you beat that mean giant."

Ivan looked at his daughter. "He's not so mean. In fact he was very polite to tell the truth. It was Claude that was mean . . . and nasty," he added, because it was true.

"If he's not mean, then why is he working for Claude Boyle in the first place?" asked Shyla with a puzzled expression.

"I can't answer that, but I am a fairly good judge of a man, and Jack seemed to be a good sort as far as I could tell in the short time I saw him. I really don't know how he got mixed up with the likes of Claude."

Shyla shrugged. "I guess it's a mystery we may never know about," she said in a matter-of-fact manner. "Not that it's important," she continued, "but when the facts don't make sense, my mind starts reasoning it out."

"Oh we know that dear," replied Grace, as she lifted the cup of cool water that had been placed in front of her. She took a drink but didn't comment further.

"I'm gonna see to Bill and that wagon load of wood," said Ivan as he rose from the table.

"You need some help?" offered Cade immediately.

Ivan looked at him suspiciously. "Why the sudden urge to help deliver firewood Son?"

Cade looked sheepish. "No reason," he said, clearing his throat. "I just thought you might need a hand." Ivan shot a glance at Grace, who was grinning. He gave her a quick smile and then took Cade up on his offer.

After the perfect meal, the Hardens returned to their chambers. Ivan and Cade went out to deliver the wood, Grace had some mending to attend to and Shyla stayed in her room. She lined up the dolls and stuffed toys, that had been thoughtfully put there by the baron, onto the chairs and benches she had placed along the wall. She then put on her best dress and practiced doing pirouettes and curtsies before her captive audience. "Lovely weather we are having," she said, addressing the rather large bear that sat in the corner. He didn't respond, but she said, "Oh, I am just fine. Thanks for asking." She lifted her dress for another curtsy and noticed how dreadful her shoes looked. *Not for long*, she thought, and smiled to herself. Tomorrow she was going into Woodvale and picking out a shiny new pair, thanks to the baron's kindness. That made her wonder what her other gift would be, and she got so excited she started jumping up and down. The dolls all stared at her disapprovingly, and the big bear wouldn't even look at her. "Forgive me," she said, feigning embarrassment, "I forgot myself for a moment." She straightened her dress and pranced along the line in regal stature. *This sure does beat the chicken coop*, she thought, then spun around twice and jumped onto the feather bed.

CHAPTER

14

Love and Archery

I van and Cade unloaded the baron's wood and then drove to the outer ring. They stopped at the Catcher's first and then went over to the Brundle camp. Theirs was an easy one to spot because there were kids everywhere, running this way and that. Tad and Camille quickly ushered the children to a new play area before greeting their guests. They welcomed them readily and thanked them for their generosity.

"Did you hear about the decree?" asked Tad, as he helped unload the wood.

"I don't think so," answered Ivan, wiping his brow.

"It seems the baron has put forth a royal decree banning all use of coal, in any form, during the Woodcutting Competition."

Ivan shook his head, "I hadn't heard."

Tad smiled and continued. "And furthermore, anyone caught violating the rule will be ejected from the grounds immediately."

"I think it's brilliant!" exclaimed Ivan, and they both laughed.

As they were leaving, Camille came running over with a basket of her delicious cookies and insisted they take them for the rest of their rounds. "You need to keep up your strength," she said, handing them to Cade.

"Thank you so much," he said, "but what about the basket."

"Oh, just drop it off at our booth at the market quarter any-time this week," she answered, and waved as they moved on.

As they visited each new camp, and unloaded more and more of their cargo, Cade's hopes rose and fell with each one. Finally the suspense was too much for him and he let out a deep sigh.

"What is it Son?" asked his father. "You haven't been your-self the entire afternoon."

"If you must know, it's Wanda Starling. I've been looking forward to seeing her again, and now it appears as though she isn't here this year."

The woodcutter covered his mouth and looked perplexed. "Wanda Starling?" Ivan's expression changed to a bemused look. "Why didn't you say so? The Starlings don't stay with the others. They have their own camp on the east side. The baron had a special area built for them with an arena, corrals, and a stable to house their prizewinning horses. In fact," he said with a touch of laughter in his voice, "that is our last stop."

Cade looked at his father suspiciously. "You knew all along didn't you?"

Ivan looked puzzled for a moment, then chuckled. "Of course I did Son," he confessed. "I was young once too you know, and there was nothing that could keep me from your mother. Now let's go see that Wanda girl."

The men drove into the Starling camp in the late afternoon. The sun still had some room before it reached the horizon, but Ivan was glad it was the last delivery. He had enjoyed seeing old friends, and some of his best customers, but right now he just wanted to see his wife and be with *her*. His talk with Cade had reminded him of how much she meant, and how much he needed and loved her.

He was glad Cade had feelings for someone and wondered if they were as strong as the ones he had felt, and still felt for Grace. *It will run its course,* he thought, but was nonetheless excited for his son and his first encounter with those overwhelm-ing feelings.

As they approached the living area, Ivan could see at least six horses to the north, tethered in the tall grass. There were a few more in the corrals, and he assumed the stables housed a few as well.

Each year, four days before the festival, the baron sent two wagons loaded with riders and helpers to assist the Starlings with the major endeavor of transporting their magnificent horses to the grounds. Many interested buyers would show up on the first day to inspect the new additions to the Kings Breed. They all hoped to find that special mount, but whether they purchased anything or not, they usually stayed for the entire competition, calling it a business trip.

Ivan pulled back and called out, "Whoa boy!" stopping Old Bill beside the fire pit. He secured the reins, jumped down and went to the back to remove the rear gate. While he was getting ready to unload, he saw Big Ben Starling moving toward them from the stables. Ben Senior was about six and a half feet tall and kind of wiry, but weighed well over two hundred pounds. He was a very powerful man, due to his lifestyle, and very passionate about his horses. The last time Ivan had seen Ben he had looked like a beaten man, much older than his years, but today he had a spring in his step and his easygoing demeanor had returned.

"How's our giant killer?" he asked as he shook Ivan's hand.

"Ready as I'll ever be," replied the woodcutter. He was about to reveal the recent news about Jack, but something stopped him. He had never been one for gossip, nor did he have all the facts, so he dismissed the thought and changed the subject.

"How's Little Ben been feeling?" he asked as he began unloading the last of the wood.

"He's doing great, thanks to your daughter," he said in an appreciative voice. "But I'll let you ask him," he said, as he motioned to the young boy who had just appeared from inside the tent. He came running over and stopped by the wagon, his eyes darting back and forth.

"Is Shyla with you?" he asked eagerly.

"No, she stayed behind at the baron's," he answered, noticing how healthy and alert the boy appeared. Little Ben didn't hide his disappointment to Ivan's reply, and frowned intensely. His father picked him up and held him above his head.

"Would you go tell your mother and sister that we have guests?" he asked his son, then lowered him back to the ground so he could carry out the request. Cade looked up from his work with an apprehensive expression. The thought of seeing Wanda again triggered the butterflies in his stomach, and he felt light-headed. He put his mind back to the job and tried to calm himself.

"It seems my boy is quite infatuation with Shyla," said Ben Senior. "A case of puppy love I believe. I guess it makes sense though. It's not every day a beautiful young girl comes along and saves your life." Ivan nodded his agreement as Little Ben came running up again.

"Mom says she will have refreshments ready inside when you are finished."

"Thank you Son," he replied, and the boy ran off again.

Ivan could see the love in his eyes when he looked at the boy, but there was more. Every parent loves their child, but it becomes more apparent when they are faced with the realization that they might lose them. He could see that deep bond whenever Ben talked about, or looked at his son.

When they finished unloading the wood, Ivan led Bill into the tall grass to graze. They stopped at the washstand and then continued into the tent.

It was richly decorated and the many candles gave it a warm atmosphere. It was nothing like their rooms at the baron's, but was nice just the same.

Maggie invited them to sit at the table, and brought out a large pitcher of fruit juice, which she poured into each of their cups. "Thank you so much for the firewood," she said, as she sat down and filled her own.

"It's my pleasure, and it's very good to see you again," said Ivan, lifting his cup in a friendly gesture.

The butterflies that Cade had calmed earlier, started back now in full force as Wanda entered the room carrying a plate of squirrel cake squares smothered in wild honey. She set them on the table in front of him, and when she looked at him he thought for sure he would fall into those bright blue eyes. She was so pretty it left him speechless, but he managed to croak out a weak thank you as he took one of the squares from the tray.

"You're welcome." she answered, flashing him a smile.

The grown-ups were busy talking at the far end of the table, which left Cade sitting beside Wanda, trying to keep his heart from beating out of his chest.

"How have you been?" she asked as she filled his cup.

Cade's stomach was still doing a flip-flop, but he managed to gain enough composure to answer. "I've been fine. And you?"

"I'm doing very well actually. We are very busy with the horses and the ranch."

"Oh yes," agreed Cade, "extremely busy at the Harden residence as well, what with my dad being champion and the competition coming up." She seemed interested, so he continued. "Well, you know, practicing and living the woodcutting life." She looked puzzled and Cade felt stupid. "I'll be shooting in the Archery Tournament," he recovered quickly, trying to save the conversation.

"Oh how exciting," she said in a silvery voice, and placed her hand on his. He pulled away instinctively, but regretted it instantly. She giggled and topped off his cup again. "I shall be in the front row cheering you on," she promised, and once again placed her hand on his. This time he didn't pull away, but had a hard time catching his breath. She left it there for a few moments, then sat back and folded her arms. "It's an unprecedented turnout this year," she observed. "We should do a good business with the horses."

He barely heard her words; he was so fixated on her grace and beauty. The way she moved, and the sound of her voice were intoxicating to him.

"Yes," he replied vaguely, not really knowing what was said.

"You're very brave to take on the *Gatou*," she remarked, in an admiring tone.

Cade's face heated slightly with the compliment, and he said, "They are the best, but I will go out there and see what happens."

She looked at him, her eyes twinkling. "That takes a lot of heart," she remarked, then leaned over and kissed his cheek. "For luck," she added, and sat back down.

Cade's eyes widened and it felt like he would explode. He grabbed his cup and drank vigorously, trying to dampen the flames that arose in him, but no amount of fruit juice could contain that fire. All he could do was sit there breathing deeply and stare at the object of his desire. She met his gaze without falter, until finally he looked away. He had never known a girl like this. Not that he knew many girls, but she was fearless and straightforward, and it was very exciting to him.

His emotions had begun to settle when she asked, "Do you have a partner for the Woodcutter's Ball?"

He was caught off guard again. "Um . . . I hadn't really. Um, I didn't. . . . Well, no I don't," he answered, feeling a little off balance. She raised her eyebrows and looked at him. He sat there feeling a bit silly, but worked up the courage to speak. "Would you like to go to the ball with me? That is if you haven't been asked yet, and of course if you don't mind going with an awful dancer."

She laughed and placed her hand on his again. "I would love to go to the Woodcutter's Ball with you Cade Harden," she murmured, in a soft, affectionate voice. Cade could think of nothing else to say, so he just nodded and smiled back at her. Inside he was filled with excitement and anticipation, and the problem of getting dance lessons before the ball.

"Well, what do you think?" Ivan called out to Cade from the other end of the long table.

Cade stood up. "I think we had better be getting back before the girls start wondering what happened."

"Thanks again for the firewood," said Maggie, and started clearing the table. Wanda jumped up and started helping her immediately. *What a girl*, thought Cade, and felt warm inside watching her help her mother.

"Yes, thanks for everything," said Ben Senior. "Your family has brought us much joy, and we want you to know that it does not go unappreciated. If ever you need *anything*, just ask." His eyes misted but he held himself firm, then grabbed Ivan's hand and shook it vigorously.

"Your friendship is more than enough," responded Ivan, shaking his hand with equal sincerity.

Cade didn't want to leave, and watched Wanda as she walked out to help her mother with the dishes. She was nearly through the opening when she turned and winked at Cade, then vanished behind the curtain. Cade turned red and could do nothing to keep the grin from his face. He followed his father to the wagon and they started their trip back to the pavilion.

The journey didn't take long as they cut straight across, and they reached their chambers in plenty of time before the evening meal. Ivan relayed all the greetings and well-wishing that had been bestowed upon him on Grace's behalf, and generally filled her in on the high points of the afternoon. In turn she handed him a freshly darned pair of socks, which he took and quickly replaced the ones with the hole in the right big toe.

"I was wondering where those had gone," she scolded him jokingly, and sat back down to mend them.

The evening meal was as elaborate as the previous one, but the baron did not join them. This caused Ivan to worry and start wondering just how bad this giant mix-up might be.

"So how is Wanda?" Shyla started in on Cade.

"She is just fine," he replied. "And so is Little Ben, in case you were wondering. It seems he has taken quite a liking to you."

Shyla's mouth opened and she had an astonished look on her face. "Well," she said in a huff, "I don't even like boys, so there!"

Cade leaned closer. "Well I think he's in love with you," he said, enjoying his chance to tease *her* for a change. She folded her arms and stared straight ahead with an angry expression.

"That's enough you two," Grace reprimanded them. "Let's just enjoy this wonderful meal without squabbling."

The children stopped their bickering and started in on the next plate that was placed in front of them. Cade was mad at himself for snacking earlier, and barely made it through the third course, let alone the fourth or fifth. When dessert arrived he had to just sit and stare at it. Shyla was having no problem with hers, which made him even more frustrated. Finally he couldn't take it anymore and had to force some down just because it looked so delicious.

After the meal the family returned to their rooms and got ready for bed. The next day was a big one and no one minded turning in early on this night, but for the most part, sleep eluded them.

Ivan was thinking about going through the woodcutting course and familiarizing himself with the equipment before the actual tournament. Cade thought about doing some practicing of his own in the archery area, and Shyla was excited about shopping in the town. Grace, on the other hand, had no trouble getting to sleep. With the giant gone and her mending finished, other than Shyla's dilemma, she didn't have a worry whatsoever and drifted into a peaceful slumber as soon as her head hit the pillow.

Ivan was up before the dawn as he was each year on the day before the competition. He kissed his sleeping wife, grabbed his woodcutting gear and left the pavilion on foot. The sky was starting to show some light as he made his way to the tournament area. It was his ritual to walk the quarter each year on the day before, even though he knew it by heart.

As he approached he could smell the wood, and it was sweet in his nostrils. The old chips and dust blended with the new cutting from the many trees that had been brought in for the events, were a potent mixture to him. He stopped for a moment, closed his eyes and breathed in deeply. He loved woodcutting and felt sad at the thought of it being a dying art.

As he reached the first area he could see that the baron's men had already been busy sawing the trees into two foot lengths for the wood splitting event. The saw had its place in woodcutting, but Ivan defied anyone to cut down a tree faster than he could with his axe. Even though it wasn't his first choice, he did have a small-saw at home for cutting the blocks for the woodstove and one at his practice area, but these men had used a big-saw for this job. Unlike the single handle on the small-saw, this one had a handle on each end of its eight foot length and it took two men to pull it, which of course made for a faster cut. One of the side events each year, besides the archery, was the log sawing, but Ivan had never taken an interest in it. He didn't dislike it; after all it *was* woodcutting. He just preferred his axe.

Ivan walked over and set his equipment down. He pulled his axe from its scabbard and felt the blade. It was perfectly sharpened and ready to go. He placed a log on the chopping block and split it instantly, leaving the halves still standing there.

That was the key to this event besides power and accuracy. Anyone could split a log, but doing it so the pieces didn't fly off the block was the real talent. With seamless motion he moved around and split the two pieces almost simultaneously, then spun his axe three times in his hand and stood back admiring his handiwork. After his brief encounter with the wood splitting, he placed the axe back in its scabbard, grabbed his equipment and moved to another area.

The tree falling section was his next stop. In order to simulate an actual tree, they built a base for each twenty foot log, which kept them upright and ready to chop. Ivan sized up the space and footing, then moved on to the log chopping location.

As soon as he arrived he saw a few logs lying across the supports, so he jumped up and balanced himself precisely as he had done so many times before. It felt good to stand there, and even better when he jumped and spun in the air, landing in the opposite direction ready to cut through the back side. He felt invigorated as he leapt down and moved to the axe throwing area.

This event was his favorite, and although the rules stated that you could use an axe or hatchet, he preferred the latter. Not only for sentimental reasons, but because his had been meticulously crafted. From its weight, to its balance and feel, it was like an old friend to him. He pulled out the little blade and tossed it in for a bull's-eye. He loved that feeling. It was like freedom, and it made him feel more alive. He retrieved the hatchet, grabbed his gear and walked over to the tree climbing spot.

When he reached it, he noticed right away that something was different. There were usually only four trees used and four men competing at a time, but he could see that a fifth had been added. This one was twice the size of the others, and it was obvious who it was for. *I guess that's fair,* he thought. The normal one would topple under the giant's weight, and he was sure they had buried this one twice as deep also. *Oh well,* he thought, *it looks like they won't be needing that one after all.*

He was about to leave, but couldn't resist the temptation, so he grabbed the spurs from his bag and attached them to his boots. He threw his climbing rope around the back and bounded up the large tree at an astonishing rate. When he reached the bell he rang it, then hoisted himself up and sat on the top to take in the view of the entire field.

He could see that the circus was set up and ready to show their performances and spectacles. He could also see the early risers in the market quarter readying their stalls and booths in anticipation of a busy day. The camping quarter looked very colorful, especially with the smoke rising and settling with the morning chill. The most amazing vision though was the pavilion and surrounding tents. From his perch he could see how uniformly the rings were laid out, and how the colors matched in sequence, showing once again the effort the baron put into anything he did. It was so peaceful where he sat, but he knew he should get back and see if he was needed, and besides he had worked up an appetite on his morning jaunt.

Cade was also up early on this day. Not as early as his father, but by dawn's light. He had wrapped up some food from the evening meal because he wanted to get to the archery area before anyone was there, and knew he would be leaving long before breakfast. He grabbed his longbow and quiver, filled with the arrows he had so painstakingly crafted, and left the pavilion.

The location where the archery took place was in the northeast corner of the competition quarter and he had no problem finding it. This was his first time as a contestant and he was eager to see how the event was set up. How many targets, what distances and what types of targets, were a few of the many questions that raced through his mind. He didn't have any idea how many entrants there were, or how strong the competition was going to be, except for the *Gatou*, and only them through reputation. He had never really paid much attention before because he was always watching his dad, but now he wished he had. *Anything you can pick up from a champion sure can't hurt*, he thought, as he passed through the gate with the hanging sign that read, "Archery".

He was excited when he entered the shooting pit, but was startled when, not fifty feet away, there were two massive wolves eyeing him warily. He glanced around, trying to spot the riders. Finally he saw them squatting down at the opposite side with their arms resting on the great-bows that lie across their laps. *So much for my private practice*, he thought, but at least he could still familiarize himself with the place. He watched the *Gatou* for a moment and then looked away. He didn't know if he should say hello, or if they even knew the kingdom tongue. They didn't move or show any signs of friendliness, so he ignored them and turned his attention to the course.

It was set up in a long alleyway about fifty feet across, with targets at different distances and heights. The first one looked to be about a hundred feet away, and an easy shot for anyone who had the slightest skill with a bow. The next three were set at about two hundred feet, one hundred yards and two hundred yards. That last one would take more than a little expertise. He tilted his head and noticed another target even farther, and guessed it to be over three hundred yards at least. He doubted anyone could hit that, and thought it must be there for show.

He was busy gauging the distances when he noticed there was another set of targets about halfway down the alley that were attached to pendulums and suspended from poles that were leaning in from the edges. These poles were bound at the tops, creating a support for the eventual moving targets. He could see the catch that kept them secured, and his eyes followed the rope that was attached back to a set of small levers that would potentially release the targets into a swinging motion. He was impressed with the setup and decided he *would* practice, even though his main competition was there watching his every move.

Cade removed his jacket and took up his bow. As soon as he did, the *Gatou* got up and walked over. They stood a few feet away, holding their bows and watching him closely. He wasn't sure what to think, but wasn't about to be intimidated by anyone, so he grabbed an arrow and shot it into the center of the closest target. Only a moment later the *Gatou* each nocked an arrow and placed them neatly beside his. They looked at him and laughed, speaking a few words he didn't understand. Cade was quite annoyed by their behavior and decided he wasn't about to be laughed at, so he grabbed another arrow from his quiver and let it fly straight into the middle of the second target. Just as before the *Gatou* effortlessly shot their arrows directly next to his in the bull's-eye.

Cade looked at the wolf-riders, then at their bows. *These guys might be small,* he thought, *but they are strong.* The great-bows they were using had considerably more tension than his long-bow and he would defy any normal man to try to pull one of those bowstrings. He was tempted to ask them to let him try one, but thought better of it.

He looked at the two closely now and guessed them to be just slightly older than him, but they seemed more like men. This observation, and the laughter, got him going and he quickly grabbed another arrow and sent it a hundred yards down the alley, hitting the third target almost dead center. Again the *Gatou* followed suit, placing their arrows right next to his. He turned and they were smiling at him. *All right,* he thought, *I guess this is going all the way.*

This round he took his time and pulled the bowstring to full tension. He had never been as glad as he was now that he had made his bow with heavier wood, creating more resistance and a farther range. He held it steady and raised it slightly to compensate for distance. The arrow sliced through the cool morning air and hit the fourth target just left of center. The *Gatou* weren't laughing anymore, and looked rather serious now as they discussed something in their strange tongue. They weren't so quick to shoot this time, but each one in turn hit the target near the center.

The laughter was back now, and even louder. Cade wasn't sure why they were laughing, but it made him angry. He took a long look down the alley, then stuck four arrows in the ground beside him. He glanced over at the *Gatou*, then walked over and hit the release on all three moving targets. They began swinging from side-to-side, and looked to be about fifty feet in distance between each one. Cade walked back over and stood beside his arrows. He looked over at the *Gatou* once more and gave them a smile of his own. He faced the course again and closed his eyes.

He could feel the calm sweeping over him and when he opened them, the clarity was there. He moved with eerie swiftness in the eyes of the *Gatou*, but to him everything was in slow motion. Almost instantaneously he sent the arrows flying. One after another they bit into the first, second, and third moving targets consecutively. He grabbed the fourth arrow and paused only long enough to let the swinging circles clear the center, then released. The shaft arced through the air past all the previous targets on its undetermined course, which appeared to have no destination until it started its descent. As it made its way downward, the shot he had thought impossible was now more realistic. When it hit the farthest target just below the bull's-eye, it became all too real, especially for the *Gatou*.

Cade tilted his head but couldn't hear any laughter now, so he looked over at the boys and smiled, waiting for them to try to match his last shots. They made no move with their bows and seemed confused. They started talking to each other, then the talking turned to arguing. Now Cade was the one confused, and wasn't sure what to think. They argued for awhile and then the one who had led the shooting ran over to his wolf and leapt onto its back. He left the archery area at a dead run, heading south.

The remaining *Gatou* turned to face him. Cade waited, not sure what to expect. The plainsman bowed before him and said, "*Onak utuk*," then crossed the short distance and mounted his wolf. He headed east at a lope and disappeared into the morning mist. Cade was still confused as he retrieved the arrows and continued his practicing.

CHAPTER
15

An Unexpected Encounter

The girls were up just after Ivan and Cade, and wasted no time getting ready for the big day. Grace packed her small healing bag for the trip into Woodvale, just in case it was needed. She saw that Ivan's gear was gone and knew exactly where he was, but wondered where Cade had gotten to when there was no answer from his room.

Shyla was up and had her bed made and room straightened faster than ever before. She was washed and groomed and ringing her mother's bell with the question, *when is the Duchess Cavillade arriving?* burning in her mind. Her mother could see the excitement in her eyes and in her movements, and it reminded her of an earlier time when she would have felt the same way.

"The baron said the Lady Cavillade stopped in Coaldale for the night and should be arriving around noon today, or just before," she told her daughter.

Shyla frowned at her mother's words, but quickly thought of something that would help pass the morning by. "After breakfast, may I go and play with Loner?" she asked, with a pleading look on her face.

Grace thought for a moment. "I don't see why not," she replied, "as long as he's at the Catcher's camp and not at the business quarter."

Shyla's eyes got big, and with a worried tone she asked, "You don't think they would sell him do you?"

Her mother answered quickly. "No, I think he's much too special for that."

Shyla looked relieved. "He couldn't go to just anyone," she said. "He needs someone who understands him."

Grace smiled to herself. "You're right," she agreed. "Not just anyone."

"Good!" Shyla said sharply. "If he went to the wrong person, I don't know what I'd do. If he went to Claude Boyle, I think I would go there and steal him away."

Grace looked at her daughter. "Shyla!" she said in a firm voice, "that's no way to talk." Then she added, "But I wouldn't blame you." The girls started laughing, but were interrupted by the entrance bell.

Shyla ran over, then returned with the news that breakfast was being served in the main eating area, so they made their way to the large room and sat down to another exquisite meal. They were about half done when Ivan came in and joined them. The three finished up together and had a plate set aside for Cade when he arrived.

Ivan returned to his room to hone his blades again, and Grace took Shyla out to the Catcher's to see if Loner was there. Sure enough, when they reached the camp they could see him lying in his pen by the tent. When he saw Shyla, he started wagging his tail frantically and yelping. Shyla ran over and hugged the little puppy, and he licked her face in return.

"I'll send someone for you when the duchess arrives," Grace told her, and made her way back to the pavilion.

When she returned she found her husband adding the final buffing to the axes. She straightened up the room, then sat down, and for the first time since the baron had made his wonderful gesture, thought about what gift she might get on their trip to town. Maybe a new hat or one of those parasols she had seen. She wasn't sure, but it would be fun to browse.

The morning with Loner went quickly for Shyla, and when the messenger came to give her news of the lady's arrival, she was surprised. She said her farewell and hurried to her room so as not to be late for their departure. When she finally arrived, she saw a note on her pillow apprising her that her mother and the duchess would be in the eating area for afternoon tea. She got ready quickly putting on her blue dress. It was her best one besides the new pink gown she was saving for the Woodcutter's Ball, and she admired it before she made haste to her informed destination.

When she entered, she was escorted to the table and introduced to Lady Cavillade. She curtsied, then bowed and said, "It's an honor to meet you Duchess."

The older woman was pleasantly surprised and nodded to Grace. She then turned to Shyla and said, "What a sweet and well-mannered young lady you are, and please, call me Charlotte." She looked the girl up and down and asked, "What is your name my dear?"

Shyla could hardly remember it; she was so awed by the presence and beauty of the duchess. "I'm Shyla," she said in her best, most sophisticated voice.

"So you are," replied Charlotte, and motioned for her to sit. She did so immediately, still marveling at the clothes and jewelry, and the regal way the duchess moved.

"I never knew your first name," remarked Grace, after they had finished with the formalities and the tea had been topped off. "It's very lovely."

The duchess nodded. "It was my grandmother's name, and her mother's," she said proudly.

Shyla couldn't stop staring at Charlotte, watching her every move and memorizing them for future reference. She was such a lady, but not the snobbish kind, and Shyla liked her instantly.

"Your mother tells me you're quite anxious to go into Woodvale and pick out your honorary gift," commented the duchess with a twinkle in her eye. "We ladies do love our gifts, don't we," she said matter-of-factly.

"I know I do," declared Shyla without reservation.

Charlotte smiled and focused on the young girl in front of her. "Well you won't have to wait long," she announced, much to Shyla's delight. "As soon as we finish here, I will have my driver bring the carriage around and we will be on our way." With those words Shyla quickly drank her tea and stuffed the piece of cake she had taken into her mouth, then sat there waiting patiently for the others to finish theirs. It wasn't ladylike she knew, but sometimes you had to forgo etiquette in a time of great importance.

It seemed like forever to her, but finally Charlotte and Grace were done and ready to continue the day. The duchess sent word for her carriage to be brought around, and the three made their way to the front entrance. Shyla was excited when she saw the magnificent coach, and thought it must have been driven straight out of a fairytale.

It was snow-white with gold filigree up and down the sides. The wheels had spokes, and were wrapped in gold colored vines with white roses circling the center. The front seat was chair-like where the driver sat so stately in his royal red uniform and white gloves. The back was raised and richly decorated, right down to the two red-velvet seats that faced each other.

She couldn't wait to ride in it, and was almost giddy with anticipation. Her excitement was cut short though when a messenger ran up and handed Grace a note. She read it and turned to her daughter. "It seems that some fighting has broken out in the lower camps and healers are needed to tend them."

Shyla felt her stomach drop and stood there stunned. She was only three steps from paradise, and it was being snatched from her by some brawling beasts. *From the best day to the worst in a flash,* she thought. *How could this happen to me?* She regretted her thoughts immediately and felt ashamed. Those people needed her help, and she would do everything she could for them.

Grace knew her little girl was distraught, but such was the selfless life of a healer, and it was best to learn that early.

The duchess could see and feel the inner conflict that Shyla faced, and felt bad for her. Although she didn't have children of her own yet, she couldn't help thinking that a child should be allowed to be a child, and asked, "Is it imperative that Shyla go with you for this healing?"

Grace was shocked at first that Charlotte would interfere, but quickly saw the wisdom in her words. She had just been saying how she wished her daughter didn't have to deal with the adult responsibilities that had been forced on her lately, and now she was adding to them. *The selfless lesson can wait until another day,* she thought, and answered, "No, you're right Charlotte. I can handle this myself. I'm sure it's just a few cuts and bruises."

Shyla's face lit up. "Are you sure Mother? Are you sure it's all right?"

Grace hugged her. "Of course it is," she replied. "I was stitching up wounds and mending broken bones long before you were born. I don't think one more day of it will make much difference."

Shyla was elated and almost started jumping up and down, but caught herself just in time to restore the ladylike manner she was trying to uphold. "Thank you again Mother. Thank you so much," she repeated, "but what about your gift?"

Grace smiled, "Oh I'll get mine another day," she said, "but right now I had better change and go see just how serious this situation really is." Then she bowed to the duchess and went back inside.

"It looks like it's just you and I," mused Charlotte, and motioned for Shyla to go first. She felt almost faint as she moved toward the carriage. Her anticipation grew with each step, and as she accepted a hand up from the driver and sat herself down on the red-velvet seat, she imagined herself a princess on a throne.

The carriage ride was smooth compared with her old wagon, and she felt special as they passed by the many camps in the lower quarter. The view from her seat seemed different some-how from that of their old wagon, and made her wonder what it would be like to be a duchess. Not that she could ever know, but today she felt like one.

The two girls chatted on the trip, but mostly Shyla watched the Lady Cavillade and mimicked her every move. She was so prim and proper, with such poise and elegance that Shyla was dazzled just watching her, and knew that one day she wanted to be just like her.

They were moving at a good pace, and it didn't take long to reach the turn that would take them into Woodvale. "I haven't been here since last year," remarked Shyla. "I don't come into town often."

Charlotte looked over. "I haven't been back since I saw your father and brother here earlier this spring, but I do a fair bit of business here," she said, and opened her parasol to block the overhead sun. Shyla took one from the holder and did the same.

People were camped on both sides of the road as they made their way along, and Shyla was getting a lot of looks. This made her feel like quite a lady, riding in the beautiful carriage with the parasol resting on her shoulder. Charlotte could see how much she was enjoying herself and it pleased her very much.

"When we reach the town," Charlotte told her, "I have a few meetings and appointments I must attend to. They are all rather stuffy, so my suggestion is that you spend your time shopping for that gift." She reached into her handbag and produced three silver pieces. "Take these, and when you find something you like, pay for it and tell the clerk that your driver will be around to pick it up."

My *driver*, she thought, and sighed as she accepted the coins. She nodded and placed them in her small bag.

"You are welcome to join me of course, but I'm afraid you would be bored to tears," the duchess added, as she informed the driver of her first destination.

"Thank you again," replied Shyla, "but I like your first suggestion. I *do* love to shop when I get the chance."

Charlotte gave her an understanding look, "As you wish."

The carriage stopped in front of a large building with a sign over the door that read, "Mercantile & Goldsmith". The driver helped them down and was instructed to wait until the duchess returned.

Lady Cavillade straightened her dress and fixed Shyla's. "Remember to take your time and pick out the perfect gift," she advised the young girl. "I'll meet you at the cookhouse when I'm through. It's right next to the Inn," she added, remembering the child's infrequent visits to Woodvale. "Oh, and be sure to get yourself something to eat if you start to get hungry," she told her. Then walked up the steps and disappeared inside.

Shyla watched her until she was gone, then copied her walk and movement as she strolled along the wooden sidewalk. She didn't want to make any rash decisions with so many choices in front of her, so she paused for a moment to think, then started forward again in search of the first shop she would visit.

The time went by quickly as she moved from building to building, trying their wares. She put on hats, gloves and dresses. She tried handbags, jewelry and hair combs, but new shoes were still at the top of her list. Finally she saw the sign she'd been looking for; "Finney's Fine Shoes". It was situated at the far end of the business area and on the opposite side of the road, so she crossed the dusty thoroughfare and started toward it.

The town was busy and Shyla hoped there was still a decent selection of shoes to choose from, but she would have to *get* there first. It was so congested that it seemed like she was being swept along in the wrong direction. "This just won't do," she told herself, so she held her head up and put on her most regal walk, which seemed to be working. The men tipped their hats and made way for her, and the women moved aside as she came. She giggled to herself, "Maybe they think I'm a princess," which caused her to strut even more. *What a great day this is turning out to be,* she thought, as she passed by the various shops on her way to Finney's.

The smell of broiled meat filled her nostrils, and she realized that she was walking by the cookhouse, which she took note of. The Inn was next and then only two more buildings before the shoe place, but as she got close to the tall structure she started to feel nauseous. She stopped, leaned against the wall and breathed deeply, trying to settle her stomach. This worked for a moment, but then another spasm hit her and she almost wretched. She covered her mouth and swallowed hard. The bile was bitter and acidic and she fought hard to keep from being sick. Finally it overwhelmed her and she moved into the alley, emptying the contents of her stomach onto the ground. This helped, but the sick feeling was still there.

Once she got herself settled she realized what it was and a chill ran through her. Somewhere nearby, that dark wrongness was festering. Her inner light tried to flare but she held it at bay. Lately she had become very good at ignoring that constant burning, but with the darkness near, it was trying hard to overtake her.

She gave herself to the white energy just long enough to take hold of it, then let it flow just under her skin while keeping a tight grasp. She had control now and knew it.

It felt so good to have it running through her again, and she decided to try something. She held her hand out and concentrated, just like she had done in her dream. Channeling the searing light down her arms, she watched as a small white ball began to flicker above her outstretched palm. Shyla increased the flow and the ball grew. The light beckoned for her to abandon herself, but she knew better now. Thanks to her unconscious vision, or whatever it was, she now had a better idea of how to manipulate the manifesting energy, but reluctantly pushed it back as it fought for domination. It wasn't gone from her, just boiling beneath the surface, and it felt good to have at least a little confidence in her ability to control it. Again she wondered if it truly was a dream or something else entirely, but there was no way of knowing without experimenting, and right now she felt she had to find the source of the wrong and deal with it.

The nausea had faded now, thanks to the light, and she was able to start moving again. Her senses told her the darkness was coming from somewhere in the building she was next to, so she walked over and entered the front door of the Inn.

The main entrance was dimly lit and smoke filled the room. To her right was an old man sitting behind a long desk, and straight ahead, in what looked to be a parlor, there were people playing dice and smoking their pipes and cigars. They didn't interest her though because the wrong she felt was emanating from the hallway that opened to her left.

Shyla started down the large opening, but was called back by a loud voice. "You can't go in there!" barked the old man behind the desk, his face in a frown and his accusing eyes squinting under long bushy eyebrows.

She turned and walked back toward the grumpy looking clerk. "I'm sorry," she said in her most sincere voice. "I was looking for my uncle," she added quickly, noticing that all the patrons were men.

"Well, you can look in the parlor, but that area is off-limits," he said, gesturing toward the large hallway. "At least until the Woodcutting Competition is over." This piqued Shyla's curiosity, but she wasn't about to ask any questions that might make him crankier. Obviously her winning smile and princess-like ways were not going to sway this old grouch, so now she had to figure out a way to sneak down that corridor without being seen.

She strolled over to the parlor and moved her head back and forth, pretending to look for her uncle. She returned and informed the old man that he wasn't about. "I'll just wait here," she suggested, motioning to one of the big armchairs that sat by the entrance. "He should be along at any time." Again she smiled her sweetest smile and sat down.

"All right," agreed the clerk begrudgingly, "but you had better stay out of mischief young lady!" He frowned at her a last time, then went back to writing in his ledger.

The sickly vibrations of the darkness were coming in waves now and she knew she was the only one who could sense it, or counter it, but she couldn't do anything if she couldn't get to it.

She sat back, watching the old man. She waited patiently for him to go check his customers, go to the outhouse, or even fall asleep, but he just kept writing and watching her out of the corner of his eye. *I should leave*, she thought. *This isn't any of my business anyway.*

She wanted to get up, but for some reason she couldn't bring herself to. Each time she had faced the wrong it had been trying to harm someone. She knew she was the only one who could help, and felt compelled somehow to do what she could to stop it.

Shyla thought long and hard, trying to figure a way past the wary old man, when suddenly an idea started to form in her mind. Would it work? She wasn't sure, but she had to try something. This plan involved using the light in a way she had never tried before. She closed her eyes and breathed deeply, concentrating on the inner power that lie there smoldering. Like a starving animal it heeded her call. It was wild and random, but she strained hard and bent it to her will until she felt confident enough to explore her idea.

She opened her eyes and they shone with the light, then slowly regained their color as she fought to maintain a balance. It was easier this time compared with the first encounter, which felt comforting, yet also frightening. Was she more in control now, or was the light engulfing more of her? She pushed the thought away and focused on the task before her.

With her eyes on the clerk, she moved her hand next to the desk where he couldn't see it. With her palm facing upward, she conjured a small ball of light that hovered there waiting. She scanned the room to make sure no one was watching, and then proceeded.

Relaxing her hold slightly, she became one with the tiny white globe. Just that slight release gave her an incredible feeling of power, almost overwhelming her, and for a moment she wondered how it would feel to completely give herself over. She snapped back quickly though, knowing instinctively how dangerous a thought like that could be, and took an even firmer hold on the brilliant sphere that floated there in front of her.

Slowly she willed it away from her body and it responded to her thoughts. She kept it about a foot off the floor, then moved it along the desk until it reached the corner. Holding her breath, she slowly sent it around and out of sight. Although she couldn't see it now, she sensed it and kept it moving until it was halfway across. It was all feel now as she raised it up and stopped it just under the counter's edge. She held it there and checked the room again to make sure no one noticed. No one appeared to, so she turned a part of her attention to the candle that sat on the far end of the desk. She concentrated on the flame and adjusted the white energy to match its visual intensity and shape. She then brought her light onto the desk, directly behind the candle. After observing the clerk and making sure he wasn't aware of her actions, she moved the white energy up the stick and even with the real flame.

Now came the hard part. Sweat beaded her brow as she wrapped her light around the candle's, extinguishing and replacing it at the same time. It wavered slightly as she struggled to regain its integrity. The old man pulled his nose from the large book and looked around. Shyla fought hard to keep her flame intact without appearing suspicious. She managed to hold her composure, even under the glare of the clerk, long enough for him to revisit his work.

That was close, she thought, as she got ready to execute the next part of her deception.

Her forehead glistened now and she blinked away the perspiration that ran onto her eyelashes. Slowly she increased the intensity of the light that flickered above the candle. The old man looked up again. She increased it more, until the light's glow filled the room. The clerk was standing now, watching the candle, not sure what to make of it. Shyla would only have one chance to do this, so she readied herself. She could feel her control slipping, so she increased the brightness even more.

"What kind of trick is this!" exclaimed the clerk as he stepped back, his eyes fixated on the light. With the last of her strength she raised her flame into the air. Now the old man's attention was completely captured by the strange occurrence that had him both curious, and scared.

Shyla made her move. She quickly ran for the hallway, and as she reached it, lost her hold on the light and it fizzled out. She pressed herself against the shadowed side and waited. The little diversion had kept the clerk's attention drawn, but had he noticed her absence? She listened, but heard nothing to make her think that he had. After awhile she was satisfied and began making her way along the wall.

"Excuse me," said the clerk. Shyla froze and started to turn around. "May I help you sir."

When she realized the words weren't directed at her, she let out a deep breath she hadn't realized she'd been holding, and continued on her way.

As she moved into the opening, the sense of wrong grew stronger, causing her internal conflict to increase. She held the white energy back, but kept it ready. She wasn't going to be caught off guard again, especially when she had the knowledge of the last encounter, no matter if it was real or not.

As she reached the end of the hall she could see a big set of double doors, so she stopped and concentrated. She didn't have to focus to sense the foul darkness on the other side. She reached for the handle, but stopped when she heard a voice coming from inside. She leaned closer and listened.

"What's wrong with him?" came a man's voice.

"I'm not sure," answered another man. Shyla thought she recognized one of the voices and put her ear to the door so she could hear better.

"This sickness is beyond me," said one man.

"Well that makes you about as useless as this giant."

Shyla recognized the voice now and knew that Claude Boyle belonged to that condescending tone. More conversation vibrated in the other room, so she listened carefully as she wondered about the giant.

"Well, I'm not going to stay here and be talked to that way," said the other man. "I've got others who need my services."

She heard Claude laugh. "And you call yourself a soother. I feel sorry for those others if *you're* treating them." Shyla heard *shuffling* and *clanging*. "And you, you overgrown useless idiot. If you aren't better by tomorrow, everything will be ruined."

She heard footsteps approaching, so she backed to the wall and waited. The doors opened suddenly, and were slammed shut again by Claude, as the two men exited the room. They were so busy arguing that they didn't notice the little girl huddled in the corner. Shyla waited until they were out of sight before she opened the doors and entered the room.

It looked like a large banquet hall, and was decorated extravagantly. There were paintings on the walls, a bright red carpet on the floor, and in the middle, a long wooden table surrounded by high-backed chairs. As she approached, there before her stretched out on the table, was the giant.

There was no doubt the wrong was within him and even from ten feet away it made her skin crawl and the light within her strive for freedom. Every ounce of common sense warned her to run away, but still she moved toward the hulking mass that lie there shuddering helplessly. It was obvious he was fighting the darkness, but it was too much even for him.

Shyla climbed onto the table, that was already creaking from the weight, and placed her hands over top of his huge feet. His boots were made of fur and the size she couldn't even guess. Slowly she moved her hands over his legs and up to his waist, probing with her mind, searching for the evil that had violated him. She could feel that the darkness was in his upper body somewhere, but wanted to make sure she isolated it. Her hand moved over his stomach and up to his massive chest, and even though he was lying flat, she had to get on her tiptoes to reach it. So far his body contained no hint of the wrong, but as she got closer to his head, she knew it was concentrated there entirely. A shiver ran through her as she moved her hands up and onto his cheeks. His head was still, but his face was strained and tight with the obvious torment he was being subjected to.

She closed her eyes and brought the white energy down her arms and into her hands. She could sense the foulness beneath his rough skin and a feeling of terror tried to overtake her, but she fought it back and continued.

Gently she released the light into the giant and quickly found exactly where the wrong was located. It was stronger this time, and she could feel a trace of the red lightning along its surface. Memories stirred in her and she got angry. She moved the light right up to it and held it there in defiance. It *was* stronger, but only a small amount, so she blanketed it with the sizzling power that was now at an intoxicating level. The foulness, now aware of her presence, dug in deeper. Shyla could feel that it was attached to the giant's brain, so she circled it and ever so gently, began to pull. The giant stiffened and his face twisted into a grimace. Quickly, without letting go, she eased her hold. She knew she could extract the darkness and crush it, but without a doubt, that action would kill him. "Think fast Shyla," she told herself, "or he's a goner either way." She made her voice softer now, and promised him everything was going to be all right, but wasn't sure who she was trying to convince.

Why was the wrong trying to finish him now? What did it want? In an instant, like a load of bricks, it hit her. *Of course*, she thought, *it wants me. It has always wanted me.* With that understanding, she released her hold and drew back the light. When she did, the giant's face relaxed noticeably, so she brought the energy back into herself. She waited to see if that would help, but the foulness just took a deeper hold and the giant lurched in agony, his face stretched into a silent scream.

Shyla had to move quickly now if she was going to save him. She knew what the darkness wanted, so she pushed the light deep inside, leaving herself open to the onslaught that she knew would be coming.

Everything happened in an instant. The wrong left the giant and came at her. Just before it entered, she wove the light shield around herself, then around the dark cloud of pure evil. In that same moment she brought forth every ounce of pure energy she had and burned her captive until there was nothing left but cinders. Then something happened that she wasn't prepared for. When all that pain and torment left the giant so suddenly, he lashed out, involuntarily striking Shyla on her left side with his stone-like fist. Sparks exploded with the force and she flew through the air. She hit the wall hard and fell to the floor, unconscious.

The giant opened his eyes and sat up slowly. He was dizzy and his head felt like someone had dropped a boulder on it. He wasn't really sure where he was, or what had happened, but when he saw the little girl lying on the floor, memories started coming back to him.

He could hear the sweet voice telling him to hold on; the warm hands on his face and the release of the torture in his mind. That child had helped him and he had caused her harm. He felt helpless and sick. He tried to think through the pounding in his head, but his only thoughts were that of self-loathing. *Maybe I am a monster like so many have called me before,* he thought. *What other type of creature would hurt a little girl? I never meant her harm. I would never–.* But you did, his own thoughts answered, and the words of his family filled his aching head.

Your fascination with the small-folk will cause you nothing but anguish and hardship. You should keep to your own kind like we have done for so many generations.

He hadn't heeded those wise words, but right now he wished he had.

He stood up, walked over and knelt beside the motionless body. *Have I killed her?* he wondered, terrified to find out, but as he leaned in he could see her chest rising and falling ever so slightly. The giant sighed a deep rumbling sigh, and then took her in his arms like a newborn baby and walked toward the large double doors.

CHAPTER
16

A Giant Misunderstanding

Grace had her hands full when she reached the camp where the injured had been taken. It wasn't that the wounds were so severe, but that there were so many. She was informed that an argument had started as to whether the giant would have beaten the woodcutter if he had remained in the competition. The argument had then turned physical and increased in numbers until three entire camps were involved. They said it would have kept going if the baron's guard hadn't been called in to regulate the mess. When the dust had settled, over fifty men and a few women had been banged up in one way or another.

She tended the severe cases first, bringing some of the local women in to help clean the wounds, then she administered her remedies and addressed the minor cases in turn. Grace worked through the afternoon without stopping, all the while shaking her head and wondering how men could be so stupid sometimes.

She was sure it was the usual mix of ale and pride, topped off with too much food and not enough energy expended. Although she knew that most of the men were aware of who she was, not one of them mentioned their competition preference to her.

The afternoon was closing fast as she finished with the last of her duties. The air started to cool as the sun got closer to the trees, and Grace realized how exhausted and hungry she had become. She had been offered food by many, but right now she just wanted to have a peaceful meal with her family.

She finished the final dressing and asked the women to contact her if there were any signs of infection. Although she had inspected each one, you could never tell for sure how some people would react to treatment. When she was sure that everything was looked after and her job was finished, she packed up what was left of her supplies and placed her bag in the carriage.

So many had tried to pay her for her services, but she refused them all. She told them the only payment she asked was that they all try to get along for the rest of the competition.

She surveyed her handiwork one more time, then climbed into the carriage, sat down and took a deep breath. *What a day,* she thought, and asked the driver to take her back to the pavilion. She felt bad for him having to sit there all afternoon, but she thought she had noticed him napping earlier, so her concerns were eased somewhat.

The carriage started moving toward the upper tier. It felt good to rest her feet and mind after such a long healing. She leaned back, closed her eyes and wondered what the kitchen would be serving this evening. As she started to drift off, she was brought back by the sound of hoof beats coming up fast. *Not another crazy rider,* she thought, and opened her eyes. She couldn't see who it was from inside, but knew the voice instantly.

"Grace!" yelled Ivan in a panic.

Her heart stopped and she jumped from the moving carriage. "Who is it!" she cried, knowing it was something bad with one of her children.

Ivan dismounted and grabbed her. "It's Shyla," he said, trying to keep his voice steady. "The giant has taken her." Grace fell to her knees and her imagination tried to take over, but she stopped it and clenched her jaws. *Calm down,* she told herself, *there has to be an explanation for this.*

Ivan picked her up and held her in his arms. Once she had pushed away the panic, she asked, "Why would he do such a thing?"

Ivan looked at her, and she had never seen his eyes so wild. "I don't know," he said coldly, "but when I find him, he's going to answer to me. If he's harmed our daughter, I don't know what I'll do."

Grace felt scared and helpless. "Doesn't anyone know where he's taken her?" she asked frantically, trying to make sense of it.

"No," he answered, lifting her onto the front seat of the carriage. He jumped on, grabbed the reins from the driver and snapped them over the horse's back, causing the animal to break into a gallop along the narrow trail leading to the baron's.

"Who saw him take her?" asked Grace, trying to get some answers to all the questions that ran through her mind.

"Half the town of Woodvale saw him carry her from the Inn and head east, but no one tried to stop him . . . cowards!" he finished off, almost spitting the word. He snapped the reins harder now, urging the horse up the incline and on to the pavilion.

"We have to find her Ivan," urged Grace, and he could hear the pain in her voice.

"Don't worry my love," he assured her, "I won't rest until out little girl is safe in my arms. Even as we speak, Vero has his best men out gathering information and trying to pick up the trail."

When they reached the pavilion, he pulled the carriage to a halt and jumped off. He helped Grace down and asked the driver to look after the lathered and winded horse. He and his wife hurried inside, hoping to hear some positive word on Shyla.

When they reached the banquet chamber they could see the baron and the duchess sitting at the large table. As soon as they were seated, the Lady Cavillade spoke up. "I'm so sorry Grace," she apologized. "I should have taken her with me to the meetings instead of letting her shop alone but she had her heart set on it. Can you forgive me?"

Grace reached out and put her hand on Charlotte's shoulder. "It's not your fault," she said sincerely. "Let's keep our focus on the giant. He's the villain here, and we need to find out where he's taken her."

Ivan looked at Vero with a worried expression. "Have you received any news from your men?" he asked, trying to will the proper response.

The baron could see despair in his friend's eyes, but could not help him. "I'm afraid I have nothing for you, but Cade is out with my scouts now and I expect word back at any moment," he replied, trying to ease the tension-filled room.

Unfortunately the tension only increased as they waited. Grace sat with her hands clasped in front of her and was rocking back and forth while Ivan paced the floor. No one spoke again until one of Vero's men came in from the side entrance. Ivan sat back down and waited patiently for the two men to finish the discussion, that he couldn't quite make out. Finally the man exited and the baron spoke. He looked concerned, and chose his words carefully.

"I am told," he began, "that during the giant's stay in our land, he spent most of his time in a cave east of here. My scouts have scoured the countryside and found tracks and signs that would indicate that he has taken the child there." He paused for a moment to let this new information sink in, then continued. "I have ordered my men to assemble, and they will await us at the edge of the competition quarter where the trail is fresh."

There was silence in the room once more as each person tried to grasp the situation without panicking. Vero looked at Ivan and added, "I've arranged for my two best horses to be saddled and brought to the front entrance as we speak."

Grace shot the baron a glance. "You had better make that three horses," she said with conviction in her voice. "I *will* be joining you."

The baron was slightly taken aback and said, "I'm sorry Grace. I assumed you ladies would remain here while we retrieve your daughter."

Grace stood up and faced the baron. "Whether I'm a lady or not," she said in a clear tone, "as a young girl I rode the great wolves of the plains, and on horseback, traversed mountain trails that would make a goat shudder. So a little jaunt into the hills to rescue my baby seems only natural to me, and *will* be taking place!"

It was the baron's turn to stand now, and he replied. "You my dear, are a lady no doubt, and if I did or said anything to offend you then you have my deepest apologies. Of course I would be honored to ride with you and will send for another mount forthwith." The baron bowed, then rang the bell loudly.

"While I, on the other hand," said the duchess, "will remain here and await your successful return."

Grace thanked Vero and left for her room to properly dress for the ride. Ivan followed her, his head still spinning from the good and bad tidings. The baron waited for the servant to arrive and instructed him to have a third horse saddled, then he and the duchess retired to his chambers where he readied himself for the hunt.

Shyla's head was buzzing as she tried to open her eyes. Her shoulder and side ached, and she was completely drained from so much use of the white energy. She could feel every muscle in her body, and most of them were sore. She finally blinked her eyes open and took a look around. When she saw the rock walls and floor, fear tried to overtake her, but she quickly realized it wasn't the place of her nightmare. As her vision adjusted to the dim light, she could see that she was lying on some type of animal fur that covered a stone bench about four feet off the floor. She tried to sit up, but winced in pain and cried out as she fell back onto the soft bedding. She laid there waiting for some relief, but with each breath the severity increased like a dagger twisting into her. Finally it was too much, and she lost consciousness once more.

When she started to become aware again, she felt warm, and the pain had subsided to a tolerable throbbing. She opened her eyes and realized where the warmth originated. Someone had covered her with a fur blanket and started a fire. She didn't try sitting this time, and just laid there wondering where she was and who was looking out for her. Her second question was answered quickly when a huge being entered the room carrying a pot with steaming contents. Shyla saw the giant moving toward her, but for some reason, wasn't frightened. Maybe it was because she had been so close to him during the encounter with the darkness, or because he had given her a blanket, but somehow she instinctively knew he meant her no harm.

"You awake now little one?" he rumbled, in a voice lower than anything she had ever heard before. As he approached she saw his face for the first time without the stress and strain upon it.

He was almost handsome, in a rugged way. His jaw was wide and his nose prominent. His cheek bones were high and he had pale blue eyes that were set beneath a heavy brow. His head, compared with a normal man, was huge, but it matched his body proportionately, and was topped with thick black tufts of wiry looking hair. The giant's skin was pale and appeared almost stone like in texture, but she remembered its warmth, and knew there was flesh and bone beneath.

As he got closer, he knelt and set the pot down. "You feel better now?" he asked in his deep tone.

She stared at the extraordinary man before her and answered, "I believe so, and please, call me Shyla."

"So pretty," he said as he reached down. Shyla wondered if he meant her or her name, and decided it must be both and thanked him. "You drink please," he said, handing her a bowl of hot liquid. She was careful when she sat up this time, using her left arm to assist her. There was still much pain, but she managed to get herself upright and accept the giant's offer.

The broth was thick and reminded her of one of her mother's healing recipes. "What is this?" she asked between drinks.

"Family recipe for hurt . . . uh, I don't speak very good your words. I sorry," he stumbled through the sentence.

He was so cute it made her giggle, which in turn caused more pain, so she tried hard to contain it. "That's quite all right Jack, I understand you just fine," she said, trying to comfort him.

The giant looked at her and frowned. "Name not Jack. Name is Mok. Boss man call me Jack for competition of woodcutting," he corrected her in a voice that sounded like a rockslide.

Shyla was grinning as she finished the last of the contents in the bowl. "Mok it is," she corrected herself, and handed it back to him. "I thank you for your help, but where are we?" It was Mok's turn to grin now, and he did so without reservation.

Shyla continued to study him, and was surprised at how big, white and perfect his teeth were, but then again, she knew nothing of giants.

He sat on the floor and stretched out his arms. "Welcome Mok's place. I bring help you." he said, shaking his head enthusiastically. "You save Mok. . . . Mok hurt you. . . . Mok help you," he added, grinning once again.

She couldn't help liking the giant, but needed to know where she was. How long had she been out? Did anyone know she was gone? These were just a few of the questions she had, but at least she was feeling better after drinking the giant's recipe.

"You strong for small-folk," he interrupted her thoughts. "My hit crush men, but you only bruised."

Shyla hadn't thought about the cause of her injury until he mentioned it, and now it all came back in a flood of memories. The darkness coming for her, and the shield of light she extended around herself. The same shield that saved her from the giant's blow. She learned more about the white energy with each summoning, but if she never had to use it again, she would be very happy. Every moment that she held it was so tempting and intoxicating that it became harder and harder to let it go, and that scared her. She didn't know what would happen if she embraced it fully, and wondered if the hit from the giant had been the only thing that had brought her back again. There were so many questions with no way to know the answers.

She decided against telling Mok about her ability even though she knew he must suspect something, but as they continued talking he never mentioned it.

"What ingredients were in the liquid you gave me?" asked Shyla. "I can already feel it working."

The giant looked pleased. "It family mixture for hurt but watered down for small one," he answered. "Maybe no should for strong girl." He laughed when he said it, and the rocks vibrated with him.

"Thank you so much for your help," she told him in a kind voice. "I am feeling much better already." He nodded and then gestured to the bowl to see if she wanted more. "No thank you," she replied. "I think I've had enough."

She was amazed at how she felt now compared with before she had drank the remedy, and made a mental note to ask the giant for a sample to take to her mother. This thought brought her back to her earlier concern, and she continued. "Not to seem ungrateful or anything, but I should probably return to the pavilion as soon as possible."

The giant could hear the urgency in her voice and answered, "Yes, you ready travel by sunset. I take then. You back before late." She could see the sincerity and honesty in his eyes and her worries and fears melted away, leaving her feeling safe once more.

Before she asked any more questions, she made herself more comfortable, and was still in disbelief at how much better she was feeling. "So where exactly are we?" she asked, as she leaned back against the soft fur bundle she had rolled up.

"Mok's cave," he answered in a proud voice. "It few miles east woodcutting place."

She cocked an eyebrow. "Why did you bring me here?"

Mok looked confused. "This where healing powder. You need healing. Mok bring you." Suddenly he looked sad. "People yell. Call names. Need help little one. She help Mok."

Shyla smiled and nodded, trying to cheer him up, and it was working. As soon as he saw her smile, his smile returned. "You did good Mok," she said reassuringly, "I'm grateful you brought me." His smile increased until it beamed, and she was sure she had never seen one quite like it.

The giant left, then returned with some wood, and soon had the fire roaring once again. Shyla wasn't sure why, with the air already warm, but it did feel good.

Mok must have read her mind because not a moment later, he said, "The heat help healing. I don't need, but you body do."

That statement made Shyla curious, and she asked in her straightforward manner, "Where are you from?"

The giant didn't answer right away and sat there looking as if his mind were far away. Finally it returned and he replied, "I in far north land from mountains beyond mountains where snow never leave."

Suddenly she felt a chill and snuggled a little deeper into the fur. "They have woodcutting in the mountains?" she asked, wondering how he had learned it, or if he really knew how.

"I born Arcana," he began, "past northern borders you kingdom. There Frosty Pines and Highland Tamarack grow. As small boy I woodcut with family, then I older I hire with northern logging camp. My family don't like, but I love woodcutting. They don't cut enough for Mok." He paused for a moment to clear his throat, and Shyla thought it sounded like a small avalanche. "I work for loggers," he continued. "All day . . . no rest . . . many seasons. They like Mok. One day men talk Woodcutting Competition and legend who dominate. I ask hear more stories. They tell Ivan and woodcutting feats unequal by man, and more story this greatest woodcutter in land."

Shyla's eyes widened at the last part as she realized that he had no idea who she was and wasn't sure how or if she should tell him. She thought for a moment and decided she would, but didn't want to interrupt his story. She loved listening to his deep rumbling voice, with its warmth and timbre that soothed and drew her in like magic. Then to her delight, he started again right where he had left off.

"After years, every victory I hear, so practice all events to one day challenge hero. I walk down from Arcana and Land of Gales, through Miner's Pass in Bitter Mountains, to you land where find cave. Then go town. Many scared. Boss man help get into contest, after show what can do with axe."

Shyla frowned. "More like helped himself," she said under her breath.

The giant looked over. "You speak little one?"

Shyla smiled again, "No, please continue," she said, very interested now in hearing how the darkness took him.

"Boss man pay fee then get new clothes made. Then new gear and nice room at Inn. He good Mok, until Mok sick. Then very angry."

Shyla sat up straight, surprised at how little pain she felt, and asked, "Mok, how did the sickness take hold of you?"

The giant sat there deep in thought, then answered slowly. "I lie big table, fancy room. Very late I see shadow move. I sit up, see what make, then it move onto table. I reach out and go onto hand, then gone. Soon Mok feel pain. Head hurt, and fight it. Boss man yell Mok. Soon go black. Wake up, see you on floor."

He looked sad when he spoke those words, so Shyla decided to try to cheer him again. "You know Ivan the legendary woodsman," she prompted, and Mok's face lit up.

"Yes," he said with excitement in his voice. "One day be like him."

She could see he was cheering up already, but still wondered if she should tell him. "Well," she continued, "he is my father."

Mok stared at her and his mouth opened, but no sound came out. His hands began to tremble and his eyes welled with tears. Shyla was really wondering now if she should have told him, but it was too late. They sat staring at each other, and before either one could speak, their attention was drawn to the cave entrance where the sound of horses' hooves on rocks filled the air.

Ivan, Grace and Cade, along with the baron and the rest of his men, reached the scheduled meeting place just before the sun started to set. The plan was simple. Follow the giant's trail to his cave and rescue the girl, hopefully without incident. Ivan was eager to get moving, but understood that some organization and preparation was needed, so he helped as much as possible with the horses and equipment.

Grace too was impatient, but waited silently while she checked her healing bag for items she hoped she wouldn't need.

Cade was busy working up front with the scouts and had his longbow strung, just in case it was needed. He was angry about what had happened and was ready to track the giant right through the *Whispering Forest* if necessary.

Finally, after what seemed like forever, the hunting party was ready to ride, so Grace mounted her horse and fell in line behind the baron. As she pulled up, she glanced to the side and saw Claude Boyle riding in on his black stallion. She turned to Vero and asked, "What is he doing here?" The baron shrugged and turned his horse to engage the newcomer, but Ivan cut him off and rode straight up to his rival.

"What brings you out tonight Claude?" Ivan asked with disdain.

"Well," answered Claude nervously, "we all want to see your daughter returned safely, and I do need to get my giant back to the Inn and rested for tomorrow's activities."

Ivan frowned and shook his head. "Do you care about anybody but yourself?" he asked, in an almost threatening manner.

"Now Ivan," replied Claude with a hint of fear in his voice, "that's no way to talk to your neighbor." He put on a phony smile, reached into his jacket pocket and pulled out a silver cigar case. He opened it and gestured for the woodcutter to take one.

It was made of pure silver and polished so brilliantly that he could see himself in it. He could discern intricate engravings along the edges, and knew it was worth more than he made in half a season.

Now Ivan wasn't one to begrudge a man his fortune or wealth, but he knew exactly what Claude was doing, and it was getting to him. It took all of his strength not to let him know, and he declined the offer as graciously as he knew how.

The woodcutter pulled on the reins and started to move off, but stopped suddenly and turned toward Claude once again. "What sort of activities is the giant up to tomorrow?" he asked. "He *has* withdrawn from the competition, has he not?"

Claude smiled his wicked smile and replied, "No, that was just a rumor. I mean Jack *did* have a bit of a fever, but you know how people exaggerate."

Ivan switched his gaze from his neighbor to the baron, causing Vero to chime in. "It is true that the giant did not officially withdraw, and therefore may compete tomorrow, *if* he is able."

Claude smiled again and bowed slightly to the baron. "If you want I can send for my dog," offered Claude graciously. "He *is* the best tracker in the land."

"That won't be necessary," answered Vero. "The trail is quite clear."

Ivan reined his horse around, and as he passed his old friend he whispered, "Can we go?"

Vero stood in his stirrups and yelled, "Mount up!" so the hunting party made their way along the trail they hoped would lead them to the giant's cave and the little girl he had taken there.

Cade hung back, following the lead scout as they climbed the gradual incline. As night fell, and torches were lit, the trail swung southeast and the ground became steeper and rockier. Heading this direction, they would reach the Horseshoe Creek and the *Whispering Forest* within a few miles, so Cade knew the cave must be close now.

He had been so worried about his sister that he had forgotten to mention his earlier encounter with the *Gatou,* but it was probably of no interest to anyone but him anyway. Still, all-in-all it was a very unusual day thus far.

When he had finished his practice and decided to check out the business quarter, word had spread about Shyla's abduction. The following events had brought him here, riding at dusk along a clearly marked trail, to a cave to rescue her from a giant. This sounded like something out of one of those story books she loved so much, and when she was safely home again they would no doubt laugh about it. *Oh Mother, please let her be all right,* he pleaded silently, urging his horse closer to the front.

The tracks turned east again, and the terrain became more rugged as they made their way steadily upward. The horses were starting to tire now, and you could see their laboring breath in the cool night air. Even with the beginning of summer the evenings still had a bite left in them, and this one was colder than normal.

Cade's horse stumbled, jarring him from his thoughts, and as he looked up he noticed a light in the distance. "That must be the cave," he said to the scout leader, who began barking orders to the men.

The hunting party circled and approached from the north side, stopping about two hundred yards back to plan the rescue. Once the main course of action was agreed upon, Ivan took charge immediately.

"When we reach the cave I'll call the giant out, and I want each of you to keep your weapons trained on him," he instructed the men. "Don't make a move without my order. I would like this night to end without bloodshed if possible, but if my daughter is in danger, then I will do what has to be done." His words were hard and direct, and no one questioned them.

The woodcutter led the scouts up the final slope and only a few yards from the mouth of the cave. He yelled into the opening and his voice cut the air like a knife. "I know you're in there Jack, and I know you have my daughter." He hesitated for only a moment to let the echo die and then continued. "Now bring her out, and she had better be unharmed or you will not live to see the dawn." His words echoed along the rocks, but no sound came from the cave. "Be ready men!" Ivan called out, and squeezed the handle of his freshly sharpened hatchet.

Everyone held their breath waiting for something to happen, but still there was no sound or movement. It seemed like a half-night before they finally heard shuffling from inside and then a shadowy figure emerged from the entrance. It was the giant, but he had no one with him.

"Where is my daughter!" yelled Ivan, raising his blade. The men all followed his lead, raising axes, bows and spears.

The giant looked devastated and answered slowly. "She inside resting from hurt," he replied, glancing from one person to another.

Ivan could feel his stomach tighten, and shouted, "Did you hurt my daughter!"

Mok looked down at his hero and replied, "I . . . I hit her, but not mean to."

Ivan wanted to throw his axe. He wanted to slice the air between the giant and himself, but something in the big man's eyes stopped him. There was a sincerity and regret in his voice that stayed his hand.

The men were eager now, almost frantic waiting for Ivan's signal, and he could almost feel the tension of the bowstrings. Cade though, watching his father, lowered his bow at the same time Ivan lowered his hatchet.

Then it happened. One of the hunters loosed an arrow and it flew past the giant's left side and glanced off the rocks. Ivan could see this ending badly, but before he could do anything, he heard Shyla scream, "Stop!" as she ran in front of the giant with her arms raised. She could barely feel the pain as the light within her began to roil and shimmer, and her only thoughts were of saving her new friend.

The energy raced through her veins and along her skin, pushing ever outward until it pulsed at her fingertips, waiting for release. Shyla basked in the glorious power that was hers to wield, and embraced it fully as it grew stronger and brighter.

Grace saw her daughter run from the cave. She saw her skin start to glow silvery white. She saw the sparks dancing above her fingers and the wind blowing through her wavy black hair. Her heart sank and she hesitated only a moment, realizing the air was calm this night, then she ran toward her little girl.

Shyla felt magnificent as she got ready to punish the people who had threatened her friend, but something wasn't right. She was losing control of the light and her will was being cast aside and replaced by the white energy. She could feel her essence being pushed into some small corner of her mind, and fear gripped what was left of her. She tried to grasp the light like she had done earlier, but it was too strong now and she was still weak from her fight with the darkness.

It was too much for her, and she was about to surrender herself completely, when she felt another force which she recognized right away. It was her mother's binding spell. She could feel it envelop her, attempting to force the light back into her. She knew her mother could only hold the spell in that capacity for a short while, but it was enough for her to regain her hold. Together they pushed the white light back into the small place where it burned continuously, tempting her every waking moment.

As the energy imploded, a blast of air was released, knocking Mother and Daughter down, but they didn't hit the stone. Two large hands caught them and helped them to their feet.

"You all right little one?" asked Mok, kneeling down so his eyes were level with hers.

"I'm fine," she said, still out of breath. "What about you?"

Mok was noticeably relieved to see that she was unharmed after what he had just witnessed, and answered, "Don't worry about Mok. He good," then grinned at her. Shyla threw her arms around his huge neck and hugged him tightly. Mok put his hand on her back and patted it gently.

The baron yelled, "Stand down Men!" as he analyzed the situation, then rode up and dismounted. Ivan had already covered the distance and was making sure his girls were all right, while Cade, bow still ready, was watching the giant warily.

After the emotional reunion, Shyla turned to her father and said, "Please don't let anyone harm him. He was only trying to help me."

Ivan put his hand on his daughter's cheek and said, "I never meant for any harm to come to anyone. I just wanted my little girl home safe."

Shyla looked up at her father, then at the giant and said, "Daddy, this is Mok, and Mok, this is my dad, Ivan."

The woodcutter extended his hand and once again the giant's engulfed it. "We meet again," said Ivan, "and again the circumstances are not the best, but if you helped my daughter, then I am indebted to you."

The two men finished shaking hands and the giant spoke. "You daughter save Mok, and Mok indebted to little one."

"No," came a voice from the group, "*you* are indebted to me." Ivan knew that sound, and was never happy to hear it. Claude Boyle rode up and motioned to the giant. "Come on Jack. Let's get a move on. We need to get you back to the Inn and rested for tomorrow's competition."

The giant ignored him and spoke directly to Ivan. "If don't want Mok in competition, Mok withdraw."

Claude interrupted again, "Oh no you don't, unless you want to spend the rest of your days in a dark coal mine."

It was Ivan's turn to ignore him now, and he answered, "I would be honored to compete against you Mok, and I want you to give me your best."

Claude was speechless for a moment, then added, "Yes and that unfortunately will be too much for you. Now come on Jack, move it!"

Mok just stood there facing the woodcutter and said, "I honored again," then turned and followed Claude down the hill toward Woodvale.

Ivan cradled Shyla in his arms and sat her on his horse. He got on behind and held her as they rode down the hill on their way to the pavilion. The baron's men scouted ahead, but Cade stayed back to be with his sister. He hadn't realized how much he cared for her until she had been taken, and when he wasn't sure if he would see her again.

"I don't like how Claude talks to Mok," said Shyla out of the blue.

"I don't like how he talks to anyone," said Grace, reaffirming her daughter's statement.

The woodcutter held his daughter closer. "Once I win the tournament," he said with confidence, "we won't have to worry about Claude and his questionable ways any longer."

The breeze had a chill, so Shyla snuggled in closer to Ivan, and the family remained silent until they reached the pavilion.

CHAPTER

17

Disquieting Discoveries

fter the horses were led away, the baron, who had
instructed the kitchen workers to wait for their return,
invited the Harden family to a late supper in the large
banquet room.

Vero and the Lady Cavillade were already seated when the
four arrived. Charlotte was so relieved to see Shyla that she burst
into tears and hugged her repeatedly, apologizing all the while.
Shyla assured her it was no fault of hers, but the duchess felt
responsible nonetheless.

The mood was light and joyous as the baron and his guests
started the meal. Grace, who realized she hadn't eaten since
noon, was enjoying every mouthful, and Shyla, whose appetite
was returning quickly, was attempting to finish every dish that
was placed in front of her.

Once they had settled in, and the wine had been served, the
baron held up his glass and said, "To good friends," which
prompted everyone to raise their glasses and repeat his words.
Cade and Shyla were drinking fruit juice, but held up their
glasses just the same, very happy to be included in the adult
rituals.

Everyone had eaten their fill and were deciding whether or
not they had room for desert, when the baron turned to Cade

and said, "I heard through my sources today that you ruffled some *Gatou* feathers this morning on the archery course." Cade looked sheepish, then nodded, wondering if he was in some sort of trouble. "Oh don't worry," he reassured the boy, "I'm not upset, but it may not have been a good idea to show your talent so early in the game." The baron's face became serious now, and he continued. "I'm told that, as we speak, the legendary *Gatou* bowman, *Onak*, is on his way here and will represent his people in the Archery Tournament tomorrow."

Cade looked at the floor and tightened his jaw. He had done it again. In every single situation where he let his emotions get the better of him, it always ended badly. If he had just walked away from their taunts he could have beaten them tomorrow and had the silvers for his family, but now he had no idea what would happen. He almost asked the baron how *Onak* could enter the contest after the entry deadline, but thought better of it considering *his* somewhat controversial addition. That question was still in his mind when Vero unknowingly answered it.

"Each year *Onak* enters the archery, but never attends. Instead he sends a couple of young boys, who of course always win. He feels that this creates a mystique, and solidifies the *Gatou's* reputation, not to mention his legend status." The baron shook his head and then looked at Cade. "You must have done some extraordinary shooting for them to send for their greatest bowman, and for him to be riding here now."

Cade's face turned red and he looked at the floor again. "Well," said Ivan, "this season could turn out to be the biggest challenge yet for the Harden family."

The baron raised his glass again, "To the Hardens!" he said in a loud voice.

As Grace lifted hers she added, "May we always stay safe and together."

Dessert arrived, and was served. It looked wonderful and tasted even better. When the group had finished, their attention was drawn to the little girl who was sitting there wondering why everyone was looking at her.

Finally the duchess spoke. "You've had quite an adventure today Shyla," she stated, giving her a warm smile. "I'm sure we would all like to hear what exactly happened with you and the giant."

Shyla cleared her throat and began her story. She told them about the giant's sickness and how she cured him, leaving out the details that weren't necessary, or that she didn't want everyone to know. She continued until she had filled in everything up to when she had ran from the cave.

The room was silent when she finished, as each person realized what an emotional and trying day she had gone through. Cade reached over and squeezed her arm, and Grace gave her a knowing look.

"So what you're saying," began Ivan in a stern voice, "is that *you* healed my competition."

Shyla's eyes got big and her mouth opened. "I . . . um, well." She tried to defend herself, but no real words would come.

Ivan's face softened and soon he was smiling. "I'm only teasing, my girl," he offered, in a loving voice. "What you did was a selfless and honorable act, and I couldn't be more proud to have you for a daughter."

Vero stood and started to clap. This caught on quickly, and soon everyone was applauding her, and of course she got up and bowed, then curtsied, then bowed again.

"Vero, my old friend," said Ivan, who was still standing, "I thank you for your help in bringing my daughter back, and for another fine meal, but tomorrow is a busy day and I must bid you goodnight."

The baron nodded, and replied, "As you wish, and you are welcome always. Have a peaceful evening and good luck on the morrow."

The rest of the group stood and Grace said, "Yes, I think we all need some sleep. It's been a very eventful and exhausting day." She thanked her host, said goodnight to Charlotte and went with her family to their chambers.

As they walked along, Grace looked at Shyla suspiciously and raised an eyebrow. "You will have to fill in the parts of the story you left out, when you get a chance," she said, still eyeing her.

"Of course Mother," she answered in a direct manner. "I just don't want people to know about me."

Grace felt sad to hear her daughter speak those words, but couldn't deny reality, and the fewer people who knew, the better. Already too many had witnessed too much, so discretion and secrecy were of the utmost importance.

Just before they reached their hallway, Cade turned to his father and said, "Dad, something has been bothering me all night and I was hoping you could help me understand it."

Ivan looked concerned and replied, "I will if I can Son."

Cade thought for a moment. "Well," he started, "not that I wanted it to happen, especially after the way things turned out, but honestly, how in the name of the Mother, do you miss a giant from fifty feet away?"

Shyla's face scrunched up and her mouth opened, but Cade winked at her and smiled, and the whole family had a good laugh before retiring to their adjoining rooms.

Surprisingly, they all fell asleep almost instantly, even with the excitement of this day and the next in the forefront of their thoughts. All except Shyla. She laid there trying to relax, but it did no good. It had been an exhausting experience and sleep should have come easy, yet the events of the day kept flooding in, and she was worried about Mok. She was certain she had purged all the darkness from him, but what if it returned. Her imagination was trying to run away, so she caught it and reeled it in. She would see him tomorrow and make sure he was well.

Finally sleep started to overcome her and her eyes closed. As she began to drift off, she could sense that something wasn't right. She knew her body well, and it did not feel proper. Slowly she started to probe her inner self, starting at the feet and moving upward. When she had finished, she was amazed. There was no sign of any injury. The bruising on her side and shoulder was completely healed, and that was impossible. A wound like that would take days to mend, even with a skilled healer working on it. *Had the giant's elixir been that potent?* she wondered. She wanted to believe it, but something was tugging at the edge of her mind and she couldn't ignore it.

Shyla scanned herself again, and now she saw it plainly. Fear gripped her and she felt sick as she realized that the light she had once held in her core was now imbued throughout her body. Instead of that tiny ball burning at her center, there were thousands of smaller points of light firmly attached, from her head to her toes.

She still held it at bay, like before, but the feeling was completely different now, and it frightened her. *Was this one of the steps to a Sol'mar's burn out?* she asked herself. *Am I that much closer?* She hadn't discussed it with her mother, but remembered Zarina's words, and she was no fool.

Tears filled her eyes and trickled down her face. She wasn't going to give up without a fight, and was determined to break the pattern of the many *Sol'mar* before her. She knew now that the light had healed her when she almost lost herself to it, and that made her see just how little she actually understood it.

She checked her side and shoulder once again and found the same result. It was as if she had never been hurt, but there was more.

When she was a little girl she had taken her father's axe, and was playing woodcutter, when it glanced off the log and cut her leg. It had taught her a good lesson, and left a deep scar on her thigh. Either her mind was playing tricks on her now, or that scar was gone. She pulled back the blanket, and sure enough, there was no trace of it. A shiver ran through her body and it wasn't from the night air. Suddenly she realized she knew nothing about the light, and was a silly little girl playing with fire.

She pulled the blankets tight around her and curled into a ball. Her thoughts went to her grandmother Zarina, and wished she could see her. Her mother was probably the best healer in the kingdom, but Zarina knew a great deal more about the old ways and had access to knowledge that was forbidden to most. *When I go to train with her this summer it should be quite different,* she thought, *and maybe I can learn how to get rid of this accursed energy of the Sol'mar or hopefully learn to control it better.*

Zarina's teachings were still etched in her mind. *No Sol'mar has ever made it past her twenty-second year without burning out.* Another shiver ran through her, but what could she do about it besides never use the light and hope that Zarina could help her. Before she went to sleep, she vowed never to let the white energy overtake her again.

The family was up at dawn the next morning and the pavilion was teaming with activity as they came in for breakfast. The baron was already half finished when they sat down.

"Sorry I couldn't wait," he apologized, "but I have a very hectic day." He rang his bell and their meals began to arrive. "The Lady Cavillade won't be joining us this morning, but wishes you both good luck today in your competitions. She has gone into Woodvale to meet with her sister and nephew." He finished his last bite of food and added, "But she will be there later cheering you both on."

Ivan was confused by his words, but the baron cleared it up with his next statement. "It would seem," he said, addressing Cade, "that you have started a rather big incident with your bow skills. In fact, it's big enough that I've had numerous requests to move the Archery Tournament to the afternoon, after the first round of the woodcutting." He smiled and shook his head. "It appears that with the arrival of *Onak*, and he *is* here, that everyone wants to watch both events and therefore I've had to reschedule and post it on the board." His eyes never left Cade's. "I hope you can chew what you've bitten off Son," he added with a serious expression. Cade felt ashamed and bewildered, until the baron said, "Of course you can, and I look forward to watching it."

Cade was relieved and replied, "I will do my best sir."

Vero turned his attention to Ivan now and spoke. "As for you, oh great woodcutter, I will see you in awhile for the cutting of the first notch." With that, he rose from the table, bowed to the girls, and left the room.

Ivan waved as his friend exited and thought about what the day held. He had the honor of cutting the first notch to open the Woodcutting Competition, as he had done each summer since its beginning.

The first time, he had been asked by the baron, and then it was the winner of the previous year that performed the ceremony, and of course that had been him ever since. Usually the woodcutting and archery were held simultaneously, but it seemed that Cade had altered that tradition, which made Ivan happy because now he could watch his son take on the legendary *Gatou* bowman.

"This is a good change," said Grace. "Now I can witness both of my men best opponents that were brought in especially to beat them."

Ivan hadn't really thought about it before now, but his wife's words were true. The giant had been sought out, and helped by Claude, for the sole purpose of defeating him, and now *Onak,* the *Gatou* legend himself, was called in to defeat his son. *Strange times,* he thought.

Grace noticed that Shyla was unusually quiet during breakfast, and asked, "Are you all right child?"

"Better than ever," she replied, rubbing her leg where the scar had been.

She had decided not to mention that, or the spreading of the light until after the competition because she had been the cause of too much distraction already. She also didn't mention that she had lost her handbag with the gifted silver coins in it, and would have to wear her old shoes for another year.

After breakfast the family got ready, then met at the front entrance to take the carriage to the competition quarter. Shyla was delighted to see Rufus there waiting for her and thanked the guard for looking after him. After only a small delay they were loaded up, dog and all, and on their way to take on all comers.

The woodcutting area was packed with people and they cheered and clapped vigorously when Ivan stepped from the carriage. He waved to the crowd, then walked up the steps that led to the platform where the opening ceremony would take place. From his vantage point he could see how truly large the turnout was. It was almost overwhelming, and he had never seen so many people in his life. There were hundreds more than any previous year and it felt good to be recognized by so many. He had spent a lifetime perfecting his craft, and this was one of the few instances where he felt genuinely appreciated for his efforts.

The cheering increased in volume and intensity as he reached the center, which prompted another wave and nod to his fans. He acknowledged the baron, who stood behind the log that would be used, and stopped next to him. An axe was brought over by one of the servants and placed in the baron's hands. He held it high in the air. This caused even more yelling and cheering, until it almost hurt Ivan's ears.

The axe was beautifully crafted with a polished blade and designs carved along the handle. It was used only once a year for this ceremony, then placed back in its case.

The baron held it up for a few moments, then lowered it and raised his hand. The crowd hushed almost instantaneously with his gesture, and Ivan knew it was out of respect and admiration, rather than fear of consequence. Vero moved his hand toward Ivan and said, "I give you your champion," and handed him the axe.

The people went wild now, and the applause became thunderous, but one sound carried above the rest. It was the giant, who he now saw at the edge of the field, bringing those huge hands together in honor of his hero. Ivan smiled and the giant nodded and waved, but only long enough for Claude to grab his arm and lead him back to the contestants' camp.

Ivan hesitated a moment, then lifted the axe and made two deep cuts at opposite angles, causing a big piece to fall from the log. The applause continued until the baron raised his hand again.

"First off I would like to thank you all for coming," he began. "It is an unsurpassed turnout, and is shaping up to be the finest competition yet." There were hoots and yells, and excitement on every face. The baron smiled and continued. "Remember, there is entertainment, food, and drink throughout the grounds, and we have a lineup of contestants that could prove to be the best ever. So without further ceremony, I would like to announce that the Woodcutting Competition has officially begun. Now please make your way to your favorite event. Round one will begin shortly."

People were hurrying off to get a good spot at each area, but most were still hanging around, which puzzled the woodcutter until he started to move. As he grabbed his gear and headed to his first event, the spectators followed right behind him.

The morning went well for Ivan and he breezed through the wood splitting, tree falling and log chopping for day one, but saw no sign of the giant. Even after he aced the tree climbing and axe throwing, moving him into day two, there was still no giant to be seen. Finally it dawned on him as to who was organizing the tournament. Vero of course, being the brilliant man that he was, would never pit him against Mok until the final day, if they were both still in it. He chuckled to himself, then went over to his family to celebrate his advancement to the quarterfinals and help his son get ready for the archery event.

Ivan and his family explored the competition quarter on their way to the contestants' camp. They saw jugglers and acrobats from the gypsy camp, and some unusual looking animals that were on display to advertise the circus. Many of the merchants had samples on display from their stalls in the business quarter, and there were lots of different foods being cooked and sold by the plate-full.

After some deliberation, the family decided on what they wanted to eat, and stopped at the cook-fire of an old friend.

Nat Bonner and his people had been raising the Highground Longhaired Cattle for generations. Each year they cooked and sold their meat to future clients and hungry spectators, and there was no denying the unique and wonderful flavor of the tender beef. They said it was due to the northern sweetgrass that they grazed on and the pure mountain water, but it also had to do with the way they served it.

A large roast was cooked to a precise temperature. Then strips were cut from it and placed on a round piece of flatbread. Then wild lettuce, herbs and spices were added, along with a creamy sauce that blended perfectly in texture and taste. The bread was then folded and rolled into a meal that you held in your hand. It was quite brilliant actually, and sold faster than they could make them.

Shyla enjoyed hers, while looking around at the many people and sights. Ivan and Grace were busy eating and talking to Nat, but Cade could only go through the motions. His mind was overtaken by the tournament that was coming up much too fast. He was upset with himself for creating the circumstance he now faced in *Onak,* but there was nothing he could do now except give his best.

After the Hardens had finished their meal they walked to the contestants' camp and the guys found their appointed tents. Their quarters were situated next to each other and had their names attached. They contained a bed, washstand and fire pit. This was meant to give a contestant some privacy and keep him warm and well rested between events.

Ivan opened the flap for his wife, but before he entered, he noticed a huge tent off to the side and didn't have to guess who it was for. Cade went into his temporary quarters to do the final checking of his bow and arrows, but mostly to try the private mental preparation his father had shown him just before they had left for the competition.

Shyla was tired of tents and stayed outside to play with Rufus. She was so happy to see him again, and had been so worried that something had happened to him. She had saved some of her food from lunch and was feeding it to him when she heard someone behind her. She turned and looked up, and then up some more. "Mok!" she squealed. "How are you feeling?"

The giant knelt down and answered, "Mok feel great, but how little Shyla feel?"

She had forgotten about her vanished wounds and replied, "I'm just like new thanks to your family recipe." She stretched the truth only a little, but still felt bad not telling him about what her gift, or curse, had actually done.

"Mok glad to hear that," he said, and hugged her carefully with his left arm. He brought his right arm from behind his back. "Mok have something for little one," he rumbled, and held out his hand. Shyla saw her handbag resting in his palm and a feeling of relief washed over her. "You leave Mok's room," he told her, smiling again.

"Thank you so much for returning it," she replied, taking it and discretely checking its contents. Everything was still there, including the silver pieces. Those new shoes were back on her list, and she had to grin just thinking about it.

"So how did you do in the events today?" she asked, as direct as ever.

"Mok make next day, but not see woodcutter," he answered, his face looking disappointed at the last part.

After meeting the giant and getting to know him better, Shyla was starting to understand why he wanted to be in the competition. He wasn't necessarily here to best her father as much as he was here for the honor of competing against the legend, his hero.

"Jack! . . . Jack!" a loud voice sounded from across the way.

The giant stood and said, "Mok must go now."

Reaching up, she grabbed his hand and squeezed. "Thank you again for returning my bag. You are a true friend," she said, looking up at him.

The giant stared at her and appeared somewhat shaken. "Mok have friend," he voiced out loud, then smiled from ear to ear. Shyla nodded and smiled back. *It's wonderful to see him happy,* she thought, as he moved off to his tent.

She watched him walk away, and was still in awe of his size. *He has a heart to match,* she thought, then went back to playing with the four-legged friend that she had missed so dearly over the last days.

They didn't get much playing in before the others emerged ready to go, so she followed her family across the grounds to the archery area, where Cade would take on the greatest *Gatou* bowman since *Zalak* Belden.

CHAPTER
18

Gatou Lessons

There was a lineup outside the main gate when they arrived, but they were ushered straight in and escorted to the baron's private seating box directly behind the shooting pit. The public seating on either side was filled to capacity, while others stood row-on-row, hoping to get close to the *Gatou* legend. Normally this event was just a novelty and drew maybe forty or fifty people, but today it was crawling with spectators from every corner of the kingdom.

Grace and Shyla took their seats while Ivan and Cade made their way to the contestants' ring.

The girls were just getting comfortable when the duchess walked up and greeted them. "You ladies are looking fabulous today," she remarked, in the most eloquent fashion.

"As are you," said Shyla, standing to curtsy, then sitting back down.

"Hello Charlotte," Grace added, which brought a frown from Shyla, who thought her propriety was lacking.

The duchess motioned to her left and said, "Grace and Shyla, I would like you to meet my sister, Bridgette Willington and her son Stafan."

"So good to meet you both," replied Grace, shaking their hands.

Shyla, who was still miffed at her mother's lack of etiquette, decided to put on her best. She rose and in a sophisticated voice said, "Duchess," and curtsied once again. She wasn't sure if she *was* a duchess, but it couldn't hurt. Now she stepped past her mother to greet Stafan. She wasn't sure either if he was a duke or not, so she decided to say, your grace, and that should almost cover anything. She looked up and opened her mouth, and that was it. He was the most handsome boy she had ever seen. His blonde hair was thick and wavy, kind of long in the front and shorter in the back. He had big brown eyes with thick lashes, and his features were perfect. He looked to be a couple of years older than Cade, and was so refined and dignified that it made her feel weak.

"Miss Shyla," he said after a long pause, "I have heard so much about you." He took her hand and continued. "You are most certainly everything they described and more, but they should *not* have tried to explain your beauty, for there are *no* words to capture it." Then he bowed deeply and kissed her hand.

"We should be getting back to our seats," said the duchess, "but we will be seeing you later at the pavilion for dinner."

Grace nodded. "I look forward to it," she said, loudly enough to be heard above the crowd.

She looked at her daughter and commented in an amused tone. "You can breathe now my girl." Shyla hadn't realized it, but she was still standing there with her hand out, her mouth open and her heart racing. Feeling ridiculous, she quickly regained her composure and sat back down.

Grace caught her daughter's eye. "I thought you didn't like boys," she teased, raising an eyebrow.

"I don't!" exclaimed Shyla, folding her arms and sporting a huge pout.

She was staring straight ahead, ignoring her mother, when she saw the Starling family go by. She smiled and waved, and there was Little Ben waving frantically back at her with the dumbest expression on his face. *Oh . . . My . . . Gosh!* thought

Shyla, *if I never see another boy again it will be too soon*, and her pout increased.

Ivan and Cade made their way through the crowd toward the other archers, and as usual Ivan's presence caused a turmoil. As he walked along, he shook so many hands he lost count, and said thank you so many times his voice was raspy. Finally they entered the ring and left the expectant fans behind.

"Wow Dad," commented Cade, "you really are a legend."

Ivan coughed and swallowed, clearing the dust and dryness, and replied, "If you shoot the way I know you can in this event, you won't be far behind." Cade liked the sound of that and the thought warmed him. He was proud of his father and didn't mind standing in his huge shadow, but now he felt excited to step up and cast his own.

Cade was surprised to be the first one there, until he saw the other men off to the side in a large circle. This seemed strange, so he went over to see what was going on. As he approached he could see an old gray wolf lying in the grass, and it looked much bigger than any he had seen so far. He heard a loud, powerful voice as he got closer, and stopped behind the wall of bodies to listen.

"Come on gents," the voice urged, "who will try next? It doesn't cost you anything, and you could earn yourself a shiny new gold coin. This one was freshly minted at the king's treasury out of pure *Gatou* gold, not that darker stuff from the Westlands."

That's got to be Onak, thought Cade, and pushed his way into the circle. The men were bunched tightly together and it took some effort to get through. As he did, he tripped on someone's bow and fell to his knees in the center.

"That's what I like to see," came the loud voice, "someone eager to test their manhood, although this one looks a little green." The men roared with laughter, and Cade turned red. "Come now boy," the voice taunted, "you don't have to kneel before the great *Onak*. Just walk over and give your best try." He gave a hearty laugh when he finished speaking and the rest of the men joined in again, except for Ivan who listened intently to each of the plainsman's words.

Cade stood up and dusted himself off, still feeling embarrassed. He looked up and saw the *Gatou* standing on the other side of the circle. He was leaning on his great-bow, and had a big smile on his face. He looked similar to the other *Gatou* bowmen, but was about a head taller and layered in dense muscle. His body was so muscular in fact, that it looked unreal, and Cade didn't even want to try to guess how strong he was.

"Are you gonna stand there all day boy, or are you ready to prove yourself?" he asked, still smiling.

Cade looked him up and down again and really hoped he wasn't talking about wrestling, but that seemed unlikely considering he was holding the bow, so he asked, "What is this challenge you speak of *Onak*?"

The *Gatou* held up his bow and said, "It's quite simple really. All you have to do is take my weapon and pull it to full tension to walk away with a gold coin."

Cade was relieved at first, but then his guts tightened and he felt trapped. He had wanted to try a great-bow since he had first seen one, but not with everyone watching him.

"Come on boy, don't be shy," *Onak* goaded, holding the bow toward *him* now. "Unless of course you're not up for it," he added in a mocking tone. "I'm sure no one will blame you if you back down," he continued, looking at the faces before him. "I mean each man here has tried and failed miserably," he finished, shaking his head and hanging it down. The archers burst into laughter once more, and Cade knew he had just been baited. He could see no way out now, so he reached out and took the great-bow from *Onak's* grasp.

He held it in his left hand and placed the fingers of his right hand on the string. It was smooth and cool to the touch, and there was some strange looking wax covering the taut cord. He pulled it slightly at first, just to test the tension, and knew right away that he had been put to an almost, if not, impossible task.

A gold coin would mean a lot to his family now, so he took a firm stance and began to pull with all his might. The string moved inch-by-inch until it was a quarter of the way there. This feat had obviously impressed his peers by the sounds they were making, but he was still so far away. He could see *Onak* beside him with a smug look on his face, so he reached deep inside and increased his efforts. He brought the string farther and farther back, until it was almost to half tension.

The strain was getting to him now and his muscles were on fire. Sweat dripped off his chin, and he could feel his strength draining with every heartbeat. He fought to keep his grip, and had to concentrate hard to maintain his position. Finally he went to the place where he had gone so many times when shooting, and everything began to slow. The clarity came, giving him new resolve, and he inched the string back. Now he was past the halfway point and still moving toward victory, but he was almost spent, and the resistance felt like it was increasing even more now. With one final burst he pulled with everything he had, but the great-bow proved too much for him and he had to let go before it got to three-quarter tension.

Cade felt devastated after coming so close then failing, and handed the bow back to its owner. "That was a fine attempt," said *Onak*, in a neutral voice. "Maybe you could come back in a few years and try again." He turned and the men made way for him as he walked out of the circle.

Soon all the contestants had moved off, leaving Cade standing there alone. Ivan walked up and placed his hand on his son's shoulder and asked, "How do you feel?"

Cade frowned, "Well, I am exhausted," he replied, still breathing heavily, "but fine other than that."

Ivan held both of Cade's shoulders now and asked, "No, I mean how do you *feel*?"

Cade looked puzzled, then thought about it and answered, "Actually, I feel humiliated and defeated."

The woodcutter walked his son over to one of the benches and sat him down. He looked him directly in the eye and said,

"That is exactly how *Onak* wants you to feel. He knew who you were as soon as you arrived, and set you up for the fall." Cade listened carefully as his father continued. "The *Gatou* were notorious for their strategic warfare. In fact, one of their principal moves was to leave one of their great-bows behind for the enemy to find. Of course they would try it, which would result in the same outcome as today, causing their rivals to lose heart, and consequently, the battle that ensued." He patted his son's back and added, "The *Gatou* pride themselves in not only outdoing their opponent physically, but mentally as well."

Cade thought for a moment and replied, "I know what you mean, and when I think it all through, I can see exactly what he did. It was very clever, but knowing it just might give me an edge." The two stood, and Cade said, "Thanks for the insight. I feel much better now."

Ivan shook his son's hand and wished him good luck, then gestured toward the men who were gathering by the shooting pit. Cade glanced over and said, "Looks like it's almost time to start." He picked up his bow and quiver and made a motion to leave, but stopped. "I really hope *Onak* enjoyed his little mind game," he said with a gleam in his eye, "because I've got a surprise of my own planned for him." Cade winked at his father and walked over to the other archers.

The woodcutter felt proud of his boy as he made his way through the crowd and took his seat beside Grace and Shyla.

Multiple horns sounded from the baron's box as Vero himself stood and began speaking the words that would get the competition started.

"Welcome spectators, honored guests and competitors. Before we begin I would like to say that this year's festivities continue to surpass all others, and are shaping up to be the greatest ever. If you hadn't noticed already, the legendary Ivan Harden is here to watch the event." With those words the crowd erupted and the woodcutter stood and waved. Vero raised his hand and continued. "We also have a legend from the *Gatou* tribe who has graciously joined us today. *Onak* is here representing his people." The crowd exploded again, almost out of control now as the *Gatou* bowman jumped up on a bench and took his bows.

The respect for the baron was evident as the place quieted with a motion. "I would also like to introduce a new face to the event. Cade Harden has joined us this year, and is the reason that *Onak* has returned." He gestured to the boy and gave him a smile. The people didn't respond quite as enthusiastically as before, but it was a respectable reception nonetheless. Cade was shocked at receiving the recognition, but enjoyed it thoroughly as he waved to the crowd.

The baron raised both arms now and spoke in a loud voice. "And now I am pleased to say that the Archery Tournament is officially underway." The horns sounded again in a melodious cascade as the first two contestants entered the shooting pit.

There had been many entries close to the deadline this year, bringing the field up to twenty-eight archers. That number was cut in half by the end of the first round, and they hadn't even triggered the moving targets yet. By the end of the second round they had incorporated the fourth target, at the two hundred yard distance, and that took the contestants down to four men, *Onak*, Cade, and two bowmen from the baron's scouts.

The spectators quieted as Vero's voice cut through the air. "Ladies and gentlemen, let's hear it for your finalists." The crowd responded with a loud cheer and applause that continued as the closest moving target began swinging back and forth. Cade wondered why they hadn't used the fifth target, but he sure wasn't going to complain.

The first scout took aim and missed the target a little to the left, which eliminated him according to the rules, unless of course everyone else missed also. The second scout hit his mark right of center. *Onak* and Cade placed their arrows close to his, advancing the three and prompting the release of the second moving circle. The remaining scout took careful aim and let go with what looked to be a perfect attempt, but it fell short, putting him in danger of being knocked out. *Onak*, with a smile on his face, walked up and quickly sent a shaft close to the bull's-eye. Cade stepped up, and with an even faster shot, placed his right next to the *Gatou's*. Now it was down to *Onak* and Cade for the championship.

It was an unexpected pairing to most of the people, but a welcome one as many were rooting for the underdog.

The second moving target was being reset now, like the first one had been before the previous round, so the two archers took advantage and rested for the next challenge.

After only a short break, the third target was moving back and forth across the alley, and *Onak* opted to shoot first. As he passed Cade, he whispered, "Now we start your training, pup."

Had it been a different place in his life, that statement might have unnerved him, but now it only made him more determined to prove himself.

The wolf-rider pulled the bowstring back, but didn't release as fast with this shot. He angled it to allow for distance, then after a few moments, let it go. It arced through the air and bit into the wood just below center, bringing the fans that weren't already standing, to their feet.

It was one thing to make a shot like that, but altogether different to watch it executed, and even Cade was impressed, but not intimidated. He walked up, put an arrow in place, and lifted his bow. He adjusted for distance, movement, and the wind factor with a thought, then sent the shaft along its intended path and into the target, just slightly above center.

The people were starting to warm up to Cade now, and the yelling and clapping was almost as loud when he hit *his* mark.

The last mover was reset now and there was only one target left to determine the winner. Cade was glad he had come earlier to practice, even if it had created a tougher challenge, because he knew now that he could make the shot.

According to tournament rules, the one closest to the bull's-eye each round determined who went first in the next, so Cade decided to take the honor. He felt it held an advantage, and besides, it was the perfect opportunity for him to reveal the surprise that he hoped would rattle even the great *Onak*.

The crowd grew quiet on its own now as Cade entered the shooting pit. He knew he should be nervous, but on *him*, pressure had the opposite effect. For some reason he felt exhilarated and ready for battle.

He checked his bow slowly, making sure it was sound. He tested the string for any fraying, but mainly he was watching *Onak* and waiting for him to notice the delay. He checked each end of the bow now to ensure that it was strung properly, and that's when *Onak* glanced over to see what was taking so long.

As soon as he did, Cade reached into his quiver and pulled out one of the red *Gatou* arrows he had acquired during practice, and was glad now that the younger plainsmen had hurried off and left them behind. He watched closely and saw *Onak's* face tighten and his eyes narrow for just a moment, before returning to the carefree expression. That's what Cade had wanted to see, so he quickly nocked the shaft in place.

He turned and smiled to himself before seeking out the target. He looked down the alley, and there it was facing him. The shot still seemed impossible even though he had made it only a day ago, so he took his stance and raised his bow in defiance of what his senses were telling him.

He was glad to have the *Gatou* arrow, not only because it bothered *Onak*, but because it had been crafted for distance, and this *definitely* qualified. He pulled his longbow to full tension, and brought all of his concentration to the circle that appeared so small at the end of the lane. He let his mind go, but the place of clarity was slow to come. He tried to will himself there, yet couldn't achieve the same focus as when he had been taunted by the young *Gatou* bowmen. Everything became slightly clearer to him, but he soon realized that this was the extent of his ability at the moment, so he loosed the red missile and watched it soar high into the air. The arrow flew straight and true, eventually finding its mark in the ring outside the bull's-eye.

The people were back on their feet now in amazement, and the cheering was out of control. Cade acknowledged them with a wave, but was not happy with himself. He had watched *Onak's* skill from the beginning and was almost certain his shot could be beaten, and according to the rules, the contestant closest to the center on the final target was declared the winner.

Cade grabbed his quiver and moved to the side. All he could do now was wait and see if his attempt at mental warfare had worked.

Onak passed him by and walked into the shooting pit like he owned it. He placed his right hand above his eyes, blocking the sun, and took in the distance between himself and his future conquest. He knelt, placed his bow across his legs, then reached down and grabbed a handful of soil. Letting most of it fall through his fingers, he threw the rest in the air to test the wind. He pulled an arrow from his quiver before setting the leather container on the ground behind him, and slid the nock over the string of his great-bow. *Onak* placed the shaft just above the grip, where he liked it, and took his stance. Slowly, and without so much as a waver, he pulled back until the tension was maxed, then lifted and locked his arms in position.

It was like watching an artist at work, and Cade could see now why this man was a legend.

Onak released, and the arrow left the bow with such force that you could hear it slice the air on its fateful flight. Only moments later it hit the target dead center and the crowd erupted.

Cade felt sick, but knew he'd been beaten fairly, so he walked over to congratulate the *Gatou*. He hadn't quite reached him when *Onak* raised his bow and shouted, "Now we start the true test of manhood!" The words confused Cade, but he soon saw what they meant.

One of the baron's men ran into the shooting pit and waved a black flag in the air. At the far end of the alley, the turnkeeper, who was in charge of measuring and removing arrows, waved *his* black flag, then walked to the side and released the catch on another moving target. It swung back and forth on its pendulum, a few feet above the one they had just shot at, and Cade knew instantly that it had been set up at *Onak's* request.

He could see now that the wolf-rider didn't want to merely beat him. He wanted to annihilate and humiliate him completely.

The whole situation seemed daunting to Cade as he watched the small circle swinging from side-to-side. How could he hope to succeed when it was all he could do to hit the one that was standing still? Fortunately he didn't have the chance to over think it too much because *Onak* had already claimed the right of first shot and was on his way back to the pit. As he went by, Cade stopped him and held out the other *Gatou* arrows. *Onak* took them, shoved them in his quiver, and whispered, "Now I'm going to put you in your place boy," and continued on his way.

The people were quiet again when *Onak* reached the shooting area, and the air was thick with tension and excitement. The legend turned and looked at the expectant faces and shouted, "I can't put on a show without a live audience!" and threw his arms up. Everyone responded with yells and whistles, and a steady supply of whoops and hollers.

One woman in the front screamed, "I love you *Onak*!"

The wolf-rider faced her, flexed his muscles and bared his teeth, causing her to fall back in a faint.

The enthusiasm increased now, until it broke into a chant. "*Onak*. . . . *Onak*. . . . *Onak*," came the steady rhythm. The *Gatou* smiled. Now he was ready.

He went through his ritual as he got ready for his shot, and the volume of the chanting increased with each movement. Finally he was in position with his bow held high and the crowd reaching a crescendo. The legend stopped only for a moment to make a final adjustment, then let go of his bowstring, sending the bright-red projectile into a high arc. Once it reached its maximum height, it started on a downward angle like a hawk diving toward its prey, and hit the target with a *thud!* very close to the center.

Cade didn't think the noise could increase anymore, but it did substantially the moment *Onak* pulled off his impossible feat of bowman-ship, and he found *himself* cheering the great warrior.

Onak bowed slightly to the right, then slightly to the left, then deeply to the center and everyone knew it was directed at the baron. Vero stood and applauded, and *Onak* placed his fist over his heart, then straightened his arm in respect to his host.

Cade felt defeated and couldn't shake it. The thought of matching his shot was overwhelming, and he felt weak. He had almost given up mentally, when something his father once said came to his mind. *Son, if you enter a circumstance with the attitude that you cannot succeed, then you won't.* The words ran through his head a few times, and he started to feel better. He wouldn't give up so easily, and if he didn't succeed, it wouldn't be from lack of trying.

The spectators were still on their feet when Cade grabbed his gear and headed for the pit. He met *Onak* about halfway and the *Gatou* stopped and spoke to him, only this time it wasn't in a whisper. "There will be a lot less humiliation if you just withdraw boy," he said sarcastically, then laughed and continued on his way.

Cade's face heated, but he kept moving until he reached the place where he was alone among hundreds, facing an all-but-impossible task. Turning around he could see his father, mother, and little sister. They were waving, and he could see the love and support in their eyes. He looked up at the baron and received a nod. He could see the people clapping and cheering him on, and that's when he noticed Wanda Starling.

Her smile was bright and her blue eyes sparkled. She waved to him, then blew him a kiss. Cade felt a tingling sensation all over his body, and a warm feeling in the pit of his stomach. He waved back and then turned to face the alleyway so she wouldn't see the silly expression he knew was on his face.

Now it was just him, the small circle and the distance between, not to mention variables like the wind, bow tension, and the movement of the target. Everything had to be calculated perfectly to make a shot like this, so he cleared his mind and brought it all into focus.

Everyone had quieted down now, but it didn't matter to him. He was totally immersed in the calm before a violent storm.

The storm being the outcome of the challenge he now faced. As he placed one of his own arrows on the string, he searched once again for the clarity that made him one with the bow. It came slowly, much too slowly, and that just wouldn't do at a moment like this. He fought for it, but it just wasn't coming, and of course he had never known where it came from or how it happened. It wasn't triggering now however, and without it he knew he was lost. The more he thought about it the farther away it seemed, so he closed his eyes, took a deep breath and let it out slowly. He had to make his shot soon or he would be penalized, and at this point in the tournament that would mean defeat, so he raised his bow and hoped for the best.

Slowly he pulled the arrow toward himself, still fighting to find the clarity, when he heard Wanda's beautiful voice.

"I believe in you Cade Harden," came the words, and they struck him deeply. He could hear the love and admiration they carried, and it caused him to pause. He hadn't realized how strong his feelings were for her until now, and it became a catalyst for the events that followed.

The clarity came now in a way it hadn't done before and the calm was like a tranquil meadow on a hot summer day. His vision became so vivid that the target appeared to grow in size and almost slow to a halt. As he let go he could follow the arrow inch-by-inch as it cut its way through the afternoon sky, and it was fantastic. Never before had his senses felt so keen and alive, and the sensation was empowering.

"Yes!" he cried, as his arrow sank deep into the wood almost dead center, and the people answered with a deafening roar. He snapped out of his trancelike state, and as he did so, felt a sudden loss. It passed quickly though, as the reality of what he had just accomplished sank in.

Nothing was decided yet, because the shots were too close to be called from the archers' end of the alley, so everyone waited for the turnkeeper to do his measuring. If he held up a red flag, that meant *Onak* was champion, and if a white flag was waved then Cade would be declared the winner.

The crowd was buzzing now, voicing their opinions on the outcome, but only the flag would truly tell. *Onak* approached, and following him were the two *Gatou* that Cade had seen at practice. The legend stopped and stared at him with a puzzled expression on his face, then directed his gaze down the alleyway. They could see the man at the target now, and all they could do was wait. The anticipation and excitement grew with each moment, and everyone was on pins-and-needles waiting for the results.

Finally the turnkeeper raised his arm in the air, and at the end of it was a white flag. Cade's knees almost buckled when he saw it, and he felt overwhelmed. The fans erupted, and cheered louder than ever for their new champion. Cade could see no change in *Onak's* demeanor when the flag came up, just the puzzled look that remained on the wolf-rider's face, like there was something strange that he didn't understand.

The people were moving now and yelling out their congratulations to him, and as he turned to accept it, Wanda ran up and kissed him on the lips. He was caught off guard, but didn't pull away. Normally something like this would have embarrassed him, yet this felt so right that he kissed her back and held her close.

The next to offer their felicitation was Ivan. "Good work Son," he said in a proud voice. "You were remarkable." Cade had waited a long time to hear those words, and they felt like a warm blanket on a cold night.

Shyla came up and gave him a hug. "I guess you *can* beat the *Gatou* after all," she giggled, but her face became serious when she saw *Onak* staring at her, and she turned quickly with a worried look on her face.

Grace was standing there and she had tears in her eyes. "Look at you my boy," she said in a trembling voice. "I just couldn't be any prouder." They hugged, and Cade fought back his own tears.

As he held his mother, he noticed that *Onak's* expression had changed and he was coming over, presumably to commend him on his victory, but as he started to speak, Grace stopped him and they began talking in *Gatou*. The conversation went on for awhile, and when they had finished, the three *Gatou* walked up to Cade, knelt before him, and *Onak* spoke. "*Uladan majah Zalak*," he uttered in his native tongue.

All he could think of to say was a hesitant, "Thank you," then the three plainsmen stood and walked away.

Cade was the one with the puzzled look now, and asked his mother what *Onak* had said. "He said that *Zalak* would be proud," she answered. "And it is considered quite an honor among the *Gatou* people to be compared with that great legendary warrior."

Cade was pleased with himself and feeling rather important until the baron walked up in all his splendor and majesty. "Congratulations Son," he chimed, in his official voice. "Now come with me and receive a real champion's welcome."

As he started to follow, Wanda grabbed his arm and kissed his cheek. "I'll see you at the Woodcutter's Ball," she whispered in his ear, then left to rejoin her family.

With everything that had been going on, he had completely forgotten about the ball, and for the life of him couldn't remember a single dance step his mother had showed him when he was small. He hurried to catch the baron, and made a mental note to ask his mother for some brush-up lessons before the dance.

Vero led him up the steps to his seating box and placed one hand on his shoulder while making a sweeping gesture with the other. "Good people of the Northern Kingdom," he spoke in a loud and commanding tone. "I give you your new archery champion." The whole place exploded now, like lightning splitting an elder tree, and Cade enjoyed every ounce of adoration they doled out. He could never see himself tiring of the attention and appreciation that came with the title, nor did he mind receiving the pouch with the twenty-eight silver coins the baron handed him for all to witness.

After the enthusiasm had died down, Vero leaned in and said, "The people are extremely happy that you are their new champion.

They love your adeptness with the bow and that you are Ivan's son, but also you are the first one of their own to best the *Gatou* since the inception of this tournament. You will be greatly honored for each of those reasons, and I tell you this now so you can fully understand what is transpiring here and enjoy it for what it truly is." Cade understood the baron's wisdom and thanked him for everything, then left to finish celebrating with his family.

The first thing he did when he saw them was hand his mother twenty silver coins from the pouch, which was equal to one gold coin of the kingdom. She didn't want to take any of his winnings, but knew his heart was set on helping the family, so she accepted it graciously and thanked him for his generosity. When she took the gift she could see the pride and satisfaction on his face, and knew how good he felt to be able to contribute when they needed it most.

The family stuck around while Cade greeted old friends as well as new fans and supporters. His voice was getting raw from saying thank you, and he was just beginning to understand how his father must feel. The whole tournament was an incredible experience, and he was cherishing every moment.

When he was through, they took the carriage back to the pavilion where the evening meal was ready for serving. The baron and Charlotte were seated already, along with Bridgette and Stafan. There was minimal conversation throughout dinner, other than a toast to Cade for winning, and some small-talk between the girls. Shyla didn't speak to, or even look at, the young man who sat across from her, and decided she would never be joined if all boys were as silly as the ones she had encountered lately. She and Stafan had nothing in common, and for the life of her couldn't understand why she felt so flustered whenever she was around him. It wasn't like she hadn't seen a boy before, and hoped it would pass soon.

When they finished, everyone went to their rooms for the night. Cade stopped his mother before she went in and asked her if she would show him some dance steps before the ball, which brought a smile and a, "Yes," from her.

Shyla thought for a moment and then asked, "Maybe you could show me some as well. . . . I mean if you're going to be doing it already." Everyone stared at her, which brought forth a, "*Humph!*" as she rolled her eyes and stomped off to her room.

"Goodnight to you too," said Grace, then took Ivan's hand and led him through the curtain.

Cade was mentally and physically exhausted from the day, but was still floating on a cloud, and as he drifted off to sleep, he dreamed of Wanda Starling.

CHAPTER
19

Business and Pleasure

T he pavilion was bustling again the next morning as servants and workers moved about getting everything prepared for the second round of the Woodcutting Competition. Shyla ignored Stafan through breakfast, and managed to secure a large juicy bone from the kitchen for Rufus just before everyone left for the carriages.

The reception was overwhelming when Ivan and Cade stepped onto the competition quarter, and the woodcutter was happy to share the stage with his son. He felt good this day, throwing, climbing and chopping his way to the third round and a semifinal position. All was as it should be, but still there was no giant to contend with.

He heard that the big fellow had made it through as well, and after watching Cade take down a legend, he felt a little apprehensive, but was still looking forward to the challenge.

It was still early in the afternoon when the family got back to the carriage and Ivan was acting strangely. He stopped everyone before they got in and looked to the driver. The man nodded and smiled, so the woodcutter took Grace in his arms and carried her up and inside.

To her delight she was greeted by dozens of roses and wild flowers that decorated the interior, as well as a huge basket filled with meats, breads, fruits, cheeses, and a large bottle of apple cider.

Grace looked at her man with a loving expression and said, "You remembered," then squeezed his hand and kissed it.

He looked at her with warmth and love in his eyes and replied, "Of course I did. You don't think I would forget the anniversary of the day we met, do you?" He took her hands and kissed them in turn, then pulled her to him.

"Well, I wouldn't have blamed you with how busy you've been and all the pressure you're under," she answered, yielding to his touch.

"I would have," he said, and kissed her neck.

Cade and Shyla stood outside the carriage, knowing better than to enter, but were still wondering what was going on when the door opened and Ivan stuck his head out. "Children," he said in a fatherly tone. "Your mother and I are going on a picnic, so you will have to take the next carriage back. It should be along shortly."

The two weren't surprised, and said simultaneously, "All right Father," and waved as the driver sped away.

They looked at each other and started to giggle, then Shyla said, "I hope one day I find someone who loves me the way Father loves Mother," and then sighed.

Cade looked at her and said, "I don't see how."

Shyla's mouth opened immediately and she was about to give him a tongue-lashing, when another carriage pulled up. She recognized that it belonged to the Willingtons, so she made no move toward it.

She had almost forgotten she was mad at Cade and opened her mouth again to berate him, but heard a voice that she had unfortunately become very familiar with over the last two days.

"Are you two waiting for a carriage?" asked Stafan, as he walked up.

Shyla gazed up at the dashing young man and the feelings started again, so she pushed them away and answered, "We have been abandoned here by our parents who are off on some romantic picnic. So yes, we are quite carriage-less at the moment," and with that, she tilted her head and looked the opposite direction.

"Well, my lady," he said, bowing low, "look no further, for mine is at your disposal . . . and yours," he added, finally acknowledging Cade. *Why does he talk like that?* thought Shyla, *and why does it make me feel the way it does?*

She pushed the feeling away again, and answered, "I accept," and walked briskly forward. Stafan hurried over and took her hand, helping her up the step and inside. Cade shook his head and followed.

Once inside, she could see that it was as lavish as Charlotte's, but was covered so you couldn't tell from the outside. She liked the privacy and mystery of the covered carriages, but preferred the open ones, with the sun shining on you as you sat upon the throne-like seat for all to see.

"Would you like some juice?" asked Stafan, producing a tray with cups and a container.

"I would love some, kind sir," replied Shyla, vowing never to let him see her flustered or shaken in any way. Cade took one also and thanked him.

Everyone quietly drank their juice and looked around the carriage, then Stafan asked, "Before I give the driver his instructions, what would you think of taking a small diversion this afternoon?"

Cade wiped his mouth with his sleeve, which prompted a disgusted look from Shyla, and asked, "What did you have in mind?"

Shyla tried to appear disinterested as she daintily sipped from her cup. She listened intently though as Stafan replied, "Well, my mother is off somewhere with my aunt and the thought of spending the rest of this beautiful day in that stuffy pavilion is not to my liking. I suggest we take a trip down to the entertainment and business quarter to see what wondrous sights they may have to offer."

Shyla was thrilled but didn't show it, and Cade shrugged. "I'm with you on the pavilion thing," he agreed, "and I've been waiting to see the circus since we first arrived." Stafan looked at Shyla and his gaze made her feel weak, so she nodded and turned to stare out the window.

"It's settled then," he remarked in an enthusiastic voice, then leaned out the door and said, "Driver, make haste to the entertainment quarter." When he was back inside he saw the look of disappointment on Shyla's face, so he leaned back out and said, "Please." Her heart melted when he did that, but she remained vigilant despite herself.

The carriage rolled along smoothly and the dust was minimal, which for Shyla, added another plus to the covered variety.

As they passed the pavilion and started down the hill, Stafan commented, "That was some excellent marksmanship you performed yesterday sir."

Cade, who wasn't used to being called anything except his name, nodded his head and replied, "Thank you. I was having a good day."

"If you say so," returned Stafan, his eyes narrowing slightly as he smiled a knowing smile. Cade looked away and wondered what he knew exactly.

Shyla's excitement grew as they got closer and she wondered what amazing things she might see, or whether she might finally get that new pair of shoes she wanted. She knew her choices wouldn't be as plentiful at the booth as in town, so she didn't get her hopes up too high. She also found herself wondering about the giant. She wasn't sure why, but she felt a special bond with him, like she needed to protect him, which was rather comical considering his size and strength.

She was still thinking about Mok when the carriage stopped. Stafan looked out the window and asked, "What will it be, entertainment or business side first?"

Cade sat up straight and in his most formal voice replied, "You know what they say; business before pleasure," which brought a smirk from Shyla and a chuckle from their host. It *was* funny, yet beneath the humor Shyla knew exactly why he wanted to visit the business side but, circumstances being what they were, wasn't about to say anything.

Stafan politely instructed the driver, and soon they were pulling up in front of the many booths and stalls the vendors had set up to showcase their merchandise.

The three strolled between the many rows of mini-shops. Shyla realized that she had already visited most of their main buildings back in Woodvale, but still kept an open mind, browsing a little at each one even though new shoes were still at the top of her list. Cade was more interested than usual, and Stafan was just enjoying the company of individuals close to his own age.

Many of his daily activities revolved around duties and customs, and that meant dealing with adults. He was glad to finally get a break and be with some younger people, and of course he didn't mind Shyla's company either.

As they turned the corner and started up the next row, Shyla saw the booth with the shoes displayed, so she hurried over and started searching. She was surprised at how good the selection was, and even more surprised when she found the exact style and size she had wanted.

They were leather, covered in silver cloth, with a flat heel and pointed toes. The top was open halfway to the tip and there was a shiny silver buckle just past that. The buckle was for decoration, and had a loop on it to put a ribbon through so you could tie a bow. The neat part was that depending on what dress you wore, you could change the ribbon color to match. She was so excited to get them and bought a red, green, blue, yellow and pink ribbon, just to be safe. Of course she didn't have all the dresses to match, but she was optimistic.

When she was done, the total came to two silvers, which left one still snug in her bag. The merchant wrapped them in light parchment, tied it up with string and handed it to her. She took it with a smile and walked over to Stafan, who was standing there looking across the street with an amused expression on his face. Curiosity got the best of her so she followed his gaze, and there was Cade standing at a dress shop, bartering with the vendor. He had purchased dresses before that she and her mother had already picked out, but she couldn't believe what she was seeing now, and it got worse when he turned around and stepped into the walkway holding a bright blue shawl.

"What do you think?" he asked, raising it in the air.

Shyla was totally confused, but replied quickly, "I don't think it matches your eyes."

Cade looked exasperated and spoke in a frustrated voice. "No, I mean for a girl."

Shyla had caught on now and gave him a coy look. She put her hands on her hips, raised an eyebrow and said, "A girl?" with a questioning lilt.

Cade was growing quite impatient and replied, "You know. Wanda Starling."

Shyla's face became serious now and she answered, "Well in that case it will match the eyes rather nicely."

Cade seemed pleased and went back over to the shop, then returned with a wrapped up parcel of his own. He felt guilty for buying something *that* frivolous, but he had given his parents a gold's worth of silvers, and it felt good to have coins of his own for a change.

The companions walked up and down the rows, pointing out odd interesting looking items, but mostly they were enjoying the warm weather and watching the people. They saw men and women of all shapes and sizes, with their strange looking hats and mustaches that were simply too big. They laughed and joked around, and were having fun just being silly. Shyla started feeling bad because Stafan hadn't found a single item that he needed or wanted. Of course what would a boy of his stature need that he didn't already have, and probably of much better quality than anything here.

She had just finished her thought when they came upon a *Gatou* booth. The pieces that were hanging there demanded attention, but not as much as Cade it seemed.

Since they had started browsing through the rows, many people had stopped and congratulated him, but that was nothing compared with the *Gatou*. There were two males and two females from their tribe, and they were acting like the king himself had just dropped in for a visit. They were obviously in awe of his recent win and didn't hold anything back in showing it. Cade, of course, was soaking up the attention, and Stafan it seemed, was enjoying the lack of it, while Shyla was ignoring all of it and concentrating on the exquisite jewelry and clothing in front of her.

She had seen a couple of *Gatou* trinkets and an outfit that her mother owned, but she was still amazed at the quality of craftsmanship and attention to detail these people could create. Each necklace and ring was a work of art, and the etchings and carving of the little statues must have taken weeks to complete. The leather clothing was always the fashion in the cities, and even the royals were often seen in their garments.

Shyla knew that even the smallest of these items was well beyond her means, so it didn't surprise her to see Stafan finally interested in something. He had his eye on a necklace and asked her what she thought.

"I think it's just the most gorgeous piece I've ever seen," she answered, holding it to her neck.

"Do you think my mother would like it?" he asked, for reassurance.

Shyla held it up again and replied, "I think that any woman would absolutely love it," and ran her fingers over the leaf-shaped gold.

Stafan was inspired by her enthusiasm and said, "Very well, I will purchase this as a birthday gift for her." He took the necklace, walked over to one of the *Gatou*, and after haggling for a short while, took fourteen gold pieces from his purse and handed them to the smiling woman. Shyla could see many more coins of the same color inside, and wondered what it would be like to be rich.

Soon they were moving down the row again, each with a package in their hand and a smile on their face. Shyla stopped in to say hello to the Catchers, and was glad to see that Loner wasn't there for sale. The thought of that made her feel awful inside, and she hoped he would go to a good home.

The little shops were starting to thin out now, but Shyla knew there was still one more stop before they made their way to the entertainment side, and it was coming up at the end of the lane.

The Starling's area was a lot bigger than the others to accommodate the horses that they were showing, but Cade wasn't interested in that. His mind was occupied with one thought only, and that was Wanda.

When they arrived, he looked around but saw no one. Disappointment clouded his face until Ben Senior came out and told him that Wanda was at the corral working with the stallion. Cade thanked him and quickly made his way there. Stafan and Shyla followed right behind, and Shyla hoped she didn't run into Little Ben, especially right now.

When they reached Wanda, she was inside with the animal and didn't notice them at first. She was wearing her riding clothes and had a whip in her hand. She raised it and shook it, and the white stallion reared up, striking the air with his front feet. She lowered it and he dropped down, then snorted and shook his head.

Shyla was impressed with his muscularity and obvious pure blood, and thought that Stafan must have at least two of his own back home.

Next Wanda raised the whip, then lowered the end in a downward motion and the powerful animal dropped to his knees, tucking his head against his chest in a bowing position. He stayed there until she lifted it, releasing him from the pose. When he was on all fours again, she swung the whip over her head three times in a circle, making a loud crack as she snapped it. This caused the horse to run along the edge of the round corral at a fast lope. As she turned in the center to match his speed, she noticed her visitors and stopped the stallion with another flick of her wrist. The sun was bright, so she shielded her eyes with her hand. When she saw that it was Cade, her face lit up and she ran over.

Shyla studied her as she approached and thought that, for her age, she looked much more like a woman than a girl. She carried herself so well, and the way she was looking at Cade reminded her of the way her mother looked at her father. She could see that Cade felt the same way, and until this very moment, could never have pictured him getting serious about a girl. Everything was changing and she didn't know if she liked it.

She glanced at Stafan, who didn't appear to be impressed by Wanda's grace *or* beauty, and she *did* like that very much, but of course he was probably used to seeing pretty girls.

"So how is the champion doing today?" asked Wanda, as she stopped on the other side of the wooden railings.

Cade leaned on the fence and replied, "About the same as I was before I became champion."

Wanda removed her gloves and laid them on a post. "I'm glad that all the attention hasn't swollen your head too much," she teased, then took his hand in hers.

Cade knew that whether he was shooting in the forest or in front of hundreds of people, it made no difference as to who he was, or how great a bowman. No one could argue that, but legends weren't created in the woods, and you couldn't buy shawls with pinecones, which reminded him.

"I brought you a gift," he said, handing her the package. "If you don't like the color you can exchange it for another, and if you don't like the gift you can exchange it. I talked to the shop owner and he wrote the stall number on the inside, and if you–."

Wanda stopped him, took the package and replied, "I love the color *and* the gift, and thank you so much."

Cade felt slightly confused and asked, "Aren't you gonna open it?"

She held it to her and replied, "If it's all right, I would like to open it later, in private."

Now he was really confused *and* disappointed, but answered, "Sure."

Shyla sighed and thought, *Welcome to the wonderful mystery of girls, Cade Harden.*

"So who is your new friend?" asked Wanda, changing the subject.

"Oh I'm sorry," Cade apologized. "This is Stafan. Stafan, this is Wanda."

The young man took her hand and bowed low, but didn't kiss it, much to Shyla's delight. "So good to meet you," he said as he let it go.

"And you," she returned, performing a small curtsy that didn't match her outfit at all.

"Will you be attending the woodcutting tomorrow, or the final day?" Cade asked Wanda, still puzzling over her reaction to his gift.

"Unfortunately no," she replied disappointedly. "I have to be here, but I will see you at the ball," she added, leaving Shyla wondering if it was a question or not. Cade nodded and Shyla smiled, holding her new shoes a little closer.

"We should be going," said Cade finally, not wanting to leave.

"Thanks for coming over," said Wanda, looking at each of them. "Thanks for the gift," she directed at Cade, "It was very thoughtful of you."

Shyla and Stafan moved off a ways, and he said, "It was nice to meet you, Wanda."

Cade was about to turn when she stood on her tiptoes, leaned over the top rail and kissed him on the cheek. Cade's face started to redden, so he turned and led the other two toward the entertainment half of the quarter.

CHAPTER
20

A Magical Night

When they entered, the place was alive with activity and excitement filled the air. The circus and gypsy camps took up most of the area, and there were some solo attractions set up around the outskirts.

They saw sword swallowers and fire-eaters, jugglers and contortionists, and even some minstrels and dancers advertising for the gypsies. They stopped to watch, but each act only performed a small sample of what you would experience if you paid to enter and see the full show.

The sun was still well above tree-line, so if they hurried they would be able to take in most of the fun before dusk, and that's exactly what they planned on.

As they entered the first few tents, Stafan insisted on paying because he was the one who had invited them, to which Cade couldn't argue, and Shyla thought was very gentlemanly of him.

The acts were unbelievable with their feats of strength, demonstrations of balance, and daring stunts. Shyla enjoyed them all, but was really looking forward to the animal enclosures. She loved to see the different creatures from far and distant lands. They looked so interesting and unusual, and the essence they gave off made her wonder what it would be like to visit their true homes.

When they'd finally been to every tent, Stafan suggested they break for dinner. This time Cade insisted on paying and Shyla didn't really care which of them paid, as long as she got some food soon. With the Woodcutting Competition, then the trip through the business section and the entertainment area, she realized she had only eaten a portion of the Bonner's wrap since breakfast.

They looked around and found a suitable place to eat. Shortly after they were seated, a large man brought them each a long stick with skewered pieces of cooked meat that had been basted with what he called his family sauce. Next he brought out three plates of baked beans and thick pieces of heavy-bread. In the open-air, the meal tasted so good that the trio barely said two words until their plates were completely clean.

"Well, I certainly needed that," remarked Stafan, as he stood and pulled Shyla's chair out for her.

She thanked him and said, "Now I want to go see the unusual animals and birds they have displayed."

"Are you sure?" asked Stafan skeptically. "I once went to one of these where they had a flying dog advertised on a big sign. Of course the wings were made of wood with feathers pasted on and strapped to his back, and there was a guy in the rafters swinging him across the stage with a rope."

Shyla frowned at him. "Of course there are phony ones," she agreed, "but there are also many rare and unique species as well."

Stafan loved how her face scrunched up when she was trying to make a point, and he just stared at her without responding. Shyla blushed and looked away. *Why does he have to be so handsome?* she thought in frustration, and started walking faster.

There were many sights and sounds tempting them from their path, but Shyla was determined not to stray from her intended destination. This was finally realized when she saw a huge banner that read, "Come see the Wondrous and Wonderful Four-legged and Feathered Friends from the Southern Regions and Across the Seas".

She was excited as they went through the opening, then another smaller poster caught her eye. "Are you Brave enough to Look upon the Ferocious, Man-eating Panthadon? It has the Body of a Cat, the Claws of a Bear, the Teeth of a Wolf and the Horns of a Dryland Springer. Come if you Dare to the Pit at Sundown and be Prepared to Tremble!". She read the words again, then studied the picture below.

The artist's depiction made it look like an overgrown wild-cat with horns and long fangs. It was black with white stripes and there was a man standing next to it, making it appear nearly five feet tall.

Stafan laughed when he saw it and couldn't help himself. "Now let me see," he said slowly. "First, the reason for sundown is for using torchlight so you won't notice that the horns are tied on the cat's head, and the pit is so you can't see its size relative to your own. Lastly, if they do have a trainer or beast-master with it, he will be one of the small people to make it seem larger, when it is probably just a painted up mountain cat." Cade thought it was extremely funny as well, and he and Stafan had a good laugh.

"You may be right," agreed Shyla, "but I think I will see for myself."

There was still plenty of day left, so they started checking out the other attractions.

The first one, much to Shyla's dismay, was, "The Incredible Snake Girl". This one consisted of a thick coil of rope, covered in cloth and painted to resemble a snake's body. In the center was a girl's head, which was painted to match, and the rest of her was beneath the floor in a hole they had dug earlier. Stafan was looking at Shyla with an, I-told-you-so expression, and all she could do was shrug and nod in agreement.

The rest of the day improved though with only a few more ridiculous attractions, and Shyla just marked them down as entertainment. She was *taken* with all the different kinds of animals. She especially loved the exotic birds with their sudden movements and vibrant colors.

By the time the sun had started to set they had seen most all the entertainment side of the quarter and were almost ready to take the carriage back. They decided to rest while the torches were being lit, and Stafan treated them to a sugar-apple on a stick that he had purchased from a passing vendor. While they waited, they talked and laughed about the sights they'd seen during the day, and how good it was to get out and have some fun.

The mood had changed now that the torches were burning, and so had the music drifting in from the gypsy camp. It was livelier now and Shyla knew they would be feasting and dancing. The melodies were alluring and haunting, and reminded her of the first time she had seen the traveling people as a small child. They had treated her very special, and she planned on visiting them before she left, but first she wanted to go see the panthadon. She knew Stafan was probably right about it being a fake, yet she still needed to make sure. If by chance it wasn't, then it would be the most unusual creature she'd ever seen, replacing the wolves of the *Gatou Plains*.

They all stood up, and Stafan leaned toward Shyla. "You're going to see that cat, aren't you," he said as a statement, rather than a question.

"As a matter of fact I am," she replied, folding her arms. "I'm assuming you two won't be joining me."

"No," answered Cade, "we are going over to watch the strongman take on the locals. He's offering a gold coin to anyone who can best him."

Shyla looked amused, "I hope you do better than you did with the great-bow," she said, trying not to laugh.

Cade wasn't sure how she'd found out about that, and he could feel his temper trying to surface. "*I'm* not trying him, but I would love to see his face if the giant walked up," he retorted, and the tension faded. "Actually," he continued, "I do hope that Wanda's dad shows up. I think he could give him a real run for that gold coin."

Bells started ringing, which meant that events would be starting shortly, so Shyla made her way to the panthadon pit, while Cade and Stafan headed for the strongman contest.

Shyla hurried along the torch-lit path, not wanting to miss the spectacle. When she reached the entrance, a big man stopped her and said, "That'll be five coppers miss."

All the other shows and sights had been one or two, but she didn't want to miss this one so she handed him her silver coin and received fifteen coppers back.

She could see how packed it was as she walked down the path that led to the pit, and the people were at least three and four deep standing around the circular arena. Shyla decided that standing behind everyone most certainly *wasn't* going to happen, so she tried pushing her way through.

"No cutting in front!" yelled a man, placing her back where she started, and the other men just glared at her.

She moved around the circle in frustration until she finally decided to try a different approach. She tapped the man in front of her on the back, and when he turned around, she said, "Please sir," pointing ahead, "my father is up front." The man smiled and ushered her in, and after a couple more white lies, she was standing at the edge.

The pit itself was about ten feet deep and fifty feet across, with some logs and a few old carcasses scattered along its floor. Around the top was a large wooden rail about two feet high, with a post every eight feet. Sunken into that were inch-thick metal bars, four inches apart and six feet high. Attached to the top of each bar, was a ring of the same size that circled the entire perimeter.

That's a lot of work to contain a phony cat, she thought, *but maybe it's for effect and to impair people's vision.*

The lighting was poor, with only a few torches on the pit walls, and even though she was in the front now, she was still having trouble seeing clearly. She moved to the right and then the left, but nothing helped. The crowd noise increased as a man on the far side grabbed a rope that was attached to a door in the pit wall. He was starting to pull it up, and she didn't want to miss anything, so she dropped down and ducked under the railing. Now she could see every part of the pit and the door was fully open.

The crowd fell silent in anticipation of what would come through the opening, and her heart beat faster as she watched closely to see if it was real or not.

Suddenly the panthadon leaped into the ring and let out a fierce roar. The startled mob shifted and you could hear screams and yells all around. Before she knew what had happened, Shyla felt a hard kick to her back and lost her balance. She fell forward and over the edge. She tried to catch herself, but caught only a few splinters on her ten foot plummet to the hard surface below.

The light exploded on impact, and it was all she could do to contain it and regain the wind that had been knocked from her. Finally she got her breath back, and the tiny bits of white energy pushed into place, but her head was still swimming from the fall.

Once her mind had cleared, she checked herself for injury. Everything seemed fine, except for a couple of fresh bruises on the same side that the giant had hit her. She felt lucky to have come out virtually unscathed, and even luckier when she realized that she'd fallen behind one of the larger logs and out of the animal's view.

The pit seemed a whole lot smaller now and she was glad there were only a few torches illuminating it, but she couldn't just lie there and wait for the beast to find her. Shyla's instincts were screaming at her to make a run for the open door, but her common sense knew the beast would overtake her long before she reached it, so she remained still and tried to think.

She needed to know where in the ring the panthadon was before she could decide anything, so she sat up slowly and peeked over the log. Sure enough there it was in the center, and in a direct line with her only means of escape. *How long will they keep that door open?* she wondered. *I may not have much time.*

She watched closely as the creature sniffed and pawed at something on the ground, and suddenly realized how beautiful it was.

The panthadon was nearly five feet high and had a shiny black coat. It had four white, lightning-shaped stripes on an angle circling its body, and a long curved tail. Its horns were about a foot long, and definitely real, but she was more concerned with the knifelike fangs that protruded, even when its mouth was closed.

Worrying about that right now would do her no good, and she had to figure a way out of this without being seen. She could tell the animal was completely focused on the thing between its paws, so she decided to make her move while it was distracted. Her plan was to crawl to the edge and keep crawling along the outside until she reached the doorway.

Slowly and quietly she backed up, keeping an eye on the panthadon in case there was any change. The wall was only a few feet away now, but then she noticed that the object between its paws was the package that contained her new shoes. *I must have tossed it when I fell,* she thought, then stopped when she saw those big teeth sink in and start chewing. Rage filled her and she stood up. She started forward and yelled, "What do you think you're doing, you Big . . . Dumb . . . Cat!"

The spectators, whose attention had been fixated on the panthadon, were now noticing the little girl, and one woman screamed, "There's a child in the pit!"

The predator, not used to being attacked, left his curiosity and backed up a few paces. He sniffed the air and watched with his keen eyes to see how many, and how big his assailants were. When he saw such a little thing making the loud noise, he moved forward again, then stopped beside the shredded package and crouched. He let out another deafening roar to show his fierceness, which jarred Shyla from her state of rage. With her anger gone, she realized what a mistake she had made, and froze.

The cat was moving fast now, closing in. She knew running wasn't an option and she couldn't just stand there and wait, so she took the only action left to her. Raising her arms high in the air, she began to chant.

She called to the sweet loam beneath her feet, and the rocks and roots that lie within. She felt the tiny spring that trickled below, and drew from all of the elements that bound man and woman to the animals of the lands. Her voice rose and fell as she wove her incantation, but the panthadon seemed unaffected as he came for her.

Villam Stanky owned the circus and had built it from a small sideshow. He was the one who found the great cat and took it from its jungle home in the Deep South. Each day the coppers rolled in from his various acts, but at night his ferocious man-eating panthadon brought in more coins than all the others combined. It was his pride and joy, but only because it made him a wealthy man. For this reason alone he hurried into the pit, whip and chair in hand, yelling, "Fear not young damsel, for *I* Villam, will save you from certain death!"

He could hear the crowd cheering as he entered, but soon realized it wasn't for him. He looked over and his blood boiled at the sight. There was his fierce killer lying on his back purring, while some little whelp of a girl was scratching his belly and having a chat with him.

Villam ran over and shouted in an exasperated voice, "What have you done to my panthadon!"

Shyla was startled, but answered, "I'm playing with my new friend," and continued to scratch the soft fur.

She knew she didn't like the man when she saw his face. He had a dark complexion and dark shifty eyes. He had a thin mustache, pointy eyebrows and a big hooked nose that moved when he talked.

"Are you trying to ruin my act?" he snapped, dropping his training gear and grabbing her arm. "Wait," he said before she could answer. "Aren't you the girl that the giant kidnapped?"

Shyla pulled herself from his grasp and scowled at him. "I was *not* kidnapped," she corrected him. "He was helping me."

The tall, thin man moved in her direction, but she kept her distance. "Well he hasn't helped me," said Villam. "I've asked him many times to join our great show and he has refused. I told him he wasn't wanted elsewhere, and how people consider him a monster, but that our happy family would welcome him like one of our own. Maybe you can talk to him for me to help make up for wrecking the act."

Shyla could feel her rage starting again, but calmed herself and replied, "I would never help you take advantage of my friend. People have been doing that since he left his home and it sickens me." She brushed the hair from her face and continued. "And you, a man who exploits people and animals for his own gain, are the worst kind. Storm told me you keep him hungry and tired, and he longs to be back in the jungle."

Villam looked at her like she was crazy. "Storm?" he said, rolling his eyes, then put his hand on his chin and scratched. "That's not bad," he decided, glancing at the great cat lying there. "I think I'll use it, but why did you call him that?"

She went over, knelt down and started rubbing the panthadon's ears, causing him to purr loudly. "That's his name," she answered, "or at least a loose translation from the visions, and it suits him."

Now the circus man was frustrated and getting angry. "Well young lady," he said in a huff, "you have single-handedly destroyed my main attraction, and are going to pay for it. I know who your father is, and when he wins the competition he will be hearing from me."

Shyla laughed, much to his chagrin, and spoke in an amused voice. "There's nothing wrong with Storm," she remarked. "The affects will wear off before tomorrow night, but I *beg* you, please return him to his homeland."

The circus man looked doubtful, yet somewhat relieved, and replied, "Yes of course. Next time we are down that way, he will be a free cat."

Villam helped her up and said, "It's getting late, so let's get you out of here and on your way again."

She could see that most of the crowd was gone, and wondered just how long she'd been in the pit. She said goodbye to Storm, grabbed her shredded package and followed the tall man to freedom. She wished her new friend could come with her, but that wasn't realistic, and she knew it.

The encounter with Villam had been very unpleasant, and right now all she wanted was to find the boys and get back to the pavilion.

As she walked along in search of her brother and Stafan, she understood that the nasty man would never set his main attraction free, but at least Mok wouldn't have to endure his cruelty.

She reached the main path and found the boys waiting at the place where they had last departed each other's company. When they saw her torn dress and tattered package, they were full of questions. She answered most of them, leaving out a few details as usual, and that seemed to satisfy them.

Their adventure, though entertaining, hadn't been quite so daring and even somewhat disappointing when at the end of it not one person had beaten the strongman. Of course Big Ben hadn't made an appearance, so Cade found some solace in that.

Stafan had instructed his driver to wait at the northeast corner of the entertainment section, which took them past the gypsies on their way to the carriage. It was getting late but that was when the many talents they possessed were on display. Shyla hadn't seen the old gypsy woman for quite some time, and the ordeal with Storm had reminded her of the kindness and generosity she had shown in sharing her knowledge and wisdom. Even with her blind eye she could see more than most, and had taught Shyla how to tame the beasts of the wild and sense the weather. She had never really gotten that last one down, which was her own fault, and something she intended to work on.

"Would you guys mind very much if we took a small detour through the gypsy camp?" she asked, smiling sweetly and looking as cute as she could. Both Cade and Stafan had already wanted to go, but hadn't asked because of what she had just been through, so they agreed readily, and the three changed course toward the colorful wagons and roaring fires.

As they approached, they heard the sound of music and singing. There was also the noise of cheering and applause. Above that was a loud voice announcing the different acts and describing some of the feats they were performing. It was exciting to hear, and even more exciting when they passed between two wagons, entering the huge area where the vocalized actions were taking place.

It reminded her of the circus, except there were no tents or buildings. All the performers did their shows in the open-air, and to her eye seemed far more talented. There were at least twelve different acts around the center, each with a bucket in front so the crowd could show their appreciation through coin. Stafan must have agreed with her about the talent because he went around the ring and threw a silver in each one. She wondered if they made more by not charging admission and letting the people decide what to donate. According to Stafan's contribution they just might, but she wasn't here to see more entertainment. She wanted to seek out the friend she hadn't seen for a couple of years.

When the music had died down somewhat, she asked a gypsy fellow where she could find the old woman and he pointed her to the next set of wagons. She thanked him and led the boys to another camp, with a *completely* different atmosphere.

The fires were smaller here and the customers a little more subdued. "We are looking for a yellow and green wagon," she told the boys, scanning her surroundings.

There were wagons of all different colors here but she didn't see the one she was looking for. She saw a blue one, advertising a weaver and a red one selling remedies. Some had gambling and others dancing, but the one that really caught her eye was the purple and black wagon that had, "Sindra the Seer", printed on its side.

Shyla had never been to a fortune-teller, but had always been intrigued by them and wondered if they could *truly* see the future. She started forward, and when she got close, could see a table set up at the wagon's rear. At it sat a woman with black and silver hair.

Stafan stopped and asked, "You aren't seriously thinking of giving payment to that gypsy so she can feed you a bunch of nonsense, are you?"

Shyla giggled, "Oh come on," she replied. "It might be fun," and continued along the path.

"Well don't say I didn't warn you," he offered, following behind.

As they approached, the seer turned her head and eyed them up and down. Shyla couldn't tell how old she was in the dim candlelight, but her face appeared smooth.

"Well my dearies," she said, not changing her expression, "come to have your fortunes told, have you?"

Shyla moved forward another step and answered, "Yes, I believe we will."

The gypsy removed her scarf and shook out her hair. It hung down and onto the ground from her sitting position and was thick and straight. Next she reached into the trunk beside her and pulled out a wooden box with pictures and writing on it. She placed it on the table and removed the lid, revealing a large round object that was dark green in color and appeared to be made of crystal or glass. She took it from the container, placed it in front of herself and began polishing it with the scarf. Shyla watched her closely and wondered what it was for.

The woman finished, pulled the candle to her, then looked up and asked, "Who is first?"

Shyla was shocked when she saw her, for she had never seen eyes that color before. They were violet with a black ring around the outside, and her skin was ageless. That, along with her black hair and silver streaks, made her look very mystical indeed. When she was done staring, Shyla decided that this Sindra woman reminded her of her grandmother Zarina, and felt a pang of loneliness at the thought.

"I'll go first," Stafan volunteered, and sat down on the chair across from Sindra.

"It will be five coppers," she said, pushing a cup toward him.

He took a silver from his pouch, tossed it in and replied, "That should cover all of us." The gypsy nodded, placed her hands on the table and motioned for him to do the same. He did so against his better judgment, not wanting to seem apprehensive to his new friends.

Sindra took his hands in hers and closed her eyes. She started chanting softly and rocking back and forth. Then without any apparent reason, stopped and opened her eyes again. When she did, the green ball in front of her began to glow. Faintly at first, but after a few moments it lit up the faces of the two seated at the table. Stafan was watching closely and wondering what trick she was using to create the effect.

Its illumination remained constant as the seer began to speak. "You are weighed down with responsibility," she began, "like a chain around your neck, but it is not without reward. You will be the master of many estates and wealth will be yours, but the cost will be your freedom."

Stafan looked at her skeptically. "Will I be happy? Will I marry? Will I have children?" he asked all-at-once.

She leaned back and chanted some more, then stopped and said, "You will marry, but not until your latter years, and she will bear you a son and a daughter. Only then will you know *true* happiness." The green light faded and Sindra let go of his hands. "That is all," she said in a strained voice.

Stafan stood up and shook his head. "You can't be serious," he countered, obviously frustrated. "Other than the fairytale at the end, anyone could have told me those facts."

The gypsy met his gaze. "I only tell what I see. No more. No less," she replied in a convincing tone.

The air was calm now and smelled of cooked meat and pan-bread. Shyla thought the woman might pack up her stuff after what Stafan had said, but she just sat there waiting.

"Do we have any other nonbelievers?" she asked, looking at Cade and Shyla with her strange eyes.

"I'll go next," said Cade, taking Stafan's place on the chair. He was rather enjoying the gypsy camp and couldn't wait to find out what was waiting for *him* in the future.

The seer went through the chanting once more, then grasped his hands as she leaned forward. Again the emerald sphere glowed as she began her prediction.

"I see for you a life of freedom and adventure. You will travel to many lands and partake in many cultures. You will become very well-known for your craft and will use it to help others, but as always there is a tradeoff." She straightened her body and let go of his hands. "You will never be a wealthy man," she finished, leaning back again.

He sat there for a few moments taking it all in, then thanked the woman and returned to the others. "Did you hear that Shyla?" he asked in an excited voice. "I'm gonna be an adventurer."

She smiled. "Yes, a poor one," she replied, and they all laughed.

The sound of dogs barking filled the night air and the customers around the wagons were thinning out.

"Maybe we should go," said Shyla, almost insistent. "I don't really need my fortune told, and I still want to find my friend, and it is getting late."

The boys frowned. "Come on Sis," urged Cade. "It's fun and it's paid for."

"Yes," agreed Stafan. "And who knows, maybe she'll tell you that you don't marry until your latter years either," he added, winking at her. Her mouth opened, then she blushed and looked away.

Shyla was feeling anxious about the seer looking into her life. Whether she was real or just a good con-artist, she wasn't sure she wanted to chance it. There were so many things she didn't want the others to know about her, and maybe some she might not want to hear either. It would be safer to leave, but she was tired of running from her problems or hiding them away. This woman might have answers that could help her, or information that could prevent her from burning out. She decided to act before she changed her mind, and with a forced resolve, walked to the table and sat down.

She could see the gypsy up close now and thought she was beautiful in a frightening way. Her skin was so white and her small hands revealed long nails that were colored black with silver stars and crescent moons painted on them.

"What is that jade globe and why does it light up?" asked Shyla in her direct way.

Sindra didn't seem to hear her, but replied, "That is an ancient artifact which has been handed down in my family for generations. When the seer who possesses it rejoins the balance, the next oldest girl with the vision receives it and keeps it until she is gone. After that it goes to the next, and so-on."

Shyla stared at the green ball, but wasn't satisfied. "Where did it come from and what is it doing when it glows?" she asked as direct as before.

"It is called a Cantra, and I don't need *it* to see that you have a very inquisitive mind," she answered, still very serious. "As to where it came from, that I don't know for sure. The elders say that it was found deep within the ground."

She stopped and prepared to do her telling, but could see that the young girl would not be satisfied until all of her questions were answered, so she continued.

"The flux, or glowing as you call it, is a flow of energy triggered by a seer that magnifies her ability to look into a person's path of being. It enhances the visions and increases the depth of seeing."

Shyla was surprised the woman was as direct with her answers as she was with her questions, and started to worry again. She was having second thoughts once more, but it was too late, so she put her hands on the table and waited to hear what the seer would say about her life.

Sindra grabbed her hands, leaned back and started to chant in her strange tongue. She spoke softly at first, then increasingly louder until the Cantra began to glow a beautiful deep sea green.

She leaned forward, opening her eyes, and they mirrored the globe in front of her.

Shyla was startled when she realized it wasn't a reflection, and became more worried as a result. She could feel the gypsy trembling, and the words that came from her lips ceased.

Sindra grasped her hands tighter and moved closer. "I see a happy childhood," she began, and the trembling stopped. "You will travel as well, and visit many lands. You will be blessed with loving and loyal friends, and mentored by a wise and powerful ally."

She paused, and Shyla could see the strain on her face and sense a conflict within her. The seer tightened her grip even more and continued.

"You will embark on a perilous journey that will bring you to a crossroad. You must choose wisely or. . . ." She stopped and the trembling started again, only it was even more severe. "I can see no more. . . . You are blocked and I sense a great power . . . and something else." Sweat ran down her face now and she was almost convulsing. "Something coming . . . a darkness . . . an evil beyond imagining . . . it's coming. I can . . . see it. No! Noooo!" She screamed until no sound would come, and her eyes rolled back in her head.

Shyla tried to pull away, but the woman's grip was like iron. The Cantra's brightness was increasing now and she could feel it trying to weave its way in. The light flared as it detected the intrusion, and she had to harness it quickly to prevent another situation where she would be compromised.

It seemed that without the seer's control, the Cantra's power was increasing and flowing right at her. She knew instinctively that if she didn't stop is soon, it would harm her.

She took a tighter hold on the light and brought it to the forefront, right up against the green energy. It was a lot easier to wield now that it was spread throughout her, which was good, but also cause for concern. Slowly she started to push, but was met with equal force. She increased her effort, and again the Cantra's power matched her own, and then increased. It was apparent now that this was not going to be as easy as she'd hoped, so she gathered all the white light and drove it straight at the intruder. The green energy fought to fulfill its intended task and Shyla could tell she was going to have to call on every ounce of the energy. She straightened her body and concentrated all of the power at her core. Then like a bolt of lightning, released it, driving the green aura back into the Cantra, splitting it in two.

Cade was watching from behind and saw the flash of light, then noticed the gypsy woman coming out of her trance. Stafan was impressed and wondered how much better the act would have been had he tipped her a silver instead of the five coppers.

Sindra released her grip on Shyla's hands as her presence of mind returned. Shyla knew her hands should be in pain, but was so busy reining in the light that she barely noticed.

Finally the seer came to her senses and stared at the broken Cantra that lie before her on the table. "What have you done!" she yelled, mortified by what she saw.

After seeing the blinding flash and hearing the commotion, gypsies from other wagons were starting to gather and voices were buzzing in the air.

Shyla wasn't sure what to tell her, so she lied. "I think you must have lost control when you blacked out, and overloaded the Cantra," she answered, hoping the fortune-teller didn't recall any of what had actually happened.

Sindra leaned forward and stared into her. "Oh yes," she replied, her penetrating eyes fixed on Shyla, "it overloaded all right, and thanks for bringing me back." Her gaze turned to a look of sympathy now and she spoke softly. "It must be difficult for one so young to carry a burden of responsibility so great." Shyla could see the concern in the gypsy's eyes as Sindra held her cheeks and kissed her forehead.

Well so much for trying to hide things from a seer, she thought, and realized that the gypsy must know everything; the light, the darkness, and that sweet, sorrow-filled voice calling to her. She had seen it all and it had almost destroyed her.

Shyla stood and apologized to her for what she had done. "Nonsense," replied Sindra. "Through you I have seen more, and farther than I ever dreamed possible, or had wished to," she added, with a hint of fear in her voice. "Before you go," she continued, "there's something I would like you to have." She stood and reached between the pieces of Cantra, picking something up. She held out her hand and Shyla could see a fragment of the ancient artifact about two inches long, and in the shape of a heart. "Please take this," she offered, placing the shard in Shyla's hand. "It may yet hold some of the Cantra's power, and I have a feeling you are going to need it more than I."

When she placed the green piece in her bag, the pain in the gypsy's eyes was evident, so she asked, "Are you sure you don't need it?"

The woman's face turned expressionless again and she replied, "It was created by your will my dear, and who are we to question the balance? Besides, it's a turning point and a chance for our kind to revisit our roots and stop relying on an external crutch to perform our natural ability."

Shyla felt a bond with her and couldn't help but like the seer. "I will see you again," she told her, and rejoined her brother and Stafan.

"What was that all about?" asked Cade, who had been quite impressed by the performance.

"Oh she was just giving us our copper's worth," replied Shyla, feeling a tinge of guilt at her deception.

"Well I hope you're satisfied," scoffed Stafan. "I mean surely you didn't think she had real vision. There is no such thing. And honestly, I don't see how anyone could actually profess to see the future."

The woodcutter's daughter looked at the young nobleman and felt disappointed. With the words he had just spoken, she was pretty sure there would be no *future* for them, but he was still the most handsome boy she had ever seen.

"Shyla. . . . Shyla my precious girl," came a raspy voice from the onlookers. "Aren't you a sight for a sore eye."

She recognized the voice instantly and ran over to the old gypsy woman and gave her a big hug. "I see you haven't lost your sense of humor," commented Shyla, and hugged her again.

The old woman cackled loudly and replied, "When you're as old as I am, it's one of the few luxuries you've got left." She took Shyla's hand and cackled some more. "Come now girl, we've got lots of catching up to do," she told her, and led her away from the crowd.

"I won't be long!" Shyla yelled back.

"Don't you worry about us!" Stafan called out. "I've just spotted a dice game that should keep your brother and I entertained."

The old woman moved fast for her age and Shyla was hard-pressed to keep up without running, but it was only a short distance to her wagon. The gypsy looked slightly more hunched over than in their last visit although it didn't appear to slow her down much, and soon they were up the steps and standing inside her traveling home.

"Some tea my dear?" she asked, as they sat down at the small table.

"I would love some, Grelda," she replied, removing her coat and placing it on the chair-back.

She was one of the few people who called the old woman by her real name, and probably one of the only people who knew it. Most called her, "The old gypsy woman with the blind eye", which she seemed to enjoy.

As she poured the tea, Shyla looked at the old black patch on the left side of her face. Her long white hair hung down her back and was tied with a scarf. Her good eye was hazel in color and slightly buggy. She still had most of her teeth, but her skin had seen better days, with wrinkle upon wrinkle revealing her years. Her true age was unknown to Shyla, although someone had once told her that Grelda was nearly two hundred years old. That was hard to believe, yet nowadays she wasn't dismissing anything that seemed unusual.

The tea tasted of cinnamon, one of the spices the gypsies traded, and warmed her as it went down. She hadn't realized how cold she was and welcomed the hot liquid.

"My you have grown child," remarked Grelda, as she sipped her own tea. "And how do you keep getting prettier with each visit?"

Shyla loved compliments, but sometimes felt awkward when they were spoken. "Why thank you," she replied, taking another sip.

She looked around the wagon and could see so many books and remedies that she could barely contain herself. Most of her collection of books had been given to her by the old gypsy, and she was excited to see if there were any new ones since her last visit.

"So how have you been?" asked Grelda politely, still holding her cup. She knew something was up and waited patiently for Shyla to tell her. The old woman had witnessed the lightning and could feel a change in the young girl, but its origin was foreign to her.

On her last trip through the Woodland Vale she had stopped to see Shyla. The young healer had always been wise for her age, but Grelda could now sense that something was weighing on her that was creating a forced responsibility. She could see a hardness forming in those innocent and inquisitive eyes, and it saddened her old heart. The ability to wield the magic of the land was strong in her, but this magic was something that could be outside of, or a vital part of the balance. That in itself was very fascinating and unnerving, so she took another drink and waited for Shyla's response.

What should I tell her? thought Shyla. She was so used to concealing the truth that it was becoming easy to lie, but she would never deceive Grelda, nor did she think she could even if she tried.

"I have been better," she told her honestly, and after that it was like opening a floodgate. From her first encounter with the darkness and the discovery of her new gift and what it meant, to the splitting of the Cantra, she told it all. It felt so good to finally let it out. When she was finished, the tears were streaming down her face and the old gypsy was cradling and rocking her gently.

"There there, my girl," the old woman soothed her. "Old Grelda is here."

When she was through crying, the relief she felt was astonishing. It was like much of the weight had been lifted from her, and she wept again. "I'm sorry," she apologized, drying her eyes with the old woman's handkerchief. "I've just never told anyone the complete truth before, and I guess it must have been bottled up inside."

Grelda brushed a tear from her cheek and stroked her hair. "You don't worry about that now," she encouraged her. "What we need to do is figure out what needs to be done to control this magic."

She poured Shyla another cup of tea and went to the front of the wagon. As she drank, Shyla could see her rummaging through the books and papers. When she returned, she was empty-handed. "I can't find anything in my collection that mentions the white energy you've described," she said, pouring herself some more tea. "The only thing you can do is find someone to teach you how to control it, and your grandmother Zarina would be my first choice. If anyone is able to help you, that old she-wolf can."

Those words coming from someone else might have offended Shyla, but she knew that Grelda meant them with the deepest respect, and voiced her agreement.

"At least we know that the light only triggers when you are being threatened somehow or someone is in trouble," reasoned Grelda, "and knowledge like that should help you prevent another incident, or at least get control of it sooner." Shyla loved and respected the old gal and nodded her consensus.

Shyla had stayed much too long and needed to get going soon, so she grabbed her coat, picked up the parcel and handed Grelda her cup. "I should be getting back," she told her, "before Cade loses the rest of his winnings, if he hasn't already."

The old gypsy looked disappointed, but understood. "Before you go," she said, "I want to give you a gift. I know you love books, so I want you to look through my collection and pick out one for your very own."

Shyla's face lit up and she exclaimed, "Really!"

The front wall contained a bookshelf that was completely filled with every type of story and poem you could think of, so she hurried over to make her selection. She was thrilled and excited, but took a moment to relax and find just the right one. There were so many, but one in particular caught her eye. She felt somehow drawn to it, and when she flipped through the pages, found she didn't understand a word that was written there. The language was foreign to her, but for some reason she knew she wanted it. She brought the book over and asked Grelda what it said on the cover.

"It's strange you should choose this book," she said, holding it to the light. "I acquired it very long ago and have never been able to decipher the writings, but if you want it, it's yours."

Shyla placed it in her bag alongside the heart shaped piece from the Cantra. "I'm not sure why the book intrigues me," she said openly. "There's just something about it."

The old woman cackled loudly. "No need to explain my dear, but I want you to choose another. Something you can actually read."

She knew better than to argue, so she walked back over and, after considerable deliberation, chose *The New Adventures of the Twelve Foot Gnome*. She already had the first stories and couldn't wait to read the new ones.

"Good choice," responded Grelda. "I've always loved those books."

The old gypsy helped her with her coat and gave her some cookies for the road. "Now you be careful, and when you sense the magic coming on, I want you to think about feeling the weather the way I showed you. You know the calm that comes when the day is going to be sunny and warm. Take that sensation and try to use it to relax the light within you, and hopefully that will help," she offered in her kind way.

"I will try that, and thanks again for everything. It was so good to see you again."

They hugged, and Shyla stepped out the door.

"Don't forget to say hello to your mother and grandmother for me when you see them, and tell Grace to stop by if she gets a chance," said Grelda, standing on the top stair.

Shyla looked back and replied, "I will tell them, and you take care my friend." She waved and moved off in search of her brother and Stafan.

There was only one wagon left with any activity to speak of, so she decided to begin there.

As she started over, she realized she was still carrying the package that contained the chewed up shoes, and wasn't quite sure why. It was hard to discard something you had waited so long for, but she knew they were beyond salvaging. As she walked up, she reluctantly tossed them in the fire. *Maybe I'm just not supposed to get new shoes*, she thought, and sighed.

The boys were there, and right in the middle of a dice game called, "Crowns and Wheels". Stafan was shaking a cup and calling for one more crown. He tossed the die from the container, and when it stopped rolling there was a picture of a crown on the top side. The gamblers yelled and congratulated him as he scooped up his winnings.

"Are you up or down?" asked Shyla, clapping along with the others.

"That win pays for the day, besides the necklace, and I think Cade is one silver richer," he told her, as he passed the dice-filled cup to the next person.

"It sounds like it's a good time to be going then," she offered, not wanting to break up their fun.

"I'm ready," he agreed, "but I think Cade has the fever."

Shyla knew exactly what he was talking about and had heard stories about men who had lost everything they owned in a single night.

She moved over to Cade, who was next in line for the dice, and squeezed his arm. He looked around. "Hi Sis," he greeted her.

"Stafan and I are ready to return if you are," she said nonchalantly.

"I will be shortly," he replied, not really paying attention to her. "I'm doing well, and I think I can double my silvers this turn."

What could she do? She couldn't just stand by and watch him lose. She grabbed his other arm and turned him to her. "Cade!" she raised her voice, making sure she had his full attention. "Don't you remember when we were children and the gypsies taught us about their gambling wagons?"

At first he was startled by her actions and tried to pull away, but then a thought-filled expression came over his face.

"Better luck next time sir!" shouted the game-boss, and held the cup toward Cade. "It's your turn young man," he said with a glint in his eye. "I hope you don't take the wagon, wheels-and-all this round."

Cade looked at Shyla, then at the man, and took the dice. "Not tonight," he declined, passing them to the fellow next to him.

The game-boss looked angry for a moment, then caught himself and gave them a wide smile. "Come back and try your luck again soon," he crooned, and moved to his next mark.

Everything except the gypsy camp was shut down for the night, so they had no distractions on their way back to the carriage. They'd had a full evening, and when they began moving, were glad to be going back. When they reached the pavilion gates the guard let them through and told them there was food awaiting them in the dining area. They stopped for a quick snack and then went straight to their chambers. Shyla thanked Stafan for the day as they separated down their own hallways, and each of them was asleep as soon as they climbed into their beds.

CHAPTER

21

Relentless Doubts

The next morning was another early one and Ivan felt great. He had a good breakfast and a peaceful carriage ride to the competition quarter. The sun was shining brightly in a cloudless sky, and the conditions were perfect for a day of woodcutting.

The previous rounds had been made up of two or three eliminations per event, leaving eight men remaining in the semifinals. There was Ivan, the giant and six others. Vero had shown him the event board earlier, and again it was strategically set up. There would be six eliminations today, leaving two men standing and moving on. In the first heats, the giant was up against a fellow northerner down from the Land of Gales, and Ivan was taking on a burly woodsman from Belden's Wall. The other four would be fighting it out for two positions in the afternoon round.

If all went as expected, the giant and Ivan would beat their opponents, putting them through to the next day, and the championship round. Vero had it brilliantly planned to maximize the excitement and entertainment, and today Ivan would get a chance to see Mok in action. He wasn't sure if that was a good idea or not, but really wanted to size up his competition. From the stories that had been going around, and the ranting and raving about the giant's domination in the events, his curiosity was piqued.

Ivan laid in his tent and cleared his mind. He felt relaxed and in a good mental state after his picnic the day before, and was as ready as he'd ever been at this stage of the competition. The entrants this year were quadrupled from the previous, and although he needed it desperately, couldn't let gold be the driving force behind his performance. Focusing on the craft itself, and the love he had for it, had always been his reason for competing. In all the years that hadn't changed, even with the pressures on him.

The bell rang three times and the horns sounded, so he grabbed his gear and headed for his first event.

After the wonderful afternoon with Grace he had meticulously sharpened and honed his blades to a fine edge, and felt confident the outcome today would be solely dependent on his skill.

The first event was the wood splitting, and Ivan had no trouble staying ahead of his muscular opponent. The man's thickness enhanced his strength but slowed him, and he couldn't compete with the woodcutter's agility and lightning speed. The tree falling and log chopping held the same results, but the tree climbing proved to be somewhat tougher. The man's leg strength was incredible and Ivan actually broke a sweat as he bounded up the tree, ringing the bell only a few moments sooner. The last event was the axe throwing, and of course no one could beat Ivan at that as he spun his hatchet in for the win.

He shook the man's hand and asked him how things were in Belden's Wall.

"Good," he replied, obviously enamored by the legend, "but even better when I tell everyone that I met, and competed against the greatest woodcutter in the land." He was so thrilled that he shook Ivan's hand again, then ran off to tell his story to anyone who would listen.

Grace came over and hugged her man while the rest of the family voiced their support. He was finished now until the afternoon, but decided to stay and watch the giant throw. He wasn't able to watch any of his other events because they were competing at the same time, but after lunch each event would be finished by both sets of competitors before they moved on to the next.

Ivan received so many handshakes that the faces blurred into one another, and was offered enough good luck to last a lifetime. He took a few moments for each person, and even after all the years, still appreciated their support and adoration.

Everyone quieted when the giant entered the axe throwing area. Standing there, his opponent looked like a small child next to him and Ivan had trouble not feeling intimidated by his sheer size alone. That was just fine, but all the size and strength in the land wouldn't help in this event, so Ivan watched him closely as the giant pulled an axe from his large bag. It was of normal size, but looked like a hatchet in Mok's hands.

The woodcutter watched everything the giant did, from his stance to the way he gripped the handle, and where. Mok brought his thumb over the edge of the blade to test its sharpness and then Ivan saw it. When he was finished, he caressed it and pulled it to his forehead, then rubbed the handle up and down before gripping it again. The giant truly loved woodcutting, and that was more of a worry to Ivan than his *size* or *strength*. When someone had that much passion for their craft, only then were they capable of greatness, and as a man who felt that way, Ivan could easily see it in Mok.

The man from the Land of Gales raised his axe in the air, trying to gain some support from the crowd but they were there to see the giant. After a few unenthusiastic cheers, he stepped to the line and threw his hatchet just inside the bull's-eye. There was a decent response to his attempt, but it multiplied quickly as Mok took his place to throw. The anticipation grew as he drew back the axe, but Ivan knew the outcome before he let it go. All he needed to see was the way he held the axe, and the fluid motion with which he delivered it, to know for sure. *Thunk!* the blade sank deep and inside his opponent's placement, winning him the event.

The people shouted their approval and the giant waved in appreciation.

"I knew he was good Daddy!" exclaimed Shyla, clapping as loud as she could.

"Yes he is," replied the woodcutter, starting to feel that twinge of doubt again.

Word of the giant's advancement to the afternoon round spread quickly, and Ivan looked forward to studying him some more. If his other events were like this one, he would definitely have a challenge on his hands.

They got some lunch and took it to the tent. Ivan didn't even taste the food as his mind focused on the next round. His family, who had been in this situation many times now, knew better than to try to communicate with him. They finished the meal quietly, offered him their support and left the woodcutter to his thoughts.

After he was finished, he took out his axes and began sharpening them. He ran the stone over the blade methodically and thought about his predicament. His next challenger was one of the few woodsmen from the Westlands. He was good, but Ivan had faced him more than once and beaten him. That was just it. He had gone up against all these men at least once over the years, but never the giant, and if things continued the way they were going, he would be facing him at the finals tomorrow. *Was the giant good enough to beat him?* he wondered. *Could the balance unfold in such a way that Claude Boyle would end up victorious in this?* He pushed the thought away and refocused. There was no use worrying about what might happen, and what he needed to do now was take the necessary actions to prevent it.

The bell rang, so he grabbed his pack and left the tent. When he stepped out, the giant was right there.

"I walk with you?" asked Mok, slowing to match his pace.

"Of course," replied Ivan, not wanting to seem rude. Usually he didn't associate with the other competitors until after the competition, but wasn't really up against him until the next day, if it worked out that way.

"I look forward watch you," said the giant in his deep voice.

"And I you," mirrored the woodcutter, *his* voice sounding thin and empty in comparison.

When they reached their destination Ivan could see hundreds of people surrounding the event site. They applauded as the two walked up, and Claude quickly grabbed Mok and led him away. Ivan had seen much-too-much of that man over the past few days and would be glad when he could wave the purse full of gold in his face. He knew it wasn't right to think that way, but after all that Claude had done, he didn't care.

The giant was up first, and when Ivan saw who he was cutting against, he was glad. Mok's opponent was woodsman to the king, and in charge of his private timber reserve. He was brilliant with a blade and had placed second to Ivan many times before. In fact there wasn't a better axe-man to test the giant's skill against, and that was his intention.

As they squared off, he was shocked at the big man's finesse and speed, and after three events the giant had dominated the eastern cutter completely. Ivan did the same to his opponent, but not with the ferocity and attack that Mok had shown. It was then that he was convinced that this giant was truly a woodcutter, and not just a sideshow attraction.

The next event was almost amusing as the giant raced up the hundred foot span, leaving the king's man at the sixty-five foot mark when he rang the bell. Ivan was also first to ring his bell, but was almost certain the giant's run was faster.

That left one more event, and by the end, Ivan and Mok were on their way to the final day like so many had predicted. The woodcutter congratulated the giant, and before he was finished, Claude was there pulling him away. "Looks like your reign is almost over," he said with a sneer and a smug look on his face. Ivan was still holding his hatchet, but kept his shaking hand at his side. He just stared at his neighbor until he looked away and moved into the crowd, then went to find his family.

Everyone was excited for his victory and advancement to the final day, but inside he felt a trepidation that gnawed at him.

The giant was good. Maybe too good, and that worried him. This was not a moment to falter, and he needed to forgo his negative thoughts. Sure the giant was a threat, but had he ever really been threatened by any man in his field before? This was his chance to finally face a truly worthy opponent, and he needed to embrace it rather than fear it.

Grace sat beside him in the carriage and could see that something was wrong. "Don't worry my love," she told him. "After tomorrow they will be singing songs about how the great woodcutter defeated the giant."

Ivan squeezed her hand. "I hope so," he said, and remained silent the rest of the way.

When they reached the pavilion they cleaned up and were escorted to the banquet hall where they greeted Vero and a room full of guests. Ivan hadn't realized that the baron had invited some of his friends, and a few of the royals, for a feast in his honor. Even though he didn't feel like celebrating, he took his seat at Vero's right side in respect to his host.

The night dragged on with toast after toast, but the food and wine were still tasteless to him as he sank deeper into his depressed state. It crept up on him like a foul wind and he couldn't shake it.

Vero could sense his friend's distress and cut the meal short by two courses. He had dessert served and the people on their way out in an expeditious fashion, as only he knew how.

As each person retired, they gave the woodcutter their best wishes and good luck for the finals, and he acknowledged each of them woodenly while trying to keep up a formal front.

Once the guests were gone, the baron turned to him and asked, "What is bothering you my friend?"

Ivan knew he meant well, and replied, "I think I'm just exhausted from the day and need some rest."

The baron stood and said, "I think we could all use some of that," and pulled Charlotte's chair out for her. Everyone was in agreement, so they all turned in early in anticipation of the final round of the Woodcutting Competition.

The night sky was clear, with a slight chill in the air. The moon, which had almost reached its fullness, shone down brightly on the meadow that made up the four quarters. Inside the pavilion all the guests slept peacefully in their cozy rooms. All except Ivan, whose face looked strained as he dreamed of an army of giants who were coming to take him far from his family.

He awoke in a cold sweat and sat up in bed. His stomach was in knots and he felt parched. He dressed in the dark and decided to take a walk to calm himself. The banquet room seemed like a good destination, and while he was there he would look for something to quench the powerful thirst he was experiencing. He traversed his way through the labyrinth of hallways until he reached the one that led straight to the room he intended to visit. As he got closer he could see light coming from inside, and when he entered, saw Vero sitting at the large table going through some papers.

"Couldn't sleep either?" Ivan asked as he approached.

The baron looked up from his work. "No, I'm just finishing some business for tomorrow's finals," he answered, motioning the woodcutter over. Ivan sat down, grabbed a goblet from the table and poured himself a drink from one of the pitchers in front of him.

"I hope you don't mind," he said, and took a few swallows. "I don't know why I'm so thirsty."

Vero smiled, "Help yourself," he replied. "What's mine is yours. In fact I think I'll join you. I need a break from this anyway." The baron poured himself some juice and refilled Ivan's.

There were only three candles lit, but it didn't take much light for Vero to see the worry in the woodcutter's eyes. He reached over and placed his hand on Ivan's forearm and said, "I've known you over thirty years and I think I can see when something is troubling you deeply, so don't try to tell me you're just exhausted."

The woodcutter looked up at his old friend and replied, "It's the giant. His skill and power may be unmatched even by me, and it has me shaken."

Vero smiled. "Not to make light of your situation, but now you know how every woodcutter who ever faced you has felt." Ivan thought about it and realized it was probably true, but it didn't change what he was feeling inside.

"I'll tell you what," Vero continued. "I understand your concern, and it is warranted I grant you, but I think you should have another cup of juice and think about exactly who you are. Once you get that straightened out, go back and get some rest and I'll bet everything looks a lot brighter in the morning. In fact, I'd be willing to wager that when I see you step onto that field tomorrow, it will be the mighty legend that I know and love."

Ivan stared at the man across the table and his heart swelled. "Thank you for that," he said, and stood up.

"I'm always here for you," replied Vero, then went back to sorting his papers. The woodcutter returned to his room and tried to get some sleep, but his thoughts kept returning to the giant.

He wasn't sure when he fell into slumber, but the next sound he heard was Grace saying, "Ivan. . . . Ivan wake up. We need to get ready for the morning meal."

He opened his eyes and saw his beautiful wife looking down at him. He didn't move, but kept staring at the woman who counted on him to provide for and protect her. The woman who believed in him beyond words, and now the thought of failing today made the doubt in him even heavier.

She felt his forehead and listened to his chest. "I don't sense any illness in you, but I can tell something is very wrong," she observed, with a worried expression. "If you just tell me what the problem is we can work through it together," she offered, taking his hand in hers.

He gazed upon the love of his life and saw the deep concern on her sweet face. He felt like he was betraying her with the words he spoke, but had to be honest. "I don't think I can beat him," he uttered regretfully.

The look in her eyes when he finished speaking would have scared a man of any size and he laid there waiting for the lecture, but all she said was, "You mean Claude?"

Ivan's eyes widened and he sat up. A fire kindled deep within him, and in an instant, burned away any doubt he ever had. He felt his strength returning, and his resolve wrapping around him like armor plating. He looked at Grace and she was smiling. *What a woman*, he thought, and jumped out of bed. He grabbed her and kissed her, then dressed in his best woodcutting outfit and checked his gear.

It was all in order and he was ready, so he stood by the entrance and watched as Grace finished fixing her hair. She had it up in a half ponytail and tied with a ribbon. She wore her new dress, like she had planned, and was a vision to behold.

"Well," said Ivan, offering his arm, "I've got a giant to take down, and I'm gonna need a big breakfast."

CHAPTER
22

Contest of Strength

Vero wasn't at the dining table when the family sat down and Ivan hadn't expected him to be. He knew he would be off early checking on everything, making sure the day ran smoothly.

The Hardens laughed and joked through the meal, but the children weren't used to seeing their father act like that before the big day. Usually he was very somber and focused, but they liked it much better when he was being himself. The light mood continued throughout the carriage ride, and Rufus, who got to come along again, sensed it also and barked loudly whenever the family laughed.

The crowd erupted when Ivan arrived, and kept applauding as the rest of his family stepped out. He could see well over a thousand spectators, which was by far the most that had ever attended the competition.

He watched his wife and children as they made their way over to the baron's private seating box, and felt proud. Grace looked stunning in her new green dress, with her auburn hair swaying beneath the matching ribbon. Shyla wore her cute yellow dress, and had worked so hard to make her old shoes look presentable. Cade on the other hand wore his old hunting clothes, but they were clean and he felt comfortable in them.

Even old Rufus appeared younger as he trotted behind. Ivan kept watching until they were seated, then went to his tent to await the start.

The contestants' area was quiet this day and he welcomed the silence. It was short-lived though, and he barely had a chance to relax and grab some water before the bell rang its last chime of the year. He tightened the laces on his leather boots, checked his gear once more and started over to the wood splitting event.

Mok was there when he arrived, and he was glad he had resolved his earlier issue because the giant looked very intimidating indeed. His axe was new, and twice the size of Ivan's. He looked him up and down and decided that Claude must have had an outfit made especially for him because he was dressed in full woodcutter's garb. He really did look the part, right down to his leggings and enormous boots.

The day was clear and sunny and the baron's voice carried on the light breeze. "Good people of the Woodland Vale and surrounding areas, along with our welcome guests from nearby lands. I am very pleased that you have joined me here to witness the final day of our humble twenty-second year of the Woodcutting Competition."

The crowd responded aggressively, but he didn't hush them like before, waiting for them to finish before he continued.

"As a child I was always fascinated by the art of woodcutting, and grew to love it even though I don't swing an axe. Just watching the skill it takes to perfect the craft has always held my respect, and I am honored that I can host a tournament that brings the best woodsmen together in one place. It thrills me that men who wield axes at this caliber get to show their abilities to hundreds of people, rather than a few trees and forest animals. I know each of you has learned to appreciate what these men offer and have given to improve our lives, and it's my great pleasure, once a year, to give just a little back to them. It's not so much the gold as it is the acknowledgment they receive here. They are so often overlooked and taken for granted, but to me they are the unsung heroes of our land. Ladies and gentlemen I give you . . . your woodcutters!"

All the contestants stood and waved, and the people responded with even more eagerness than before. For a second time Vero waited for them, then continued once again. "Your enthusiasm is contagious my friends, but let's save some for our finalists," he said, directing their attention to the two woodsmen who stood there resting on their axes.

"Our first man came to us from beyond the Bitter Mountains in the northern reaches of Arcana. He's been a woodcutter all his life and we are thrilled that he came to compete this year. At first people weren't sure about him, and some were downright scared, but after he helped a young girl that we all know and love, we found out he has a heart as big as he is. Would you please give a warm, Woodland Vale welcome to our first finalist, Tamarack Jack!"

The whole place broke out with an earsplitting reception which continued for so long that the baron had to stop it. He raised his arms and turned his attention to Ivan.

"Our next finalist needs no introduction, but deserves only the best. I've known him for most of my life and consider him a true friend. When I first told him I wanted to put on the competition he asked me, 'Who would want to watch that?'" Everyone laughed and Ivan looked amused as Vero carried on. "I think your question has been answered loudly today," he said, and the woodcutter smiled and nodded. "It started as an idea, and with Ivan's help, became a reality. The first year we held it there were some tough competitors, but at only eighteen, Ivan won it and has held the crown for twenty seasons since. He was a legend ten years ago, and I'm glad to see he's in fine legend form today." He turned to Ivan and they exchanged a heartfelt glance.

Vero moved forward and lifted both arms toward the woodcutter and said, "Now please make welcome the greatest woodcutter to ever hold an axe. The legend . . . the sensation . . . the truly magnificent, Ivan Harden!"

The crowd was in a turmoil now, but Vero just sat back down and let them go. He could see that his friend was back to his old self, but the encouragement from the people couldn't hurt either. Ivan saluted the baron, gestured to the fans and readied himself for the first event.

The wood splitting was a very simple contest but took a great deal of finesse and dexterity. For the finals, each man started with twenty-five blocks of wood. His goal was to split and stack them between the two posts in front of him before the other man finished his.

There were only two main rules to this challenge. First, you had to split all of the wood on top of your chopping block, and second, every piece had to be stacked between the posts before you could call to the turnkeeper.

Before they began, the blocks were stacked four-high in three rows on either side of each man, with the final one placed on the chopping block ready for the first strike. The giant's blocks were twice as big as the woodcutters due to a rule that had been implemented on the second year of the competition.

Ivan remembered when that brute of a man from the Big Timber area had come down and entered, bringing his oversized axe with him. Right away the other contestants began complaining about the difference, so a new rule was put in place to ensure the fairness of the events. From then on each axe was weighed and measured, and the appropriate sized logs were allotted to each woodsman. It didn't make that much difference in the wood splitting, but with the tree falling and log chopping, without the rule it would be quite an advantage to the giant.

Mok turned to Ivan and said, "Good luck for you."

The woodcutter looked up and replied, "And you."

The two men raised their axes and waited for the turnkeeper's words. The old man lifted his arm and shouted, "Make ready. . . . Begin!" and the blades fell simultaneously.

The woodcutter's speed, matched with his accuracy, was beyond imagining as he sliced through the lengths and tossed the pieces into a perfect stack. No one had ever seen him move like that before, but he had good reason. Beside him was a master-woodsman, and no matter how fast he cut and stacked, the giant seemed to match him strike-for-strike. He didn't look over, but could hear the force of each blow, so he gave everything he had to the last ten blocks.

Every muscle in his body strained with each hit and the sweat surfaced and ran down his torso. His lungs were on fire and his breath labored as he threw the last pieces on the pile and yelled, "Done!"

The crowd went wild, but it wasn't official until the turnkeeper checked it and gave the okay.

Ivan looked over now and saw the giant on his last piece, and noticed he hadn't slowed even with Ivan's announcement. As he watched Mok finish, he couldn't help but admire him and wish they'd met under different circumstances.

The turnkeeper stepped onto his platform. "It's official," he announced. "The wood splitting event has been won by Ivan Harden of the Woodland Vale."

Mok came over and shook his hand, "Good job," he said, and he could see the admiration in the big man's eyes. Never before in his life had Ivan had to work so hard to win an event, and he felt great as they moved to the tree falling area.

For the finals in this event they had brought in two thirty-one foot logs and buried them six feet in the ground, leaving twenty-five feet protruding. The reason for making them so high was to have enough weight to create a solid chopping area, and make it feel similar to falling a real tree.

Ivan set down his gear and grabbed his sharpening stone from the bag. He touched up his blade, then took a cup of water from one of the carriers. It was cool and refreshing going down and he drained it in a single motion. After thanking the boy, he moved up to the tree. He took his stance and looked over at Mok, who had a big grin on his face, and he could see that he *too* was truly loving this day.

The turnkeeper walked over and checked with each man, then climbed onto his perch and cleared his throat. "The tree falling is about to commence," he said loudly, trying to be heard above the crowd. He then raised his arm and called out, "Make ready. . . . Begin!"

The woodcutter's axe bit into the tree at a precise downward angle, then changed direction with an upward swing, knocking big chunks to the ground. His speed was almost a blur as he cut his way through the front side. He could hear the giant to his right, and each of his powerful blows was deafening as they shook the very ground beneath them.

Ivan finished the front and jumped to the other side. He spun his axe in the air and struck the back at the same moment his feet touched down, not missing a stroke.

Mok was pounding his way through the back now as well and you could hear a low rumble as he grunted with each forceful hit.

The chips were flying from each tree and it was an amazing spectacle. Everyone could see that both of these men were giants in their own right, and the match was too close to call.

Only a few more swings now, thought Ivan as he finished a perfect wedge. As the woodcutter drove in his final cut, Mok let out a yell and he heard the giant's tree crack. Ivan pulled his axe out quickly and watched the top half of his tree fall swiftly downward, but as he looked over, saw the giant's hit the ground just before it.

The crowd went silent and Ivan felt devastated. Never before in his life had he worked so hard and lost an event. He wasn't sure how to react, but like a true champion, he wiped the sweat from his brow and waited calmly for the results.

Everyone could see that the turnkeeper was flustered, but he called it out in a full, clear voice. "It is my official word that the tree falling event has been won by the northerner, Tamarack Jack of Arcana!"

The people were still in shock and made no sound, so Ivan began to clap. When they saw that, it caught on and went through them like a wildfire. Soon everyone was cheering the giant's win.

It was then that Ivan began to wonder where Claude was. He hadn't seen him anywhere and usually he never left Mok's side, or was at least close by. It did seem strange to not see him standing there gloating at a moment like this, but he wasn't complaining. *Good riddance*, he thought, and moved to the next area.

He congratulated his massive opponent as they walked up, then proceeded to sharpen his axe again. He took some more water and looked out at the spectators. Some of the faces he recognized, but most of them were unfamiliar to him. Grace and the children were there with the baron, and he wondered what they thought of the giant beating him.

It was a tie now at one each and there was only one way this day could end. He would have to win two more events to remain champion and bring home the gold.

The sun was getting hotter as it approached midday, so Ivan rolled up his sleeves and sat down on the log he would be cutting momentarily. He placed his axe across his lap and cleared his mind.

The upcoming challenge was similar to the tree falling, except the log was horizontal, and you stood on it while you chopped. The first man to cut through was declared the winner, and would be ahead in the competition.

Ivan remained sitting until the turnkeeper signaled for them to mount up. He jumped on and secured his footing, ready to give his all. The old man shouted, "Begin," and the woodcutter brought his axe to life. His speed, accuracy and rhythm were perfection in motion. The turnaround was completed at a staggering pace as he spun in the air and started on the back half without a moment's hesitation.

At this rate he would make short work of this event, and that's exactly what he needed to do. His blade bit into the wood like it was hungry, and he could see the tree wobble as he pushed himself to the limit. Only three more cuts and he was there. *One. . . . Two. . . .* "Done!" yelled the giant just as Ivan finished. He looked over as his log fell, but he was too late. He had been beaten again, even though he had done his best.

Now he knew how all of those other men who had gone against him felt, but they hadn't expected to win, and that made it even harder. He barely heard the turnkeeper call the giant's name in his dazed condition, and realized he had better snap out of it if he was going to have any chance of winning.

He was still fuzzy headed when he reached the tree climbing, so he grabbed a pitcher of water from the carrier and dumped it over his head. That seemed to help as the cobwebs cleared and his focus started to return.

There was only one option now, and the alternative was unthinkable. All he needed to do was beat the giant to the top and ring the bell and this contest was his.

The hatchet his father had given him was sharpened and waiting in his bag, and no one could beat him in the axe throw. He could split a hair at a hundred feet, but first he needed to climb for his life.

He knew his family would be worried sick for him, but he couldn't think about them right now. There was a hundred foot span that would be the difference between success and defeat, and he needed to concentrate on that.

Ivan pulled out his tree spurs and attached them to his boots. He grabbed his climbing rope and flung it around the log. Holding each end, he leaned back and checked it for size. Its length was perfect and needed no adjusting, so he dug in and scaled up a few feet. The spurs were tight and sharp and the rope gripped nicely, so he descended and waited for the start.

He squatted a few times to loosen up and tried not to think about the giant's climb the day before. It took some effort, but he pushed it from his mind and concentrated on the task that was in front of him.

When the turnkeeper yelled, "Make ready!" the woodcutter held his rope up as far as he could reach and squeezed it tight. As soon as he heard the next word he pulled himself up hard and began his ascent. He drove upward, one leg after another with all his might. Everything he had was being drawn from within. Arm, body and leg strength were working together to create as much speed as possible.

When he reached the fifty foot mark he could hear the giant scaling alongside at an incredible rate. He knew he had to reach deep inside and find something when he had nothing left to give. His thighs were burning and his arms were spent, but something triggered in him that pushed him through the last few feet. He thought of his wife and what this would mean to her and it renewed him enough to make a final burst to the top. He reached for his bell but the giant's sounded first. The frustration and heartbreak hit him instantly. It was over and he had lost.

Working quickly to regain his composure, Ivan looked over to show his respect to the new champion, but he wasn't there. He looked down and saw Mok at the eighty-five foot mark, holding his tree and shaking it. He was astounded at the strength the giant possessed to ring the bell that way, but still didn't quite understand until Mok smiled. It was then that he noticed all the people roaring with laughter. He joined in when he realized that he had actually won the event, but wasn't sure he liked the giant's sense of humor.

He knew that later on he would think this was funny, but right now it had brought him some unnecessary grief. It didn't take long to get over it though, and when he was back on the ground and packed up, he was feeling renewed once more.

The entire crowd was moving now, hoping to get a good vantage point for the axe throwing. This event took place in the center of the ring, with the target set at one hundred feet.

As the two men made their way across, Mok spoke up. "You very fast climbing," he said, with sincerity mixed into the gravel. "I know I not catch you so make fun joke."

He grinned when he said it and Ivan couldn't be upset with him, so he replied, "Thanks, and yes, you did have me going there."

The giant seemed pleased and responded, "Mok make people laugh," and kept grinning all the way to the throwing area.

Ivan was relaxed now and his confidence level was back up as he unsheathed his hatchet from its scabbard. He thought of his father every time he held it, and felt joy and loneliness all-at-once. It had been so long since he'd seen his parents and wondered if they would have a chance to return before the balance took them. Sailing to the many lands across the sea had been a very tempting offer, but he had never regretted staying behind, especially when he looked out and saw his precious family cheering him on. He waved to them, then turned his focus to the baron who had stood up and walked forward.

"Today is a momentous occasion," he remarked, his voice blanketing the crowd. He wasn't speaking overly loud, but was well rehearsed in projecting his words. "On one side we have a legend. On the other, a true contender. Together they have put on the finest display of woodcutting I have ever witnessed."

The people seemed to agree as the noise level rose and then fell again as Vero continued.

"It is down to one event now to determine the champion of this year's competition, and it should prove to be as exciting as the first four. Before I hand it over to the turnkeeper, I would just like to say that over the course of the tournament these two men have shown us all what it truly means to be a woodcutter. They have both brought honor to the craft, and no matter the outcome, they are both worthy of the win."

Not a moment after he was finished speaking, the turn-keeper shouted, "A round of applause for Baron Vero Salday!" Everyone showed their appreciation for the host, then turned back quickly so they wouldn't miss any of the action.

"We will now proceed with the axe throw," he continued, trying to demand the attention of the crowd. "Tamarack Jack will go first, when he is ready."

Mok stepped up to the line, axe-in-hand, and took his stance. He moved his grip down until it felt balanced. With a smooth motion he lifted the blade and touched it to his fore-head, then took careful aim. He moved it back and forth, waiting for the right feel, then released it to the air. End-over-end it spun until it sank deep into the target, a quarter inch right of center.

The reaction to the near-perfect throw was exuberant and the giant accepted it graciously as he backed away and waited to see if his attempt would hold up.

The din was so deafening that the turnkeeper's announcement could barely be heard. "Ivan Harden will throw next, when *he* is ready."

The space between the center and the giant's blade seemed tiny to those watching, but to Ivan it was huge. *I could drive my wagon in there and turn it around,* he thought, and chuckled to himself. He wasn't being cocky, he was just glad to be in the situation he found himself at the moment. This was his *best* and *favorite* event, and it showed.

He lifted his hatchet and spun it three revolutions. He flipped it in front of himself, caught it with his left hand and spun it for three more. With a quick motion he tossed it behind his back and up over his right shoulder, then caught it again. Finally he gave it another three spins before stopping it in a throwing position. The people started yelling and screaming and he could hear Mok clapping behind him.

There were some who would have called it showing off, but Ivan considered it showing off your talents, and that's what every woodcutter was there to do.

The sun was directly overhead as he took his position. The breeze had stopped, increasing the heat, and everyone's parasols and fans began to pop open. To a bird overhead it may have looked like a field of assorted wild flowers, but Ivan paid no attention to the weather or the doings of the people as he concentrated on the target in front of him. Everything had come down to this and he was totally transfixed in the moment.

He grabbed a rag from his pack and wiped the sweat from his hand. He gripped his hatchet the exact way he had done so often and raised his arm. *This couldn't be better,* he thought, as he pulled back and readied himself. He smiled as his arm moved toward victory, but then a ray of sunshine shot past his eyes and a warning went off in his mind.

Maybe it was the excitement of being so close to beating the giant, or his age catching up with him, but he ignored his instincts and continued the toss. An instant later there was a flash of light that blinded him just before his release, causing his little axe to bite into the wood a half inch left of center.

He was stunned for a moment, then quickly looked for the source. It didn't take him long to spot Claude Boyle putting his silver cigar case back in his pocket and skulking into the crowd. Emotions exploded within him and his eyes narrowed and turned cold. His first thought was to grab his hatchet and hunt the man down, but for some reason it changed and he was mad at himself for not stopping his hand when he should have. How could he be angry with Claude for doing what it was that was in him to do? That would be like beating a dog for barking, or chopping the head off a rooster for crowing. It would make no sense, and right now he could only blame himself for not avoiding the trap. Claude had won and there was nothing he could, or *would* do about it. He would stand tall and accept it like the man he was, and that was the end of it.

Everything had happened so fast, but now he started to see the mixed reactions from the spectators. He soon realized that they hadn't noticed anything except the placement he had made outside the giant's. Why *would* they notice? It had been directed at him, and everyone's attention had been on his axe; everyone's that is except Mok's, who was now moving in the direction where Claude had disappeared.

"I smash him," snarled the giant as he passed Ivan.

The woodcutter ran in front of him and put up his arms. "Don't do this," he implored so only Mok could hear, then extended his hand so no one would be suspicious of his actions.

The giant shook it and said, "He cheat you."

Ivan looked up at the angry colossus and smiled. "You are a good man," he told him, "but it's my fault for not pulling my throw when I first saw the danger."

Mok met Ivan's gaze and the look in his eyes turned from fury to sadness, then he nodded and returned to the axe throwing area.

The woodcutter followed him over and his eyes went to the baron's seating box. All of his people were standing with bewildered looks on their faces, wondering what had just taken place. He looked away and stood there waiting for the words that would vocalize the end of his reign as champion.

The turnkeeper climbed onto his platform and waited for some order to occur. This took awhile, but finally it calmed down enough for him to start.

"Ladies and gentlemen," he began. "After careful measuring, it is my official statement that the axe throwing event has been won by Tamarack Jack of Arcana, which makes him the winner of this year's Woodcutting Competition!"

Those words were hard for Ivan to hear, but he clenched his teeth and listened without faltering. It was apparent that many of the people were upset with the results, but they still applauded the giant for his incredible showing.

"And now!" shouted the turnkeeper, "if you will please make way for the baron we will begin the award presentation shortly."

Ivan went over and grabbed his hatchet. He placed it in the bag with the rest of his gear and stared at the target. He could have made that throw over and over, and hit the center perfectly with each toss, but that didn't matter now and it was best not to dwell on it.

The baron was making his way over now and Ivan could see Grace and the children on their way to join him. As they got closer, he could see the look in his wife's eyes and knew she would be full of questions he didn't want to answer right now.

When she was near he leaned in and whispered, "Later," which she accepted, and remained silent. In fact, none of the family spoke as they watched Vero walk to the center of the main platform. The very same platform the woodcutter had stood on and accepted this award year after year, until today.

Vero raised his arm, hushing the crowd, and Ivan could see the admiration in the turnkeeper's eyes at the control the baron had over the people. Vero gave Ivan a curious look before he started his speech, and the woodcutter could tell that he knew something wasn't right.

"Today is a day of great joy and great sorrow," he began, still looking at his old friend. "It is sorrowful because we have to say goodbye to a champion who ruled this competition for over twenty years. The part that brings me joy is that a younger generation of woodcutters is emerging from a trade that is said to be dying. From the turnout I see here today, and the skill with which the competitors wielded their axes, I would say that woodcutting is alive and well in the land!"

Everyone cheered in agreement, and that's when Ivan saw Claude moving toward the platform with his wife and son in tow. *He has a lot of nerve*, thought the woodcutter, and wondered if he were to attack, whether the coward would try to use Morra and Sonny as a shield.

The baron's voice interrupted his thoughts as he addressed the giant. "Before me stands a superior craftsman, and if he will join me on the platform I will make the presentation." Mok took a step up but the old structure started to tilt, so he moved back and waited by the edge.

"Well," laughed the baron, "I guess *I'll* join you," and walked over.

Ivan noticed that Vero was still a few feet shorter than the intended recipient as he continued with his proclamation.

"Today we crown a new champion and his name is Tamarack Jack from Arcana, sponsored by Claude Boyle of the Morgan's Coal Company."

With those words Claude, who was now standing by Mok, smiled and waved. The woodcutter started to burn again and it was all he could do not to think of beating that dog.

"As the winner of the Woodcutting Competition, I present you with this purse of twelve gold coins and the title of top woodcutter in the land." Mok accepted it and thanked the baron as the people gathered round their new champion. The giant remained by the platform for only a short while, then walked away, grabbed his axe and brought it back to his gear-bag.

Shyla, who was feeling strange about all that had taken place, congratulated him as he came over. At first the giant looked at Ivan and his pained expression was clear. Then he looked down at Shyla and said, "Thank you little one." She could tell something wasn't adding up, but held her tongue for once.

The five stood there in awkward silence, with only two of them knowing why. This continued until Claude came up and grabbed the pouch full of coins from the giant's hand. "I'll take that," he said rudely. "It will *almost* cover your expenses."

At first Mok appeared ready to strike the man, but his expression quickly changed to one of defeat, and he hung his head. Morra and Sonny were standing there looking uncomfortable so Grace greeted them. Morra answered with a quick, "Hello," and then looked at the ground.

When Sonny saw Ivan, his face lit up and he said, "You were great today Mr. Harden."

Before the woodcutter could respond, Claude growled in a scathing voice, "Yes, you were great, but I doubt your skills will help you in the coal mine this winter . . . if there's any room that is."

After Claude's rude statement, Mok and each of the family members were handling it in their own way.

Grace was trying hard to be a good person despite how she felt inside. Cade was unconsciously reaching for his bow which was, unfortunately, back at the pavilion. Shyla felt the light kindle in response to her negative feelings and was trying to suppress it. Ivan was now contemplating the chopping of the rooster's head, and Mok remained standing with his head down, afraid that if he looked at Claude he might hurt him.

Once everyone had ignored him for long enough, Claude turned to go, but before he did he grabbed Mok's arm and said, "Come on you big dummy, I've got people who want to meet my new champion." The giant turned and followed without saying a word.

"Oh, that man!" exclaimed Grace, obviously fuming.

Shyla looked exasperated and asked, "Why does he let Claude talk to him like that and order him around?"

Ivan could see her frustration and answered the best he could. "Mok is afraid of confrontation because he doesn't want anyone to think of him as a monster. He wants so badly to fit in with our kind, and for people to like him, that he won't stand up for himself." Shyla didn't like the answer, but it made sense, and once again her friend was being taken advantage of.

The woodcutter wished he could console her, but the day had unfolded poorly for them all and there was nothing he could do about it. The way Claude was acting, Ivan was sure he thought no one had seen him pull his little stunt with the cigar case, and for some reason he found that humorous. He couldn't imagine a person with such a high opinion of himself that he thought he could do anything without consequence, but the day had obviously gone exactly how he'd planned, so maybe he could. Surely the balance would deal with it, but what did he know about such things?

He shrugged, grabbed his gear and said, "I need to get out of here if anyone would like to accompany me back to the pavilion for some food and rest." The feeling was unanimous, so they weaved their way over to the carriage path where the driver was waiting.

CHAPTER
23

Honor in Defeat

The ride back was quiet and gloomy, and even the old dog could feel the mood, letting out a little whine every so often. Ivan was trying to figure out what to do next, but mostly he was thinking about all the things he wouldn't be able to give his family. He'd been counting on the gold for everything, and now there was nothing. As the provider it had been up to him to come through for the ones he loved, and he had failed them. Of course it would be easy to point fingers and blame it on Claude or the giant, but he was the one accountable and would make no excuses to anyone.

When they arrived, the guards were surprised to see them, but opened the gates quickly and let them through. Once they were inside they washed up and went to the banquet room for a late lunch. The woodcutter understood why the guards were confused by their early arrival, and wondered if he should have stayed and partook in the festivities that followed the contest. Had the circumstances of his loss been different he probably would have, but he needed to be away from Claude right now so he wouldn't be tempted to do something he would regret.

Hunger should have been foremost in his mind after the exhausting morning, but Ivan only picked at the food in front of him, his thoughts somewhere else completely. He sat there contemplating until he was brought back by the strange sensation that someone was watching him. He looked up, and Grace, Shyla and Cade were all staring with questioning expressions on their faces. Not one of them had mentioned his defeat, since none of them could believe it had happened, and they were all waiting for him to make them understand. He knew it wasn't fair to keep it from them so he began to explain.

"Before I tell you the details of why I missed that easy throw," he started, trying to pick the right words, "I want you to know that it was my fault for not paying attention to all things around me." Grace raised an eyebrow and waited to hear the real reason. Ivan took a drink from the cup in front of him and hoped they would understand. He explained how Claude had reflected the sunlight into his eyes with his silver cigar case, and why he hadn't called for a disqualification. Anger and hatred flashed in their eyes, but there was also a look of relief.

"I knew something was wrong," said Shyla, still processing the story.

"Yeah," Cade chimed in, "there was no way you would have missed that toss."

Grace stood and walked over to her man. She took his hand and spoke softly. "I could tell that something wasn't right, and I want you to know that I do understand why you didn't say anything." She kissed his cheek and returned to her seat. "I may understand," she added, "but that doesn't change the fact that Claude is a lying, cheating weasel!"

Cade sniggered. "Mother, you're giving weasels a bad name."

"He's worse than a porch troll!" exclaimed Shyla, pounding her little fists on the table. Everyone laughed, but each of them knew that Claude had cost them dearly.

"Let's look on the bright side," offered Ivan. "We are no worse off than when we got here, and we are all safe and together."

Cade looked worried. "We *are* still going to the ball, aren't we?" he asked.

Ivan nodded. "Oh yes," he answered. "We are definitely going, and we will show everyone that the Harden family is as gracious in defeat as we are in victory."

Grace could see the relief on her son's face and reassured him. "Don't worry, I haven't forgotten. I will show you some dance steps before tomorrow night . . . and you," she finished, looking at her daughter who was starting to worry about her shoes again. It had been easy enough to hide them at the contest, but at a dance it would be next to impossible.

"As of right now," declared Ivan, "we are putting this day behind us and looking to the future and whatever we can make of it."

When the family was finished eating they returned to their rooms. Cade decided to do some afternoon hunting, so he grabbed his bow and rounded up old Rufus to accompany him on the trip.

Shyla stayed in her room and fretted over her ugly shoes. There was no way she was dancing at the ball. She would die of embarrassment if anyone saw her feet, but she knew her father would ask her, and Stafan would, surely. This day was just dreadful. First her father had lost the competition because of their awful neighbor, and now she was going to have to wear her chicken-poop shoes to the biggest fashion event of the year. She flopped down on the bed and decided to take her mind off things by counting the points of light within her, starting at her toes.

Ivan laid on his bed with Grace cuddled next to him, but despite how tired he was, his mind kept going over the events of the day. If he'd just stopped when he should have, he could have given his family everything he wanted to, but now it was beyond his reach. It was over, but he could still provide some things . . . like a new bedroom for his daughter. Shyla was quickly becoming a young woman and needed her privacy, so when she and her mother were in the south visiting Zarina, he would build her a new bedroom to come home to. It wouldn't have the extravagant feather bed and full-length mirror, or the silver brush and comb set, but he knew she would appreciate it just the same.

With his mind off the negative thoughts he fell into a deep slumber, and the next sound he heard was the entrance bell ringing. He looked around and saw Grace walking toward him.

"How do you feel?" she asked, sitting on the bed.

"Well rested," he answered, blinking as his eyes adjusted to the newly lit candle.

"That was a messenger saying the baron wants to see you in the dining area. The children and I have already eaten, but you looked so peaceful I didn't want to wake you."

Ivan sat up. "How late is it?" he asked.

She handed him his clothes. "It's well past sundown," she told him, helping him on with his shirt.

"I must have been tired," he observed, "but I did wear myself out earlier and didn't get much sleep last night."

She smiled. "Not to mention the stress of being in a situation beyond your control."

He pulled on his boots and combed his hair. "Yeah, that too," he agreed, splashing water on his face and wiping the sleep from his eyes.

"You look great, and you don't want to keep your host waiting," she said, walking him to the entrance.

"I know what he wants to talk about," he replied, "and I hope he respects my wishes in this matter."

Grace fixed his collar. "Vero has always respected you," she assured him, "even when he doesn't agree.

"I hope you're right," he sighed. He kissed her, pulled back the curtain and made his way down the corridor.

When he entered, he could see that the dining hall was lit by only a few candles, much like their last late night visit.

"Some wine?" the baron asked him as he sat down. He took the goblet and thanked him. "I also had the cook fix you a plate," he said, pushing a large platter in front of him. It was a lot of food but he was hungry again. "We can talk while you eat," offered the baron politely, and Ivan knew he would have to explain everything before he left.

He ate a few mouthfuls and the baron watched him patiently. "I'm sorry I didn't stay for the outdoor banquet and entertainment," Ivan apologized between bites, "but I really wasn't feeling up to it." He took another mouthful and washed it down. "I'm sure it went on just fine without me."

Vero looked amused. "I guess you could call it fine," he affirmed, "if you don't mind listening to Claude Boyle go on-and-on about himself."

Normally Ivan would have laughed at that statement, but the thought of it made his insides burn yet again.

"Yes," continued Vero, "he seemed pleased with himself and couldn't help but expound on the fact that his giant had, how did he put it . . . crushed you."

Ivan finished his plate and the wine, then refilled his goblet once again. He could see Vero watching him and waiting, so he told him everything that had taken place during the axe throw.

Vero rubbed his chin. "I suspected as much," he determined. "There was no possibility of you missing that throw on your own." He looked perplexed as he took a sip of wine. "I must determine, from your lack of action directly after the deed was done, that you do not wish to pursue the matter further," he concluded, still pondering the variables.

"Yes," replied Ivan. "My opportunity to do anything passed before the act was carried out."

The baron took another drink and frowned. "I understand what you're saying, but I can't say I totally agree. I know you've made up your mind though, so I will respect your decision, although I do hate to see someone like Claude come away with the spoils."

Ivan nodded. "And I even more, but it's done now and I can only look forward."

The two men sat there for awhile contemplating different outcomes, then Vero spoke. "There are actions that are within my power to do," he began. "I could cancel some of his substantial contracts and see to it that a few of his major buyers sever ties with the coal company, but that would only hurt Sam Morgan and Claude's family."

It seemed that any way you looked at it Claude was sheltered from harm, and that was very upsetting to both of them.

Vero stood and raised his goblet. "To the silent champion," he declared, and they drank in unison.

"I don't feel much like a champion," admitted Ivan, "but thanks for the gesture."

The candles were burning low when the baron stood again and said, "It's getting late and I have much to do tomorrow with the final preparations for the Woodcutter's Ball. Oh and also, I will be making a couple of announcements there that may be of interest to you."

The woodcutter wondered what Vero had up his sleeve but knew better than to ask, so he bid him a good night and returned to his room.

The following morning the pavilion was even busier than it had been on any of the previous days. The girls were up extra early, getting their outfits ready for the evening. After they sorted out their clothing, they went to the girl's wash chamber and began readying themselves for the big event.

Ivan remembered the last Woodcutter's Ball with all the people putting on their best, trying to impress and outdo one another. Shyla had been too young to attend for very long and Cade hadn't seemed that interested, but it was incredible the difference a year could make.

After breakfast Grace brushed the children up on the three main dance steps, then all the girls went to Charlotte's rooms to have their hair and faces done.

Ivan wasn't sure he liked the idea of his wife being painted up like those ladies from the royal court, but he wasn't about to say anything. After what had happened, he wanted his family to enjoy themselves to the fullest and try to forget the situation they were in, if only for a night.

He stared at the bed where his wife had laid out his formal woodcutting outfit. It wasn't new by any means, and wouldn't be practical for falling or logging, but it made him look very distinguished.

He was pulled from his daydream by the entrance bell, so he walked over and drew back the curtain. The woodcutter was puzzled when he saw Cade standing there with his hunting gear.

"Dad, can I borrow your bow?" he asked, looking to be in a hurry. "It seems that ever since Stafan watched the Archery Tournament he has wanted to learn how to shoot, so I told him I would give him a lesson."

Ivan nodded and retrieved the weapon for his son. "Just make sure you are back well before sundown. We don't want to keep our ladies waiting," he replied, amused by the difference between boys and girls.

"No problem, and thanks," Cade assured him before turning the corner.

Ivan went back inside, grabbed his axe and started to sharpen it. It didn't need to be done, but it never hurt to have a sharp axe on hand, plus it helped him think.

He was glad his family could enjoy themselves, but he had to start focusing on creating some income. He thought of selling an early supply of winter's wood to his customers at a reduced rate, or landing a contract like his father had done with a rich businessman or one of the royals. Many ideas came and went as he sat there, but most of them were flights of fancy or wishful thinking.

He switched to his hatchet, and again tried to come up with some way to generate the revenue it would take for them to survive without having to accept Claude's insulting offer.

He wasn't sure how long he'd been at it when someone entered the room. He looked up from his task and his heart quickened. He had seen his wife first thing after she was awake in the morning and she was beautiful. He had seen her after a long day of slaving over a hot stove and she was beautiful, but the women standing before him now was absolutely, stunningly beautiful. So-much-so in fact, that he was speechless and could only stare.

"Aren't you going to say anything?" she asked, afraid he didn't approve.

"I would," he answered, "but I'm not sure how to address a queen from some exotic land, who must have just mistakenly entered the room of a lowly woodcutter."

Her smile lit up the chamber. "I am *your* queen," she said, coming closer.

"Yes you are," he replied, moving up to her and kissing her gently on the lips so as not to mess up her hair or face. She kissed him back not so gently, and they held each other tight.

"What about me?" asked Shyla, who was standing there waiting.

"And who might you be?" Ivan teased.

"Daddy!" she scolded, playing along.

He looked at her and shook his head. "Don't try to tell me that this sophisticated looking young woman in front of me is my little girl."

Shyla curtsied. "The very same," she replied, and blushed at the compliment.

"How late is it getting to be?" asked Ivan. "It would seem I've completely lost track."

Grace loosened the laces on Shyla's dress and asked her to go and change into her gown. "I am told," she answered, "that we have only a short while to get into our formalwear and meet at the front entrance before the sun will be setting."

Ivan dressed himself in the clothes his wife had laid out, then asked her to help him with the tie. He had never felt comfortable in one, but didn't mind wearing it for this special occasion.

"Cade should have been back by now," he said, trying to hold still for his wife.

"He *is* back," she told him. "He's with Stafan, who has kindly offered to help him with his wardrobe in exchange for the archery lesson."

Ivan laughed. "I never thought I'd see the day when Cade dressed up in fancy clothes."

Grace slipped into her gown and gently took her pearl necklace from the jewelry case and placed it around her neck. "There is a certain young lady attending that might have something to do with that," she replied, her face serious now as her eyes took on a sadness. "They are growing up much too fast."

Shyla came in and the girls helped each other straighten and tighten their dresses. Ivan pulled a comb through his thick chestnut hair, but it just hung down more like a mane than anything manageable.

Finally they were ready and on their way to the front entrance where they would take the carriage to the Woodcutter's Ball.

When they reached the open-air they could see the boys standing there and it was quite a sight to behold. Cade was wearing a blue velvet coat with silver buttons. He had on a white lace-up shirt, black pants with adjoining silver rings down the side of each leg and sported a white sash around his waist. He also wore white gloves and black boots with silver buckles, and bowed to his family as they walked up.

"Did I get that right?" he asked Stafan, as he straightened.

"You were superb," he answered. "And don't worry; your girl will be very impressed." Cade smiled at the thought of Wanda, but still felt awkward in his new attire.

"Don't you boys look splendid," commented Grace, as she stopped in front of them.

When Stafan saw Shyla he swallowed hard. "It is so good to see you again my lady," he said, bowing his head.

"Always a pleasure," she responded, and realized that she meant it instead of just reciting the words.

"It would seem my mother has taken the carriage with her sister, and mine is rather large," Stafan addressed Shyla. "I would be honored if you would accompany Cade and myself on the ride over."

Shyla was excited but showed no emotion. "I think that would be fine," she consented, then turned to her father. "However, I must ask my chaperone if that is agreeable."

Ivan eyed the young man. "I don't see any harm in it," he replied, "but I will continue my chaperone duties when we reach the ball," he finished, giving a stern look.

"O-of course sir," Stafan stammered, suddenly feeling a bit nervous. Ivan smiled to himself, then escorted his wife to their carriage.

Stafan helped Shyla up the step and inside, while *she* made sure not to ruffle anything. Cade climbed in behind them and the carriage creaked along the path toward the big tent that had been set up at the competition quarter.

CHAPTER

24

The Woodcutter's Ball

The sun was down now and the three could see the many lights around the large canopy as they rounded the bend. It was erected where the contestants' rest area had been, and its size and lighting made it appear much closer than it was.

Cade began to feel anxious as they approached and Shyla's tummy did a flip-flop. This was her first *real* dance and she was feeling a little apprehensive. She had been allowed to attend last year, but had been escorted back early because it was an adult function. She had matured a lot since then and everyone was looking at her like she was a young lady rather than a little girl, and she loved it. All she ever imagined when she was gathering eggs or working around the cabin, was being like one of the princesses from her story books, and now she *almost* felt like one.

The carriage came to a halt and Cade stepped out. He glanced around quickly to see if Wanda was among the many people who were entering the main opening, but didn't see her. He wasn't even sure when she was supposed to arrive, but got butterflies when he thought about it. He could hear music coming from inside and it sounded like a full company of musicians. The baron hired only the best, and they always traveled a great distance to entertain on this prestigious occasion.

The wind shifted and he began to smell the many aromas of the different foods that were cooking, and was glad he had saved enough room to partake in the baron's annual feast. This magnificent meal was one reason people came from all over to be here, and it was second-to-none.

He could see the remainder of the torches that stood along the outside of the tent wall as they were being lit, and guessed the massive structure to be about two hundred feet long. The wall itself was ten feet high and then curved in and up another ten feet to the peak. *I guess you need a tall roof if you have a giant for a champion,* he thought, then looked around to see if his companions were coming.

After Cade left, Stafan remained seated, so Shyla waited, as it was customary for the gentleman to exit first, then assist the lady.

"Before we leave there is something I'd like to ask you," said Stafan in a serious manner.

Shyla felt slightly anxious, but she answered sweetly, "Of course."

He looked unsure as he began. "I know we aren't together or anything, but I was wondering if you would honor me by accepting this gift?" he asked, reaching under the seat and handing her a package. She took it, not knowing what else to do, and set it on her lap. He looked so worried and excited that she couldn't have refused if she'd wanted, so she smiled and opened the parchment.

She let out a gasp and her eyes welled with tears as she looked down and saw the contents. It was her shoes. Well not hers, but an identical pair right down to the size and design, and lying across them were ten ribbons of different colors.

"I wasn't sure what dress you would be wearing, so I purchased all of the ribbons he had," explained Stafan, pleased that she wasn't offended.

Shyla caught her breath and blinked back the tears. "I *love* them," she said, and gave him a hug. Stafan reached into the small chest beside the seat and pulled out a knife. He took the pink ribbon and cut it in half, then pulled each piece through the silver loops and tied them in a bow.

"You must try them on," he said eagerly, feeding off her excitement. Shyla removed her old ones, stuffed them in her bag and placed her feet in the new silver ones. They fit her perfectly, and now she felt *entirely* like a princess.

Stafan got out and helped her down. They watched as the driver turned the carriage around and stopped it behind a row of carriages and wagons to await their return.

"Shall we?" asked Stafan, raising his elbow. Shyla took his arm and the three of them walked through the entryway and inside.

There were already over two hundred in attendance and the mood was very uplifting. Cade had thought he might be over-dressed, but it was the opposite if anything. The *Gatou's* designs were well represented, with their leather clothing and jewelry adorning many of the guests, along with the highest of fashions from other lands. The gowns and accessories were so breath-taking that Shyla could have spent the entire evening admiring it all, but she wanted to find her parents, and *really* wanted to see Mok.

The musicians started a lively tune and many people moved to the newly built dance floor. The floor had been constructed from wide planks that were placed on beams and secured with long iron nails.

As they made their way through the crowd, Shyla mentally rehearsed the dance steps her mother had shown her, just to be safe. Once they made it past the main group of guests, they stopped to look around.

The dance floor and stage were in the center of the back wall, and on the opposite side were a series of large tables. The first four were filled with beverages and the tables next to those were filled with food, with people lined up to sample it. Farther along the wall were four brick ovens and eight fire pits, with a cook tending each one and replenishing the tables when needed. It was all very impressive, but Shyla especially loved the Candle-lamps.

They were candleholders in the shape of a globe and covered in white cloth so they gave off a softer light. There must have been a hundred of them hanging from the ceiling, and they created an enchanted setting.

She could see now that the other half of the tent was full of tables with benches surrounding them. She scanned them quickly, and it didn't take long to find what she was looking for. Next to the stage was the largest table, and at it sat the largest man. Seated next to the giant were the baron and Charlotte, along with Bridgette and some of the royals she had met at the pavilion. Next to them, and much to her dismay, were Claude and Morra Boyle. She liked his wife, but no matter what her father had tried to say about it all being his own fault, she despised the man for what he had done.

She saw her mother and father sitting at the next table over and pointed them out to Cade and Stafan. Seated with them were Ben and Maggie Starling. Wanda, who hadn't noticed Cade yet, was on their left. Next to them were the Catchers and the Brundles, minus all the children.

Cade could see that Wanda was wearing the shawl he had given her and it made him smile. He was glad to see it because it had been his main reason for choosing a blue jacket. Even as they walked up she didn't recognize him at first, his clothes being so different from what she was used to, but when she did, her face began to glow and she looked very impressed.

Stafan turned to Shyla and asked, "Would it be all right if I sit with you? It looks rather stuffy at Mother's table."

Shyla giggled. "Of course you can," she nodded. "I'll be right there."

She stopped, strolled over and tapped Mok's arm. He was sitting with his back to the woodcutter's group, so he spun his head to see who it was.

"Little one," he said, turning on his bench to face her. "Is good see you."

She rubbed his arm. "And you," she replied, still noticing the pain in his eyes.

The other people at the table were busy talking but she leaned closer anyway, and in a quiet voice whispered, "Father told me what happened at the axe throw and you need to know that you are not to blame, even one tiny bit."

The giant's face tightened and he looked conflicted. "Mok know, but still feel bad. Mok cause sadness for little one's family. Will not forgive."

Shyla gave him a sympathetic smile and said, "We would forgive you even if there was something *to* forgive."

The sadness and pain in his eyes increased and he whispered, "Mok not forgive Mok."

Her heart ached watching him struggle with what had been done to his hero, so she changed the subject. "Would you save me a dance?" she asked, trying to lighten his mood.

It changed somewhat, but now he looked sad *and* puzzled, and answered, "Mok not dance."

She rolled her eyes and shook her head. "Of course you can. I'll show you, and I *won't* take no for an answer."

The giant sighed. "All right little one. Mok dance," he agreed.

"Jack!" Claude hollered in his obnoxious tone. "You are ignoring our guests." The giant clenched his teeth and closed his eyes.

"It's all right," soothed Shyla, placing her hands on his, "I will see you later." She felt bad for him but could do nothing, so she walked the few steps over to her table.

"And here comes my lovely daughter Shyla, who I'm sure you all remember," stated Ivan proudly, in his teasing manner.

Not one to pass up a formal introduction, she said in a charming voice, "It's so very nice to see you all again," then lifted her dress high enough for everyone to see her shoes, and curtsied gracefully.

She went over and sat down between her mother and Stafan, and as soon as she was settled, Grace whispered, "You told me your new shoes were ruined and I've listened to you complain for days."

Shyla answered through her smile. "I'll explain later," and kept smiling at all who were watching.

The tables were filling now as the people poured in, and the lines for the food and drink began to grow. Shyla knew that Cade and Stafan were hungry, and she was starting to feel it as well, so she turned to ask if they wanted to get something before it got too busy. She was just about to speak when four men dressed in white brought over several platters of food and jugs of different colors, and set them down in the center of the table. She was pleasantly surprised, then realized the lines of tables along the back wall were filled with the woodcutting contestants and their friends and families, and they were being served in the same manner.

It is good to be a woodcutter's daughter, she thought, as she sampled the different dishes, *and it is good to sit by someone who makes you feel special and pretty*. She knew she was special, or at least different, and was as pretty as most girls she had seen, but when Stafan looked at her she could see in his eyes that he thought she was absolutely wonderful.

Everyone had finished eating now and were talking back and forth, except for Cade and Wanda who were only paying attention to each other. Ivan and Grace were enjoying some wine and reminiscing with their old friends, in between frequent interruptions from people who wanted to meet the legend and shake his hand. As each one came and went, Shyla could see Claude watching, and knew he was angered by the fact that everyone was still enamored and in awe of the woodcutter, even after he had been defeated by the giant.

The musicians had stopped to eat, but were back on the stage now and starting up again. Cade asked Wanda to dance, and as they moved toward the floor, Shyla had to admit that he looked dashing, but even more-so with a beauty like *her* on his arm.

The song seemed quite popular as couple after couple left the table until finally there was just Shyla and Stafan left. She was feeling very uncomfortable, and when he stood and held out his hand, she thought she might faint.

"I think it's time we tried out those new shoes, don't you?" he asked, giving her his best smile. She looked at him with a disappointed expression, so he rephrased the question. "I mean, may I have the *honor* of this dance, my lady?"

She liked the sound of that much better and replied, "I'd be delighted," and took his hand.

Her mother and father looked exquisite as they moved across the floor, and even Cade was doing well, but she felt too nervous to move. Stafan took her right hand in his left and put his other arm around her waist. She could feel his strong hand on the small of her back, and when he moved, she concentrated hard to match his steps. It was difficult to remember what her mother had said, so she counted in her head, trying not to make a mistake. This felt a lot different from dancing with her brother, and when he spoke, she was hard-pressed to listen *and* keep the count going.

"I'm not sure, but I think I'm losing the feeling in my left hand," he commented with a smile.

She hadn't realized how hard she'd been squeezing and loosened her grip. "I'm sorry," she apologized, and felt her face flush.

"Don't worry about it," he told her, "but I think if you relax and loosen up you will enjoy it more." *It couldn't hurt*, she thought, so she quit counting and listened instead to the rhythm of the music.

The steps were firm in her mind now so she started to feel it rather than force it, and by the end of the song she felt far more at ease with the movement. The only problem was, it had just started to become fun when they had to stop. She was disappointed until the young duke asked if she would like to try another, and the two of them twirled and glided smoothly through the next selection.

"The new shoes are working remarkably well," teased Stafan, as he escorted her back to her seat.

"Yes," she agreed, "and you didn't step on them once," she added, returning the banter.

The tables were all full now and they were bringing benches in for the ones who were left standing. There were over a thousand people in attendance, with more arriving steadily, and everyone was taking full advantage of all that had been provided by their host. The temperature in the tent was increasing from the body heat alone, and the noise level rose as each person tried to make themselves heard across a hundred tables.

Vero stood and walked onto the stage, and by his sheer presence, commanded the attention of the room. The guests stopped what they were doing to hear what the baron had to say, and Ivan was curious to see if he was going to make the announcements he had talked about. The baron was dressed like a king and his voice carried to the entire gathering.

"I thank you for joining myself and all of these great contestants for our Woodcutter's Ball," he began, gesturing down the row where the woodsmen were seated. "This was a record year for entrants and visitors alike, and the skill level was beyond anything we have ever seen before. This ball was put in place to honor the woodcutters, and one in particular each season, but first let us turn our attention to our former champion, Ivan Harden."

The entire room stood and thundered their appreciation as the woodcutter rose and acknowledged them.

"But now," the baron carried on, "we are here to honor a new victor, so let's hear it for Tamarack Jack." Again the crowd went crazy cheering for the giant, but he just looked back and forth at the sea of people, not really paying them much mind. Before the applause died down the baron continued. "With that said, I want you all to enjoy the food and drink, and of course this very talented group of musicians and singers. I am told that only this morning they were commissioned by Claude Boyle to write a song about our new champion, so I will take my leave and turn it over to the Kingstown Minstrels."

The three drummers started first and were quickly joined by the lower tones of the oversized guitars. They were then accompanied by two wood whistles that played a harmony intro, leading the guitarists and violinists in a lively melody that brought a young man to the center of the stage. He lifted his arms slightly and sang in a clear, resonant voice.

He's Tamarack Jack the giant with the axe
He towers six foot o'er you
He'll fall the trees and drink the seas
And raise the rugged mountains too
But he'll be gone ere break of dawn
Never to look back
He came to town for a legend's crown
Hats off to Tamarack Jack

Tamarack Jack. . . . Timber
Tamarack Jack. . . . Timber
He came to town for a legend's crown
Hats off to Tamarack Jack

They say he hails from the Land of Gales
Where the weather's bleak and cold
With a fist of stone he stands alone
His heart so true and bold
He walked for days from that northern place
His hand upon his axe
He came to town for a legend's crown
Hats off to Tamarack Jack

Tamarack Jack. . . . Timber
Tamarack Jack. . . . Timber
He came on down and took a legend's crown
Hats off to Tamarack Jack

Tamarack Jack. . . . Timber
Tamarack Jack. . . . Timber
Tamarack Jack. . . . Timber
Tamarack Jack. . . . Timber

The crowd loved it and many were repeating, *Tamarack Jack. . . . Timber*, while they applauded. Claude seemed very pleased with himself and clapped loudly, as though he had just won some type of showdown.

It had been Mok's dream for people to like him and respect him for his woodcutting abilities, but not this way. None of it was real and the lie felt like a stone in the pit of his stomach. He had watched and done nothing as his hero was cheated out of what was rightfully his, and he was disgusted with himself.

Claude, who had finally stopped clapping, raised his cup and shouted, "Here's to Tamarack Jack, the *greatest* woodcutter in the land! He showed everyone that Ivan Harden is nothing but a washed up, broken down old woodsman who was lucky to win the events he did!"

As the words left his mouth, Vero fought hard to hold his anger back, but the giant didn't. He stood, knocking his bench back, and grabbed Claude by the front of his coat, lifting him high in the air. Everyone at the table jumped up and scrambled out of the way; everyone except Vero, who sat with an interested expression at the scene that was unfolding in front of him.

The guards, who were positioned against the wall, made a move forward but were motioned back by the baron who wanted to see where this would lead.

"You not talk Ivan that way!" yelled Mok, shaking the helpless man and baring his teeth. "You not worth speak his name!"

The whole place was silent as the giant's words carried to every corner.

Shyla was up and moving already. She ran over, and in a loud, stern voice shouted, "Put him down Mok. He's not worth it!"

The sound of her voice quelled his rage somewhat, so he stopped shaking Claude and dropped him to the ground.

"I sorry little one. Again I monster," he said, then started walking to the opening that led outside.

Claude got up, dusted himself off and sat back down. He looked at the baron. "Aren't you going to do anything?" he asked in desperation. "I'm a respected citizen of the Vale and I have just been assaulted by a beast."

Vero gave him a warning look and replied, "I wouldn't push my luck if I were you."

Claude opened his mouth to argue but thought better of it. "Oh great," he remarked, "the giant crushed my cigar case."

He pulled the crumpled piece of silver from his pocket and tossed it on the table. The baron looked at the case, then at him and had to laugh, to which Claude had nothing more to say.

Shyla went after the giant and caught him halfway across the dance floor. "Wait!" she called out. "Where are you going?"

Mok stopped and answered, "I ashamed. Must go now."

Grabbing his hand with both of hers, she said, "Please don't leave. You have nothing to be ashamed of. Claude deserved what you did . . . I'm sure of it."

He looked down at his friend. "I ashamed be part boss man's lies. Mok must go."

Shyla shook her head. "No, you promised me a dance," she insisted.

The giant kept staring at her and she could see that his big heart was breaking. "Yes Mok promise," he agreed, giving in to her.

The music stopped and the singer announced, "Here's one of your favorites folks. Everyone bring your partner to the floor for the *Woodvale Waltz.*"

As soon as the song started, Shyla took hold of the giant's hands and they rocked back and forth in a circle.

"Where will you go and what will you do?" she asked, concerned about how he would be treated. Mok couldn't hear her with the loud music and people, so he bent down and set her on his forearm, lifting her up so he could listen.

"Mok not hear you," he said, still rocking back and forth. She repeated her question and he answered, "Have couple offers now."

The tune was beautiful and it flowed effortlessly, but it didn't ease Shyla's mind. She reached up and placed her hands on his cheeks.

"Will I ever see you again?" she asked, feeling a sadness creeping into her.

"Mok not know, little one," he answered, his voice breaking up on the last two words.

Shyla quickly fought back her tears and looked the other way. She could see the crowd below her and was getting many strange looks, but for once she didn't care what anyone thought. With a heavy heart she laid her head against the giant's massive chest and wished the song would never end. When it did, he kissed her forehead and gently set her down.

"Mok never forget little one," he said, and with his long stride, was out of the tent within moments.

Shyla stood there watching the opening where he had disappeared. *You don't have to go,* she told him silently, then followed after her friend. When she got outside there was no sign of him, so she went to the carriage, leaned on the wheel and started crying. Once the tears began to flow they wouldn't stop, and she sobbed uncontrollably.

It wasn't long before she felt a hand on her shoulder and heard a familiar voice. "Are you all right Shyla?" asked Stafan, handing her his handkerchief.

"My f-friend is gone and I may n-never see him again," she answered, still sobbing.

The night air carried a chill, so Stafan removed his jacket and wrapped it around her. "Never, is a word I seldom use, and I'm *sure* you will see him again soon," he comforted her, hoping his words would help.

"Do you really think so?" she asked, wiping her eyes and nose.

"I don't see why not," he replied, trying to ease her mind, "I'm sure he will join a local timber crew and you can visit him whenever you like."

That thought calmed her and the crying slowed. Once she had gained control of herself, she realized she was wearing his jacket. "You must be freezing," she said, handing it back.

"I'll only accept that if you accept my proposal," he told her, and saw the shocked look in her eyes. "No. . . . I mean, either we go back inside, or you let me get you a blanket from the carriage."

She looked amused and told him the blanket would be fine. "Do you mind if we sit in the carriage awhile?" she asked. "I don't feel like going back in quite yet." He helped her inside, then lit a candle. He gave her a blanket and a cup of juice, and made sure she was comfortable.

"Are you feeling any better?" he asked, once she was settled.

"Somewhat," she replied. "I didn't want Mok to leave feeling like an outcast, and I still have this inner need to protect him, as silly as that sounds."

What a caring person, thought Stafan, as he took a drink from his cup. "I don't think it's silly," he assured her. "I feel the same way about my mother, and sometimes it causes me great distress."

She pulled the blanket tighter around her. "Yes, but you have your father's help."

As soon as her words were spoken his expression turned to one of sorrow. "My father was lost at sea when I was twelve years old," he conveyed in a strained voice, "and I have been the man of the family since."

When will I learn not to speak my mind so freely? she scolded herself, and tried to imagine his pain. "I am so sorry," she apologized. "I didn't know."

His face was back to normal now and he replied, "It's all right, how could you have. I would have told you before but it never really came up, so don't worry, I'm not upset with you."

She appreciated his kindness, but still felt terrible, and there was no way to take it back. "I think I'm ready to return to the dance now," she stated, removing the blanket.

"Yes," he agreed. "Let's enjoy what's left of this fine evening."

Ivan had watched, with a certain amount of satisfaction, as Mok raised his neighbor into the air and then dropped him at his daughter's behest. He had chuckled when he saw the ruined cigar case, and had exchanged an amused glance with Vero. He had seen Shyla dance with the giant and then follow him out, and had watched Stafan run after her. All of these things he had watched, but made no move; not because he didn't want to, but because he didn't need to. He was the kind of man who made few errors, and could tell that the situations he saw needed no input or interference from him. It was nice to sit back for a change—he knew the baron felt the same—and watch the balance work its magic. He had to admit he was glad to have witnessed his neighbor receiving a little payback. Just seeing the look of redemption in his wife's eyes when the giant grabbed Claude and started shaking, was worth every gold he had lost in the competition.

When another slow song began, he took Grace to the dance floor and held her close. He could see Shyla and Stafan return-ing from outside, and it was good. He saw Cade and Wanda across the floor, and the way he paid attention to her alone, reminded him of his first encounter with *his* sweetheart. It was so good to see his children having fun and feeling those first emotions of youth, and even though he knew there would be hard days ahead, tonight he felt like the richest man in the kingdom.

When the music ended, he took his wife back to the table and then stood before Shyla. "It seems with all the excitement, I didn't have a chance to ask," he said, extending his hand. "Would you do me a great honor and dance with a poor woodcutter?"

Her smile started and kept getting brighter as she took his hand. "Oh Daddy," she beamed, "I would love to."

As soon as they were gone, Cade asked his mother to the floor and they were followed by Stafan and Wanda, and for the rest of the night they all danced and laughed without any further incidents.

"Ladies and gentlemen," came a voice from the stage. "I'm sorry to say that we will only be playing one more song for you this evening, but before we finish, please welcome, the baron!"

Vero received a warm reception as he walked up, and Ivan was paying close attention. "Well my friends, it looks like we've come to the end of another Woodcutting Competition, and what an interesting one it was. I would like to thank all the woodcutters once again for participating, and I know we are all looking forward to next year's events."

He walked to the edge of the stage and brought Charlotte back with him.

"There is something I want to share with you all," he said, putting his arm around her waist. "I have asked the Duchess Cavillade to be my wife, and as of this afternoon we are pledged to be joined."

The entire crowd jumped to their feet and applauded vigorously for the couple, but there were more than a few disappointed ladies.

"As a gift to the duchess, I am having a manor built on the shores of the Misty Lake, and we will be moving there after the joining." That statement brought many different responses, but Ivan could see that the people were truly happy for them.

"There's just one more thing before I say goodbye for another year, and this should be of interest to the woodcutters in the room."

Everyone quieted, wondering what he was going to say, and Ivan waited patiently.

"I know you've all heard of the extremely rare *balbou* tree and its many extraordinary properties," he began, with the full attention of the onlookers hanging on his every word. "Well, I am prepared to pay thirty gold for a fifty-foot span, and I am in need of three such pieces. The first woodcutter who brings me one, or all three, will receive prompt payment in full."

Ivan smiled when he heard the baron's offer, and was very interested indeed.

The *balboa* tree was not just extremely rare, it was the rarest tree in the known lands and he had been fortunate enough to see three of them during his life. The first two had been brought to the palace when he was a boy, and the third he had seen in a place he dreaded to think about.

The reason it was so highly sought after, as the baron had mentioned, were its properties. The *balboa* tree was as black as night and had no bark or branches. It was the hardest wood known, and when it was cut, had the most beautiful black and white quilted grain. It was said that centuries ago the trees were plentiful in some areas, but the demand soon left them all but extinct. Their beauty and density, although magnificent, wasn't the sole reason they were coveted by so many. The main attraction was that the wood did not burn, and when exposed to a flame, gave off a scent that would put a rose garden to shame. These qualities made the *balboa* tree sought after for building fireplaces, and Ivan knew without asking that Vero planned on putting three in his new manor.

If he could get such a tree he would make more from it than he had made in all his days of woodcutting. He didn't want to think about that now though, so he cleared his thoughts and applauded Vero and Charlotte on their exciting announcement.

The last dance was a waltz and everyone took to the floor. After it was through they personally congratulated the newly pledged couple and thanked them for an amazing evening.

What a special night, thought Ivan, as the family gathered their belongings and made their way outside. While they waited, Cade made plans to meet Wanda for breakfast, and Stafan bid Shyla a goodnight, then escorted his mother to their carriage.

Everyone was exhausted when they got to the pavilion and went straight to their beds.

"Thank you for that," said Grace, as she blew out the candle. "I haven't enjoyed myself that much in a long while."

Ivan put his arm around her. "I'm glad you had a good time," he replied. "And did some of that enjoyment come at

Claude's expense?" She poked him in the ribs and he grabbed her wrist. "C'mon now," he laughed, "you can't tell me it didn't make you extremely happy to see him hit the dirt."

She didn't say anything right away, then answered, "Maybe just a little," and they both laughed until their sides ached.

Ivan was almost asleep when Grace asked, "What did you think of Vero's offer? Wouldn't it be something if any of those trees existed around here."

Ivan sighed. "Yes, it sure would," he answered, and was brought right back to the difficulty he faced. He *did* know where a *balboa* grew, but it was located deep in the heart of the *Whispering Forest*.

On his last trip into that foreboding place he had uncharacteristically lost his sense of direction and nearly panicked. This seemed strange to him because he had gotten turned around a few times when he was out cutting and had always found his way again without too much concern. This time though, it almost seemed like there was something else present that was clouding his mind. All he'd been able to think about was getting out, so he found the tallest tree and climbed to the top to get his bearings, and that's when he saw it.

Off in the distance, rising up through the leafy canopy, was that black beauty reaching toward the sky. He had been in awe, but quickly dismissed it when he spotted the Horseshoe Creek, and his way out of those woods. He had never entered that forest again except to go through on the wagon path or trade-road, and had not thought about that tree again until Vero had mentioned it. Now it was all he could think about, and no matter which way he looked at it, he always came out with the same conclusion; a conclusion that, realistically, seemed utterly ridiculous.

He would have to harness old Bill to the pull-sleigh and travel for miles into the center of a forest that seemed to protect itself against the slightest of intrusions. Then begin searching for an object that was not only extraordinary but truly sacred. It was bad enough laying axe to wood in that place, but to chop down the rarest tree in existence, then cut it up and drag it out again, was a fool's errand if ever he had heard of one. He had never considered himself a fool until now, but it seemed he had no choice.

His mind raced until he fell asleep, and although he couldn't remember his dreams, he awoke in an anxious state of mind.

CHAPTER

25

A Farewell to Friends

The girls were packed and Ivan had his gear sitting by the entrance before they were called to breakfast. Cade had gone off earlier to meet with Wanda, but the rest of them were enjoying their last pavilion meal with the baron and his future wife.

"We have truly taken pleasure in having you as our guests this season," commented Vero to Grace after they had finished.

"And you are always a kind and gracious host," she replied, and Ivan nodded his agreement.

Stafan looked at Shyla and his voice tightened as he spoke. "I have so relished your company over the last days and hope we will see each other again soon."

She smiled and felt a touch of sorrow at the thought that they might not. "We do lead entirely different lives," she admitted, "but I do hope for the same." He took her hand, then leaned in and kissed her cheek, not caring whether her chaperone was watching or not.

"I feel terrible about this," uttered Vero, seeming fairly distraught, "but with the size of the competition, and the extra responsibilities this year, I didn't have a chance to purchase my gifts for you ladies. So instead I offer my apologies and this pouch of silvers in hope that you can forgive me," he finished, passing it to Grace.

She could feel that it was a lot more than the gifts would have cost and knew exactly what he was doing, and it touched her deeply. "This is more than adequate as you well know, and I accept it humbly, but no apology is necessary," she told him as she placed the pouch in her bag.

"He is a *very* generous man," giggled Charlotte, as she flashed her new ring with the oversized blue stone in its setting. After discussing the baron's favorable character, the girls were busy talking about anything and everything to do with all events leading up to the joining.

"So what did you think of my announcement about the *balboa* tree?" asked Vero, as he set a sack on the table.

Ivan eyed the object curiously and answered, "Truthfully, I've been trying to come up with a way to deliver one directly to your doorstep."

The baron laughed as he untied the string that held the sack closed, and reached inside. "If anyone could make that happen, I'm sure it would be you. In fact, I'm hoping you will be the one who claims the reward." Ivan smelled a familiar fragrance as Vero pulled out the contents and held them in his hands. He set them on the table and Ivan could see four pieces of *balboa* wood, and the sweet, subtle aroma filled his nostrils.

"The king sent these over when I was deciding on my building plans, and Charlotte fell in love with the idea, especially when I showed her its reaction to fire." He held a piece over the candle flame and a floral fragrance began to emanate, almost as if someone had brought in a basket of roses. "Remember when we were kids," recalled Vero, "and we would light one of the palace fireplaces in the middle of summer just to smell this wood?" Ivan nodded, and it brought back a fond recollection of when they were boys together.

"Do you think I could have one of these?" asked Ivan. "It's not the same as a fireplace, but it would be nice to keep, if only for the memories."

Vero rubbed his chin, then handed him a piece. "The king wanted these back, but when I tell him who made the request, I'm positive he won't mind."

The woodcutter thanked him and stuffed it in his pocket. The girls had finished their discussion now and Charlotte had said goodbye and left with Bridgette and Stafan.

"Do you think I might bother you for one more favor?" asked Grace, as she stood and approached the baron.

"You have but to ask," he replied, standing to greet her.

"I would like to go and say farewell to one of my friends down at the gypsy camp, and I was wondering if I might use one of your carriages?" she inquired, not wanting to take advantage of his hospitality.

"I will have one brought around immediately," he replied, and rang his bell loudly.

They thanked Vero again and left the banquet hall. Ivan went to his room to think more about his plan, and the girls made their way to the main entrance to take the carriage down to the entertainment area.

The carriage was uncomfortably hot inside as they rolled down the dusty path. From the windows they could see people breaking camp, and many wagons moving toward the public road. The site was similar on either side all the way to the business section of the quarter, and as they passed by they could see that most of the stalls and booths were either gone or being dismantled.

When they reached the gypsy camp the mood was the same as the wagons that were already packed up formed a line in preparation for their departure. The girls got out and asked the driver to wait, then started their search for the old woman.

In the daylight it didn't take Shyla long to find her wagon, and soon they were sitting around the little table drinking tea.

"I'm *so* glad you could make it down to visit an old woman," rasped Grelda as she filled Grace's cup. "I have some interesting remedies to show you and some even more interesting stories I think you'll enjoy."

Shyla finished her tea and asked, "Do you think it would be all right if I went and said goodbye to Storm? I noticed the circus is ready to leave and I would really like to see him before he goes."

Grelda looked at her and interjected. "Ah yes, I heard about that. It would seem your strength in the gift is increasing if you were able to enchant a cat of that size and demeanor. Now if we could just do something about the circus owner. I hear he's crankier than a wild boar, and he wasn't very happy with you." Shyla tried to look innocent.

"Very well," replied Grace, "but don't get into any trouble. Stay out of that man's way and don't do anything foolish."

She was about to ask, *what could I do?* but after her last visit to the circus, thought better of it and answered, "Of course Mother. I will just say a quick goodbye and be right back."

She thanked Grelda and hurried out. She was excited to go see the cat again, and quickened her pace. The colorful wagons were even brighter in the sunlight and she saw Sindra's near the back of the line. She hoped the seer would be all right, but was sure she would come back even stronger than before.

When she reached the outskirts of the circus grounds she could see that everything had been loaded onto and into wagons. She carefully scanned each one, trying to find the panthadon. There were so many, but finally she spotted the bigger ones on the far side.

All of the circus hands were gathered and enjoying a bite to eat before the journey, so she made her way between the smaller wagons, hoping to find Storm before anyone saw her. She stayed low and ran from row to row until she was directly across from the large wagons and could see them clearly. Storm *had* to be there.

She was thinking about running over and searching when she heard someone coming, so she peeked out and saw Villam moving down the row toward her. She jumped back, ducked down and waited for him to pass. Her heart was racing as he walked by, but she did her best to stay quiet. Once she was sure he had gone, she crawled out and hurried across to try to find the big cat.

These wagons looked more like cages on wheels. There were ten of them in a line, so she started at the back and made her way forward. It could have gone faster and been a lot less risky, but each one was closed in on three sides, leaving the side with the bars as the only way to see in.

The first one contained an old bear that didn't appear too ferocious, and confined in the next was the Wolfman who didn't look nearly as scary in the daylight. One-by-one she checked them, recognizing most of the exotic creatures, until she reached the second-to-last cage where she saw the cat lying in the corner. *He* still looked as incredible in the day, and she called to him. Storm lifted his head, and as soon as he saw her, jumped up and ran over to the bars.

"How are you boy?" she asked, reaching in and petting his nose. He licked her hand and began purring loudly. She was startled at first by his sharp tongue, but quickly got used to it and it actually began to tickle. "It's so good to see you again," she told him, as she reached up and scratched his ears. "I just couldn't have you go without saying goodbye." She had forgotten just how majestic he was and thought, *it's such a crime to keep a proud and magnificent animal like this locked in a cage*

She stayed awhile longer, not wanting to leave, but knew that her mother would be waiting, so she said a last goodbye and hugged him through the bars. "I *truly* hope you get to see your home again," she told the panthadon, and walked away.

She hadn't gone more than a few steps when she heard a deep sigh. At first she was worried she had been found out, but that sound was all too familiar, so she followed it to the front wagon and peered in. Her heart almost stopped when she saw Mok sitting there leaning against the back wall. There were shackles on his wrists and ankles, with large chains attached that were secured through the floor.

"Mok, what's going on!" she asked, in a raised voice.

The giant looked up. "Little one," he rumbled, his voice sounding strained and weary.

"Who did this to you!" she yelled, not concerned any more if anyone heard her.

"Little one," he repeated, not really paying attention to the question. "I sorry," he uttered, looking down again.

"Don't worry Mok, I'll get you out of there," she promised him, pulling on the door.

"Not you again!" shouted Villam, his frustration apparent. "Are you here to try to ruin another one of my acts?"

The light inside her pulsed in anticipation. "If you don't free the giant," she threatened, "you *will* be sorry." The white energy was building as her anger increased and she knew that if Villam didn't release Mok, she would try to melt the bars and chains, no matter the cost to her.

The circus man could sense that she meant every word and didn't want any trouble with the locals, so he quickly explained. "You've got it all wrong miss. The giant isn't a prisoner. He is here because he has joined our happy family and will be one of the featured performers."

She looked at Villam and shook her head. "I don't believe you," she protested. "If you're not keeping him against his will, then why is he in chains?" She held the light at bay, waiting for his reply, knowing that if he tried to deceive her she would do what was necessary to get her friend out of there.

"Now listen to me girl. The reason for the chains is only for effect. When we are leaving or coming into an area where we are doing a show, we dress things up for appearance' sake. As soon as we are out of sight, the chains come off and we all ride in comfort to the next town." He was very believable but she still wasn't convinced, and he could see that in her eyes, so he continued. "We have a contract," he declared, "and he is signed to my circus for three years, for fair compensation and lodging."

How could this happen? she thought, and tried to reason it out in her mind. "Is this true Mok? Are you working for this man?" she asked, afraid to hear the answer.

He lifted his head again. "Mok sign contract. I sorry," he told her, and his eyes looked hollow. Her anger turned to despair and she pushed the light back into place.

She was sick inside and felt helpless as she looked upon the giant, then turned to Villam and said, "Please be good to him."

The circus man put on a concerned expression. "Don't you worry miss. He will be treated like a king. Now if you would please move aside, I need to get this caravan rolling. We have a show in the Westlands and we are late getting started."

She nodded and stepped back. "Goodbye Mok!" she called out as the wagons began to move.

"I sorry, little one," he rumbled, his head hanging low.

Tears streamed down her face as she watched him go, and her heart ached at the sight of the words that she saw on the side of his cage. "Mok the Monster", was printed in bright red letters, and she fell to her knees and wept until well after he was gone.

The next thing she heard was her mother's voice. "Are you all right my girl!" Grace called out as she ran up to her.

"Oh Mother!" she cried, and a flood of tears started again.

When Grace saw her child hurting that way, her instincts took over and she knelt down and comforted her daughter as only a mother can. She held Shyla, rocking her gently until the crying had turned to sniffles, then asked, "What has happened that has made you so sad?" She helped her to her feet as Shyla explained what had befallen the giant and how she felt like she had let him down.

They returned to the carriage and Grace knew that no amount of consoling would help. Only time and the balance could ease her pain.

Shyla was quiet on the trip back and Grace let her be. As they pulled up to the pavilion she could see their wagon, and it was completely loaded. Old Bill looked well cared for during his stay and seemed eager to get moving. Ivan, Cade and Rufus were there to meet them, so they left the comfortable carriage and the entire family climbed aboard the old wagon and started for home.

Ivan could tell something was wrong as he turned Bill through the outer gates, but decided to wait to be told, rather than ask. Cade was too busy thinking about Wanda to notice anything, and Grace could see her man's concern, so she slid closer and took his arm. Shyla was oblivious to everything around her as she thought about Mok and how she had just stood there and did nothing to help him. *How could I have done that?* was the question in her mind as the wagon began to slow. The woodcutter pulled up as a rider approached and stopped beside him.

"Ivan Harden," he began. "I have a delivery for your daughter, from the giant," and handed him a rolled up hide. The woodcutter thanked the messenger and passed it back to Shyla who was now very aware of her surroundings and took it eagerly. She untied the leather cord that secured it, began unrolling it and quickly recognized the blanket Mok had wrapped her in when she was hurt. She buried her face in the warm fur and remembered his caring words and kind eyes.

Pulling it closer, she could feel there was something inside the fold, so she reached in and drew out a leather bag. She didn't have to open the drawstrings to know what it was, and it made her smile. He had sent her the healing powder from his homeland, but it only cheered her temporarily and then she felt even worse.

"Would you like to stop in Woodvale and pick up some supplies?" Ivan asked, as they turned onto the public road.

"Let's just go straight home," replied Grace. "I miss our little cabin." The children didn't say anything so the woodcutter set the old horse on a steady pace, and his mind returned to his perilous plan.

Trying to find a positive side to the day, Shyla had folded her new blanket and was using it as a cushion on the hard wagon seat and was showing Grace the powder Mok had sent her.

Her mother was very interested as she smelled the contents and held a pinch of it up to the sunlight. "I wonder what plant this was rendered from?" she pondered. "I've never seen it before." She tested it a little more and then returned it to her daughter.

"Believe me Mother it works, and he had it watered down." As she spoke of the giant, her stomach clenched and she knew that nothing could chase the gloom away on this day, and hoped that tomorrow everything would look brighter.

The trip went fast, and soon they were pulling into their little meadow. Rufus was the first one down and was running around sniffing the ground to see if any strange animals had moved in while he was away. They unloaded the wagon and drove it around the back. Shyla grabbed her egg basket and ran to the chicken coop to gather the eggs that had accumulated, but mostly she wanted to see if the chicks had hatched yet. The boys unhitched Bill and turned him out while Grace unpacked and started to think about what to make for the evening meal. Her stay at the pavilion had been great, but she was ready to get back to looking after her family.

Shyla brought in a *full* egg basket and set in on the counter, but was disappointed because there had been no chicks to play with. Her mother assured her they would be hatching any day, but she just moped to her room and shut the door.

The boys came in and Ivan was carrying a good-sized piece of smoked venison, which he handed to Grace. She took it and asked, "Would anyone protest to me making a big breakfast scramble for supper?"

"Sounds good to me," answered Cade, as he left to grab some wood.

"Yes, I see we have a few extra eggs," chuckled Ivan, eyeing the overfilled basket.

He put away his woodcutting gear and went and sat in his chair where he thought about the *Whispering Forest*, and when and how he would make his journey in.

Cade did the same with *his* hunting gear, then grabbed the water bucket and headed for the creek. Grace went to Ivan and told him what had happened with the giant, then started slicing the venison in preparation for frying and serving it with the scramble. Shyla stayed in her room, covered up with her new blanket and was feeling terrible.

Right after Cade returned and set the bucket on the counter, Rufus started to bark. It wasn't a warning bark, but more of a friendly, familiar kind. Cade ran onto the porch and saw Brant and Leslie Catcher coming in from the public road. They were driving a big two-horse wagon and pulling another, all filled with dog cages. They made a wide turn and pulled up beside the cabin.

Ivan and Grace went out to meet them and asked if they would like to come inside and rest awhile.

"We would like to," replied Brant, "but we've got to get these dogs home. We just thought that, with everything that had happened, this might be a good time to give Shyla her gift."

Grace smiled. "You have no idea how good your timing is," she replied, in a relieved tone.

Brant went to the back, opened a cage and lifted Loner out. He set him on the ground, and right away he and Rufus were circling each other, getting reacquainted.

Grace went inside and knocked on Shyla's door.

"What is it Mother?" she asked in a glum voice.

"There's someone here to see you," answered Grace. "It would seem a boy has come calling." She tried hard not to giggle and give it away.

Shyla sat up and tried to think of who it might be. "Mother, I'm really not in the mood to play this game, so *please*, just tell me who it is."

Grace waited until she had regained her composure to answer. "I'm sorry dear," she pretended to apologize, "but you'll just have to come out and see for yourself." And with that, she turned and walked back outside.

Shyla flopped down and pulled the blanket tightly around her. *I don't want to see anyone right now*, she thought, but soon her curiosity got the best of her and she sat back up and slipped on her old shoes. She left her room and walked to the front door.

She opened it and her face lit up when she saw the pup. She ran over to him and picked him up.

"Loner!" she exclaimed, "I've missed you *so* much." The little dog yelped with joy and licked her face, causing her to laugh as she held him in her arms. Rufus didn't look impressed, but Ivan and Grace were happy to see their daughter smile again.

"Thank you so much for bringing Loner by to see me," Shyla said, noticing the Catchers were ready to leave.

"Oh we didn't bring him here to *see* you," he explained. "We brought him here *for* you, if you'll have him."

She looked at her mom and dad, wanting to believe it, but afraid to after all that had happened earlier. "Is it true?" she asked. "Is he *really* mine?"

The grown-ups laughed. "He's all yours," affirmed Brant, and Ivan and Grace nodded to her. She couldn't imagine how a day that started out so terrible, could end so wonderfully, and she couldn't quit smiling.

"We've got to get these animals home and fed," said Brant, "but we'll see you soon," and he and Leslie climbed up and drove out of sight.

"Can I show Loner my room?" asked Shyla, in a pleading voice.

"Just this once," replied her mother. "After that he's an outside dog."

She called him onto the porch, then opened the door and coaxed him inside. It seemed he'd never been in a house before and he stepped cautiously, sniffing everything before he followed her to the bedroom. Rufus wasn't missing out on this and darted through the doorway behind them before anyone could grab him. It was all out of the ordinary but no one minded considering what she'd been through. The indoor visit didn't last long though, and soon they were out adventuring around the property.

The breakfast scramble went well with the smoked venison and it felt good to sit down with just the family again. Shyla was back outside playing with the dogs as soon as she was finished cleaning up, and Cade went off to hunt for game birds.

Grace was making a list for the garden and trying to stretch their purse. The gift that Vero had given her was over a gold's worth of silvers, and Shyla had refused to take any. With that and the silvers from Cade, she had well over two gold coins to put toward preparing for the winter months. It wouldn't be enough, but if Ivan could land some jobs they might just make-do.

The woodcutter was back in his chair now and had his plan worked out. If any of the woodsmen from the ball knew the whereabouts of a *balboa* tree they would be making haste to get it to the baron first, so he had to *hurry* or it would be too late. He had to leave the next morning to have a chance, and everything depended on it. It would also have to be before first light so Grace wouldn't see the direction he went.

He hated to deceive his wife, but if he told her his plan she would never agree to it. He did tell her he would be gone, but had said he was going to look for and mark good building logs for Shyla's new bedroom. Even though he felt bad, he knew the deception was necessary to complete this undertaking, but when he returned with a pouch full of gold it would make the apology a lot easier.

Ivan was already in bed when Shyla returned, and Grace was boiling some eggs for breakfast. It had been awhile since she'd cooked anything and it was good to be back in her own kitchen.

"Could I speak with you Mother?" asked Shyla, in a serious tone.

"Of course," answered Grace, a little concerned, but not wanting to make any rash assumptions. She followed Shyla to her room and sat down beside her on the bed.

"It's about the white energy of the *Sol'mar*," she began, trying to think of the best way to explain the transformation. "You remember when I lost control at the cave and you helped me to regain it? Well, it seems that when I did so, it healed me and repositioned itself inside me."

Grace wasn't sure if she knew exactly what her daughter was trying to tell her, so she sat quietly and listened. She could hear the crickets singing and hadn't realized how much she had missed that sound while they were staying at the pavilion.

"I don't mean healed the bruises from Mok—she felt a pang when she said his name—but I mean, healed me anew." Her hands were shaking as she pulled up her dress and showed her mother the smooth skin where the scar had once been. The worried look on her mother's face was no surprise to her, but she needed to tell her everything.

Grace looked down in disbelief. "Not even the most accomplished adept could manage a healing like that," she remarked, mainly to herself. "What else did you say about the energy?" she asked, still studying her daughter's leg.

"You know how the energy was a ball deep in my center," she explained. "Well, now it's spread throughout my entire body, situated in tiny points of light."

She waited for her mother's reaction, but this time she *was* surprised as Grace just sat there deep in thought.

"I'm sorry I didn't tell you earlier," Shyla apologized, "but I wanted to wait until the competition was over and we were home again."

Grace sighed and took her daughter's hands. "It is I who am sorry for knowing so little about something so dangerous. I have no idea whether this new manifestation is a good thing or bad, but Zarina arrives at Belden's Wall again the middle of next month, and we will be there to meet her. If anyone can help us, it's her." She hugged her daughter and stood up.

"That's not exactly all," added Shyla, her inflection causing Grace to sit back down. "Well," she started, "I went to a seer at the gypsy camp and she used an ancient artifact called a *Cantra* to increase her powers, and it kind of conflicted with the light in me, and I sort of cracked it in half. Luckily everyone was all right, and she gave me this." She reached into her bag and showed her mother the green shard. "She said it may help me someday, but I don't sense any power left in it, so I think of it as more of a keepsake."

Grace studied the fragment and listened as her daughter went on.

"I also found a book at Grelda's that I was hoping you could help me understand," she said, pulling *The New Adventures of the Twelve Foot Gnome* from her bag. Her mother looked confused and Shyla shook her head. "No, not that one," she corrected herself, and produced the proper text.

Grace took the book and looked it over, but the sun had gone behind the trees, so she lit the candle and held the aged tome up to the light. "Grelda had this you say?" she muttered to herself, studying it closely. She could tell from the thicker parchment pages, and the way it was bound, that it was very old. The writing was in a language she couldn't decipher, but there was something familiar about it. She leafed through it, and there was more of the same, tickling her memory. It wasn't until she studied the symbol on the black leather-bound cover, that it came to her.

"What is it Mother?" asked Shyla, seeing the recognition in her eyes.

"A very long time ago," she began, "the renowned healers of the Council got together and formed their own language so they could document their secrets and keep them protected. If I am correct, this book is written in that rare tongue and could hold some of the answers we seek. The only problem is that most of the healers that studied the old ways are no longer with us, and any that are may not even know anything about this forgotten writing."

She studied the ancient symbol in more detail, staring at the silver etchings depicting the Children of Balance, and was transfixed by the Mother's eye in the center. Now she was almost certain of her discovery. "Maybe Grelda knows something. She *is* the one who gave it to you."

Shyla shook her head. "She didn't hand it to me. I was drawn to it and chose it on my own. When I asked Grelda about it, she had no idea what it said."

Grace handed it back to her. "This book found its way to you, so I leave it with you to keep safe until we can show it to Zarina. Maybe she can make sense of it, or knows someone who can translate it. Until then, we won't speak of it."

Shyla had never seen her mother this way before and could tell by her expression that this was a serious matter.

Grace heard Cade come in, so she bid her daughter goodnight and went out to wish her son the same.

CHAPTER
26

The Whispering Forest

I t was another brisk morning and the moon was still shining as Ivan secured the last strap on the pull-sleigh harness. Old Bill was feeling frisky, but only because he had no notion of where they were going. They passed the cabin and Ivan reined him down the wagon trail that led straight to the creek. He hopped onto the sleigh as they crossed, then guided him through the low-hanging branches and into the *Whispering Forest*.

As they entered, it seemed like the moon had gone out, and it took a moment for Ivan's eye to adjust. It didn't seem to bother Bill though as he plodded along to the creaking and jingling of the harness.

The path had been well-worn once, but now the woodcutter could see grass and small willows sprouting up through the ruts. This had been the main road when the trade route had first been established, but as the town of Woodvale began to grow, they had branched it off and cut a path there. His plan today was to take this path to the trade-road, then move straight east toward the Crooked Mountains and into the center of the forest where the *balboa* tree awaited him. It seemed so easy, but that was usually when things went awry.

After almost ten miles they came to the fork that joined the trade-road, so he let Bill rest while he looked for the best place to begin the journey. After a thorough search he found an opening about three miles south that appeared more sparsely treed and would be less likely to encumber the sleigh. They went in with caution, but were soon making good progress as the runners moved swiftly across the moss covering of the forest floor.

The sun was up now but the thickness of the dense growth blocked the light, so Ivan decided it was time to take a look around. He stopped beside a massive tree, pulled out his spurs and began to climb. It wasn't a race but he bounded up at a quick rate and his anticipation grew more and more as he got closer to the top.

When he finally rose above the forest ceiling, he blocked the sun from his eyes and searched extensively. He smiled when he saw the majestic *balboa* in the distance, and gauged it to be about ten miles away. If he kept up a steady pace he could be there before noon, and then to the baron's before the evening meal.

He knew Vero would be remaining for a few days to oversee the cleanup at the competition grounds, and it would feel so good to deliver the tree right to the pavilion.

As they moved along with ease, he started to think that maybe all the stories he'd heard about this place were just that . . . stories. He'd had one bad experience, but that could have resulted in his dwelling on what the people had said about this forest.

He felt good as he climbed down and hurried Bill along, moving straight to the one thing that would change all of their lives forever.

The going was good as the terrain moved gradually up and down, flattening out in between. By the time midmorning arrived he figured they were about halfway there and laughed at himself for being so superstitious. It was funny how a tale could change with each telling and this place seemed harmless, but he still kept his wits about him just in case.

He stopped for a quick bite of the venison he'd brought and admired how vibrant, rather than scary, the forest actually was. After a short rest they continued, and the slope of the land remained the same as they ventured ever onward. Bill moved with ease, pulling the empty sleigh, and Ivan was whistling a song as he walked in front, leading the way.

Suddenly he stopped whistling and slowed up. About a hundred feet ahead was a thick fog moving steadily toward them. This was a normal occurrence in the deep woods, but it still gave him a chill. *It's just fog*, he told himself, and continued forward. As soon as the mist surrounded them, he started to feel strange, like he'd had too much wine the night before, and his head felt like it was stuffed with sawdust. No matter how hard he tried he couldn't shake the feeling, so he sat down on a log and tried to clear his mind.

The tales of the *Whispering Forest* started to creep in again, but he berated himself for being silly and put it down to an overactive imagination. *Fog often has that affect on people*, he thought, and as soon as he did, the misty veil lifted and his head cleared. It did seem weird, but maybe he was just a little jumpy. *That must be it*, he thought, and soon they were off again.

The forest had been dimly lit since he'd entered and he had relied on the occasional place where the trees thinned out to check how far along in the day it was. As he approached one such place, Ivan could see that the sun was directly overhead and knew he must be getting close now.

It wasn't long before he saw an opening in the distance and could see the sunshine cascading brilliantly on the other side. His heart raced and he quickened his gate. He knew he was late, but if he hurried he could still have the *balboa* on the sleigh and over to the pavilion before dark. He pushed past the last few trees and into the opening.

He stood there in amazement, not believing the sight in front of him. It was a road. Not just any road mind you, but the trade-road that went into Woodvale. He had gotten completely turned around and came right back out the way he had gone in.

Ivan felt embarrassed for allowing himself to be tricked that way, and for underestimating the power of the forest. He had entered like he owned the place and had been readily dismissed like an unwanted visitor. His pride was dented, but he had definitely gained a new respect for the life around him, and vowed he would not be fooled a second time. It was too late now to start in again, so tomorrow morning he would continue his journey, only this time he would be ready.

He headed home, but after he crossed the creek he decided to unhitch the pull-sleigh and leave it in the trees for the morning. He jumped on Old Bill and rode the rest of the way, hurrying by the cabin in hopes that no one would see the direction he had come in from.

"I missed you at breakfast," Grace commented, as he entered the house.

Ivan walked to the counter. "I wanted to get an early start," he told her. "Good building logs are hard to find." He dipped himself a cool drink of water and offered her some.

"So, did you find any?" she asked, as she fixed him some lunch.

"I'm going to go out again tomorrow. I really want everything to be perfect," he answered, meaning every word.

"That sounds good," she said, "but we need to go into Woodvale soon and get some supplies. I need to get the garden planted before I take Shyla down to Belden's Wall."

Ivan nodded and thanked her for the food, but his mind was on the challenge he faced the next day. When he had finished eating, he went to his chair and began touching up his axe blade while he thought.

He didn't sleep much that night, and was up before the rooster. Bill greeted him with a nicker and was raring to go, which amazed Ivan. After twenty years of woodcutting together, the old horse had always been eager to get moving and had never let him down.

When they reached the creek, Ivan harnessed him up and they made their way to the place on the trade-road that they had, *unfortunately*, become all too familiar with the day before. He had it worked out this time and was going to use the trees as a guide. His plan was to line up two of them in the direction he wanted to go, then walk straight to the next one and continue the same way to the next. This way he could travel in a straight line no matter what else happened. He cleared his mind and headed in.

He lined up the first tree and started toward it, but stopped when he heard something coming. *If the forest can alter my mind,* he thought, *maybe it can sway the beasts of the wild to protect its borders.* With that idea forming, he grabbed his hatchet and readied himself for an attack.

His eyes had adjusted to the meager light now and he was ready to defend against whatever it was. The sound drew closer, maybe fifty feet away. He positioned himself in front of Bill and strained to catch a glimpse of his assailant, but the undergrowth was too thick to see anything. It was close now, and in the next instant a dark figure bounded at him. He had almost released his hatchet when he saw Rufus running up, and he let go of the deep breath he'd been holding. "You gave me a scare boy," he said, rubbing the dog's head, glad to have his company.

Over the next while he went from tree to tree and climbed the tallest ones to keep the *balboa* in line. The plan seemed to be working, and he was definitely getting closer, but he made sure of every move this time and there was no way this forest was going to beat him twice.

It was misleading how normal everything appeared though. The birds were singing as they nested in the branches and searched for food. He could hear the frogs and the squirrels creating the sounds that always made him feel at home in the woods, and even the odd game bird ruffled its call to whoever was listening. The trees here were old, even beyond a guess from Ivan, and he had never seen a more vital forest in all his years of woodcutting. Normally he would have been intoxicated by the sheer magnificence of it, but today he was all business and wasn't letting himself be distracted.

There was a slight breeze moving through the trees now and it felt good as the morning began to warm. From his few trips up he knew the sun was shining in a clear sky, and was absolutely certain he was moving to his intended destination with each step. Old Bill seemed content to trail along behind, but Rufus was up ahead following one scent after another that his keen nose had picked up.

The next tree in line was on the other side of a small glen where the sun was filtering through, so Ivan decided to stop and eat some of the venison and heavy-bread he had brought. He tied Bill near some tall grass and found himself a patch of thick moss to sit down on. It was soft and inviting, and it felt good to relax awhile. The bread and meat were tasty, and he called Rufus over to join him. He hadn't really brought enough for two, so he checked his pockets to see if he had anything left from the day before. He came up empty-handed except for the sample of *balboa* wood, which he'd forgotten he had with him. He never tired of that smell, and gave him an interesting idea.

He held the piece up to Rufus and got him to sniff it. The old hound was at one time the best tracker around, and once he was locked onto a scent, you couldn't drag him off with a team of horses.

Rufus licked the wood and put his nose to it again.

"Can you find it boy! Can you find it!" exclaimed the woodcutter, trying to get the dog excited. He wagged his tail rapidly and circled the glen with his nose to the ground, then lifted his head high into the air and began to howl. Ivan laughed. *It looks like his old sniffer still has some life left in it*, he thought, and walked over to get Bill.

Before he started moving he made sure of his bearings, lining up the next tree and heading right to it. If his prediction was correct, the *balboa* should be about six miles straight east of his current position, and Rufus appeared to agree, his nose in the air while moving in that direction.

He had gone about a mile when he stopped and listened, but couldn't hear anything. In fact, that was the problem. He could hear nothing at all. Not a bird or squirrel. Not even a frog was croaking, and a warning sounded in his head. He called

Rufus back and checked his surroundings for any signs of danger. It didn't take long for him to see it moving through the trees like a white blanket covering a mossy bed. The fog was back, but he knew its affects this time and was ready for it. He waited patiently as it crept in around him and his companions, then pulled his jacket up to his face and took a deep breath. He held it as long as he could, but the mist was becoming thicker as it rolled in. Slowly he let the air out of his lungs and waited as long as he could before taking any back in again. When he was forced to, he took small breaths and concentrated on keeping his mind alert. It seemed to be working and he didn't feel any of the dizziness or grogginess he had experienced before, then suddenly, as fast as it had appeared, the fog was gone and everything was back to normal.

It was comforting to hear the forest sounds again and he took a few moments to regroup. He smiled and was proud of his small victory, but the day was getting shorter and he needed to get moving. *Bill must have been spooked in the confusion and gotten himself turned around*, thought the woodcutter as he straightened him out and lined up the next tree. He moved swiftly and directly now, keen on getting to the *balboa*.

He had just lined up a tall pine, when he heard a bark. He looked over his shoulder and there was Rufus facing the wrong direction and looking back like he wanted him to follow. Ivan felt sorry for the old dog, but no one, neither man nor beast can stay sharp forever, and it was apparent that his old friend was slightly confused.

"Come on boy!" he urged. "It's this direction," but Rufus only barked again and kept looking the opposite way. "I guess your age has finally caught up with you old friend," he remarked, feeling sad about the way everything had gone over the last while. "Don't worry," he chuckled, "I'm probably not that far behind you."

The lead rope pulled tight in his hand as he led Bill forward, but Rufus wasn't following. He called the dog over and took out the piece of wood, placing it up to his nose again.

"Let's get you back on the scent," he said, giving him ample time to regain it. He put the wood away and bent down. "All right boy, let's go get that tree," he told him, then straightened and started forward once more.

Again Rufus ran back the way he had just come and barked for him to follow.

"Come boy, it's this way!" he scolded in frustration.

Something wasn't right here. He had watched that old mountain-hound track a rabbit through a snowstorm and never falter; so why now? Ivan was absolutely certain he was heading straight for the tree, but he had thought that the day before and ended up back at the road. *Had the fog gotten to him without him noticing this time? Was he making the same mistake again?* All these questions running through his mind, and no way to know the answers for certain.

If he climbed a tree he would at least know if he was right about the direction, but if his mind *was* being manipulated, he wouldn't know for sure. There had to be an answer here some-where, and when he had become almost completely discouraged, it came to him.

"Of course!" he said aloud, and started searching the area. It didn't take long to find what he was looking for . . . tracks. He saw tracks; his own tracks, and they were going the opposite direction than he was headed now. The fog *had* turned his senses against him again . . . but not the dog's. *Could it be that the forest didn't alter the animals, and only kept people out?* He called Rufus over and apologized to him, then turned Bill around and put his trust in the one he should have all along.

It felt strange as he followed. Even though he knew the dog was leading him to the *balboa*, his instincts were telling him to turn around before it was too late. It was difficult to ignore the urgent feeling of despair that increased with each step he made, but he still had his free will and stayed close behind Rufus.

They had only traveled about half a mile when Ivan saw the fog again. He called Rufus back and waited. It swept in quickly this time, but he didn't bother covering his face or breathing any differently. It hadn't helped before, although in his arrogance he thought it had.

He had been so sure he could beat a bunch of trees. He was Ivan Harden, the master of the woods, but this forest had humbled him and made him feel small and insignificant in its presence. Now all he could do was wait and see what would happen next.

It was much thicker this time than in his previous encounter and he couldn't see anything, so he held onto Rufus and the lead rope to keep everyone together. Soon, like it had done previously, the mist lifted and was gone within moments.

The woodcutter's mind felt muddled now, and he was having trouble remembering where he was or why he was there. *I know I'm here to find something,* he thought, but his memories eluded him as he tried in vain to concentrate. He looked at the horse, and the pull-sleigh, then at the dog beside him.

"I must be here to get some logs," he whispered to himself. "Some logs for my daughter's new bedroom perhaps." He was trying *so* hard to remember, that his head began to hurt.

"No . . . that's not it. I'm sure I'm here for something urgent. Something I need right now," he mumbled, but still couldn't grasp it.

Frustrated, he leaned against a tree and shoved his hands in his pockets. "Why can't I remember?" he asked himself, and Rufus looked up at him, not sure what his master wanted.

An overwhelming desire to leave overtook him now, but he knew there was something important. He stood there for awhile trying to straighten his thoughts, when he noticed a smooth object touching the back of his hand. Curious, he pulled it out and looked at it. When he saw the beautiful black and white grain of the *balboa* sample, a memory started to form. He wasn't sure why, but he brought it up to his nose and smelled it. The sweet pungent fragrance drifted into his nostrils and completed the memory.

"That's it!" he called out, startling Old Bill. "We need to find the sacred tree!" Rufus barked at his enthusiasm and once again began to lead them onward.

His head was still fuzzy, but at least he was aware of what he was there to do, and knew they were getting close. The land started to slope gradually downward now and Ivan could hear a *swishing* sound. All the plants and trees were bigger here, like they had been enlarged somehow, and he could smell moisture in the air. Then, without any warning, it began to rain. Big drops fell straight down and it confused him. He had seen the sky earlier and there were no clouds or any signs that would have indicated a weather change, yet here it was, coming down hard.

Turn back, came a whisper, and the woodcutter looked around. *Go no further,* the voice came again, and Ivan stopped. He turned in a circle, trying to establish its source, and noticed something unusual. Back the way he had come, and not fifty feet from where he stood, the ground was completely dry.

He had ridden out of storms before, but never had the rain ended in such a perfectly straight line.

Heed my warning, the whisper continued, and again he felt a strong desire to leave the forest. *There is only deep sorrow ahead,* the soft voice murmured, causing Ivan to turn and start back.

He took two steps and then faltered as a vision of his family formed in his mind. They were his reason for being here, and the reason he needed to get to that tree. He spun around and moved quickly, talking to himself all the while, trying to drown out the voice that seemed to be coming from the drops themselves.

Finally, after a few hundred yards, both the rain and the voice stopped, along with the desperate urge he was feeling to run far away from this place.

He looked back and everything was calm and serene once more. At least now he knew for sure how the forest had got its name, and wondered how many others had ventured in unaware.

He stopped to rest and called the dog back. Rufus trotted up to him and the moisture sprayed from his fur as he tried to shake himself dry. Ivan held up his arms but could only block a portion of the watery assault. Now it was Bill's turn, and his attempt to shed the accumulated drops was a lot quicker but not quite as effective. Nonetheless, most of it managed to find Ivan as well and he knew that if someone happened to be watching, they would have found it very amusing. He didn't mind though, and brushed himself off. He was just glad to be feeling almost normal again, and when he saw the bright light about a half mile in the distance, his spirits began to lift.

The ground leveled out now and the trees thinned and increased in size even more as they got closer to the opening. Ivan started to feel even better than normal as they covered the last two hundred feet, and Rufus began to howl softly, knowing he was so near his wooden quarry.

CHAPTER
27

The Balboa Tree

The sun was bright as they burst into the meadow, and Ivan couldn't believe his eyes. The grass was greener than he'd ever seen before, and the colors of the flowers were so deep and vibrant that it almost seemed exaggerated. A hundred feet from the tree-line he could see a lake, and its waters were so blue that it looked like a shining jewel set in the middle of this extraordinary place. He was so fascinated by the vision before him that he almost forgot his true objective.

The lake was about two hundred yards across, and on the far shore he saw the *balboa* rising up from the meadow floor like an enormous ebony candlestick. Rufus was already moving toward it, skirting the water's edge, so Ivan followed his lead.

He marveled at the lush plant life as he walked along the shore, and wished he could take some of this soil to put on Grace's garden. *Wouldn't she be surprised,* he thought, *when her tomatoes grew to the size of cabbages.*

As he rounded the lake he could see the dog circling his black prey and howling his victory to the finish of a successful hunt. He took Bill to the trees and tied him out of reach of where he planned to fall the *balboa*, then made his way to Rufus and his new prize.

391

He called the old dog over and praised him on his brilliant tracking skills, and he could see how good that made him feel. *Now to the tree,* he thought, and felt relieved to have finally made it.

It was a magnificent specimen, not that Ivan had seen many, and it was at least twice the size of the ones that had been brought to the castle. *Vero might even pay extra for this,* he thought, and set his gear-bag on the ground.

He took out his axe and checked it for sharpness. Pulling a thumb across the blade told him he could easily shave with it. This was simple now. All he had to do was chop it down, cut it into fifty-foot lengths and secure it to the pull-sleigh. He wasn't too worried about leaving this place either. Getting *out* of the *Whispering Forest* had *definitely* not been a problem.

With his axe gripped firmly, he walked up and mentally marked where he would make his first cuts. He had never actually seen a *balboa* growing before, and was surprised at how much its surface looked like skin rather than wood. It intrigued him so he lowered his axe and leaned in, placing his hand on the trunk. He was shocked when it felt warm to the touch, and it wasn't from the sun. He couldn't believe the vitality and vibrant life he sensed beneath the outer layer, and if it were any other circumstance, he would never harm a tree this incredible.

He stepped back and raised his axe again, and his heart hurt at the thought of killing such a wondrous creation, but his family came first, and that's how he had to think of it.

Lifting the blade high, he took his stance and prepared to strike, but he just couldn't bring himself to do it. He knew this single tree was the difference between a continuous struggle to make a living and providing a comfortable life for his loved ones, but he was still having trouble carrying out the deed. For all he knew, this *balboa* could be the last of its kind, and he would be destroying an entire species. He debated back and forth, and wrestled with his conscience until he was exhausted. *All right, that's enough,* he told himself. *Just harvest the tree, take it to the pavilion and be home for a late dinner.*

With all the resolve he could muster, he raised his axe for the last time and brought it down hard. As it sliced through the air, toward its intended placement, Ivan did something he had never done in all his years of woodcutting. He looked away just before he finished his swing, causing his axe to glance off the hard surface and fly out of his hands.

End over end it sailed through the air until finally it landed in the lake, a goodly distance from the shore. He ran to the edge, but all he could see were some ripples and a few bubbles where it had sank.

He quickly removed his boots and socks and started wading toward the remaining bubbles, but soon realized, contrary to how inviting it appeared, the water was freezing. He hurried back out even faster than he had gone in and began rubbing his already numb legs.

Once the feeling started returning to his lower limbs, Ivan began to realize the severity of his situation and a hopelessness crept over him. Everything had gone wrong since he'd left his cabin, and now he had lost his only axe. He was so devastated and sick inside that he fell to his knees at the water's edge and began to weep.

Ivan hadn't cried in a very long time, and he couldn't control it. All those years of frustration poured out. All the times he'd watched his family go without so he could continue woodcutting. This had been his one chance to really prove himself in their eyes, and he had failed them.

Rufus came over and laid down beside him. He looked up at his master and whined, wondering what was wrong. Ivan looked down, blinked away the tears, and stroked his old pal's head.

His faithful dog had brought him here when he wasn't able to think straight. Even the horse had pulled the sleigh all the way from home, and he felt he had let them down as well. The woodcutter hung his head in shame and continued to weep.

There was nothing here for him now, so he pulled on his socks and began to lace his boots. When he finished, he stood up to leave, but stopped when he heard a loud *gurgling* coming from out on the lake. His eyes moved in the direction of the sound, and he could see the water in the center swirling in a small circle.

It must be currents from underground springs, he thought, but as he looked on, the circle increased in size and began to swirl faster. Small waves were lapping the shore now and Ivan moved back a few steps, never taking his eyes off the strange whirlpool.

He has seen something like it before in the back-eddy of the creek, but it was much smaller, and that water had been moving.

The waves were crashing on the shore now as the pool's intensity grew, and Ivan could see a pillar of water rising from its center. Dark clouds formed above the lake as the pillar continued to ascend, and bolts of lightning flashed along its surface, seeming to accelerate the already cascading tempest. Icy winds whistled past him and he pulled his jacket closed, but knew his actions were wasted as he felt its deep bite.

His instincts were screaming at him to run, but again Ivan had never been one to do that, so he waited and watched as the pillar quit rising and started moving forward.

The wind was gusting now, and the thunder and lightning blasted in a violent chorus as the pillar came closer. Ivan stood his ground and had already decided to face whatever it was that he may have offended, but was still in disbelief at what he thought he saw.

Is the fog still altering my reality, he wondered, *or have I entered into some magical nightmare?*

The pillar stopped by the shore and floated there motionless, but the water within still spun in turmoil. Then suddenly it began to glow a deep blue and the woodcutter heard a voice.

Who dares enter my domain! it wailed, and the sound echoed through the meadow. Ivan was too stunned to answer, and again words sounded from the great vertical pillar.

Why were you kneeling in sorrow before me? The voice was louder this time, and was answered by claps of thunder and dazzling streaks of lightning. The icy wind felt like it had reached his bones now, and he stood there shivering and speechless.

Finally he found his tongue and answered through chattering teeth. "M-my name is Ivan Harden, and my axe s-slipped out of my h-hands and f-flew into your l-lake." He was shaking so much now he could hardly get the words out.

How dare you raise an axe in my forest! roared the voice.

"I didn't realize it was yours. I-I only wanted the *balboa* t-tree to provide for m-my f-family. I—."

Silence! it boomed, cutting him off and sending a misty blast that knocked him to the ground.

Rufus, who wasn't a coward, but far from foolish, was hanging back and watching to see if the strange creature was going to make a move to harm his master.

Ivan stood up and watched as the pillar moved back. Then he saw something come up from the lake and enter its watery mass. It came forward again and stopped just off shore. The woodcutter could see the object inside, and though it was distorted by the water, appeared to be his axe. After a few moments the axe moved out of the pillar and was being held in plain sight.

Is this the item you seek? sounded the voice, and Ivan had to blink a few times to make sure his eyes weren't playing tricks. There before him was a double-bitted axe like his own, only oversized, that looked to be made of solid gold. There were strange etchings up the sides and on the head, and the fine detail and crafting rivaled even that of the *Gatou*.

He stared at the thing of beauty and almost forgot how cold he was. *If only that were mine,* he thought for a moment, then answered, "No, my axe is old and worn."

Thunder crashed, and the voice bellowed, *this is the only article I have fitting that description. Are you certain this isn't yours!*

The woodcutter paused. It would be so easy to say yes and take that golden trophy home to his family, but that wasn't his way, and he repeated, "No, mine is old and worn."

Almost instantly the clouds were gone and the misty force stopped blowing. The lake became still and the monstrous pillar transformed into a beautiful young girl that looked like one of the fairies from Shyla's story books. This was too much for Ivan and he fell to his knees again. His mind was racing to comprehend what was happening, while Rufus remained behind him whining softly from his grassy hideout.

Ivan looked up, and even though he had just witnessed all that had taken place, had a hard time believing what he was seeing.

This 'Water Fairy' was shaped like a girl, but her body was translucent and blue in color. She was very pretty and her long hair flowed down her back like a waterfall. She made a gesture, and the woodcutter's axe rose to the surface on the crest of a wave and was brought to her. Now she was holding Ivan's axe and the gold one, which made his look *really* worn.

"It appears I did have another axe," she giggled, and her voice sparkled and shimmered as she spoke. The woodcutter was shivering as he listened, and was still trying to accept the vision that was right there in front of him.

"I apologize for the theatrics," she continued, "but you are the first one *ever* to enter my sanctuary. I had to make sure you weren't a threat, and your honesty and bravery have spared you harsher treatment. There are strange and disturbing events that have occurred over the last while and I need to know how you made it through my outer defenses, when no one has since the beginning."

He still couldn't feel his hands or feet and his lips were numb, but he finally found his voice. "The beginning of what?" he asked, trying hard to keep his body from shaking.

"Why the balance of course, but you haven't answered my question. How *did* you make it through?"

The balance? he wondered. *How can she speak of it like it was yesterday? Can she really be that old?*

She set the axes down and two small pillars rose to hold them.

"It was actually my hunting dog Rufus who followed the scent of the *balboa* tree and brought us here," he replied, and the dog popped his head out of the grass when he heard his name.

Now that the storm had blown over, Rufus decided to leave his sheltered lair and join his master, so he trotted up, cautiously eyeing the strange being.

"Very interesting," she concluded. "Forgive me. I see you are in pain. Please come and immerse yourself in my waters and ease your discomfort."

Ivan looked confused. "I'm afraid that's how I gained the discomfort in the first place."

The Water Fairy giggled again. "Don't worry," she assured him. "I have changed it to suit your needs."

He was skeptical, but *surely* didn't want to get on her bad side again, so he walked forward and placed his hand in the lake. It was hot, and he was amazed. He pulled off his jacket and his shirt, then his boots and socks and waded in. He sat there neck-deep and relaxed, while the heated liquid soothed away the numbness. It felt so warm and refreshing he wanted to remain, but it was time to get going.

He thanked her, moved to the shore and waited for the afternoon sun to take the moisture. A moment later the Water Fairy raised her arms and two thin walls arose and began spinning. This caused a hot wind to blow in off the lake, and both he and his clothes were dry almost immediately.

"That feels much better," remarked Ivan. "Now if you would be kind enough to hand me my axe, I'll get out of your h . . . way as fast as I can get Old Bill moving. Oh, and I'm sorry for the intrusion. I had no idea this forest belonged to you."

The golden axe dropped beneath the surface and the Water Fairy took Ivan's in her hands.

"Now that we're *sure* this is your axe, I still need to decide what to do."

Her voice was soft and unsure and she seemed so meek, but Ivan knew better.

"I've never had to deal with this situation before and I really want to make the right choice. You *are* the only one who has made it past my traps. If I were to let you leave here, you could show others the way through, and it is forbidden for anyone to be here!"

Her voice became louder with each word, and she increased in size as Ivan's axe began looking smaller and smaller.

"Wait!" he called out. "Before you become angry again, please listen to me. I too have a sanctuary with my family, and like you I also want to protect them and keep them from harm. I must get home because I love them and need them, and they need me. If you send me back, I give you my word that I will never tell anyone the location of your meadow, or stray from the road again."

By the time he was finished she had returned to normal size again, and he hoped she had at least considered his plea. He felt sick and devastated at the thought of never seeing his family again and had to make sure that didn't happen.

The Water Fairy set his axe down, and he could see her struggling with the circumstances. She beckoned him closer and he moved to her.

"I *do* understand your responsibility and desire to be with your family," she told him, in her soft shimmering voice, "but I also have a responsibility here as well, and it goes much deeper than you can imagine. The only way I can know for sure that you are truly earnest in your statement is to read you. If you allow that, then I can make my decision with all I need to understand the problem that vexes me."

Ivan wasn't sure what she meant, but he would do anything to be with Grace and the children again, so he agreed readily.

The being reached out and placed her hands on his cheeks, and much to his surprise, they were warm and not at all wet. It was as if the water were contained by some unseen force. Her hands heated and Ivan's head started to become itchy, only from the inside.

I wonder if this is how the animals feel when Shyla reads them, he thought, just as she took her hands away.

The woodcutter wasn't sure if she was finished, so he remained still and waited.

"All has been revealed," she said, and looked very concerned.

Panic started to rise in Ivan but he didn't want to let his imagination get the better of him, so he pushed it back down and watched as she was busy contemplating.

Finally she spoke again. "I can see that your heart is pure and your word is good, but there are certain things going on in *your* sanctuary that you don't fully understand, or can possibly fathom."

Ivan had to smile. "You're referring to the women in my life, and yes, I've never understood a lot of their ways, nor do I ever expect to. It's been like that since the beginning . . . of my joining that is."

The Water Fairy spoke again, and this time she was very forthright. "I have decided to let you leave my domain, but only if you agree to my conditions and swear an oath to uphold them."

Relief swept over Ivan, and he replied, "Of course. Just tell me what they are and I will swear to them." She raised her hand and held up a finger, and her voice increased in volume as it suddenly became all encompassing.

"First, you must vow never to cut down a tree in my forest again. Second, you must swear to never show anyone how to get past my outer barriers, or divulge the location of this place." Ivan was nodding in agreement as she listed them, but his gut twisted when she revealed the final condition. "Third, you must promise to send your daughter to see me on her sixteenth birthday."

The woodcutter's head was reeling from the last statement and he didn't understand. *What could she want with Shyla?* he wondered, and couldn't keep the question silent. "Why do you want to see my daughter?" he asked bluntly, no longer worried about offending the one holding his fate in her hands.

"I only want to speak with her. She was recently shielded from me and then I saw through you that she has been warded by the powerful 'Spell of the Unseen'. This means she is also mentally invisible to those seeking her, who might covet or fear her new gift. You are not consciously aware of this, nor is she, but I can sense it although I do not recognize its origin. Do not worry Ivan William Harden, I mean Shyla no harm and she will be free to leave here anytime she wishes. That is my vow to you."

Ivan knew he didn't have a choice unless he wanted to spend the rest of his days away from his family, so he raised his hand and made his pledge. In return the Water Fairy made her vow, then returned his axe and disappeared beneath the surface.

This day definitely didn't turn out like I'd hoped, he thought, as he walked over and placed his axe back in the gear-bag. He looked at the *balboa* and sighed. *The king of all trees,* he told himself, and was glad he hadn't harmed it. Still, a part of him *was* disappointed he hadn't been able to pull up to the pavilion with his trophy.

There was no use dwelling on what could have been, so he went over to Bill and untied him. He checked the harness over, then proceeded to lead him back around the lake to the place where they had entered the meadow.

When they were halfway there, Ivan could see the water bubbling again, so he stopped. He wondered if it was just random, but soon the Water Fairy emerged from the depths.

"There's one more thing," she said, addressing the woodcutter.

I was almost free of this situation, he thought, *and now there's more?*

"Before you go I would like to extend my gratitude for the sincerity and courage you have shown this day. I would also like you to consider this as a token of my devotion to our arrangement." She waved her arms and the golden axe rose from the lake and she handed it to Ivan. He was dumbfounded as he took it, and could only manage a nod in his shocked state.

The Water Fairy left again as fast as she had arrived, and the surface was still once more.

The act that just took place was sinking in slowly, and the woodcutter began to get excited. The axe was *very* heavy in his arms, but he *sure* didn't mind. Again the day had changed, only now he hadn't had to cut down the tree, and possessed something worth a whole lot more. He couldn't even guess the value of his new acquisition, but it had to be worth an incredible amount, and somehow the burden seemed lighter as he began moving again.

When he was well into the forest, the actual weight of the golden axe began to slow him down as the heat of the day reached its fullness. He thought of sticking it in his bag, or tying it to the pull-sleigh, but it was much too fine for such treatment, so he bore the burden, periodically switching shoulders to offset it.

He reached the area where the ground started its incline and the rain began to fall again.

Good luck, came the whisper. *May the balance protect you.*

The rain stopped before the voice had faded and Ivan wasn't sure if he was supposed to respond, so he said, "Thank you," and continued up the hill.

The air grew very warm as he climbed, and when he reached the place where the terrain leveled again, he had worked up a sweat carrying the extreme weight. They had only gone a mile when he saw the fog, so he called Rufus back and waited like he had done before. It rolled in, and when it was only a few feet away, parted and let them through.

The rest of the journey went smoothly, and soon they had reached the trade-road. Ivan couldn't believe how relieved he was to be back out, and switched his treasure to the opposite shoulder to even the pressure. He hadn't really examined the axe yet, and was waiting until he got home to take a good look. "Only twelve more easy miles boys," he remarked in a chipper voice, and quickened his pace.

CHAPTER
28

A Master Plan

Claude stood on his porch and watched his hired man planting the grain in his front field. He had arrived back from the Woodcutting Competition the day before, and had taken that time to recuperate. He had been humiliated by his ordeal with the giant, but was feeling himself again this afternoon.

The Woodcutter's Ball was not his favorite memory over the past week, and his pride had been crushed, along with his cigar case, but at least his arrogant neighbor had finally been defeated. He wasn't sure what had become of the giant and didn't much care. Jack had served his purpose nicely, and now Claude had Ivan right where he wanted. He would *have* to work in the mine now and more than likely be forced to sell him his property at a low price.

The sun was hot, yet the fire that burned within him at the thought of bringing the legend to his knees was all consuming.

I bet Sonny won't think Ivan's so great when he sees him shoveling coal, he thought, and had to smile at the irony. When he purchased the woodcutter's homestead he might let him stay on as a renter, but then make sure he only made enough at the mine for a meager existence. *It will be so nice to see him put in his place,* he thought. *I've waited so long for this,* and again he smiled.

He felt great and was enjoying some quiet time at home. The mine had been shut down during the competition, and Morra and Sonny had stayed behind to visit with Sam for a few days.

Claude was just about to go back inside when he saw a flash of light from the direction of the creek. Curious, he shaded his eyes and saw Ivan coming through the opening with his old nag and bag-of-bones hound. *This is as good a time as any to pressure him into selling,* he thought, *and maybe set up a schedule for his work in the mine.* He felt like the king of the land as he walked toward the fence, and couldn't wait to watch the woodcutter squirm. He leaned on the railing and waited as Ivan came closer.

When he was about a hundred feet away, Claude noticed that he was carrying something on his shoulder and it was sparkling brilliantly in the sunlight. Now his curiosity was jumping and he strained to make out the shiny object. Soon Ivan was in range and he could see the golden axe clearly. His stomach knotted at the sight, and his face heated.

How is this possible? he wondered, while keeping a straight, yet slightly red, face as the woodcutter came up and stopped beside him. *All those years of wearing him down until I finally had the high ground, and now he shows up with a golden axe. This has to be a trick,* but Claude knew real gold when he saw it.

If there was one talent he excelled at, it was thinking on his feet, and his mind was racing now. It made him sick to think that all his planning and scheming might have been for not, then he reminded himself, *Claude Boyle never loses.*

Already his sharp mind was hard at work, and he said, "I am glad I caught you Ivan. I was just thinking about how badly things have gone between us since I moved here, and I came over to see if we could bury the hatchet . . . uh, so to speak." He could see the surprise on Ivan's face, but the woodcutter leaned the axe against the rails and grasped Claude's extended hand. "That's a mighty fine axe you've got there," he continued. "Don't tell me it's another trophy that you won with your extensive talent in woodcutting."

Ivan didn't know what Claude was up to, but he could see that behind his friendly mask he was spitting with rage, and the woodcutter just couldn't keep quiet. After all the times Claude had gotten the better of him, he finally had the advantage and couldn't help but rub it in.

He didn't tell him the location or the whereabouts of his adventure, nor did he reveal the method or details of his entry into the meadow. In fact he left everything out except the story of the tree and the Water Fairy, and how he had received the axe as a gift after losing his the way he did. He knew how much it would irk Claude to know that he had been given something so valuable, and he smiled as he finished his tale.

It was all Claude could do to smile back after listening to Ivan's story, but he did, and was already thinking of a way to best him.

"It looks like you've been through a lot today," he remarked, and handed the woodcutter his handkerchief. "Wipe your brow neighbor," he offered, insisting that Ivan take it.

He obliged, and it felt good to wipe away the sweat and travel dust. "Thank you," he replied, handing it back, "but I must be getting to my cabin. I *really* want to see my wife and children."

Claude waved as he left and cursed under his breath. He had much to do now if he was going to make his new idea work, so he hurried to the house and went straight to where Morra kept her diamond jewelry set. He took them all and placed them in a bag, then went out and saddled his fastest horse. Those jewels meant a lot to his wife, but if this worked she wouldn't even know they were missing before he had them back again.

The afternoon was waning and he had a good ride ahead of him, so he headed out at a full gallop, heading east on the public road. When he reached Woodvale his mount was heavily lathered and favoring his left front leg. He rode directly to the stables and told the stable-master to provide him with a fresh horse and have it ready when he returned.

With his bag held firmly, he hurried to the goldsmith building, where he proceeded to bang on the door until someone answered.

"We're closed," started the owner, until he realized who it was, then opened up and let him in. Claude emptied the bag of dazzling jewels onto the counter and informed the man that he needed fifteen bars of gold. He told him that he would leave the diamonds as security and be back to claim them in no more than two days. The shopkeeper knew these diamonds, and retrieved the gold immediately.

"Remember to keep these safe until I return," he instructed, then placed the gold in the bag and carried it out the door and down to the stables. The other horse was ready when he arrived, so he placed the bars in the saddlebags and left the town at a dead run.

The sun was setting as he hit the public road and raced for home. He didn't let up on his mount for the entire ride, and with the extra weight, it was totally spent by the time they reached Claude's estate. He didn't stop until he reached the bunkhouse, then dismounted and pushed open the door. The men were playing dice, but paused when they saw the frantic look on his face. Claude called on the blacksmith to fire up the forge and another to look after his horse. The men hurried out, wondering what could possibly need fixing so late in the day.

The blacksmith worked hard bringing the coal to a bright orange color as he worked the billows. Claude laid the gold on the bench and started going through the molds that were stacked against the wall. He found the ones he wanted, brought them over and set them beside the bars.

The blacksmith was watching him, and looked confused as he fanned the furnace to the desired heat. When Claude was satisfied everything was ready, he informed his man to place the melting pot on the coals. He did so without question, but was more curious now than ever.

"All right Bruno," he said, motioning to him. "I'll tell you exactly what I want."

The blacksmith walked over and looked at the mold he was holding. It was the double-bitted axe-head mold, so what should have been obvious, baffled him even more.

"I want you to take eight of these gold bars and craft an axe head with them. Then I want you to take this large rod-mold and fashion a handle for it. It doesn't have to be *Gatou* quality, but try to make it look good."

Bruno nodded. "You're the boss," he answered, and took the gold to the forge where the pot was just starting to glow.

It didn't need to be fully heated to melt the gold, so he waited until the bottom had brightened just enough and dropped the bars in. He tightened the clamps on the mold and readied it for pouring, then watched as the gold gave way to the high temperature.

Bruno guessed each bar to weigh about seven pounds, so when he was finished his creation it would be just over one hundred. That was more than he could earn in a few lifetimes, and here was Claude making an axe with it for who knows what.

The gold was liquid now, so he took the tongs, lifted the melting pot out of the coals and poured its contents into the mold. He replaced it, dropped the last of the bars in, and readied the next mold. Soon he had both pieces poured and setting, waiting for them to cool. Next he separated the molds and began attaching the handle to the head. That part wasn't difficult, but the shaping proved much trickier. It took awhile, especially with Claude standing over his shoulder, but finally he had formed it into a fairly decent replica.

"That will be all Bruno," Claude dismissed him, eyeing the golden axe.

"You have a good night sir," replied the blacksmith as he left the building.

Yes, a short one, thought Claude, and went over the plan in his mind. He would leave well before daybreak, and if all went as designed, he should be back in plenty of time to ride into Woodvale and bring back Morra's diamonds.

He climbed the stairs to the next level and found two leather straps. Returning, he grabbed the axe and took everything up to the main house. He ate some of his leftover stew and made himself a lunch for the next day. He was tired after his ride, so he retired for the evening and dreamed of riches beyond imagining.

It was still dark when he awoke, so he lit a candle and made his way downstairs. He took one of the leather straps and fashioned a makeshift harness for the axe so he could carry it easier. He took the other one and placed it in a bag, along with his lunch. He secured the axe in the harness and put his arms through the loops, and the weight was distributed nicely. So with the axe on his back and the bag in his hand, he left the house and headed to his kennel.

He reached the closed-off area and called to his prize hunting dog. "King! Come here dog, we've got a big day ahead of us."

He had always wanted a Royal Hunter, but they were always spoken for, even before they were born. His dog had been bred by the Catchers for the king, but had been passed over because his majesty had only taken two of the three pups. The little dog had cost him dearly, so he called him King and found it very amusing. For all the breeding and acclaim he was supposed to have, the hunter had been almost useless to him until now, but today he should be able to earn his worth many times over.

He grabbed a leash that was hanging there, and waited. The dog approached warily and cowered as Claude reached for him. He grabbed his collar and fastened the leash. King needed to be alert and in top form today, so he led him back to the house and brought him a bowl with the last of the stew in it. The dog wasn't sure what to think, but finished it quickly and looked around for more.

"I'm not trying to fatten you up. I just need you strong for our little journey," he taunted, then moved across his yard toward the creek.

The air was mild this morning and Claude knew they were in for a hot afternoon. King was excited to be out of his cage and having someone pay attention to him, as he sniffed the ground and scented the air instinctively. They reached the Horseshoe Creek and found the best place to cross. Once they'd reached the opposite shore, he sat the dog down and knelt in front of him. He pulled out his handkerchief and put it up to King's nose. He knew that Ivan's smell would still be strong on it, and hoped the trail was still fresh enough for his dog to follow. He wasn't really worried though, because he knew King was the top breed for tracking, and could follow a scent that was many days old.

Claude turned the hunter loose and he started in a small circle. Gradually it got bigger, as he went round-and-round with his nose to the ground. Soon, as he neared the entrance to the old wagon path, he stopped and began a low growl, then looked back at his master.

That was one of the unusual traits about the Royal Hunter breed. When they found the target scent, they would growl rather than bark or howl like most dogs. This made it easier to sneak up on their unsuspecting prey.

Claude hurried over and attached the leash once more, then encouraged King to continue tracking. It didn't take much coaxing before he found himself being pulled along the path that lead to the main trade-road.

Excitement heightened in him at the thought of what the day might hold, and the axe pulling steadily on the leather straps was outweighed by his greed as he hurried his step to match the dog's. He had listened carefully to every word Ivan had said, and if this 'Water Fairy' had offered the woodcutter a golden axe when his old one flipped into the lake, Claude couldn't even imagine what he would be offered when *his* golden axe happened to find its way in there. All he had to do was find the meadow, and he would show Ivan Harden that he *couldn't* be beaten.

When they reached the fork, the dog turned south and continued until he came to a slight opening on the left side, then started his low growl again. Claude followed him forward and they made their way east, straight toward the heart of the *Whispering Forest*.

Claude wasn't aware of any of the stories about these woods, and was oblivious to everything around him. He just held on to the leash and followed along blindly.

They traveled easily and were making much better time than Ivan had, but as the light started to touch the morning sky, the weight of the axe began to wear on him. He decided to rest for awhile, so he laid the axe down. It was a relief to shed the load, but he knew it was just the beginning. If everything went right, his trip back would be a lot slower, yet worth every step.

He ate half of his sandwich and fed the rest to his dog. He was impressed with the absolute way he tracked and was beginning to think he might be worth every gold coin he'd paid, but he would reserve any true judgment until he was standing by that lake.

He strapped on the axe and they resumed their trek. It wasn't long before Claude noticed a large fog bank directly ahead so he slowed King down before entering. He wasn't sure if this would cause the dog any problems, and it didn't appear to, so he urged him along again hoping to get clear of the annoyance.

The farther they moved in the thicker it became, until Claude was completely relying on King for every step he was taking. Suddenly his mind began to feel clouded and he shook his head trying to rid himself of the fuzziness he was experiencing.

The fog was performing its duty as an outer guardian, but its efforts were being countered by unknown factors. The man following the dog was not the usual trespasser and had certain qualities that rendered its affects inert.

Claude had no sense of direction to begin with and had no idea where he was, so trying to disorient him was impossible. As far as trying to confuse or alter his mind into giving up or forgetting his purpose, that was futile as well. Between his self-importance and the greed that drove him, his mind was full and nothing could penetrate it.

After causing him only a slight discomfort, the fog gave up and dissipated, leaving the twosome moving ever closer to the meadow.

When they reached the place where the land began to slope downward, Claude decided to stop and finish the rest of his food. It was getting on toward midday and he knew he must be getting close. He wasn't worried about rationing because he remembered his neighbors words clearly. Ivan had made it to the lake and returned by late afternoon of the same day, and he had been leading a horse that was dragging a pull-sleigh. If his figuring was correct, he should be there and back with his treasure before supper time.

They started up again and he invited the downhill terrain. It made the going a little easier, but after about a mile if flattened out once more. Within another half mile he saw a rainstorm ahead and wondered where it had come from. He thought about waiting it out, but didn't have time, so he moved headlong into in.

After only a few feet King stopped and looked around.

Has he lost the scent? Claude wondered and felt panic at the thought. "You worthless mutt!" he yelled above the rain. "If you don't pick up the trail, you won't be fed for a week . . . if you're lucky!"

Almost as if he'd understood, King started his low growl and resumed the hunt. Claude felt relieved as they continued, and tried to ignore the weather.

Soon the voice came. *Turn back, there is only peril ahead,* it whispered.

All Claude could think of when he heard it was that it was trying to keep him from the riches that awaited, and again his greed saved him from the outer defenses.

Soon the rain stopped, along with the voice, and he could see a light in the distance. *It has to be the lake,* he thought, and forgot all about the harness that was cutting into his shoulders as he increased his speed in anticipation.

Claude was almost sprinting when they came through the opening, and the sun's brightness was overwhelming compared to the dim light of the forest. He stopped and covered his eyes, waiting for them to adjust. He could hear the low growl from the Royal Hunter, and had to keep a firm hold as the dog pulled steadily, trying to continue the chase.

Finally Claude's daylight vision returned and he gazed out over the meadow. He could see the *balboa* tree and the vivid colors of the plant life, but his only interest was in the lake and what lie beneath it.

Standing there wasn't accomplishing his goal, so he tied King to a tree and made his way toward the shore.

As he got close, he loosened the axe and pulled it free, but kept the harness secure. When he reached the shore he tossed his former burden as far as he could, and it landed about twenty feet out. Claude watched the bubbles as the golden axe sank into the deep blue water, then fell to his knees and waited.

After awhile, with nothing happening, he pretended to cry . . . rather loudly. Soon the lake began to bubble and he knew he'd gotten the Water Fairy's attention. *This is going to be easier than I expected,* he thought, and began to exaggerate his former efforts.

The bubbling grew more intense now, almost to a boiling state. Suddenly it stopped and the Water Fairy emerged and glided over to Claude.

"Why do you kneel in sorrow by my waters?" she asked in her shimmering voice.

He readied himself. *This doesn't get any sweeter,* he thought, and looked up with the saddest of faces. "Well," he began, sniffling slightly, "I was on my way from Belden's Wall to the City of Kings to deliver a precious gift to the orphanage there, when I decided to take a shortcut through your forest. Me and my trusty dog King," he said, motioning to the tree-line, "had almost given up hope when we found your meadow, and the life-giving waters of your lake. Having traveled for all those days, I was so parched," and he coughed for effect, "that I rushed over and began to drink. As the cool liquid renewed my fading strength, I failed to realize that the gift I was so selflessly carrying, fell from its harness and sank into the icy depths of your home. Now I'm afraid all the little orphan children are going to go without proper food and shelter, not to mention clothing, and I feel responsible for their suffering." Claude sobbed as he finished his tale, and waited for a response.

The Water Fairy didn't say a word as she slipped beneath the surface. A few moments later she arose holding Claude's golden axe in her hands. "Is this the gift you speak of?" she queried, lifting it up.

He looked at the axe and felt quite confused. His anger flared, but he never fell out of character. "That *is* similar," he admitted, "but the gift I carried was *much* finer than that."

The Water Fairy only hesitated a moment and was gone again. When she returned, what she held in her hands made Claude's eyes grow wide and his heart pound in his chest.

It was a golden axe, only much bigger than his, and the craftsmanship was unimaginable. It was hard to see it clearly though, because the jewels that adorned it kept catching the sunlight and blinding him.

Set generously in the handle, up and down both sides, were emeralds, rubies and sapphires. Encrusted on either side of the blade, were diamonds the size of chicken eggs.

Claude stood up with his mouth hanging open and almost forgot to breathe.

"Is this your axe?" she asked, holding it up.

He was in shock and fought hard to get it together. As his faculties returned, he realized that the four words she had just uttered were the most beautiful he had ever heard in his life.

"Yes," he replied eagerly, then added, "it's for the children." He walked forward and reached out to grab it, his mind reeling at the sight. Just before he could get his hands on it, the Water Fairy let go and it fell into the lake and disappeared.

Claude was so distraught at the sight that he almost dove in after it, and then he felt warm hands on either side of his head. He tried to pull away but her strength was too much for him.

"You don't mind if I read you?" she said, not really asking, and her voice seemed louder, and the shimmer was replaced with a harsh edge.

Dark clouds began to form over the meadow and the wind started to pick up. The Water Fairy began to grow in size and Claude felt a sickening fear run through him. Lightning split the air and the booming storm answered, but he could do nothing at all except wait in her iron-like grip.

The icy winds were gusting and the rain was pounding down when she finally released him, and what once looked like a beautiful young girl, had become a gigantic pillar of swirling frenzy.

He tried to run but was enveloped in a cocoon of freezing water and lifted off the ground. He wasn't sure what fate would befall him as he hung neck-deep in his watery prison, but even in his peril, he still thought of the jeweled axe.

I see you Claude Boyle! thundered a voice that seemed to come from everywhere. *You tried to take something that didn't belong to you, and that makes you a thief. Every word you spoke was false, and that makes you a liar.*

The liquid shell tightened around him and he winced in pain as the judgment continued.

I have looked into your heart this day and what I saw befits the conduct you have shown here. Claude Boyle . . . you are a thief, a liar, and a coward, and have caused others much suffering in your lifetime. What do you have to say for yourself?

The water surrounding him loosened somewhat, making it possible for him to breathe normally again, and he was trying to think of some way to calm the fairy. *How am I going to talk my way out of this one?* he wondered, and when he did speak, all he could think of to say was, "Could I have *my* axe back?"

The grip tightened again and he was slowly being drawn toward the spinning tower. It was ten feet across and twenty feet high now, and roared like waves crashing against the rocks.

He knew that if he were pulled into that violent column he would be lost, and felt relieved when he was stopped a foot away.

If you don't change your wicked ways, came the deafening voice, *you will experience tenfold the misery you have inflicted throughout your life. Before I release you, I warn you not to return here, or ever utter a word about this place to anyone. If you do, I will find you. Remember, I am every drop of rain and every puddle and stream, and you can never hide!*

Suddenly he felt himself being thrown through the air. As he sailed helplessly backwards, he heard the voice echoing through the meadow one last time.

I'll be watching, were the last words he heard before he felt something hard hit the back of his head.

CHAPTER
29

The Balance

Right after he left Claude, Ivan knew he shouldn't have said anything to him about his trip into the *Whispering Forest*. He hadn't broken his word to the Water Fairy, but he still shouldn't have said anything. He could understand more easily now the reason why Cade had bragged to Sonny about their big delivery that day, and even though he knew what he'd just done was wrong, it sure felt good. *This is no time for regrets*, he thought, and walked the last few steps to his cabin.

His excitement escalated as he dropped the reins and stepped onto the porch. He looked at the axe as he leaned it against the logs and it all still seemed like a dream to him. He opened the door and saw his wife sitting at the table with her quill moving swiftly. She was writing on a parchment and had every silver they possessed stacked in front of her. Ivan couldn't believe the joy he felt, knowing that he would never have to see that worried look on her face again.

"Hello my love," he called out.

Grace jumped in her chair. "Oh!" she exclaimed, "you startled me. I didn't hear the door. I guess I was too caught up with trying to figure out how much we can spend on supplies this trip. We still have plenty of smoked venison, so if we go without bacon we can—."

"No," interjected Ivan, "we will get the bacon."

"I just thought we would wait and see how your contracts go before we spent too much, and then—."

"No," he interrupted again. "From now on my beautiful wife, you are going to have anything your heart desires."

Grace stood and looked at her man. She knew he meant well, but she had to be the realist. With the loss at the Woodcutting Competition, coins were scarce and it was going to get a lot worse. "That's generous of you to say my dear, but you know you're my only heart's desire."

Ivan gazed into his wife's eyes, and as she moved toward him, his smile started and kept getting bigger until he was grinning like a fool.

"I've got something to show you," he said, unable to wait any longer. He reached over, grabbed the golden axe and held it in front of him.

Grace stopped and stared. She looked at Ivan, then back at the axe and seemed frozen in place. Ivan could see the confusion in her eyes but just kept smiling, waiting for it to sink in. She was having a hard time accepting what she saw, but finally found her voice.

"Is that what I think it is, and where did you get it?" she asked, still somewhat in shock.

"I'll explain everything," he told her and led her to the table. He laid the axe down and lifted her into his arms. He carried her to his favorite chair and she snuggled with him while he told her of his journey into the *Whispering Forest*.

He told her everything he was allowed, except the part about Shyla. He just couldn't bring himself to say it out loud and still wondered if he'd made the right choice. The Water Fairy *had* promised that she only wanted to talk with his daughter, so he found some comfort in that, but wasn't prepared to speak with his wife about it just yet. He would tell her of course, but when the time was right.

Ivan stood and set his wife down, and they walked over to the table to look at the axe. Grace marveled at its magnificence and as the magnitude of what it really meant began to hit her, she had to sit down.

"Are you all right?" asked Ivan, concerned at her reaction.

"Let's just say I'll be more than all right once my mind catches up," she answered, still staring at the object that would secure her husband's dreams. Now he could remain a woodcutter *and* provide the things he so desperately wanted for his family.

"I better go tend to Bill," he remembered. "He's had a long day as well." He left Grace to admire the axe and went out to unhook the horse. As he stepped outside he could see Claude riding like the wind out to the public road. *That man has sure been in a hurry lately*, he thought, and took Bill to the back to put away the sleigh and turn him out.

Everything felt different now as he walked back to the cabin. That underlying feeling of stress that had constantly nagged him had vanished. He knew gold couldn't buy happiness, but it sure relieved the pressure.

When he reached the porch he saw Shyla and Loner emerging from the trees, so he waited. She saw him and chimed, "Daddy!" and ran up.

"I'm not Daddy," he growled. "I'm the porch troll and this time you're mine fair princess." He growled again and grabbed her, lifting her high in the air. When Loner saw this, he barked protectively at Ivan. "And don't think your beast can save you either!" he snarled, lifting her even higher.

"Evil porch troll," she said, very serious. "If you don't release me, my trusty guardian will gobble you up."

Ivan looked at Loner, then back at Shyla. "No fair!" he grumbled, and set her down. "One day I'll get you princess."

"Not today," she giggled, then rushed past him and into the cabin. Ivan entered and saw Shyla standing at the table staring at the axe.

"Where did it come from?" she asked, in obvious disbelief of what she saw.

"Your father brought it home with him," replied Grace, who was still sitting where Ivan had left her.

"Is it real?" Shyla questioned, trying to understand what she saw.

"It's very real," Grace answered again, "and it's all ours."

Shyla stood there for a moment, then started jumping up and down. When she'd finished jumping, she started skipping around the table singing, "We're rich, we're rich, we're rich . . . la-la-la-la la-la. We're rich, we're rich, we're rich . . . la-la-la-la la-la." Ivan and Grace had to laugh at their daughter's antics, and for the first time it really dawned on them that what she was saying was true.

The woodcutter sat down beside his wife and looked the axe over. He hadn't studied it thoroughly since he'd received it and was impressed even more than before. Not only was it breathtaking because of the gold that it had been created from, but it was a stunning piece of art, worthy of any palace wall. Ivan continued surveying his treasure, seeing something new with each glance, while Shyla continued to skip around the table singing the song she had just written.

Cade walked in carrying three dressed out rabbits and took them to the counter. He placed them in a pot and proceeded to pour water over them. He looked over at Shyla. "Who's rich?" he asked, washing the meat and adding some salt to the water.

"We're rich, silly," she answered, continuing her song and dance.

"Yeah right," said Cade as he moved to the washstand and began cleaning the blood from his hands. He looked at Shyla again and asked, "Why are you singing that dumb song, it's annoying?"

"Because it's true, silly," she replied and resumed where she had left off.

"You're the one who's silly!" he blurted. "We are the *opposite* of rich, and you have a whole lot of nonsense in your head!"

"I'm not the one who's silly, silly, and if you don't believe me, just look on the table."

Cade dried his hands. "Why, did you and Loner find a pot of gold in the woods today?" he asked sarcastically. When he got no answer, he turned and saw his father, mother and sister all smiling at him. He knew something was up and when he finally looked on the table, his knees almost buckled at the sight. "Is this some kind of trick?" he asked, trying to maintain his balance.

"Nope," answered Shyla. "It's the real thing, and it's all ours." She started her skipping and singing again but Cade ignored her and stared down at the golden axe. He moved to the table and ran his hand along its handle.

"Where did you get this?" he asked his father.

"I acquired it today in the *Whispering Forest*," replied Ivan nonchalantly.

Cade looked at Ivan and his eyes got big. "You went into the *Whispering Forest*?" he asked in an astonished voice.

Ivan sat both his children down and told them everything he had told Grace, again leaving out the part about Shyla, and they sat there in silence hanging on every word. When he was done, they all sat there quietly and it seemed like the axe had everyone in a trance.

"Well," said Grace, "rich or not we still have to eat," and went over and started preparing the rabbits for cooking. Shyla jumped up and sang her new song all the way to her bedroom, but Cade remained seated, still in wonderment at the object before him.

"Isn't it something?" remarked Ivan as he left the table.

Cade didn't answer, but was in full agreement as he continued to study everything about it. While he was marveling at its beauty and obvious worth, a relief swept over him that almost made him weep. He hadn't realized how much their financial state had been bothering him until now, and the release was unexpected. He had been carrying an unknown burden, and with it lifted, he felt light-headed. Now he understood the guilty conscience he had experienced after buying that shawl for Wanda, and spending the coppers at the circus. It also explained why he had wanted so badly to double his silvers at the gypsy camp, and why he hadn't spent any since. He had been accepting the responsibility of providing for his family without even knowing.

Cade stood and placed his hand on the axe, then smiled. *This means that I am truly becoming a man,* he thought, then walked over, grabbed the water bucket and walked to the creek to fill it.

At mealtime the food tasted better than usual and Grace had baked a cake to celebrate their good fortune. The mood was light and the family joked around and enjoyed one another's company. There was a calmness in the air, and when they held hands to give thanks, it was genuinely heartfelt.

After the meal, Shyla went out to play with Loner, and Cade went for a walk. He couldn't believe the sensation of freedom he was experiencing, and remembered a similar feeling when he was a small child.

Ivan put the axe in a safe place and was going through the same emotions as his son, only magnified. Grace was happy for her man and most all of her worries had already begun to fade.

That evening, when each of them had climbed into bed, although they didn't feel that much different, they knew that after today their lives would be changed forever.

The next morning Grace was up before Ivan for the first time since she could remember. She didn't know if it was from the fatigue of his ordeal or the lack of stress he now enjoyed, but it gladdened her heart to see him deep in slumber.

It was warm out so she refrained from building a fire until she was ready to prepare breakfast. By that time everyone was out of bed and looking very chipper indeed. As they sat down to the morning meal, everyone's mood had already brightened even more and Grace was really starting to appreciate the golden axe. Not for its worth in coins so much as what it symbolized, and the positive affect it was having on her family.

They had almost finished, when the dogs started barking. Cade excused himself and ran out to see what it was. He was thrilled when he saw the wagons rolling into the yard. It was easy to see, by the bright colors and vivid designs, who they belonged to, and by the time all ten had pulled in, the entire family was on the porch watching the spectacle.

A large gypsy man climbed down from the lead wagon and engaged Ivan in conversation. "Good day sir," he offered, extending his hand. Ivan took it and greeted him. "Our purpose for stopping today, is that these wagons from our caravan are in need of repairs and we were wondering if you would have time to take on the job?"

Before the woodcutter could answer, Grace came over and asked, "Is the old gypsy woman with the blind eye with you?"

The big man looked puzzled. "She's not with us at the moment, but should be here shortly, although *her* wagon doesn't need fixing."

Grace smiled. *That old fox,* she thought. When they were visiting, Grace had mentioned their current predicament to Grelda and knew that she was the one who had arranged this, just to help her family.

"Why aren't you getting the work done in the Westlands where the rest of your caravan is headed?" she questioned the man, as Ivan listened with a confused look on his face.

"The old woman suggested we stop here for repairs and catch up with them later. Her suggestions are always taken seriously, so here we are," he replied, and just after he spoke, the old gypsy could be seen coming in off the public road.

Everyone watched as her wagon stopped beside the cabin, and Shyla ran over to help her down.

"How are you Grace?" she croaked, as she made her way over. "It's good to see you again so soon." Grace hugged her and thanked her for her kind gesture, motioning to the wagons. Grelda cackled, "Well, they do need attention and your husband is the best, so I thought that, with your current plight, we could all benefit from the decision."

Ivan had caught on now and stepped up. "The gesture is much appreciated," he told the old woman, "but our plight has taken a positive turn recently. I do welcome the work though and would be glad to fix whatever needs repairing, but

I would much rather trade craft for craft on this job, if you are willing."

Grelda looked somewhat perplexed for a moment, then cackled again and asked, "What did you have in mind?"

Ivan looked at the wagons and thought about it. "I'll tell you what," he said, addressing Grelda. "I'll work on the wagons during the day and then you and your people supply the evening meal and provide the nightly entertainment. That way we all get to take advantage of, and enjoy each other's talents without any coins exchanging hands."

Grelda looked him up and down, then in a raspy voice announced, "You've got yourself a deal."

Cade and Shyla were excited by the news and couldn't believe the gypsies were going to be performing in their own yard.

"Would you like to come in for some tea while your camp is being set up?" offered Grace.

"I would love to, thank you. I *do* enjoy your company," replied Grelda, and the girls went inside.

Ivan and Cade walked over and checked out the first wagon, and Rufus and Loner followed behind, sniffing at the new smells and watching protectively over the boys. "It looks like some of the floorboards need replacing and one of the wheels needs to be redone," commented Ivan to his son. "Let's get it off and take it to the work-shed."

As Ivan and Cade removed the wheel, the woodcutter noticed that Sam Morgan and two other men were riding up to Claude's house. This seemed strange to Ivan, because in the eight years that Claude had lived there he had never seen Sam visit his neighbor's place. It was always Morra and Sonny who would go and stay with Sam at his property outside Coaldale.

Before they had the wheel off, the men were heading back toward the public road. Ivan was puzzled, but didn't give it any more thought.

The day was hot and the work went fast, and they had almost finished three of the wagons when the sun started to set.

The girls had enjoyed a pleasant visit, and Grace had informed Grelda of her findings concerning the mysterious book. It was unusual for a healer to divulge information like that to someone who wasn't part of the Council, but for some reason she trusted the old gypsy implicitly.

Ivan secured the last of the floorboards just before dark. When he stepped from the third wagon, he could smell the different dishes for the evening meal being prepared over various cook-fires, and *knew* they were in for a treat.

Soon everyone was sitting around a big fire in the middle of the camp, enjoying the many gypsy delicacies that were being served. After they had eaten their fill, the entertainment began. Cade and Shyla remembered most of it from their night at the circus, but it had been a while since Ivan and Grace had observed their magnificent skills.

The woodcutter and his wife held hands as they watched the performers, and Ivan couldn't recall a time when he had been happier.

Claude awakened with a splitting headache and groaned as he struggled to sit up. He felt his head, and could see blood on his fingers as he drew them back. When his blurred vision had cleared he could see that he was just inside the tree-line, and not far from King, who was still tied there. His head was pounding and his body ached, but his fear of the water creature was foremost in his mind. His only thoughts were to grab King and get out of this place.

Nothing he'd planned had worked out and now he just wanted to go home and forget any of it had happened. When he tried to walk he stumbled and fell, but after a few moments, found his balance and moved over to the dog.

He untied King and checked the sky. The sun was well along in the day and he realized he had been out for most of the afternoon. He would have to push hard to make it to the trade-road before dark, even unencumbered, but there was no choice. No matter what lie ahead, it was time to leave. He took one last look at the lake and for an instant thought of what could have been, then turned his dog toward home and started out.

There were no encounters with rain or fog on his way back, but it was near dark when King finally led him onto the road. Although his head was still killing him, all he could think of as he made his way down the wagon path to the creek was, *how can I get Morra's diamonds back?*

Soon the wagon path opened up and he saw the Horseshoe Creek, and was glad to be out of the *Whispering Forest*. He stopped on the shore and washed his face and hands in the cool water, then dumped some over the back of his head. It stung at first, but felt soothing after a few more attempts, and eased the throbbing and cleared his mind somewhat.

He crossed the creek and climbed the fence onto his property. He could hear voices and music coming from the woodcutter's place and wondered for a moment what was going on. He didn't have time to worry about what Ivan was up to though and had to find a way to get those diamonds back. He didn't have anything that compared in worth to those jewels, and the few gold coins he had stashed away wouldn't even begin to buy back one of those pieces. Sam actually owned the land and buildings where he lived and the paintings and furniture belonged to his wife.

As he stopped at the kennel and put King inside, he started to feel a touch of panic setting in, but he still had at least two days to come up with some way to recover those gems.

He reached his house and felt relieved as he stepped inside. He was starving, so he made himself a cheese sandwich and took it to the table. When he sat down, he saw a parchment with his name on it, propped up against the candle. Apprehension filled him as he opened it, and those sick feelings returned as he read the words that were written on the page.

I know about your dealings with the goldsmith, and what you've done can never be forgiven. You have broken my daughter's heart and I must take action. You are never allowed to see Morra or Sonny again, and if I see you, I will have you horsewhipped and thrown in a dark dungeon somewhere. I am sending some men from the mine out there this evening to make sure you are gone, and if I were you, I'd ride as fast and as far away from the Woodland Vale as I could.

Sam Morgan

Claude's hands shook as he read the note again. Sam Morgan was not a man that you crossed, and the more he thought about it, the more he was gripped by fear. He ran upstairs and threw some clothes in a bag. He grabbed the pouch of coins he had tucked away, and hurried to the stables. It was dark, but he fumbled around until he had his best horse saddled.

Running into Sam's men was something he wanted to avoid, especially after the way he had treated them, so he threw his meager belongings in the saddlebags and headed out.

As he galloped to the public road, he could hear laughter coming from the woodcutter's yard and could see a celebration taking place. *How could he have beaten me?* Claude wondered, and was truly baffled by the notion. When he reached the road, and turned his horse toward the Westlands, he could smell the wood smoke from Ivan's fire as it drifted down the vale.

The woodcutter applauded as the jugglers finished, and then looked over at his wife. It was so good to see her enjoying herself, then for an instant he thought he saw something out of the corner of his eye. He turned toward his neighbor's field, and was sure he'd seen a rider, but no one would be out this late. He turned back around just in time to see the big gypsy swallow a long sword, and everyone in the camp clapped enthusiastically.

As the night went on, the different performers showed their expertise and flexibility, and it was turning into a truly wondrous evening. Once everyone had finished their acts, they traded in their costumes and paraphernalia for musical instruments and began playing a haunting gypsy song.

It was incredibly beautiful how the violins and wood-whistles complemented each other with their harmonies and layered lines, as the guitars and drums brought in precise rhythms and strong percussive flavoring.

Ivan had learned to sing at the castle, and people had always told him they liked his voice, but the entertainers he was listening to now were professionals of the highest quality, and he took it all in with wonderment.

What a great way to finish the day, he thought, and closed his eyes to better appreciate the sounds that flowed so gracefully from each minstrel.

When the song finished, he opened his eyes to see Shyla standing there holding his guitar. "Please sing for me Daddy," she pleaded, handing him the instrument.

Ivan had mixed feelings as he took it, but he had never been able to refuse his daughter. "Let's do one we all know," he suggested to the players, and tried to think of a good selection.

"I know!" exclaimed Shyla, "how about, *The Tale of the Twelve Foot Gnome.* Everyone knows that tune."

The woodcutter looked to the musicians and they all nodded, so he showed them the chord and began to sing for his little girl.

> *Here's a tale of the Twelve Foot Gnome*
> *Who didn't have a home*
> *Cause he was tall and his people small*
> *So they sent him on his own*
> *They didn't see, or want to be*
> *Kin to a Twelve Foot Gnome*

His shirt was a billowing sail
His pants the tail of a whale
He made his socks from the skin of an ox
His hat a castle dome
And each of his shoes was the hide of a moose
A well-dressed Twelve Foot Gnome

One day the rains came down
And flood the gnomish town
So they climbed the tree that stood in the lee
Of the land they loved so dear
They reached the top, but drop by drop
The water drew ever near

Far off the Twelve Foot Gnome
Was walking all alone
But with ears that size he could hear the cries
Of the folks who'd done him wrong
But still he raced all through the day
To the place he'd once belonged

Into the churning foam
Jumped the Twelve Foot Gnome
And as he sank, from the tree to the bank
He stretched himself out wide
Then down his arms, and free from harm
Ran the gnomes to the river's side

Now legend stories say
That he was washed away
But on a rainy night, you'll see a sight
That'll chill you to the bone
There in the lee by the elder tree
The ghost of the Twelve Foot Gnome

No more to roam, he's finally home
The ghost of the Twelve Foot Gnome

When he was through, Shyla ran up and threw her arms around his neck. "Thank you Daddy!" she cried. "I love that song." Everyone else seemed to like it as well as the applause escalated, and Ivan felt honored to have been able to sit in with such a great gypsy band.

He set his guitar down and listened as the music continued. The next pieces of music the travelers selected were woven seamlessly together like a well told story and Ivan could have sat there all night, but wanted to be up early to work on the rest of the wagons. He stood and thanked everyone for the brilliant entertainment, then picked up his guitar and walked to the cabin. He didn't mention to Grace or the children how late it was getting because they were having so much fun, and it gave him great pleasure to see that taking place.

Once inside, he hung the guitar on its nail, grabbed the water bucket and headed back out. When he opened the door, Grace was standing there looking up at him with a twinkle in her eye. She got on her tiptoes, put her arms around his neck and leaned into him. "Are you ready for bed?" she asked in a sultry voice.

"I am now," he admitted, lifting her a few inches off the porch. "I'll just get some water for morning and be right there."

"I *really* enjoyed your singing," she told him, and went inside.

As he made his way to the creek, he could see Cade and Shyla sitting by the fire, still enthralled by the musical splendor, and he had to smile. What a day the family had gone through, and especially him. From not knowing whether he would ever see his loved ones again to carrying two hundred pounds of gold, in the form of an axe, back to his little cabin, had been unimaginable to say the least.

When he reached the creek, he filled the bucket and set it down. He cupped his hands and dipped some of the cool water, drinking his fill. Before he left, he looked at the *Whispering Forest* silhouetted in the moonlight. He thought of the *balboa* tree and the Water Fairy, and was once again relieved that everything had turned out the way it did.

Almost everything, he thought. Had he made a mistake agree-ing to her third demand? He knew it would bother him until it was resolved, and wondered what a being with all that power and ageless wisdom could possibly want with his daughter.

The End

of the First Book of

The Balance Series

GLOSSARY

Adan: Marcus and *Jadax's* twin son (taking after the *Gatou* side). His name means "moon" in the *Gatou* tongue.

Adept Healer: The final stage of a healer's training, and the name they use when they acquire this knowledge. This is the highest rank for a healer, and only then do they receive the ring of the healer's seal. After this title is given an adept can go forth and heal on their own.

Air Child: Fabled eldest daughter of the Mother of Balance, placed in a sanctuary at an undisclosed location in the land and attached to her mother with an invisible line that is said to help secure the stability of the balance.

Albert: Blacksmith in the town of Woodvale.

Arcana: Land far to the north of the Woodland Vale, through the Miner's Pass in the Bitter Mountains and then just north of the Land of Gales. Homeland of Mok the giant. (see map)

Back-strap: The strip of meat alongside the backbone of an animal that runs from the shoulder to the rump.

Balance, the: An invisible power throughout all the lands that creates an equal distribution of energies and probabilities that seek to stabilize good and evil. It is believed that good deeds will be rewarded and malevolent ways will be justly punished in accordance with the laws of this force. It is said to have been brought to the land by the Mother of Balance and maintained by her and her children since the beginning.

***Balboa* Tree:** A sacred tree, black in color with no bark or limbs. It is known for its hard wood, black and white grain and pungent aroma. It is impervious to fire and when exposed to flame, gives off a floral bouquet and is thus used mainly in the building of fireplaces for those who can afford it.

Barrem Harden: Grandfather to Ivan Harden. A woodcutter by trade who bequeathed the Harden homestead to Ivan.

Belden's Pass: A pass through the Crooked Mountains that was discovered by Frank Belden on the settlers' first journey north from Southport. (see map)

Belden's Trail: The trail from Southport, north through the Drylands to the Crooked Mountains, and then through the Belden's Pass to Belden's Wall. It was the route taken by the first settlers on their journey north from Southport. (see map)

Belden's Wall: The town formerly known as Marshside. After extenuating circumstances a wall was built around the marsh to protect the town, so its name was consequentially changed to Belden's Wall. (see map)

Ben Starling Junior: Son of Ben Senior and Maggie. Brother to Wanda.

Ben Starling Senior: Owner of the Starling ranch and breeder of the King's Breed horses. Father of Wanda and Little Ben, and husband to Maggie. Very big and tall. An easygoing man who is good friends with the Hardens

Big-saw: A saw, eight feet long with handles on each end to accommodate two men for the purpose of falling or cutting trees into uniform lengths.

Big Timber Area, the: Place where loggers and woodcutters go to harvest large timber for clients. Located in the northern part of the Woodland Vale, bordering the Bitter Mountains to the north. (see map)

Binding Spell: A spell of the land used in healing to staunch excessive bleeding and prevent ruptures.

Bitter Mountains, the: Mountains located north of the Woodland Vale and south of the Land of Gales. (see map)

Black Buffalo: Roaming the *Gatou Plains*, a mature bull is twelve feet in height and weighs in at over four thousand pounds.

Bone-knife: Knife made of bone, used by the *Gatou* tribe.

Brant Catcher: Breeder of dogs in the Woodland Vale. Husband to Leslie and good friends with the Harden family.

Breakfast Scramble: A meal made with eggs that are mixed with leftovers from the night before and scrambled together.

Bridgette Willington: Younger sister of the Duchess Charlotte Cavillade, and mother of Stafan.

Bruno: Blacksmith hired by Claude Boyle.

Cade Harden: Fourteen years old. Son to Ivan and Grace Harden, and brother to Shyla.

Camille Brundle: Wife to Tad Brundle and co-owner of "Brundle's Brick Yard". Mother of five small children.

Candle-Lamps: Globe-shaped candle holders covered in white cloth to further soften the candle's light and create a pleasant atmosphere.

Cantra: Large green ball made of an unknown glassy substance, said to have been found ages ago, deep underground. Used by a seer to help enhance their ability to see into their subject's path of being.

Chance: Black wolf of the *Gatou*. Named by Marcus Belden after he was chosen by the *Vallah-von*.

Chickory Willow: Willow wood used in the smokehouse to give the meat a unique, dark spicy flavoring.

Children of Balance, the: Children of the Mother of Balance. Keepers of the sanctuaries and protectors of the Lines of Balance. Two daughters: Air and Water. Two sons: Land and

Fire. It is believed that together with their mother they hold order and balance throughout the lands.

Chintau: Head *Gatou* healer.

City of Kings, the: Located in the northeastern most part of the Woodland Vale, it is the western city of the twin cities and home to the king. There the royal palace sits high on a bluff overlooking the Northern Sea, and the higher workings of the kingdom are conducted there. It is also known as Kingstown. (see map)

Claude Boyle: Manager of the "Morgan's Coal Company". Husband to Morra, and father to Sonny. Son-in-law to the owner of the coal company, Sam Morgan, and neighbor to Ivan Harden.

Coaldale: Town built by Sam Morgan, located in the central area of the Woodland Vale. (see map)

Cold-cellar: A room dug into the side of a small hill, used to keep items cool and fresh.

Common-trough: A watering trough used by the community of a city or town. Maintained and kept full by the local stable-master.

Competition Field: The hundred acre field, east of Woodvale, that accommodates all of the activities, entertainment and guests for the entire duration of the Woodcutting Competition.

Competition Quarter: The southeast quarter of the competition field. It is used for all of the side events and the five main events of the Woodcutting Competition.

Council, the: Group of elders formed by Frank Belden to help make decisions for the structured building and expansion of the town of Marshside. Also put in place to make educated choices for the greater good of the settlers.

Council of Healers, the: Sect of adept healers whose primary function is to oversee that the integrity of the healer's code is upheld by every healer, and to study in depth, the magic of the land. This magic is used by those healers who are gifted, to assist in their healing. Only one out of every hundred healers has this gift, and it is only strong in a few.

Crooked Mountains, the: Mountains that run between the Drylands in the south and the foothills and *Gatou Plains* in the north. At their easternmost point they swing north and run along the South Seas until they reach the Northern Sea, where they dissipate just before King's Port and the City of Kings. This change in direction, from east to north, is the reason they were given their name. (see map)

Darkness, the: A being that consists of an unknown dark energy. It seeks out and tries to destroy those who wield the light of the *Sol'mar.*

Double-bitted Axe: An axe that has a blade on each side of its head.

Dryland Brigands: Marauders that roam the Drylands, pillaging and instilling fear in unsuspecting travelers.

Dryland Springer: Deer-like animal with long spiral horns, indigenous to the Drylands. Able to leap very high and bound very fast.

Drylands: Area of desert-like terrain between the Crooked Mountains to the north and the jungles of the Southern Lands. (see map)

Duchess Charlotte Cavillade: Influential investor and land owner. Eldest sister to Bridgette Cavillade and pledge interest to the Baron Vero Salday.

Eastern Lands: Lands east of the Northern and South Seas.

Faline: Grace's wolf, who chose her when she was a child.

Falseapple Tree: Ornamental tree used for decoration in many courtyards, public venues and residences. It resembles an apple tree but never bears fruit, constantly blooming throughout the entire summer.

Fanta: *Adan's* wolf. Mate to Chance.

Fire Child: Fabled youngest son of the Mother of Balance, placed in a sanctuary at an undisclosed location in the land and attached to his mother with an invisible line that is said to help secure the stability of the balance.

Fire-rock: A black rock that, when struck, discharges sparks. Used to create fire.

Flame-stick: Stick used with a soft-bow to create a fire. The bowstring is wrapped around the stick and spun to create enough heat to ignite the fuel source.

Flatbread: Bread that is cooked in a frying pan after the dough is flattened.

Foothills: The rolling hills beside a mountain range.

Frank Belden Junior: Marcus' son. Also known as *"Zalak-diche"* in the *Gatou* tongue.

Frank Belden: Leader of the original settlers who came up from Southport to build a new home and create a trading route to the north. Co-founder of Belden's Wall

Frosty Pines: Large pine trees that grow only in the northern reaches of Arcana. Harvested by the giants and used for building.

Frozen Lands: Lands to the north of Arcana. Not suitable for habitation due to the low temperatures. (see map)

Game-boss: The overseer of the gaming in a gypsy gambling wagon.

Gatou Plains: The rolling plains between the *Whispering Forest* to the north, and the foothills and Missing Marsh to the south. (see map)

Gatou: The brown-skinned race who make their home on the *Gatou Plains.* They are short in stature but possess at least twice the strength of a normal man. They are known for their prowess with a great-bow and their wolf-like mounts.

Grace Fallow: Maiden name of Grace Harden.

Grace Harden: Wife to Ivan Harden and daughter of Zarina Fallow. Adept healer blessed with the gift, and mother of Cade and Shyla Harden. Member of the Council of Healers and youngest ever to join that prestigious sect.

Great-Bow: A very heavy bow used for hunting, with the power to shoot over very long distances. Used mainly by the *Gatou*, reason being that most men can only draw the bowstring a few inches.

Grelda: Gypsy healer and wise-woman also known as "the old gypsy woman with the blind eye". She is the one who taught Shyla how to further harness the magic of the land and has since mentored her in its intricacies.

Hatchet: A small axe used for throwing or meticulous woodcutting practices.

Healer's Seal: Ring given to an adept healer upon her initiation, and the design upon its face is pressed into wax to seal confidential documents. This ring is spelled by a gifted healer and the seal can only be safely opened by another adept healer.

Heart of the Land, the: Name given to the Mother of Balance during her fabled first contact with man and woman.

Heavy-Bread: Bread baked without a leavening agent, therefore giving it a heavier consistency. Often found in remote areas where supplies are limited.

Heavy-Cake: Cake made with nuts, and fruits if available, and mainly used as a sustenance-based food with a hearty consistency and sweet flavor.

Highground Longhaired: Cattle bred and raised in the Big Timber area by Nat Bonner and his family. They created the breed and feed them a specific diet that results in a tastier, more tender meat.

Highland Tamarack: Large leaf bearing tree that grows only north of the Bitter Mountains. They are harvested by the giants and used for building. With great value attached due to their hardness and large size they are also harvested by the northern logging crews and brought south through the Miner's Pass for trade or sale.

Horn Vines: Vines that produce very large thorns that look like the horns of a bull. It is used in many healing remedies and grown along perimeter fences or walls as an extra deterrent to unwanted guests. It is also entwined on the band of the healers ring due to the significance of its potent healing properties.

Horseshoe Creek, the: Creek that separates the *Whispering forest* and the Woodland Vale. It flows from the Crooked Mountains in the east, to the Westlands, where it joins the Traveling River that flows down from the north. (see map)

Ivan Harden: Husband of Grace Harden and father to Cade and Shyla. Woodcutter by trade and legendary woodsman in the land.

Jadax: Princess of the *Gatou* tribe. Daughter of *Shadak* and wife to Marcus Belden. Mother to *Zalak* and the twins, *Adan* and *Sada*.

Jinda: Zarina's *Vallah-von.*

Joining: A celebration where a man and woman become husband and wife. The man's joining is witnessed by someone close to him, and traditionally, the woman is walked across the fertility line by her father and left under the protection of her new husband.

Kast: Sada's wolf.

Kau-diche: Means "cunning warrior" in the *Gatou* tongue.

Kau-diche-rah: Means "cunning warrior's son" in the *Gatou* tongue.

Kau-diche-rah fal von Jadax: Means "cunning warrior's son protector of *Jadax*" in the *Gatou* tongue.

King: Claude's dog. Bred by Brant and Leslie Catcher, he is a Royal Hunter renowned for their expertise in tracking.

King's Breed: Horses bred and raised by Ben and Maggie Starling. They are white in color, very spirited and eight-gaited.

King's Port: Located in the northeastern corner of the Woodland Vale, it is the eastern city of the twin cities. Resting on the Northern sea, it is the fortification city that plays guardian to its western sister, the City of Kings. (see map)

Kingstown: See - City of Kings.

Kingstown Minstrels: Traveling musicians from the City of Kings. Group that plays the annual Woodcutter's Ball.

Korak: *Gatou* warrior. Son of the chief, *Shadak*. Brother to *Jadax*.

Lake of Falls, the: Lake that rests in the arm of the Crooked Mountains to the east of the Missing Marsh. It gets its name from the five waterfalls that plummet from the western face of the mountains into its icy depths. (see map)

Land Child: Fabled eldest son of the Mother of Balance, placed in a sanctuary at an undisclosed location in the land and attached to his mother with an invisible line that is said to help secure the stability of the balance.

Land of Gales: Area located south of Arcana and north of the Bitter Mountains. Prone to storms and violent weather. (see map)

Leslie Catcher: Wife of Brant. Dog breeder and friend of the Hardens.

Light, the: Ancient power that rests within a chosen *Sol'mar*. Unknown magical energy source that has been studied by the Council of Healers for centuries.

Lines of Balance: Invisible cords that are said to connect the Mother of Balance to her four children who are situated at strategic points throughout the land.

Loner: Puppy that Shyla met at the Catcher's dog farm. Very intelligent, with white ears and a black body.

Longbow: A bow used by most bowmen. Shoots a medium range and mainly used for hunting.

Lookout Hill: Highest hill in the foothills. Discovered and named by Frank Belden. (see map)

Maden: Motherly, heavyset woman. Writer and caretaker to Marcus Belden. Penned most of the scrolls on Belden's Wall that reside in the museum in Southport.

Maggie Starling: Horse breeder and trainer. Wife to Ben Senior. Mother of Little Ben and Wanda.

Magic of the Land, the: An energy that flows within the land and all living things, and can be tapped into by those who have the gift. Some say its source is the Mother of Balance.

Mallah: Scholar and scribe. Curator of the museum in Southport during her life. Daughter of *Zalak* and Mina Belden.

Marcus Belden: Son of Frank Belden and husband to *Jadax*. Father to *Zalak* and the twins, *Adan* and *Sada*. Visionary and architect. First person to negotiate trade with the *Gatou* and co-founder of Belden's Wall. Also the man who spearheaded the building of the Wall of Belden.

Marrine Harden: Wife to William. Mother of Ivan.

Marsh-Dwellers: Scaly lizard-men indigenous to the Missing Marsh, who walk upright and hunt in packs.

Marshside: See - Belden's Wall

Melting pot: Metal pot made to withstand high temperatures. Used in a smith to put metals in for melting and molding.

Mina Belden: Wife of *Zalak*.

Miner's Pass, the: Pass found by the early day miners leading north through the Bitter Mountains to the Land of Gales. (see map)

Missing Marsh, the: Swamp found east of Belden's Wall comprising six hundred square miles. (see map)

Misty Lake, the: Lake situated northeast of Coaldale. Future site of the baron's manor. (see map)

Mok: Name of the giant. Woodcutter from Arcana.

Morgan's Coal Company, the: Coal company founded by Sam Morgan.

Morra Boyle: Wife to Claude and daughter of Sam Morgan. Mother of Sonny.

Mother of Balance, the: The being that is said to have brought her four children from beyond the stars to the land, and brought order to the chaos that existed when she arrived.

Mountain-hound: Dog bred for tracking and endurance. Rufus, the Harden's dog, is one of these breeds.

Nat Bonner: Breeder of the Highground Longhaired Cattle.

Northern Kingdom: Land mass from the Crooked Mountains in the south to the Bitter Mountains in the north, and encompassing all of the Westlands.

Northern Sea: Sea off the coast of King's Port. Its runs south to Falling Rock Point and north to the Frozen Lands. (see map)

Northern Sweetgrass: Grass that grows in the western half of the Big Timber area and is used by Nat Bonner to graze his cattle. It is said that it is the main reason the beef is so tender and tasty.

Old Bill: Ivan's horse. A blue-roan workhorse, half again the size of a normal horse. Very old and has been working with the woodcutter for over twenty years.

Old Gypsy Woman With The Blind Eye, the: See - Grelda

Onak: Legendary *Gatou* bowman. (still living)

Onak Utuk: Means "*Onak* will come" in the *Gatou* tongue.

One River, the: The River that, at its head, cascades from the south side of the Crooked Mountains from its underground source, then makes its way through the Drylands where it eventually drains into the South Seas near Southport. (see map)

Pan-bread: Bread dough cooked in a frying pan rather than an oven. Heavier than regular bread and sometimes sustaining ingredients are mixed in for consumption while traveling over long distances.

Panthadon: Large catlike creature with long spiral horns and protruding fangs. It is five feet tall and black in color, with four white diagonal lightning shaped rings surrounding its body. Can be found in the jungles of the Southern Lands.

Papa Bar: See - Barrem Harden

Plainsman: Name for a *Gatou* tribe member.

Pledge: Promise given when a couple agrees to be joined as husband and wife.

Porch Troll: Imaginary creature that lives under the Harden's Porch. Created by Ivan to tease his daughter.

Pull-Sleigh: A sleigh constructed for pulling fallen trees out of wooded areas.

Royal Hunter: Dog bred for tracking. Considered the most superior of trackers and usually purchased by the king or one of the royals.

Royals, the: People of the royal bloodline.

Rufus: Dark red mountain-hound owned by Cade Harden. Given to him by the Catchers when Cade was born.

Sada: Marcus and *Jadax's* twin son (taking after the *Gatou* side) His name means "sun" in the *Gatou* tongue.

Salt Spring, the: The hidden spring that Frank Belden salted to attract the Black Buffalo during the settlement days of Marshside. (see map)

Sam Morgan: Owner of Morgan's Coal Company. Father to Morra Boyle.

Shadak: Chief of the *Gatou* nation. Father of *Jadax* and *Korak*.

Shamus: Merchant from the town of Belden's Wall. Stood up for Ivan at his joining.

Shau-muai-din vay: Means "blood brother of the plains" in the *Gatou* tongue.

Shyla Harden: Daughter of Ivan and Grace. Sister to Cade. Apprentice healer and the first *Sol'mar* in a thousand years. Gifted in the magic of the land and able to communicate with animals.

Simon: Son of Albert the blacksmith.

Sindra the Seer: Gypsy seer who uses a Cantra to enhance her predictions.

Small-folk: Name that the giants give to normal sized people.

Small-saw: A saw, about three feet in length with a curved handle. It is used to cut logs into uniform blocks for different uses.

Soft-bow: Bow used in making a fire by wrapping the string around a fire-stick and spinning it to create enough heat to ignite the fuel source.

Sol'mar: Name of the individual whom the energy of the light magic inhabits. This phenomenon only occurs every thousand years, and no healer occupied by the light has ever exceeded the age of twenty-two before burning out.

Sonny Boyle: Son of Claude and Morra.

Soother: Modern healer, relying on new methods in the art.

South Seas, the: Seas off the coast of Southport, encompassing the waters north to Falling Rock Point and south to the unknown waters. (see map)

Southern Kingdom: Area from the northern border of the Southern Lands, north to the Crooked Mountains encompassing the Drylands and Southport.

Southern Lands, the: Uncharted area below the Drylands. Home to jungles and hostile creatures. (see map)

Southport: City on the coast at the southeast end of the Drylands and the northern border of the Southern Lands. (see map)

Spell of the Unseen: An enchantment placed on an item that is cast by four of the gifted to render its possessor physically and mentally undetectable by any who wish to locate them through magic, and can only be detected by its creators.

Squirrel-cake: Much like heavy-cake, this hearty mixture of nuts and berries is very nutritious and sustaining, not to mention tasty.

Stable-master: Person in charge of the stables and the common-trough. Also a member of the Town Council and contact to the blacksmith shop.

Stafan Willington: Son of Bridgette. Future duke and land overlord.

Sugar-apple: An apple coated with melted sugar. These apples are brought up from the south for the Woodcutting Competition.

Summer-sleigh: Sleigh built with wide runners to enable easier movement through the forest. Used to take loads of wood from the timbered areas.

Tad Brundle: Owner of Brundle's Brick Yard. Husband to Camille and father of five small children.

Tamarack Jack the Giant with the Axe: Name given to the giant by Claude Boyle to try to enhance interest and further intimidate competitors. See - Mok.

Traveling people: Name for the gypsies.

Traveling River, the: River that flows south, then east, from the western end of the Bitter Mountains in the Westlands. Waterway used to transport goods to the western sections of the territory. (see map)

Tree Spurs: Metal attachments that strap on to a woodcutter's boots. They have two sharp points on each inside edge and are used to climb trees.

Twelve Foot Gnome, the: Fictional character brought to life in children's stories and songs.

Ucho: Means "good" in the *Gatou* tongue.

Ucho tan: Means "good luck" in the *Gatou* tongue

Unknown Waters: The waters south of the South Seas. (see map)

Uladan majah Zalak: Means "*Zalak* would be proud" in the *Gatou* tongue.

Utai: Means "thank you" in the *Gatou* tongue.

Vallah-von: *Gatou* name for their wolves meaning "protector and friend".

Vero Salday, Baron: Wealthy land owner. Ivan's childhood friend and right hand to the king. Suitor to the Duchess Charlotte Cavillade and respected leader of the people.

Villam Stanky: Circus owner and exploiter of animals and people. Nasty demeanor and selfish attitude.

Wall, the: Slang name for the town of Belden's Wall.

Wall of Belden, the: A rock structure built by the citizens of Marshside and the *Gatou* tribes. Designed and spearheaded by Marcus Belden, it is fourteen feet tall and eight feet thick. It runs from the Crooked Mountains south of Belden's Wall, north to the *Gatou Plains,* then swings east and runs all the way to the Crooked Mountains in the east. (see map)

Wanda Starling: Daughter of Ben and Maggie Starling. Sister to Little Ben.

Water Child: Fabled youngest daughter of the Mother of Balance, placed in a sanctuary at an undisclosed location in the land and attached to her mother with an invisible line that is said to help secure the stability of the balance.

Water Fairy: A water being taking the shape of a young girl. Very old and very powerful.

Water-skin: A leather, watertight pouch used to carry water for drinking.

Westlands, the: The land west of the Woodland Vale. (see map)

Whispering Forest, the: Ancient forest to the north of the *Gatou Plains* and south of the Woodland Vale. (see map)

White Energy: See - Light, the

William Harden: Ivan's father. Woodcutter and mason by trade. Husband to Marrine.

Wolf-Riders: Name given to the *Gatou* warriors.

Wolves of the *Gatou:* Also called "*Vallah-von*" in the *Gatou* tongue, they are the wolf-like animals ridden by the *Gatou* tribe.

Woodcutter's Ball: Annual dance and celebration following the final day of the Woodcutting Competition.

Woodcutting Competition: Annual contest hosted by the Baron Vero Salday, bringing the best woodcutters in the land together to match their skills against each other for a winner-take-all purse of gold.

Woodland Vale: Area of land south of the Bitter Mountains, west of the Northern Sea, north of the *Whispering Forest* and east of the Westlands. (see map)

Woodvale: Town in the central area of the Woodland Vale. Host town of the Woodcutting Competition. (see map)

Woodvale Waltz: A beautiful ballad inspired by the breathtaking scenery throughout the Woodland Vale. Named after the town of Woodvale.

Wrong, the: See - Darkness, the.

Zalak Belden: Son of Marcus Belden. Husband to Mina and father of two sons and a daughter, Mallah.

Zalak-diche: Means "strong warrior" in the *Gatou* tongue.

Zarina Fallow: Mother of Grace Harden. Wife to Hawkins and an adept healer. Versed in the old ways and very powerful and influential throughout the healing community. Prominent member of the Council of Healers.

About The Author

Lorn Wolf was born in 1963, in Northern British Columbia, Canada, where he spent his childhood adventuring around his parents' thousand acre horse ranch. His imagination was first sparked by the bedtime stories his mother would tell him, and then, at age ten, his schoolteacher read to the class, *The Hobbit* and *Lord of the Rings* trilogy by J.R.R. Tolkien. This truly solidified his absolute infatuation with fantasy. Lorn's other interest was music and that is where his writing skill began. At the age of eight he wrote his first song, and along with learning to play many instruments and becoming a recording artist, he continued to write many songs for himself and other performers. After spending eight years in Nashville Tennessee, honing his songwriting craft, he began to feel confined in that style and decided to combine his dedication to writing with his love of fantasy, and become an author of fiction.